PRAISE FOR HOLT MEDALLION WINNER VICTORIA CHANCELLOR'S PREVIOUS ROMANCES

MIRACLE OF LOVE

"Victoria Chancellor is a master of re-creating the magic and the miracle of love. A heartwarming read. I loved it."
—Evelyn Rogers, bestselling author of *Wicked*

"Miracle of Love is a beautiful, tender and touching story that is sure to delight fans of special author Victoria Chancellor. A wonderful reading experience."
—*Romantic Times*

BITTERROOT

"Victoria Chancellor wastes no time drawing the reader into this intriguing tale of love and treachery. Bitterroot is an absorbing time-travel . . ."
—Rosalyn Alsobrook, bestselling author of *Love's Image* and *The Perfect Stranger*

"Victoria Chancellor works magic with her clear, crisp prose, drawing the reader deeper and deeper into the story. She weaves history, past and present, together, making this a truly believable and heartwrenching tale."
Romantic Times

FOREVER & A DAY

"A mesmerizing adventure with star-crossed lovers who will leave your heart pounding!"
—RITA award winner Helen R. Myers, author of *After That Night*

"Victoria Chancellor has penned an exciting, eerie and romantic tale of obsession, true love and sacrifice."
—*Romantic Times*

WHERE BLUEBIRDS FLY

David stepped even closer. Analisa smelled his scent, so unique and clean, and experienced the heat of his body. He was burning hot, as hot as the embers in the hearth. She wanted to step back, but she'd taken root at this spot. All she could do was wait, her heart beating fast, her breath shallow and rapid.

"I couldn't have imagined a more lovely woman to share this dream," he said, his voice as soft as a snowflake. "I've been telling myself that I was hallucinating this visit to the past, that I was really still up in my plane, unconscious."

"You are not in your plane," she whispered. "You're here in this cabin."

"Whatever you say. All I know is that you're here with me, and you obviously want me as much as I want you."

"I want you?" His words made no sense, but somehow her body understood, warming, tingling with awareness and a sudden yearning to be closer still to this man.

"Yes, you do," he said, his head angling closer, his lips parted.

Her heart seemed to skip a beat. Time stopped as the combination of his words and her body's reaction seeped into her consciousness. "I don't know what you mean," she said carefully. That panicky feeling returned, cooling the heat of her body, breaking her free from the strangely exhilarating lethargy that had stolen over her like morning clouds easing over the highest peaks.

"Then let me give you a hint," he whispered, their lips nearly touching.

Across the Rainbow

Victoria Chancellor

LOVE SPELL BOOKS ◆ **NEW YORK CITY**

LOVE SPELL®

November 1997

Published by

Dorchester Publishing Co., Inc.
276 Fifth Avenue
New York, NY 10001

ISBN 0-505-52236-5

Printed in the United States of America.

To all my special "friends" who have crossed the rainbow bridge before me. I hope we'll meet again someday because I miss you with all my heart.

ACKNOWLEDGMENTS

Special thanks to the Jackson Hole residents who helped with research:

Steve Kerley of Jackson Hole Aviation, who told me exactly what David would see and do from the pilot's seat.

Grand Teton Natural History Association, for their excellent reference materials.

Nell Fay of the Jackson Chamber of Commerce, who told me about the rainbows and other important facts.

And thanks to author Carole Howey, who provided a great map and procured that phone book page I couldn't have gotten anywhere else.

Chapter One

Jackson Hole, Wyoming
June 1997

"Daddy, Daddy, look!" Jamie ran into the airplane hanger, her new sneakers squeaking across the shiny concrete floor. "Daddy! Where are you?"

She squealed to a halt in front of the office. "Daddy!"

"What is it, Muppet?"

Uh-oh. There was a big stack of papers on his desk, and he looked really serious. But he just had to listen. She was too excited to wait for him to get finished, because grown-ups could work forever.

"A rainbow! A really neat one. I think it's the one, Daddy. If you go now—"

"Jamie, I'm not going anywhere. I have to finish the logbooks and then order some supplies for the weekend. I'm going to be really busy, remember?" He smiled just

11

a little bit before he picked up the boring old papers again.

"But Daddy . . ." Jamie just couldn't make him understand how important the rainbows were. She just knew that if he'd listen, they'd all be happy again. He'd get a new wife and she'd get a mommy. And not just any mommy, but a princess. A beautiful, nice princess who would smile all the time and bake sugar cookies with sprinkles on top.

"Jamie, I know you think that rainbows are special, but they're really just an optical illusion. The sunlight passes through water droplets and refracts into the colors of the spectrum. We can see the rainbow, but it really isn't there in the sky."

Jamie planted her fists on her hips and frowned at her daddy. He was the most stubborn daddy in the whole world. "I know the rainbow is real because I can see it. And you could too if you'd just come outside."

"I'm sorry, Muppet, but I'm really busy." He didn't even look up from his ugly old desk. "Why don't you show the rainbow to Aunt Holly?"

"She's talking on the phone. And besides," Jamie said, wishing her daddy would listen to her, "the rainbow is for *you,* not for Aunt Holly."

He finally looked up, a serious look on his face. He was really handsome—a lot better than those men on the calendar in Aunt Holly's office—but most of the time he didn't smile enough. Aunt Holly said that he used to smile and laugh more, when Mommy was alive. Jamie didn't remember Mommy, but Daddy missed her a whole bunch. All her friends had mommies, and most of them were really neat. Jamie wanted one too.

"Sweetie, I know you believe in magic rainbows, but I can't just fly my plane up every time we get a little shower and the sun comes out."

"But Daddy, how are you going to get happy again if you won't try?"

"When the time is right I'll start dating again. I'm just not interested right now." He sighed and picked up a pen, twirling it in his fingers.

"But I want a new mommy! This summer would be a really good time, so I could show her around the house before I go to first grade."

"I can't just order up a new mommy for you, Jamie. It doesn't work that way."

"Well, it could if you'd fly across the rainbow!"

"Jamie," he said in that voice he used when he was getting tired of talking.

"Okay," she said, miserable because he wouldn't listen. "But you'll be sorry."

Her daddy laughed. "I thought that was my line."

"Daaad-dy!"

He pushed back his chair and held out his arms. Jamie ran to him, throwing her arms around his neck. Her daddy always smelled so good. And he gave big, strong hugs that made her happy.

"Jamie, honey, how can I convince you that flying across the rainbow isn't magic?"

Jamie pulled back so she could look at his face. "Why don't you just do it, Daddy? You know, like the commercial says. Just do it." She smiled, raised her eyebrows the way that made him smile, and waited for his answer.

He looked like he didn't want to smile, but he did. Her daddy was the most handsome when he smiled. Any princess would be happy to marry him and come back to live in their house.

"If I go up in the plane, fly across the rainbow, and make a wish, you'll be happy?"

She pushed out of his arms and jumped up and down.

"Yes! Yes! That's all you have to do. I promise I won't ever ask you again!"

"Okay, Muppet," he finally said.

"Yeah!" Jamie grabbed his hand and pulled him outside the office. "Come on, Daddy. The rainbow might be all gone."

"Let me get my jacket," he said, pulling her toward the wall by the big doors. He always hung his soft leather jacket on a peg by the door.

"It's not cold, Daddy. Hurry!"

He laughed. "I'm coming."

Her sneakers squeaked as she ran ahead of him toward the doors that let the planes come inside so her daddy could fix them. Outside the wind was kind of cold, but not like wintertime, when it snowed lots.

"Daddy! Hurry."

"I'm coming." He stopped just outside the doors and looked around. Daddy always did that, like he could see the wind or something.

"See the rainbow! Isn't it beautiful?" Jamie pointed away from the airport, out where the ground was real flat.

"It's a beauty all right," he agreed, zipping up his jacket and checking his watch.

"Come on, Daddy!"

Aunt Holly came out of the big building. "What's going on?"

"She finally talked me into it."

"You're kidding!"

"No! Daddy is going to fly across the rainbow and make a wish. And then we'll all be happy again."

"I thought we were pretty happy the way we were," Aunt Holly said, ruffling Jamie's hair. "I'm happy. Aren't you, Muppet?"

"I'd be happier if Daddy had a new wife," she admitted. "You're a good aunt, Aunt Holly, but I think a mommy would be neat."

"And you think your daddy is going to get one by flying up into the sky?"

"Yes. And he has to make a wish." She turned to him. "Don't forget to make a wish, Daddy."

"I won't."

"David, this is silly," Aunt Holly said.

"Is not!" Jamie protested. What did Aunt Holly know about this really special rainbow?

"It'll make Jamie happy," Daddy explained.

Jamie smiled.

"Besides, I could use a break from all that paperwork."

"Whatever," Aunt Holly said, shaking her head. She wasn't very excited about things except for working at the airport and going to her meetings. And she always told Jamie that her daddy was spoiling her rotten. Jamie didn't know what that meant, but she didn't like being called *rotten*.

"Why don't you two watch me and make sure I get across that rainbow up there? I'll need some technical help."

"Why, Daddy?"

"Because when I get up in the sky, I won't be able to see the rainbow. You and Aunt Holly will have to tell me where it is."

Jamie frowned. "Oh. Okay, we'll do that, won't we, Aunt Holly?"

"Sure. Let's get inside and get the headphones on."

"I'll see you soon," Daddy said to Aunt Holly. "And you, Muppet, need to watch very carefully and make sure that I get this right. I'm only doing it once. You understand?"

15

Jamie nodded. "I understand. I'll tell you exactly where the rainbow is."

"Okay." Daddy smiled. "You behave while you're on the radio, you hear?"

"I will, Daddy. I love you."

"I love you too, Muppet." He leaned down and kissed her forehead. "I'll see you in just a little while."

"Will you bring the princess back with you?"

He laughed. "I don't think so. I won't be landing my plane anywhere, you know. I think that if this wish is granted, she'll probably show up later."

"Then how will we know she's the princess?"

"You can always tell a princess," Aunt Holly said. "And if we can't, we'll just put a pea under her mattress and see if she tosses and turns all night."

Jamie laughed at Aunt Holly's joke. Daddy had bought a bunch of fairy tale and folk story books, and Aunt Holly read them to her at naptime. Jamie loved them, especially the ones about magic kingdoms and handsome princes. She loved them almost as much as her favorite Muppet movie.

"Bye, Daddy." Jamie waved to her daddy, then took Aunt Holly's hand and skipped toward the building, humming her favorite song, "The Rainbow Connection."

She was going to be so happy with Daddy's new princess.

David banked his Cessna 185 to the left, circling the airport so Holly and Jamie could see him before he climbed toward the rainbow. He'd told himself many times that her idea was silly, that he wouldn't give in and fly into the sky after something that didn't really exist.

16

But here he was, spending time and gas to humor his Muppet.

He smiled, remembering the expression on her face when he'd agreed to indulge her fantasy. He dipped one wing as he soared over the right runway, then leveled off and climbed into the clear blue sky. She'd jumped up and down, her new red bibbed overalls and striped T-shirt a blur of color. Holly had separated her hair into puppy dog ears, and they'd bounced above her ears like soft little golden wings.

Jamie looked so much like her mother that he knew he'd never forget Catherine. Golden skin, gold-streaked hair, and hazel eyes with—what else?—gold flecks, he'd always called them his golden girls. Only now there was just one. He'd changed Jamie's nickname to Muppet because he couldn't call her golden girl without remembering what life had been like before Catherine climbed onto that ledge to get the perfect shot.

Photographing bald eagles had been more important than her family. At least, that's the way he thought of her avocation. Knowing that he wasn't being fair to Catherine didn't help; he wished she'd been happy photographing roses or fruit or children. Anything but wildlife.

"Daddy, you're going the wrong way." Jamie's voice cut into his thoughts, bringing him back to the present, to his little Muppet.

"Is that proper protocol?" he asked, hoping he sounded serious enough to put the fear of the FAA in her, even if they were using his own channel on their separate transmitter.

"No, but I got to let you know. You need to turn— which way, Aunt Holly?"

"Left fifteen degrees. And climb to eight thousand."

17

"That's right, Daddy, so you can get over the top of the rainbow."

"Okay, Muppet. Turning left, climbing to eight thousand. Let me know if I'm off course."

"Will do," Holly said in her practical, efficient voice. He didn't know what he'd do without his "little" sister, who took care of Jamie when he was away with a charter, sometimes overnight or even a weekend, depending on the destination. For someone who swore she possessed no maternal instincts, Holly was great with Jamie. He couldn't have continued his charter air service without her.

Glancing down at the instruments, he saw that he was nearing eight thousand feet. He leveled his climb, checking the other gauges. Everything looked fine. There were no other planes in the air, the sky was nearly cloudless now that the morning rain had dissipated, and even the wind was calm. He couldn't have picked a better day to grant Jamie's wish.

"Two-one-two-five-Robert to base. How am I doing?"

"We can barely see you, Daddy, but the rainbow's still there."

"You appear to be on course, but maybe a little low."

"If I climb much more I'll be out of my lane. Should I go to ten thousand?"

"No, stay on your flight path. You should be able to loop back in about five kilometers."

"Will do." He steadied the plane at eight thousand feet. "Jamie, what am I supposed to do when I fly over the rainbow?"

"Make a wish, Daddy! A wish for a princess."

"You're my princess."

"No, a real one. One who can get married to you so we'll live happily ever after."

"How about the poor princess?"

"Daddy! You promised."

David laughed. "I know. I was just teasing. I'll make a wish. And I'll see you soon."

"Okay. Make a really good wish."

"I will. Over."

He hadn't planned to make an actual wish. Not really. But part of his promise to Jamie was that he would ask for happily-ever-after. But what did he really want? A wife to replace Catherine? No, he would never want that. His wife had been a unique, vibrant woman with her own career and an infectious love of life. She was the kind of person who others flocked to, for her insights, her humor, her beauty.

After Jamie's birth, he was sure Catherine would cut back on her assignments, especially the dangerous ones. But she hadn't. Motherhood had barely phased her.

He didn't think he could survive marriage to another Catherine.

Who, then? He couldn't imagine what kind of woman was his "type." Oh, he'd had his share of relationships: brief ones in the four years since Catherine's death, longer ones before they'd met. They weren't serious affairs. He couldn't imagine spending the rest of his life with any of those women, much less bringing one to his home as a mother for Jamie. Not that they'd been . . . bad. They just weren't maternal. Or wifely, come to think of it.

But they had been fun.

Maybe if he'd gone back down to Denver and spent a long weekend with Amy What's-Her-Name, he wouldn't have seemed unhappy to Jamie. But the weather had been bad, with late snow when he was free to travel, and besides, Jamie had wanted to go skiing.

Hell, in the end, he just hadn't cared enough to make

the trip. Not even for a weekend of mindless sex with a fun-loving woman who wasn't looking for commitments.

That brought him back to making a wish. What would make him happy? If not "another Catherine," then what? He'd loved her, appreciated her, even liked her. They'd shared the idealism of youth and the joy of bringing a new life into the world. For Catherine, giving birth was enough; being a mother wasn't as interesting as she'd imagined. Always, the call of the wild beckoned. Endangered species, new vistas, exciting assignments. Catherine had loved her work—more than she'd loved him or Jamie.

No, not another Catherine. He wanted . . . he wanted someone who needed *him*. Someone who cared for him, and for Jamie, of course. Not some fairy princess, but a real woman with dreams of her own, and the capacity to share those dreams with her family instead of shutting them out.

"Okay, that's what I wish for. A woman who needs me and wants to be part of my family," he said aloud, feeling foolish for participating in his daughter's fantasy. But hell, what harm could it do? Keeping his word to Jamie was important—more important than talking to himself about his own personal wish.

"Two-one-two-five-Robert to base. Jamie, I've made my wish. I'm getting ready to turn around now. I'll see you in a few minutes."

"Will you have the princess with you, Daddy?"

He heard the yearning in her young voice, the desire for a storybook mother because she didn't remember her own. "No, Muppet, I don't think I'll have the princess with me. Will you still be glad to see me?"

"Sure, Daddy," she replied, her voice reflecting a degree of disappointment. "The princess can come later. I just want to meet her."

"There might not be a princess, Muppet," he warned, hoping she could understand that not all wishes were granted. But that would be like telling her that Santa Claus didn't stuff presents down chimneys, and the Easter Bunny bought his candy at the grocery store just like everyone else.

"I can't hear you too good, Daddy."

"You're breaking up, David," Holly said. "Just turn around and get back to the airport."

"Will do."

He had no idea why the radio receiver wouldn't be working properly . . . until he looked closely at the sky. Although visibility had been clear just minutes ago, directly ahead some misty clouds obscured his line of sight. Sunlight reflected off the thin layer, throwing prisms of light. Casting an almost magical glow. A rainbow of colors.

Now he was getting maudlin. Perhaps he'd been listening to Jamie too long; He'd certainly read enough magical stories to her at night. Or maybe celibacy was the problem; he should have gone to Denver, slept with Amy.

He'd told his daughter dozens of times that there was no such thing as a real rainbow, but damned if he wasn't flying into one.

"Two-one-two-five-Robert to base. You're not going to believe this, but I can see the rainbow."

He waited for Holly or Jamie to respond. Nothing. No static, just dead silence. He checked the frequency.

"Two-one-two-five-Robert to base. Come in."

Again, nothing.

The colors of the rainbow reflected throughout the cockpit. A tingling started in his hands, which gripped

21

the wheel tightly, continued up his arms, then radiated out through his body. The feeling of color, he realized. The warmth of red, the vibrancy of green, the peace of blue. Each one ricocheted through him like shock waves.

And then the colors were gone. The sky loomed clear and cloudless around him. David took a deep breath, eased his hands from their death grip on the controls, and checked his gauges. Okay. Everything was okay. He'd just experienced some atmospheric anomaly. Probably a drop in pressure or a pocket of high humidity. There was nothing to worry about.

"Two-one-two-five-Robert to base. Can you hear me?"

Nothing.

"Dammit," he muttered, taking the plane in a wide right turn, back toward home. He checked the navigational coordinates, but that frequency was dead too. The radio must have malfunctioned.

Leveling off, he couldn't make out any landmarks except the Tetons, west northwest of his location. He checked the controls, which seemed to be working normally. Still no highways or power lines, although the geographical features looked familiar.

A sense of panic washed through him. His hands tightened on the controls as his heartbeat accelerated. Ahead, the green foothills of the Grand Teton National Park rose rapidly toward the mountains. Snow capped the familiar jagged peaks. To his right, the red rocks of the Gros Ventre range formed a natural horizon in the south. West of his location, the Snake River twisted a muddy path through valleys and canyons.

The airport should be directly below.

There was nothing down there but grass.

*   *   *

Analisa Ludke reined her mare to a halt, listening to a strange, far-off sound. If she were lower in the valley, she'd be able to tell where it was coming from. But up here in the foothills, what she heard seemed to be a large honeybee, flitting everywhere. Coming first from the stand of pines behind her, then from the direction of the stream to her left. Or maybe from the mountains, jagged and snow-capped ahead.

Her mare stamped her foot, bobbed her head up and down with impatience, and flicked her ears.

"Easy, Tommelise," she said in a soothing tone. "We'll find out what is making such a noise."

Analisa pivoted on her mare's broad gray back. From here in the high meadow, she could see in every direction. Not even a cloud marred the blue sky. The sound of buzzing grew louder, yet no swarm of bees appeared. As she listened, she realized that the noise wasn't really a buzz. It was different, a sound she'd never heard before. A sound that seemed to echo through her whole body.

Tommelise stepped sideways, snorting in disapproval.

"Easy, girl." Analisa slid from the mare's bare back, not willing to take a spill and have her horse run home without her. Walking back to the homestead wouldn't be difficult since it was downhill, but she didn't want to risk a bump on her head or worse. Not since she lived alone.

A year ago, she wouldn't have been so concerned for her safety. No longer. She had to accept that neither Papa or Jurgen would come looking for her if she was late to dinner.

She shaded her eyes from the glare of the sun, looking everywhere for the steady, deep buzz. Tommelise danced, her hooves crushing the bright green grass, filling the meadow with the smell of damp earth and summer.

Suddenly, sound roared through the meadow. Tommelise reared, pulling against the reins. When Analisa looked up, she saw the source of all that noise.

A huge white bird—or maybe not a real bird. The wings didn't move, yet it glided through the air like an eagle in an updraft. The body had an unnatural shine to it, and the shape of the wings and head did not look like any real bird she'd ever seen.

The thing swooped from the sky, coming closer each moment. Analisa cried out, afraid of this monstrous winged creature. She ran for the tree line, Tommelise snorting, pulling, dancing beside her. The air in the high meadow seemed too thin. Her lungs burned as her heart beat faster, as the sound grew louder.

A shadow passed over her as the flying beast swooped low, two strange, round claws extended straight from its belly, below the wings, and another coming from far back on the body, below the tail. With a cry, she stumbled across some loose shale, falling to the ground on her hands and knees. Curse her luck! She'd nearly made it to the sheltering trees.

Tommelise whinnied in fear, pulling against the reins. But Analisa would not let them go, even when her arm felt as though it might be pulled from her body.

She couldn't worry about her mare or any injuries now. The noise of the flying creature changed to a lower hum. Analisa levered herself to her feet, watching as the thing glided toward the ground.

She'd seen an eagle do that once on a lake. When it rose into the sky again, a fat trout dangled from its talons.

She would not be a fish for this strange creature.

"Whoa, girl. Whoa. You must quiet down. We must get away from here, and fast."

Her knees ached, her hands burned, and her shoulder throbbed. Still, she wrapped the reins tightly in her fist, grasping Tommelise's thick mane with one hand to pull herself onto the mare's back. Why hadn't she taken time to throw on the old saddle? She'd never been able to mount without a tree stump or fence, but this was a good time to try. If she failed, she might not get another chance.

"Please, be still. Whoa," she called, hearing the panic in her voice. Her fear would not calm the horse. She needed to get down the hill fast, back to the safety of her house, hidden from the grasp of the winged creature.

"Tommelise, please!" The mare stepped sideways, her eyes rolling, nostrils flared. "Stop your antics. I have no mounting block here, so you must . . ."

Analisa stopped, her heart pounding in the stillness of the meadow. She heard only Tommelise's breathing as her hooves struck a cadence on the ground.

The creature rested silent and still in the middle of the meadow.

Fascinated against her will, she looked closely at its long smooth sides, huge narrow wings, and straight rigid legs. Except for a few black and red marks, it was entirely white. What would it do now? Begin the awful noise again? Fly into the sky?

Even Tommelise quieted, standing still as she gave her full attention to the meadow's strange visitor.

Analisa reminded herself that she must leave, that now was the perfect time to flee. But she wanted to know what would happen next. She had the crazy urge to creep closer to the thing, to see if it was alive, if it had eyes to see her and a mouth to eat her.

If it wasn't alive, what could it be? Houses and wagons didn't fly; she knew that for a fact. But it didn't look alive. Even from this distance, she noticed lines on the sides and tail, like seams on a quilt. This thing had been built by someone! But who, and for what purpose, other than to terrify women and horses?

With trembling legs, she walked toward the unknown object, dragging her reluctant mare behind her. *You shouldn't be doing this,* she told herself. *Get away now, while you can.* But her legs refused to obey her mind's wishes. She continued to walk until she was close enough to read the writing on the side and the odd tail that pointed toward the sky.

"Two-one-two-five-R," she whispered. In smaller letters, the words TERRELL AIR CHARTER were printed neatly on the shining white surface. What did that mean?

As she watched, a part of the side opened away from the body. She tightened her grip on the reins, ready in case her mare bolted again. But Tommelise seemed as fascinated as she, trembling as she watched the wonder of this monstrous object.

And just when she thought that she couldn't stand the tension any longer, something began to emerge from the side. A leg? Yes, and then the rest of a man.

He jumped to the ground.

The man's black hair gleamed with silver-blue highlights in the bright sun. His eyes were covered by odd glasses, dark and shiny. On his body he wore a short leather jacket, and on his legs, tight blue pants.

Even from this far away, she could tell he was frowning. He placed both hands low on his hips, bent one leg slightly, and looked around the meadow. Obviously, he didn't like what he saw. He pulled off the dark glasses and rubbed his eyes, then pinched his nose up high, just like her brother used to do when he was tired and angry.

He said something, but she couldn't hear the word.

Only the tone. She suspected he'd just cursed. Her brother had done that also.

Suddenly he looked up, stared right at her. With slow movements, he placed the dark glasses back over his eyes. His body came alive with movement, striding toward her with such masculine force that she took a step back.

And collided with her mare.

Tommelise danced away. Analisa regained her balance, gripped the reins tightly, and prepared to run. This was no boy or old gentleman. This strange visitor was a man in the prime of life, blessed with a lean and strong body. His hands fisted at his sides, he seemed to stalk her as a mountain lion tracks a deer. She didn't know why he was angry, but she had no intention of allowing him to take his fury out on her.

If only she could find the strength to run. . . .

He stopped as suddenly as he'd started, tension radiating from his body like mist from a hot spring. Whipping his dark glasses from his face, he stared at her, his full lips turned down and his wide brow furrowed.

She was too astounded to speak . . . or to run. He was the most handsome man she'd ever seen. More handsome than she'd ever imagined a man could be. More handsome than the princes in her precious fairy tales. Could he possibly be real?

She watched, fascinated, as he parted his lips. Would he speak her language? Would he greet her or threaten her? Her heart beat faster as she listened to his first words.

"Where in the hell am I?"

Chapter Two

Confusion was not a normal state of mind for David. He prided himself on possessing a firm grasp of reality—even in the face of his daughter's belief in fairy tales and make-believe worlds. But this scenario made him think he'd stepped right into an episode of "The Twilight Zone."

Standing before him was a young woman who looked like every man's fantasy. Blond, beautiful, tall, with legs that went on forever. Her clothing was right out of a history book on the American West—kind of a Calamity Jane outfit of calico shirt, cotton twill pants, and a wide leather belt. She also held the reins of a huge, pale gray horse that resembled a knight's trusty steed.

He'd seen them—a flash of movement and color in a sea of green grass—as he'd circled the area. Since he couldn't land where he'd seen other traces of human inhabitants, he'd landed in this very familiar meadow, thinking the rider might have answers to his questions. Except now his mind seemed frozen.

The young woman looked at him expectantly from wide, blue eyes, as though she wanted him to say something profound.

He had no idea what to say. Or what had happened up there in his plane.

So he blurted out the first thing that came to mind. "Where in the hell am I?"

Her pale brown eyebrows rose, her full lips parted in a silent *o*, and she stepped back. Had he shocked her? He didn't mean to. But he was just so damned confused.

"I'm sorry," he said, pinching the bridge of his nose. "I didn't mean to snap at you. It's just that . . . I don't know how to explain what happened."

"Who are you?" she asked, her tone hesitant. Her voice had a soothing, lilting quality, with just a touch of an accent, matching the other-worldliness of the scene in front of him. Majestic, nearly unbelievable scenery, a beautiful young woman with flowing blond hair, and a noble steed. And him—a baffled visitor who didn't know where he was.

Except that he knew every square mile of land from Yellowstone to the western slopes in Idaho to the Wind River Range. And his plane was right in the middle of all those landmarks.

"David Terrell," he answered, forcing his mind back to her question. "I have an air charter service in Jackson Hole." He should walk toward her, shake her hand, but he didn't think she'd react well to such a forward move. She possessed a shy, innocent aura he found intriguing, despite the fact that with a change of clothing and some makeup, she could pass for a supermodel in any ad, any magazine.

"What is that . . . thing?" she asked, pointing at his plane. She seemed to be as confused about him as he was about the geographic anomaly where he'd landed.

"It's a Cessna 185. Haven't you ever seen a prop aircraft?"

"No. I thought it was a great white bird."

David laughed, but immediately realized she wasn't joking. She stared at his plane as though it were some kind of monster. "You're serious, aren't you?"

"Oh, yes, Mr. Terrell. I live here. . . ." She paused, a flash of pain darkening her blue eyes. "I've lived here with my papa and brother for five years." She glanced at the plane again. "When we left Ohio for the Wyoming territory, there weren't such things."

"What do you mean, 'territory'? And where exactly is *here?*" David asked cautiously.

"Not very far," she said slowly, as though reluctant to say too much. "And you do know where the Wyoming territory is, don't you?"

"I know where the *state* of Wyoming is."

"Wyoming is a state now?"

David looked away from her wide blue eyes. What was going on? If he didn't know better, he'd swear that he'd become a player in some kind of historical drama. If he believed in fantasy, he'd think he'd really stepped back in time.

Or flown back, as the case may be.

But that was ridiculous. Just because he'd banked the plane toward the airport and it wasn't there, the fact that there were no roads or power lines, that his radio didn't work, that the young woman in front of him looked just like a pioneer homesteader, didn't mean that he'd traveled into the past.

There had to be a reasonable explanation—and not one that said he'd lost his mind along with his coordinates. But maybe something very down-to-earth had happened when he'd flown through that atmospheric anomaly. He could have blacked out. Or hit his head during turbulence. Perhaps this was all a dream—a trauma-induced, bizarre vision that would vanish when he woke up.

If his plane didn't crash first.

"Look," he began, then stopped. "I don't even know your name. Hell, I'm not even sure you're real. Maybe I'm imagining you."

"Analisa Ludke," she replied. "And I believe I'm very real."

"Well, Analisa, I'm having a bit of a problem. I think I'm hallucinating or something. Or having some kind of waking dream. All I know is that I flew from the Jackson airport toward a rainbow to humor my daughter, Jamie. She thinks they're magic, you see. I had a little mechanical problem with the radio and maybe the electrical system."

He remembered the tingling sensation when he'd flown through the prism of colors—further upsetting evidence that something strange had happened. He chose to ignore that piece of evidence for the moment.

"When I turned the plane around to return to the airport, it wasn't there."

"Have you flown into the sky before? And are you saying that you can fly as high as a rainbow?"

"Of course. Like I said, I have an air charter service. Flying is my job. The Cessna is a great plane for mountain flying, especially landing without an airstrip, because it's a tail-dragger. And as far as the rainbow goes, I just did it to make Jamie happy. She thinks rainbows are magic."

"And they are. Haven't you heard the stories of leprechauns and where they hide their pots of gold?"

31

"I don't believe in leprechauns and I'm not Irish. I also don't believe in magical rainbows. I just want to know what happened to me."

"What is this airport you mentioned?"

"Jackson Hole Airport. Look, it's got to be around here somewhere. I must have gotten confused when I turned. Maybe I blacked out for a minute." He laughed from the tension, even though there was nothing amusing about his situation. "Either my sense of direction failed or my mind is still at about eight thousand feet."

"I don't know what you're talking about, Mr. Terrell, but I believe you're more lost than you think."

"Why do you say that?"

"Because there are no such things as you've mentioned. Plane, airport, radio. I've never heard those words before. And I've never seen a contraption like this one," she said, pointing to the Cessna with her left hand. "We're simple people here in the wilderness, but we do read the newspapers when we can get them. There have been no stories about objects that can fly in the sky. You can be sure something that extraordinary would have received much attention."

"What are you saying?"

She took a deep breath. "I think your daughter had the right of it. You came in contact with something enchanted when you flew into the sky."

"I don't believe in mystical objects, spells, goblins, or fairy godmothers."

"Your daughter believes."

"My daughter is a child. I'm not. I know what's real and what isn't."

"Do you? Sometimes I think it's hard to tell the difference."

He prayed this young woman meant that in a very general sense. Otherwise, she'd be as loony as this dream. "Not for me," he said firmly, desperate to believe he could tell the difference. He'd always been a rational, logical person—at least until now.

She paused, her head titled slightly, a very sincere expression on her face. "I think perhaps you're from some magical kingdom, far away. To tell you the truth, I've never seen anyone like you or your plane. And no one here can fly in the sky."

David couldn't stay in the meadow with the strange woman who believed in magic kingdoms. She had no answers to his questions. Damn, she was as silly as Jamie where imagination was concerned!

Magical kingdom, indeed.

He'd explained that he had to find out where he was, and the only way to do that was to search for landmarks. She'd retreated to the safety of the trees, but he knew she watched him as he walked back to the plane and belted himself inside. Her gaze had been on him as he started the engines and taxied down the meadow. As he'd turned and checked the Unicom navigational frequency one last time, she strained to see through the darkened glass. And when he'd performed a short field takeoff and lifted into the sky, he'd circled the area to see her beside that huge gray horse in a sea of waving green.

He was crazy. Or he'd slipped into another reality. Or another time.

Maybe just the idea that he could *think* he'd misplaced Jackson Hole, circa 1997, showed that he was crazy. He didn't know anymore. All he felt was an aching emptiness for what he held dear. Jamie, Holly, his friends, his business. Warm pizza at Mountain High Pizza Pie in Jackson, the thrill of jumping off the lift at the top of Apres Vous Peak after the first snow of the season, the beauty of cresting a ridge and seeing what lay on the other side.

He'd been fully fueled at takeoff, giving him five hours of flying time, give or take. If he used it all and couldn't re-fuel, he'd never be able to leave. Lost somewhere between sanity and reality, in a place that looked like his world, but wasn't. Knowing only a young woman and a gray horse on an isolated mountain meadow.

The sky was clear and cloudless, visibility nearly forever. He found the muddy Snake River, the Tetons, and Sheep Mountain. What he didn't find were roads, power lines, or radio signals, either at the Unicom communication frequency, the navigational coordinates broadcast by VOR, or on his own private frequency, so he could talk to Holly and Jamie.

He'd known, in the recesses of his mind, that he'd see the young woman in the meadow again. After circling the area one last, desperate time, searching for Moose or Jackson or Moran, he'd flown back to the meadow to find her standing there, as though she also knew he'd return.

Because this was his land in 1997, and he wanted desperately to be home.

"Treat a stranger like a friend and he'll leave one." Words of wisdom from Analisa's mother echoed from years past. Noble sentiments from a kind, wise woman, but then, she'd had a husband and a big, strapping son to protect the family in case the stranger didn't share her goodness.

This stranger could be anyone, from a sly, ruthless villain to a prince from a fairy tale. She didn't know him. But Analisa couldn't make herself be too cautious, not where he was concerned. The fact that he'd flown into her meadow might mean something very important. At the least, his arrival was the most exciting event in all her twenty-two years.

Prince or villain, he just seemed so . . . so helpless, in an odd way. Not helpless in a physical sense, because he was a fine figure of a man. She glanced at him quickly as he walked beside her on the path. Yes, he was strong, handsome, tall. Proud, with dark hair and eyes like the Shoshone she'd seen from a distance as her father had traded with the trappers. But this man wasn't Shoshone, or trapper, or farmer. He was something else—something that made him very lost and sad.

She understood that feeling. Often, when she sat alone in her cabin, one candle to light the room and keep away her fears, she'd felt the weight of loneliness. Until last winter, she'd played chess with her brother, or read stories to her father as he smoked his pipe at night, after a hard day of labor. Now his pipe sat empty and cold, and she rarely heard the sound of her own voice inside the thick timber walls.

David Terrell needed her, both for food and shelter, and to share his loneliness as the blanket of night settled over the land. No matter that his words didn't make sense; he was still a visitor in this land. She knew he missed his daughter—the one who believed in rainbows. Perhaps his wife waited for him also, wondering what had happened to her husband. And David Terrell had no idea how to get home to them. There was nothing worse than sitting alone with memories of what would never be again. She couldn't leave him to face that by himself.

"You know," he said, startling her from her thoughts, "this is just like a movie. I've seen a bunch where people travel from one time to another, or one dimension to an alternate universe. Sometimes they're really convincing. The writers and actors make you believe—at least while you're sitting in the dark theater—that anything's possible. As a matter of fact, they sometimes create very elaborate rules.''

''Rules?''

''Sure, like for example, that if you go back in time and meet yourself, you can't touch, because you're really the same entity and can't occupy the same space. Or that if you go back in time and change one little thing, the entire future will be changed. Or maybe that if there is an exact duplicate of you, living in another dimension, you can change places.'' He laughed bitterly and shook his head. ''Maybe I've seen too much sci-fi.''

''Sci-fi?''

''Science fiction. You know, like if I don't go back, I'll mess up the future. Or maybe this isn't the past, but the future. Yeah, that might be it. Maybe I'm in some post-apocalyptic world with no technology. Bringing something into or out of the world could ruin civilization as we know it.''

''That's horrible!''

''Yeah, but those are the theories, at least from the creative people in Hollywood.''

She mulled over his words, not knowing many of them, but getting the impression that wherever he was from, he'd better get back, just as he'd come, as quickly as possible. He could ruin civilization if he didn't! And these people in Hollywood must be very intelligent to know of such things.

She decided to remain silent until she learned more about him and his world. She didn't want to do or say something dangerous.

''How much farther?'' he asked. He probably thought that she was wandering aimlessly through the hills. Surely he knew that after dark, too many predators roamed the forest, looking for an easy kill. She had no desire to become unarmed, helpless prey.

Or maybe he didn't know how menacing the mountains were at night. Perhaps he'd never been here before and only imagined that this place appeared similar to his world.

"It's just past the turn in the trail," she said. "My father built into a hill for some protection against the wind and snow. Now the cabin is nearly invisible behind the trees that have grown nearby."

"Your father is at home, isn't he?"

Analisa missed a step. She hadn't told him yet. She wondered when she would. What would he think of a single woman alone who asked a man to stay?

"Analisa?"

"No, he's not at home."

"I was hoping he could tell me more about where I am."

"I'm sorry. I'll try to explain what I can." She hoped she knew enough of history and geography to help him find some answers. But in her heart, she believed that he'd never find his family by following a map. He needed magic, and she didn't know if he'd ever look to another enchanted rainbow as the road back home.

"You mentioned your brother. Is he older or younger?"

"He . . . he was older."

"Was?"

She hesitated, knowing she couldn't talk about her family right now. Her feelings were too raw for her to face any more emotions at the moment. To distract him, she ran ahead, tugging on Tommelise's reins. "The cabin is here," she called back over her shoulder. "I need to hurry to put the animals up for the night."

"Animals?" she heard him mutter. But by then she

was skipping into the yard, her mare trotting behind her.

She stopped between the house and the barn, an area where she fed the chickens twice a day and scrubbed the clothes each week. How would David Terrell see this homestead? She tried to keep it neat, just as her mother had taught her. Her papa had continued the habit of putting every item in its place as soon as the chore was done. Sometimes, though, Analisa wondered why she tried, with no one else to see the effect of her labor.

Now there was someone else to see her home, and she was grateful that she'd emptied the wash water, hung her laundry neatly this morning, and tended to the weeds in her vegetable garden.

Her chickens and the two ducks, Louie and Marie, filed into the yard, clucking and quacking for attention. The noise wakened Daisy, who bleated in her pen next to the barn. Her sow Rose joined in the cacophony of sound just as David Terrell rounded the corner of the trail.

"Analisa!" he called out, walking into the yard, looking around at the demanding animals. "If you're in that much of a hurry, can I help?"

"No. I mean, I'll have the chores finished soon."

"Don't be silly. I'll be glad to help."

She stood there, wondering what such a man with no dirt beneath his well-cut nails or lines of worry on his handsome face, knew about farms or animals. From his expression, she'd swear that he wasn't fond of her "friends." In his land, he might not have such animals. He certainly didn't look like any farmer or homesteader she'd ever seen. He flew in the sky, for heaven's sake!

"Can you milk a cow?" she asked cautiously, thinking of Lucy, the one animal who wasn't milling around the yard or fence, looking for food and attention.

"No. But I can learn."

"She's not a very forgiving cow." Analisa rested her finger against her lips, thinking. "Can you build a fire in the hearth?"

"Is that like a fireplace?"

"I think so."

"Then yes, I can do that."

But if she allowed him to start the fire, he'd be within the walls of her house, alone with her things. With her memories. She had no choice; he'd be inside sooner or later since he had nowhere else to go. When she put the animals up for the night to protect them from wolves and lions, they filled the barn.

She had too many winged and four-legged friends. Her father would have put at least half to the ax by now, but Analisa couldn't bear the thought of losing even one. They ate too much; they were too much trouble, but they were company in an unforgiving land.

She sighed. "The kindling is in the scuttle beside the hearth. The wood is stacked on the side of the cabin."

"And the matches?"

"I'm afraid I have no safety matches. We ran out last winter. I have a flint, though. It's on the mantel."

"Okay," he said, his tone doubtful.

He probably didn't know how to strike a flame without matches, but the process itself would keep him busy. She just needed a few minutes alone to collect her thoughts—and her emotions. While she often longed for excitement and adventure, she hadn't expected such a remarkable break from routine. She'd felt as though her feet were barely touching the ground all afternoon, ever since she'd seen David Terrell swoop out of the sky.

The hard nibbles of the gander on her bootlaces brought her back to reality. "I need to put Tommelise in the barn and feed the animals."

He nodded. "I'll see about getting a fire started."

Analisa hurried away before she gave in to the temptation to follow him into the darkened interior and light the fire, then one of her precious candles. She didn't want him alone with her belongings, but she knew she'd feel quite odd when she finally joined him inside the cabin. She'd never been alone with a young man before, and she figured a handsome, exciting one like David Terrell wasn't a good choice. Even if he did have a daughter—and most likely a wife—somewhere.

Except that she didn't have a choice. Not really.

The barn was built the same way as the house, with wide, rough logs and a mixture of mud and grasses between the cracks. The back wall was packed earth, carved from the hillside. After several years, much of the roof resembled a grassy knoll. In the winter, the animals were sheltered from the wind and snow, but at times the drifts were so deep she could barely get the door open to feed them. Jurgen had always taken care of that hard work, but now Analisa had to scythe the meadow in summer to feed her small farm during the long, cold months.

The ducks followed her, quacking and fussing. Her cow greeted her with a low moo and a nudge of the stall door. "Just a minute," she said, searching the dwindling supply of corn in the bin. She hoped someone came soon to trade, or managed to raise a crop this summer, else they'd all be foraging in the forest along with the elk and the deer. Or fighting bears for the fish in the river and berries on the bushes.

Even though she lingered, making sure everyone was fed and locked securely in the barn, her chores didn't take long. She paused in the doorway with a pail of milk in her hand. The western sky was on fire with pink and orange, a few dark purple clouds resting after scaling the peaks. She took a deep breath of the cooling air, wondering again how she was going to convince David Terrell that magic had caused him to fly into her world—a world where he didn't belong.

David knew he'd stepped into another world when he entered the rustic cabin, a stack of firewood under one arm. One large room, really, with two interior doors made of pine planks. The kitchen was at the rear, the living area closer to the door. The ceiling was low and dark, especially around the wide fireplace. Hearth, he corrected himself. Analisa Ludke had some very odd expressions to go with her eccentric lifestyle.

He found the flint on the mantel, then hunkered down and cleared away the old embers, some of which were still warm from earlier in the day. Within seconds he'd stacked a decent fire, complete with kindling. He often used a firestarter or newspaper, but she didn't seem to have anything like that either. So he shredded the soft pine bark, struck the flint, and was rewarded with a small flame.

As soon as the kindling caught fire, he pushed himself up and had a look around.

Barely enough daylight came in the door and one small window to provide illumination of the interior. He ran his hands along the walls but couldn't find an electrical switch. Come to think of it, he hadn't seen any signs of electricity—either high power lines or local ones on poles.

Damn, how did these people live without modern conveniences? He searched the entire room, as well as he could, and all he found was a candleholder and one half-melted stub. Surely they had a generator, or propane, or some other source of energy besides wood. Hardly any-

41

one—even self-professed hermits—roughed it this much. Not in this day and age.

He stopped in the middle of the room, his mind reeling. What if he wasn't in his day and age? What if somehow he'd flown through some window in time, back into the past? No, that was crazy. He'd be better off believing that he'd blacked out and was dreaming all this.

"I'm dreaming," he said aloud, hoping he could convince himself. "Wake up now, buster. Get that plane back down before you do something stupid."

His words had no effect. He was still sleeping. Or hallucinating.

Did dreams usually last this long? He didn't think so. When he remembered his dreams, they were usually snatches of time, just a few minutes of conversation or a wild scenario like purple cows and castles made of ice cream. Those were usually provoked by eating pizza too close to bedtime.

This didn't feel like a dream.

"There has to be a logical explanation," he said as he lit the candle from the fire in the hearth.

So what made sense? He hadn't seen anything modern since flying through the rainbow. He'd been discovered by a young woman dressed in a calico shirt and baggy cotton pants stuffed into old-fashioned boots. She rode a horse. Every sign of civilization was gone. And he didn't feel groggy or disoriented—except for the wild idea that he'd jumped back to another era. If he was looking for clues, those were rational ones.

The idea of time travel wasn't logical, though.

How could he even consider the possibility?

Shielding the flame of the candle, he stood and faced the room again. The light didn't stretch to the corners, but it did provide enough to let him see the walls. And the shelves. And the quantity of odd trolls and other figures perched like Roger Corman movie extras.

"What in the world?" he asked himself.

He touched one of the figures, a squat man with a pointed face and large ears. Made of clay, the workmanship was remarkable, with each strand of hair defined, each wart on the odd man's face adding to his ugly, humorous demeanor.

There were more clay sculptures, from tiny fairies to large toads. Had Analisa crafted these figures, or did she collect gnomes, trolls, and other fantasy creatures? No matter. They reflected a whimsical, almost childlike personality he found . . . unusual.

No wonder she thought the rainbow was magic.

He didn't know how long he looked at the shelves full of the ugly and the beautiful, but suddenly he wasn't alone.

The evening shadows silhouetted her tall figure, reminding him that regardless of her fascination with fantasy figures, she was a young woman, not a girl. She paused, as though waiting for something. Did she feel uncomfortable with him? He couldn't imagine why, since she lived here with her family.

Where was the family?

"You must be hungry," she said, clasping her hands in front of her and hurrying into the room.

He frowned. He was beginning to recognize the confusion that always accompanied exposure to Analisa. "I suppose. I haven't really thought about it."

"I cooked a stew earlier in the day. It won't take long to warm."

David followed her to the hearth, wondering how he could broach the subject without sounding like he was interrogating her. As he pondered the issue, she stirred the mixture. The fragrance of meat and vegetables drifted upward, reminding him of how long ago he'd eaten lunch—tuna salad sandwiches with Holly and Jamie.

The memory of his daughter sent a shaft of pain through him, but he couldn't think of her right now. Not when he didn't know how to get back home.

"Analisa, I appreciate your hospitality. I don't mean to be a poor guest by grilling you with questions, but I have to know: Where is your family?"

She nearly dropped the lid, clanging it against the side of the pot. Turning quickly, still clutching the coated wooden spoon, she faced him. "What? I mean, why do you need to know?"

"I'd like to see if anyone else has an idea of what happened to me. Where I am. Does your father have any maps of the area?"

"No, he doesn't. We've never needed a map."

"You still haven't answered my question."

"Mr. Terrell, I don't think my family is your concern."

She was hiding something; she was terrible at lying or even deceiving by omission. "They're not here, are they?"

"At the moment, no," she answered, her chin going up a notch.

"Will they be back soon?"

"No, they will not." She brushed past him, retreating to the kitchen at the rear of the room. "I only offered you a place to stay and a meal because you had nowhere else to go."

Why her dismissal of him as a stray who needed food and shelter bothered him, he didn't want to analyze. "Look, I appreciate the offer. I don't mean to be nosy," he said, following her. "Nothing like this has ever happened to me before. I'm just not the type to believe in what I can't see or feel."

"I think you can see and touch this cabin. I told you already that I'm real." Her back was to him, her posture tall and straight. She had an inherent grace that drew his gaze like a human magnet.

He didn't need to dwell on that right now. He looked away, focusing on the table that stood between them. For some reason he got the idea that she'd brought it out here from Ohio—a woman's touch in the wilderness.

He fingered the lace doily on the table. "I can't reconcile what I'm experiencing with what I know to be true."

"Which is what?" she asked, pulling bowls from a rough pine cupboard.

"That I live in Jackson Hole, Wyoming. That I have a fairly successful air charter business. I have a daughter who will start first grade in September, and a sister who is probably doing her best to comfort her right now. That this place is familiar, yet entirely different from my world. Hell, if I didn't know better, I'd swear I wasn't in 1997 any longer."

She whirled around, the bowls clutched to her chest. "Did you say 1997?"

"Yes," he replied slowly. "Don't try to tell me this isn't 1997."

"I'm afraid I must tell you so. Mr. Terrell, this is 1886."

Chapter Three

She watched him across the table, the few spoonsful of elk stew sitting in her stomach like stones. He'd claimed to be hungry, but he didn't fall on his food like other men she'd seen. His table manners suited a palace more than a cabin.

The uneasiness she'd experienced earlier paled in comparison to the full-blown case of nervous affliction that currently raced through her body. The reality of David Terrell inside the cabin overwhelmed her senses. They were alone. He spoke of strange objects and used words she'd never heard before. He should be a stranger—someone to fear.

But the panic she now felt wasn't caused by fear that he might do her harm. She'd passed that point as she'd set the table and he'd fetched water from the stream. Never had he taken a threatening action or expressed any unseemly behavior. Except for his denial of what had sent him into her time and his confusion over finding his way home, David Terrell was the most polite and reasonable man she'd ever met. No, this sensation was entirely different, as though a totally unanticipated event might happen at any moment.

As though she might do something unexpected.

She couldn't imagine what that might be . . . except for the urge to see whether his black hair was sleek and smooth, or thick and coarse. Or if he smelled as clean and fresh close up as he appeared across the table. If the shadow of beard on his jaw would scratch her fingertips if she stroked her hand across it.

She'd lost her appetite. Was that common around strangers? She didn't believe so. In the few times travelers had stopped for the night—and the occasions had been very rare—she'd been excited to hear news of the world they'd left behind, to listen to rousing stories of adventure in the mountains or across the plains. Her father, Jurgen, and the travelers usually talked late into the night, passing around the dark beer Papa loved or a jug that one of the men had brought with them.

She'd sat cross-legged by the fire as a girl and viewed photographs taken by a handsome visitor named William H. Jackson. She could still recall the amazement that she'd felt at his ability to capture nature so clearly on a thin sheet of glass. The mountain peaks she'd never climbed had rested in her hands. The big lake, quite some distance on foot, appeared serene and reflective in his wondrous photographs. He'd even taken a photograph of Papa, Jurgen, and her—a treasure now more than ever.

At fourteen, she'd fashioned herself quite in love with the exciting photographer. But not even William H. Jackson, some eight years past, had made her stomach churn and her heart beat like David Terrell.

He affected her as she'd imagined the princes of fairy

tales affected the princesses—with excitement and a budding belief in happily ever after. Which was childish, she knew, because he hadn't come from the sky—or the future—to rescue her from an evil stepmother or a dangerous villain. He was here accidentally, and she must remember that he needed to go back quickly to his home and daughter. If he didn't, the whole future might be changed, according to those wise people in a place called Hollywood. The thought made her shudder.

She forced another bite of the stringy meat down her throat, knowing she must eat, because tomorrow she'd continue to cut grass and haul it from the meadow. She'd left her scythe and twine back there, forgetting everything in the excitement of the great white birdlike plane swooping from the sky for the second time that day.

She'd thought he'd flown away, that she'd never see him again. Their contact had been so brief, yet so exciting. Almost unbelievable. She'd even wondered if she'd imagined the incident.

Then he'd appeared again, and her heart hadn't stopped pounding since.

He'd been chewing a mouthful of stew for a long time.

"I'm sorry the meat is a bit tough. The elk was old, I suppose." In fact, the poor beast had been tottering, one leg injured, and wouldn't have lived out the summer. Better a quick death than the terror of a wolf pack or the sudden pounce of a lion. Still, she'd cried when she'd shot the elk through the heart. And when she'd cut the flesh, still warm, and wrapped it in oiled cloth to carry back to the cabin.

"It's fine," he said, pausing to swallow. "Really, it's tasty."

"You're probably accustomed to much finer food where you come from," she ventured, wanting to know

48

more about such a magical place that produced conveyances that flew in the sky and rainbows that sent people on fantastic journeys.

"We eat stew," he said, taking a drink of water. "And lots of other things."

"Like what?" she asked, leaning forward against the table, her own meal forgotten.

"Pizza, for one. And hamburgers. My daughter loves SpaghettiOs, but I try to limit her to one can a week."

Analisa shook her head. "I don't know those foods. Do they grow in the field or do you prepare them from meat?"

He took a deep breath. "That's right; I'm hallucinating about 1886. Okay. Well, let's see. Pizza is made from dough, tomato sauce, spices, and cheese. Then you put meat and vegetables on top and bake it in an oven. And hamburgers are ground beef, usually cooked in a skillet, and served on a big roll that's been sliced in half."

"And the last one—the food your daughter likes?"

"SpaghettiOs. Kids love them, but their tastes change around puberty. Let's just say that canned pasta is a pale imitation of real spaghetti."

"I have canned food," she said in an encouraging tone. "Peaches and milk, mostly. But that other word . . ." Actually, there were several words she didn't understand: spaghetti, pasta, and puberty.

He looked at her, eyebrows raised, the silence stretching on. Finally, he relented. "Spaghetti? It's pasta with a tomato sauce."

She shook her head.

"You don't know about pasta?"

"No."

"Noodles?"

She sat up. "Yes, I fix noodles and spaetzel. My

49

mother taught me because my father and brother loved them so.''

''Your name is German, isn't it?''

''Yes, but I was born in Ohio. My father came from Germany and my mother's family was from England, many years ago. She learned to fix his favorites.''

David nodded. ''I like German food. And German beer. They make great beer.''

''My father made beer,'' Analisa said, glad to have a common topic of conversation. ''I believe I have some left in the cold room. I can check tomorrow morning.''

David finished most of his stew and pushed his chair back from the table. ''Are you going to tell me where your family is?''

Her happiness fled as quickly as it arrived. ''I should clear the table. Surely you're tired from your journey.''

''Not particularly. And I'll be glad to help.''

''No!'' She jumped to her feet and gathered her bowl and spoon. ''That's not the work of men.''

''My sister would disagree strongly with you,'' he replied, leaning back with his hands steepled over his stomach. ''She's quite the feminist.''

''I'm not sure whether that's good or bad, but my mother taught me to clean up after the menfolk.''

''In my time, we trade off chores. Well, most of us do anyway. I suppose that some men are still back in another decade.'' He leaned forward abruptly, startling her. ''And you still haven't answered my question.''

She reached across the table for his bowl and spoon, concentrating only on grabbing them and making a quick retreat. ''Which question?'' she asked casually, hoping he wouldn't see how much she dreaded talking about her family.

His hand reached out, covering her own with the

warmth of a strong grip. "About that father and brother you mentioned earlier."

Her gaze darted to his handsome face, but she didn't dare linger. Instead, she looked back at their joined hands. In the weak candlelight, his appeared golden and strong. "I don't like to talk about them," she said, her voice sounding breathless. Even she could detect panic. Would he care? Or would he press his advantage? "Please, I must clear the table."

"What's the hurry?"

His hand remained on hers yet didn't tighten or hold too firmly. She realized that she could pull away if she wanted to, yet she found herself looking up from the common oak planks and unfamiliar masculine hand to his face. To his dark, dark eyes.

"I'm afraid," she said before she could stop herself. Something about the way he gazed deeply into her eyes made her forget every survival skill she'd learned. Made her forget that Papa had told her never to be alone with a man because she could be hurt.

"I'm no threat to you, Analisa," David said gently. "I didn't mean to scare you. I just don't understand why you're always running away." He eased his hand off hers, as though he was certain she would bolt from the room.

She didn't. She took a deep breath and stopped the trembling in her hand by holding the bowl. "We don't get many strangers out here, Mr. Terrell," she admitted, not meeting his eyes. "We were the only family here until two years ago, when a few settlers moved into the valley. Even now, we don't visit much. I don't know how to act around you."

"Just act naturally. And please, call me David." He clasped his hands together, resting them on the table. "I don't expect anything from you, Analisa. If I could find somewhere to go, I wouldn't impose on you like this."

"I don't mind sharing my meal," she said, walking away from the table. She felt him watch her back. She should have changed into a dress but had so few that were long enough. Papa had said she'd grown like a weed, some six years past.

"But you do mind sharing your cabin," he finished when she didn't say anything else.

She placed the bowls beside the sink, then turned to face him. With the table between them, she felt much more comfortable. She could even look him in the eye without flinching. "You're welcome to stay. Like I said, I'm not accustomed to having guests."

Silence had been her companion for many months, but suddenly the lack of sound became so ominous that she didn't breath for fear of setting off an avalanche she couldn't control. The horrible, exciting feeling of anticipation returned, yet this time she recognized the source. He wanted her to admit the truth, to talk about feelings she'd lived with in silence since the winter. Fears and regrets and doubts she'd shared with no one.

"Because you're alone out here, right?"

His voice cut like a bell through the stillness of the night. She straightened, inhaled, ready to deny his words. Ready to tell him that her papa and brother were hunting, or trapping. That they'd be back any time. That they hadn't gone away and left her alone in this wilderness. But she couldn't. She let out the breath she'd held and blinked away the promise of unwelcome tears.

"They're dead, Mr. Terrell. And yes, I'm alone."

David couldn't sleep. He lay on the narrow bed and stared at the wood ceiling, wondering if Holly had managed to get Jamie to sleep, if they were even home. Had the FAA come? The police? Were they looking for his

52

plane? There would be nothing to go on, since Jackson Airport had no tower or radar, just radio communications. Only Holly's word that he'd flown into the sky and . . . what? Disappeared? What else could she say?

He pictured Jamie in her bedroom, the green glow of her Kermit nightlight illuminating her huddled form beneath the covers. Each night, he'd read to her from her seemingly endless library, then they'd say their prayers and he'd tuck her in. Before he went back downstairs, he always turned back to look at her. She'd smile and wiggle one finger from her grasp on the blanket, her way of saying good night. And he'd whisper, "Good night, Muppet," as he pulled her door closed.

The memory brought tears to his eyes, but he blinked them away. Dammit, he didn't want to cry. Crying was right up there with being confused on his list of things not to do. He rested his arm across his forehead, angry because there was no way to get back to Jamie, no way he could tell if this place was dream or reality. No way he could know if he'd been gone for hours or just minutes, if he'd disappeared or simply blacked out.

He prayed this was only a momentary blackout, and this reality, a dream.

Maybe if he could go to sleep in this nightmare, when he awoke he'd be back where he belonged. He couldn't remember having a dream where he went to sleep and then awoke. Dreams were bits and pieces, not an entire day. Not every little thing that he did, from sunup to sunset.

Yes, that's what he needed to do. Just go to sleep and wake up back in Jackson Hole, circa 1997. No more pioneer cabins, no barnyard animals and stringy elk stew. No Analisa Ludke, who lived alone in the woods and believed in women's work and magic kingdoms.

No more Analisa.

Strange, how the idea caused a shaft of pain to penetrate, even past the sadness he already felt for being separated from Jamie and Holly. He'd only met Analisa a few hours ago, yet he knew her in ways he'd never known women he'd dated for months.

For one thing, she was putting on a brave front, trying to make it out here on her own. He had only a clue as to the amount of work necessary to run a homestead without electricity or modern conveniences. Hell, what did she do for supplies? For animal feed? Not even the wildlife on the National Elk Refuge could survive without a government feeding program, so he was damn sure that goat and those chickens and the huge pig needed more than what grew here naturally. He'd read somewhere that it took dozens of acres to feed one head of cattle in Wyoming.

Analisa had a damned petting zoo.

Jamie would love it here.

At the thought of his daughter, he flopped onto his side, giving up all pretense of sleep. This place was too quiet. The exterior walls must be two feet deep, and the only window was in the front of the house, by the door. He was fairly certain Analisa had bolted both before going to bed.

He couldn't even hear the buzzing of insects or the call of a night bird. In the main room, the faint light from the embers of the fire he'd laid earlier filtered through the cabin, a cozy red-gold glow. He'd left his door open, needing no privacy. He'd just never expected the silence to feel so profound. It was as if he was the only person in the universe.

Maybe he was the only person in this universe. The only real person, that is. He knew that behind the other door, a certain tall blonde had retreated after showing him her brother's room, straight razor, and comb. Yes, *retreated* was definitely the word to use. She'd avoided him like he carried some deadly disease and couldn't wait to pass it on to her.

Hells bells. He didn't like thinking about that either. She'd probably bolted and blocked her bedroom door. If she was as innocent as she looked, she didn't know exactly *why* she was supposed to be terrified of him. But she was certain that he was going to "ravish" her, or some such nonsense, based on lessons she'd learned from her family.

He'd never ravished a woman in his life. At least, not one who hadn't wanted to participate in that particular fantasy. He sure as hell wasn't going to start with an innocent young lady who was a figment of his imagination.

In the main room, the fire shifted, crackled, and spit, then settled down. He couldn't see the fireplace from his bed, but the familiar sounds of the burning logs were comforting.

He concentrated once more on relaxing so he could drift off to sleep and awake from this hallucination, but this rustic cabin and the hush of midnight seemed so real.

What was that line from *A Christmas Carol*? Oh, yes. The old miser had blamed his ghostly Christmas visions on a spot of "bad beef."

David knew he couldn't assign Analisa Ludke to the role of "vision caused by spoiled food," but he had to keep on believing that this was a dream. That he'd wake up and be back in his plane, just starting his turn toward the airport. And everything would be there. All the power lines. All the roads. Jamie talking to him on the radio, then racing to meet the plane when he landed, excited that he'd finally flown across the rainbow and wished for a new mom. Or a princess.

Everything he held dear would be back to normal in the morning. He had to believe it. If he could only close his eyes and get some sleep.

He concentrated on his breathing. He relaxed his muscles, beginning in his forehead and working down from his neck to his shoulders to his chest. He blocked all negative thoughts from his mind.

Then he heard the noise.

Analisa. His eyes popped open and he sat upright in bed.

She should never have answered his question, never admitted that Papa and Jurgen were gone from this earth. Ever since dinner, she'd thought of nothing but the loneliness and fear their passing had caused. And she remembered the anger she'd felt when she'd learned their fate—an anger she shouldn't feel toward ones so dear.

She'd loved them. Despite Jurgen's restlessness and Papa's gruffness, they'd been her only family for eleven years. When Mama died that first winter in Wyoming of a lung fever, Papa had been strong for them all. And when Jurgen grew into manhood, he'd stayed part of the family despite his need to explore new places.

He'd always wanted to see the land on the other side of the mountains, living his adventures through the tales of others who'd ventured west to Oregon and California, north into Canada, or south to the uninhabited deserts. Jurgen absorbed their stories of discoveries and developments, yearning to be part of the growth of this country.

Trappers had found his body beneath the snow, on the west side of the pass, beyond the peaks that had called his name. And Papa . . . she could only imagine that he'd gone with Jurgen to share his excitement over seeing a new expanse of this land.

Rocks and trees, dirt and lakes. The mountains were the same on either side. There was no reason to die to see the western slopes. No reason to take Papa across the pass in winter, when the snow drifted higher than two tall men and fell for days on end.

No need to die and leave her here, all alone.

She bit back another sob but couldn't help the sniffle of unshed tears. Carefully tamping down the anger, telling herself to think kindly of her brother, she hugged her arms and waited for peace to return.

"Analisa?"

She jumped, her heart pounding, sending her straight from the stool near the hearth to a stumbling halt beside the uneven rocks of the chimney.

"I'm sorry. I didn't mean to startle you."

David stood just outside the doorway to Jurgen's room, his face a golden glow from the embers she'd stirred to life just moments before, his shirt unbuttoned and hanging loose over his pants.

Thankfully, darkness shielded her eyes from the sight of his unclothed chest.

"You scared me nearly to death," she whispered, her voice as unsteady as her nerves. "What are you doing up so late?"

"I couldn't sleep." He shrugged, a movement she could barely see in the darkness of the room. "Then I heard a noise."

He'd heard her, sitting beside the fire, feeling sorry for herself when she should be rejoicing that she had a cabin and wood to warm the nights. "I'm sorry. I didn't realize I'd . . . I'm not used to having someone around."

"Don't apologize. I'm the one intruding." He stepped closer to the hearth. "Is there anything I can do to help?" he asked gently.

"No," she said quickly. Too quickly, she realized as

57

she noticed the spark of interest in his eyes. He no doubt wondered what she was doing up, why she'd felt the need to stare morosely into the fire when she should be getting a good night's rest.

She stepped back to the stool and picked up her quilt, which she'd dumped on the floor when he'd surprised her. "I'll just be getting back to bed."

She swung the soft, thick fabric around her shoulders, watching his face as she gathered the fold across her arms. And she didn't miss another spark of interest, this one directed lower—toward her chest and stomach, covered decently by the white gown. So why did his gaze make her feel . . . unclothed? Her skin burned, as if the fire had reached out and singed her belly and breasts. To her mortification, her nipples tightened.

She shifted, her feet cold against the wood floor despite the heat that coursed through the rest of her body. The cotton of her gown, once so soft, seemed coarse and stiff against her breasts. The quilt hugged her close, just as she'd imagined so many times a kind and wonderful prince would do if he ever rescued her from this wilderness.

"I think that's a good idea," he said hoarsely.

"What?" She couldn't remember what she'd said before.

"Going to bed."

"I beg your pardon?"

"You said that you should get back to bed. That would be the wise thing to do. Now. Before . . ." He stepped closer—so close that she saw the embers reflected in his dark eyes, watched the pulse beat wildly on the side of his neck. And lower, where his muscles stretched tight across his chest, the center covered in fine black hair.

She wanted to place her hand in the middle of his

chest. To see if his flesh burned as hot as hers, if the hair on his golden, tight skin was as soft as that on his head.

"Analisa?"

"Yes?"

"If you keep looking at me like that, I'm going to take your words as an invitation."

"Which words?" she asked, still distracted by the way his shirt fell open all the way to his waist. She could even see his navel where his pants gaped away from this stomach as he inhaled deeply.

"Analisa, do you know what you're doing?"

She tore her gaze away from his body and focused on his face. "What do you mean?"

"That if you're getting turned on by this whole firelight and deserted cabin scene, I'll be glad to take you to bed and satisfy that particular fantasy."

"Fantasy?"

He stepped even closer. She smelled his scent, so unique and clean, and experienced the heat of his body. He was burning hot, as hot as the embers in the hearth. She wanted to step back, but she'd taken root at this spot. All she could do was wait, her heart beating fast, her breath shallow and rapid.

"I couldn't have imagined a more lovely woman to share this dream," he said, his voice as soft as a snowflake. "I've been telling myself that I was hallucinating this visit to the past, that I was really still up in my plane, unconscious."

"You are not in your plane," she whispered. "You're here in this cabin."

"Whatever you say. All I know is that you're here with me, and you obviously want me as much as I want you."

"I want you?" His words made no sense, but some-

how her body understood, warming, tingling with awareness and a sudden yearning to be closer still to this man.

"Yes, you do," he said, his head angling closer, his
lips parted.

Her heart seemed to skip a beat. Time stopped as the
combination of his words and her body's reaction seeped
into her consciousness. "I don't know what you mean,"
she said carefully. The panicky feeling returned, cooling
the heat of her body, breaking her free from the
strangely exhilarating lethargy that had stolen over her
like morning clouds easing over the highest peaks.

"Then let me give you a hint," he whispered, their
lips nearly touching.

She pushed both hands against his chest, coming in
contact with his firm, warm skin and soft, silky hair. For
a moment the sensation of touching him distracted her—
he felt as good as she'd imagined—but then she remembered that she was in danger of encouraging behavior
no one would agree was proper.

"No, Mr. Terrell," she said firmly. Or at least she
hoped her tone was firm. Her voice sounded thin and
wavering to her ears.

"Call me David," he said, placing his hands over
hers, holding her close to his body.

The feeling of warmth shot all the way up her arms,
settling again in her midsection. "Listen to me. You are
not dreaming all this. I didn't know what you were doing
. . . I've never been alone with a man before and—"

"I know. That's a really nice touch to this fantasy."

"I am not a fantasy!" she said, shoving him with all
her strength.

He let her go, his hands falling to his sides as she
repositioned the quilt around her shoulders for protection
from his eyes.

"Analisa, I have to believe you're part of my dream.

Nothing else makes sense.'' The confusion in his eyes caused her to pause for just a moment.

"This all makes perfect sense," she said, deciding the only intelligent action was to get away from his potent charm. She backed toward her room.

"Don't run away." He took one step toward her, then stopped. "Look, I didn't mean to scare you. I saw how you were looking at me. That's a big turn-on for a guy."

"I don't know what you mean." She hugged the quilt close, feeling the chill of the room and the floor for the first time in forever. "You surprised me. And your shirt . . . You shouldn't have come out undressed."

"I wasn't the one standing in front of the fire wearing nothing but a thin nightgown."

Heat flared in her cheeks as she opened her mouth to speak. However, her voice was as useless as her good sense had been moments before. Instead of arguing with him further, she backed into her room, hitting her heel on the frame and slamming the door before he could embarrass her any more.

Not that he could have said anything more mortifying. Except maybe to remind her again of the way she'd nearly caressed him with her eyes. Hopping to the bed, she sat down and rubbed her foot.

What had come over her, so suddenly, so unexpectedly? No one had prepared her for this kind of a reaction to a man. Not her mother, before she died when Analisa was only ten, or her gruff father, who didn't speak of such things. Or Jurgen, who perhaps didn't know himself.

But David Terrell knew. He knew, and he hadn't told her what to expect. He had some explaining to do in the morning.

If she could bear to face him again.

Chapter Four

David awoke to the clang of metal hitting metal, then the hiss of sizzling grease and the smell of bacon. He sat up in bed, his heart pounding from waking so suddenly, and tried to remember where he was. Had Holly come over to fix him breakfast? And why was it so dark in here?

He blinked, searching the room for some clue. Gone was his vaulted loft, the natural wood shining in the soft morning light. Gone was the expanse of windows overlooking a stand of aspen along the creek, with the Tetons as a backdrop.

Gone.

He was in Analisa's cabin, in 1886, his plane resting uselessly in a mountain meadow.

The knowledge that this wasn't a dream left him lightheaded, his breathing shallow. David swung his legs over the side of the bed and tried to stop his mind from racing in circles. Gone. Everything he knew was gone. Jamie, Holly, his life, his business. Gone.

"Damn," he whispered, resting his head in his hands. *This can't be real.*

"Breakfast will be ready in just a minute. If you want some, you'd better be there." Analisa's cold, clipped voice broke into his thoughts. He looked up quickly, but only caught sight of her skirt as she pivoted in the doorway.

Why was she so angry? He scrubbed his scratchy eyes with his palms, trying to make sense of this nightmare. Except it was no nightmare. He'd gone to bed last night convinced that if he could just sleep, then awaken in the morning, he'd be back where he belonged. But he had slept for hours. He'd . . .

David moaned. He'd tried to seduce Analisa in front of the fire, that's what he'd done. And she'd turned him down. That fact alone should have convinced him that this was no fantasy. If it were *his* fantasy, they would have made love in front of the glowing fire. She would have responded to his touch in that wonderful, innocent way of hers. He would have taught her all she needed to know about making love throughout the long night.

His body tensed immediately at the image of Analisa, her pale skin gilded red and gold, writhing on a blanket in front of the fire.

"Damn," he muttered again, shivering as he threw back the covers and stood in the cool, dark bedroom. He needed more than cold air to douse his arousal—a dunking in the mountain stream was more like it. First, he'd answer another call of nature, then find some cold water to splash on his face and any other parts of his anatomy that needed a jolt of reality.

He carefully pulled on and zipped his jeans. He threw

on his shirt more quickly, buttoning it as he gathered his socks and boots.

"I'm putting the food on the table in one minute, Mr. Terrell, if you want any." Analisa's curt voice carried from the kitchen through the cabin like a rifle shot.

She had every right to be angry. He was lucky she hadn't brained him with the frying pan while he slept in her brother's bed. Instead, she was in the kitchen, cooking breakfast, offering—albeit somewhat angrily—to share her food.

Less than twenty-four hours into the past, and he was already in hot water. How had he studiously avoided any trouble with women in his own time, yet managed to alienate an innocent, formerly sweet-natured young lady in hers?

"I'll be right back," he called, sliding his foot into a boot. Hurrying out the front door so he wouldn't be too late for breakfast, he looked right and left for the outhouse. As soon as he pulled the heavy cabin door shut behind him, a chorus of frantic quacks, grunts, chirps, bleats, and moos greeted him. Descending like a John Carpenter version of *Animal Farm,* Analisa's petting zoo raced toward him. Ducks, a goat, and that huge pig scampered across the yard, scattering chickens in their wake. They followed his hasty retreat around the side of the cabin, toward the rough-hewn wooden structure nestled between two lodgepole pines downstream. His boots weren't made for running; he stumbled several times on tufts of grass. As he slammed the door of the outhouse, the biggest white duck he'd ever seen nipped the back of his leg.

"Ouch!" He rubbed the spot above his boot, frowning into the darkness.

Standing in the primitive porta-potty, his heart still racing, David wondered if life in the past would get any

easier. Or if he'd just blunder from one mistake to another, one bizarre incident to the next, until he discovered a way out of this mess.

Or, he thought, sobering instantly, would he ever find
his way home?

Analisa barely glanced up as her houseguest walked
toward the table.

"Sorry I'm late," he said, pulling out a chair.

"Hmpf," she muttered, refusing to look up. She
didn't need to glance at him again to know he'd washed
his face and slicked back his hair. His shirt was buttoned
and tucked in, and he looked not at all like he had last
night. So warm, so golden-skinned and taut, standing too
close. So close she could . . .

Stop it, she told herself. He'd taken advantage of her
in a very ungentlemanly fashion. She was going to talk
to him about his behavior . . . as soon as she could think
of a way that didn't send ripples of embarrassment down
her spine.

"This is very good," he said, taking another bite of
the griddle cakes and following it with a slice of bacon.
He chewed, swallowed, then continued. "I appreciate
the meal, especially after all I've done to—"

"I don't want to talk about it!" she nearly shouted,
standing so abruptly her chair wobbled. She grabbed the
wooden back, settling it on the floor.

"Analisa, I'm sorry."

"I said I don't want to talk about it." She gathered
her dishes and turned toward the sink.

"You won't accept my apology?"

"I haven't decided." Her hands shook as she put the
plate and cup on the sideboard by the sink. If he thought
he could just apologize for trying to have his way with
her last night, then he had another think coming. She

wasn't some hurdy-gurdy dancer who winked and flirted with a man. At least, that's what she'd heard those women did. Until last night, she hadn't had a clue as to the mystery of men and women.

She would have been better off not knowing.

"I'm truly sorry to have caused you such inconvenience. I know you're not used to cooking for strangers and I—"

"Cooking?" she asked, whirling around, her gaze meeting his for the first time. "You're sorry about the *cooking?*"

"No," he said carefully. "I was just starting there."

"Fine. I don't want to talk about it." She turned back to the sink and scraped her half-finished breakfast into the slop bucket.

She listened to him finish his meal as she poured water into a kettle and placed it on the hot stove. When he pushed back his chair, she almost jumped out of her skin. His slow footsteps echoed across the floor. Closer, closer . . .

She grabbed her plate, ready to get the dishes washed so she could escape his overwhelming presence.

"Let me do that," he said, his breath teasing the back of her neck where she'd drawn up her hair. Like a proper lady. So he wouldn't think she was a loose woman.

"Do what?" she asked, raising her chin. She struck what she hoped was a haughty pose, staring at the cabinet in front of her. "And please don't stand so close."

He reached around her, taking the dirty dish from her hand. "Let me wash up. You cook, I wash. Okay?" She heard the suppressed laughter in his voice. More humor at her expense.

"No!" The feel of his arm against her shoulder was more than she could bear. She let the plate go, sidling away from him. "I told you that dishes were a woman's work."

"Not where I come from," he said patiently, looking at the bucket, the dishes, and the water simmering on the stove. "I'd spend a couple of nights in the doghouse if Holly ever learned I'd let a woman wait on me hand and foot."

"Mr. Terrell, I—"

"David."

She refused to be that informal with him. Her mother had explained once that too casual an attitude invited unwanted familiarity. Finally, Analisa understood what her mother had meant. There was no way she was going to encourage David—Mr. Terrell—to become amorous.

No way would she do such a thing.

And who was Holly? His wife? Oh, Lord, of course he was married . . . and she'd almost kissed him last night. She wanted to hide her head, scream in frustration, beat on his chest. Something.

"What?" he asked, scraping the last of the eggs into the bucket for the sow.

"What?"

"You were getting ready to scold me for something."

"I was not scolding you!"

"Really?" He looked up, a smile on his face, his dark eyes twinkling.

"Most certainly."

"Then what were you going to say?"

She opened her mouth, then shut it. Truth be known, she had no idea what she'd been about to say. Her argument had flown out of her head like a startled grouse. The man was exasperating! She pitied his poor wife. He didn't act like she thought a married man should act, although he did have a daughter.

Of course, she hadn't known many married men. And

certainly not any who insisted on working in the kitchen.

He concentrated on pouring hot water over the dishes in the sink. She didn't care if he was married or not. If he had a dozen wives. She handed him the bar of lye soap.

"I'm going to feed Rose," she announced, circling around him and picking up the bucket. "Please try not to break any dishes."

"I'll do my best," he answered, that slight, infuriating smile still on his lips.

The sun was barely peeking through the line of pines as David stood by the window and watched Analisa walk toward the cabin, empty slop bucket in one hand, nearly full milk pail in the other. Two ducks and a goat trailed behind her, jockeying for position.

He'd finished the dishes—no small feat, considering he'd been forced to use bar soap instead of detergent. He finally understood what commercials meant when they described "dishwater hands." A few more days of this and his skin would be as wrinkled as one of Analisa's gnarled old trolls.

He wondered what she did with all that milk.

Turning away from the sight of her striding quickly in a too-short, too-snug dress, he returned to the table and straddled a chair. He could sure use a cup of coffee but figured in the wilderness that staple item was hard to come by.

She opened the door just enough to squeeze through. Outside, David heard the pleading quack of that damned big duck—the one with the taste for human flesh—and saw a flash of white feathers as Analisa shut the door.

"He'd make a fine dinner," David commented as she walked past him, chin high and eyes anywhere except where he sat.

"I'm sure he doesn't share your opinion."

David laughed. "Probably not." He swung his leg over the chair and stood up. "What are you going to do today?"

"Cut grass," she replied, storing the empty bucket beside the sink. "Up in the high meadow."

"Where I landed yesterday?"

"Yes."

"I'll come with you."

"You don't need to—"

"I want to help. Besides, it will give me a chance to check on my plane."

"No one will disturb your property up there."

"Why's that?"

"Because no one else is here," she said, pouring the milk into a pan on the warm stove.

"You don't have any neighbors?"

"Not up the mountain." She took a jar from the cabinet and unscrewed the lid. "Two families live closer to the river, but it's a good distance and we don't visit except to trade. There's also a new family across the ridge by the lake."

He watched her efficient movements as she stirred something into the milk. "What are you doing?" he asked when he realized she wasn't going to expound on her neighbors.

"I'm making cheese," she said distractedly, placing a cover on the pan, then wiping her hands on a towel. She finally looked at him, but not for long.

He wondered if she was remembering last night.

He hoped she forgave him soon. He didn't like this rollercoaster of emotions he felt around her: teasing one moment, angry the next, frustrated most of the time. How could he find his way home if he couldn't think straight?

"Do you need any help with the chores?"

"No, thank you."

"When will you go cut hay?"

"Not long." She nodded toward the pan on the stove. "The curd needs to set, then I'll drain it. After that, we can leave."

"I'd really like to help out with the chores. Are you sure there isn't something I could do to help?"

"No!" she said too quickly. He watched as she closed her eyes, expelled a big sigh, and swallowed. Her lids lifted slowly and she looked at him across the kitchen. "I'm sorry. I'm not accustomed to having someone else around."

"I'm getting on your nerves," David responded, wondering if she'd kick him out.

"I . . . I suppose so."

"I'd leave, Analisa, but I don't know where to go."

"I didn't ask you to leave."

"But I make you uncomfortable."

She shook her head in denial, but he guessed she didn't want to tell him the truth. Analisa was nothing if not soft-hearted, even to strange men who tried to seduce her at the first opportunity. Even to obnoxious attack ducks.

"If you can tell me where else to go, I will. Or I can stay in the barn. I don't want to inconvenience you. After all, you didn't exactly invite me to stay."

"I did offer," she said weakly.

"Analisa, I have no idea how long I'll be here. Believe me, I want to go home. I just don't know how," he said with a shrug.

"The rainbow." She said it as though the explanation were perfectly clear.

"A rainbow is an optical illusion caused by water droplets in the atmosphere." He remembered explaining the same phenomena to Jamie just yesterday, less than twenty-four hours ago. The thought of his daughter, missing him as he missed her, sent a shaft of pain through his heart. "I don't know what happened up there, but I've got to find out."

"You don't believe in the magic, do you?" Analisa asked softly.

"I believe in physics," he replied. "And I believe that there must be a reasonable explanation for this . . . journey into the past." Something that didn't involve fairy tales and superstitions better suited for children than grown men.

She shook her head. "I think maybe you'll need to believe before it will work."

"Before what will work?"

"A magical rainbow. It's the only way home, I'm afraid."

"What do you mean, we're going to walk up to the meadow? What's wrong with that huge horse of yours?"

"Nothing," Analisa hedged, placing the remaining griddle cakes and smoked, dried elk into an oiled cloth square. "But I only have one horse."

"We'll share."

She shook her head. "I don't think that would work."

"You mean your horse wouldn't let us both ride him at once?"

"Her," Analisa corrected. "Her name is Tommelise."

"That's an unusual name for a horse."

"She's named after a fairy tale."

"Why does that not surprise me?" David looked out the window, where Tommelise bobbed her head up and down, irritated at being tied to the fence so long. "So she won't let us both ride her?"

"I . . . I'm not sure." Analisa tied their lunch with a length of twine. She had no excuse to linger in the cabin, yet she hesitated. How could she admit her fears without confirming what David probably already knew—that she reacted like a loose, unprincipled woman when he came too near. She was still slightly angry with him for pushing her to respond in such a wanton way last night. If she tried to discuss her complaints, he wouldn't take her seriously. He'd no doubt smile, tease, and laugh his way through the conversation until she dropped the topic entirely. Just like he had at breakfast.

Exasperating man.

"Then let's try it," he said, breaking into her thoughts. "What's the worst thing that could happen?"

I could touch you as I long to do. I could close my eyes and kiss you, she wanted to shout. Instead, she took a deep breath, then said, "One of us, or both of us, could be thrown."

"So, we'll get on her where the ground is soft. I've been thrown before."

"I wouldn't want you to get hurt." The truth was that she wasn't about to straddle Tommelise's back with David snuggled up behind her. She knew little of men, but that situation seemed more than risky. And not because they might be thrown. Something about the position seemed very improper . . . even more improper than being in the cabin alone at night.

Although she'd changed from a dress to her shirt, pants, and boots, she didn't feel protected from his assessing gaze. Why she'd even bothered with a dress— one too short and tight—showed how ridiculous she was acting. She didn't even wear a dress when Charlie came to visit.

"Do you have a saddle?"

"Yes, but I don't use it often."

"We can use it today." He ran a hand through his hair. "Look, why don't I saddle her? Tommelise and I will get to know each other."

"You know your way around horses?"

"Yeah. I might not know much about chores or life in 1886, but I can take care of a horse," he answered with a trace of bitterness in his voice.

"You have horses where you came from?"

He nodded. "I have three of my own. We ride them for pleasure, but ranches use horses to work cattle. And there's racing, cutting horse events, police work. Lots of uses."

"I'm glad that horses are still important in your world," she said. "What about other animals? Do you have the same kind?"

He glanced out the window and produced a lopsided smile. "We have them. Although most people don't keep a zoo in their yard."

"A zoo?"

"Never mind. I suppose the saddle is in the barn."

"Yes, but—"

"Don't worry. I can saddle your horse." He turned his back and walked toward the door.

"I'm not worried, but I wish you'd consider walking," she said, her voice rising as he continued to stride across the floor.

"Analisa, this is silly. I'm perfectly willing to help you cut the hay, but I don't see why we should use all our energy getting there."

With that last comment, he went through the door and shut it behind him.

Well, he was certainly used to getting his own way, Analisa thought as she grabbed their lunch, her gloves, and the whetstone for sharpening the sickle. With a last look around the kitchen, at the curd draining into the pan and the neatly stacked dishes David had washed, she walked toward the door.

Outside, she stood near Tommelise's head and stroked her mare's soft gray muzzle and smooth, wide head. She might as well relax and accept David's help, Analisa told herself, but the concept seemed as foreign as the culture and inventions from his time.

If he insisted on riding together, she wanted to get going, even though she dreaded climbing onto Tommelise's back with him. Perhaps a saddle would be better. At least they wouldn't be quite as close. She'd ridden double on Tommelise when she and Jurgen were younger, and that hadn't been too bad. Of course, David wasn't Jurgen. She didn't feel at all sisterly toward her unexpected houseguest.

But perhaps she was making too much fuss over this fascination she felt for the stranger. She should probably accept his help, allow him to pack the soil close around the buildings against the winter freeze. Cut and stack the summer grasses. Help her gather what she'd need for the coming season.

There were so many things to do, like making cheese while she cut hay. She wondered if she'd be able to keep up this winter, when the snow fell as high as the fence and she needed a rope strung between the house and the barn to keep from getting lost while doing her chores. And where would David Terrell be when the snows came?

Would he find his way home before rainbows ceased to form in the sky? She'd never seen a rainbow late in the year. Surely not past the first snow, when the aspens turned yellow and a blanket of frost covered the ground each morning.

But she couldn't worry about winter now. Not on such a mild, sunny day.

Very early that morning, she'd escaped the sounds of David's even breathing and the images of them standing near the hearth. She'd slipped outside while the sky was barely pink in the east, leaned against the rough boards of the fence, and inhaled the fresh dawn air. When the ghostly mist drifted up from the creek, the smells of the forest became trapped low to the ground. Every time she drew a breath, she imagined she captured some of the magic of the toadstools, trees, and woodland creatures. That the mystery of the forest became a part of her, making her as strong as the largest tree, as wise as the crafty fox, as brave as the scolding jay.

Fanciful thoughts, to be sure. Perhaps she had read too many tales as a child, and tried too hard to believe as she grew older.

She shook her head to clear the images of forest and mist. The truth was that the dampness was a nuisance, not a magic tonic. Dew caused the steel sickle to rust. That's why Papa had always told her to keep the tools clean and dry.

She shouldn't have left everything out last night, but she had been sorely distracted when David's plane swooped down from the sky. And when he'd stepped into her meadow.

As if her thoughts of him had caused his appearance, he walked out of the barn carrying a heavy woven blanket and the army saddle her Papa had traded for years ago. She kept the old leather oiled, yet she knew it must be dusty from disuse.

"You weren't kidding when you said you didn't use it often," he said, throwing the saddle over the top rail. He shook out the blanket and let Tommelise smell the dusty fabric.

She snorted loudly in disapproval.

"I know, girl," David soothed the mare with a hearty

75

rub to her neck. "It's just one of those necessary evils. You're not going to give me any trouble, are you?"

"She's well mannered but spirited."

"That's okay," he replied, stroking Tommelise but looking at Analisa. "I like a filly with spirit."

"She's hardly a filly. She's fourteen years old."

"Is that the only reason she's still a filly instead of a mare?"

Analisa felt her cheeks warm. "Mr. Terrell, I don't wish to discuss such matters."

"I take it the answer is that she's never been bred."

She broke her gaze from his dark eyes and stared at the line of pines beyond her small yard.

"I didn't think so," he said with laughter in his voice. "But you've got to admit she likes me well enough."

"I think it's too soon to tell. She may buck when you try to ride."

"Oh, maybe just a little. But then, I can handle her."

"You're awfully confident." She heard the creak of old leather and looked back at him. He swung the saddle onto Tommelise's back with ease.

"Experience. I've seen how she watches me. How she reacts to my touch. I think we'll get along just fine." He smiled as he gathered the girth beneath the mare's belly. "I'd say that before long she won't be wary of me at all."

She didn't know exactly what David found so amusing, and she wasn't about to ask.

"She might have had a reason to be afraid at first, but I'm willing to go slow. If I did startle her, I'm certainly sorry."

"I don't remember her shying around you before."

"Really? I think she was definitely skittish. I probably did something she wasn't expecting."

Analisa frowned. What was he talking about? "I believe you're reading more into your observations that you should. A horse can be very complicated.''

"Much like people," he said with a grin. "And maybe I wasn't talking about the mare.''

"Then what are you . . .'' Awareness hit her like the slap of a tree limb. Her cheeks became even more warm and her fists clenched against the rails. "Was that your feeble attempt to apologize for what you did last night?''

"Yes, I suppose it was. Did I blow it?''

"Did you what?''

"Make a mess of things. Ruin any chances of redeeming myself in your eyes.''

"You . . . I'm not sure what to say to you. You twist everything around so much. Why can't you just be honest?''

He leaned one arm against the saddle and stared at her. "Analisa, I don't think you're ready for my honest confession.''

"How would you know?'' she asked, raising her chin and staring back.

"Because if I told you how much I want to hold you again, you'd gasp in outrage. If I explained that I get turned on just imagining what you'd look like in the firelight, you'd slap my face. And if I threw caution to the wind and kissed you this very instant, you'd run away. Or push me away. And I wouldn't blame you.''

"Then why are you telling me this?'' she cried in confusion. "Why say these things to me at all? Why can't you stop tormenting me?''

"I don't know. I keep telling myself to stay away from you, that you're not the kind of woman I should feel this way about. But then I look at you and all my good intentions fly out of my head. I'm left with this overpowering lust and . . . well, let's just say that I can't remember feeling this way about anyone but you.''

77

"Why me?"

"I have no idea," he replied, shaking his head. "I know I shouldn't."

"You most certainly shouldn't!"

"But at least I'm being honest with you. Since I can't seem to control my desire, I wanted to let you know that I can at least control my actions."

"And you think that I'll feel better knowing you have these thoughts? I'm supposed to be alone with you and not worry that you'll act on these . . . urges?"

"I'd never do anything to harm you. I said it before and I mean it now."

"You'll not sneak up on me in the night with your shirt unbuttoned?" she asked with a touch of lingering bitterness.

"I'm not totally to blame for last night," he said in a defensive tone of voice. "You participated pretty well yourself."

"I didn't know what was happening!" How could he be so ungentlemanly as to remind her that she'd responded to his nearness?

"I realized that this morning. But last night you were part of the fantasy, and I didn't know you were real."

"I'm very real. And I don't appreciate being treated like I'm some . . . I'm no loose woman!" she finished with passion.

He stepped around Tommelise's head, his dark eyes intense.

Analisa had the urge to run, but that wouldn't do any good. He'd overtake her if he wanted to. Besides, she had nowhere to go. She had to reclaim her confidence, to tell him that this was her home and she wouldn't be intimidated by some man who flew in the sky and made her feel in ways she'd never imagined.

But at the moment, her overpowering feeling was fear,

tinged with something else. That elusive emotion she'd experienced before.

Excitement.

Her breath caught as he cupped her cheek in his large, strong hand. His skin was warm and he smelled slightly of horse and dust. She shouldn't find that combination a feast for her senses, but on David, she did.

"I know you're not a loose woman. You're as innocent as they come. And I won't destroy that innocence."

"You promise that you won't touch me?" she whispered.

"Touch you? I'm afraid I must," he said with a tender smile. "And more, if you'd like. But I won't seduce you. I won't make you do anything you don't want to do."

Her heart beat so fast she knew he must feel the pounding. "I can't think when you're touching me."

"Never admit that to me, Analisa."

"Why?"

"Because you're too darned innocent. Too inexperienced to know what you do to me, too honest to hide your feelings, too sweet to resist."

Before she could respond, his head slanted, dipped low. She stared at his lips, parted and inviting, until the image blurred and she closed her eyes.

Chapter Five

The first touch of his lips was light as a summer breeze, his breath warmer than her heated skin. And then it was more firm, caressing her, coaxing a sigh that he sealed inside her mouth. Oh, the sudden burst of wonder that filled her! She'd never imagined such a feeling. With the first stroke of his tongue against her lips, she nearly melted into his embrace.

Then suddenly he drew back, leaving her aching for more, breathless with anticipation. She opened her eyes and found herself pinned by his dark gaze.

"You're supposed to tell me no," he said softly, his hands holding her arms in a gentle, reassuring way. "You're not supposed to encourage me to keep on kissing you until we both go up in flames."

"I am?"

"Yes. You most definitely should resist me."

"I told you I can't think when you touch me."

"And what did I tell you?"

"Never to admit that." She frowned. "I'm doing it again. Every time we . . . every time I'm close to you, my common sense deserts me."

"Please, say no more. Right now, I'm trying my best to behave like a gentleman, but you've got to do your part."

"I'll try," she answered sincerely. And she meant it. She must do a better job of resisting his powerful charm. If she didn't know better, she'd think that he'd cast some sort of magic spell over her. If she believed such a thing could happen. But then again, he'd been touched by magic. He could fly in the sky. . . .

David finished saddling Tommelise, then swung into the saddle. She rolled her eyes back and pranced, protesting a stranger on her back, but soon quieted as David kept her busy, turning in circles, stopping, and changing directions.

Analisa leaned against the fence and watched as he and Tommelise became acquainted. With a few minutes, he trotted the mare to the fence.

"I'm ready to go if you are," he announced, kicking his left boot out of the stirrup and reaching out with his hand.

"But . . . you want me to ride in back of you?" Analisa hoped the panic she felt didn't show in her voice. Could she touch him again this soon after behaving so foolishly?

"If you don't mind. Of course, if you'd rather not, I'll get behind you."

The image of them so close returned in a rush, humming through her body with delirious speed. If he were behind, he'd put his arms around her, snuggle his chest against her. No, she couldn't stand the idea. "How do I get on?"

"Just place your foot in the stirrup and swing up. I'll help."

"If you say so," she mumbled doubtfully. She wanted to grab the saddle, but David was in the way. She settled for his strong hand tugging her up as she swung her right leg over Tommelise's back.

The mare shied and danced some more. "She's not used to this. Maybe I'd better walk," Analisa said, grabbing David's waist in a desperate attempt to stay on her mare's back.

"She'll be okay. She could probably carry the offensive line of the Dallas Cowboys."

"The what?" she asked, letting go of him as soon as Tommelise quieted. She removed her hands from David's waist and held tightly to the back of the saddle.

"Some big guys in Texas." He clucked to Tommelise and soon they were off, quickly walking away from the cabin, scattering a few chickens and sending the ducks quacking and flapping their wings.

Riding behind the saddle provided a very different sensation. Tommelise's normally smooth walk seemed much more rocking. As the mare picked her way over the rocky ground, Analisa gave up her hold on the cantle of the saddle and grabbed David.

At first she held on to the fabric of his shirt, but when that didn't seem substantial enough, she splayed her fingers around his middle. She could feel his firm, warm skin and ribs. With each rolling step of the mare, the urge to slide her hands to the front and hold on even tighter grew stronger.

Remembering David's warning just minutes ago, she didn't act on the urge. But she did need to apologize for touching him. "I'm sorry. I'm not used to riding this way."

"That's okay," he said, reaching back and positioning her hands lower, against the waistband of his denim pants. "I don't mind. I'm used to riding double. Just hold on a little lower. Your fingers tickle."

"Sorry," she said, embarrassed that she'd unintentionally provoked that response. She was also extremely curious about who might have been riding double with him. His daughter, perhaps? Or the woman named Holly, who very well could be his wife?

The midmorning sun warmed her as they left the shadows of the pines for the wide grassland that stretched between the sloping hills.

"You'll have to show me the trail," David advised as they proceeded up the gentle incline. "I'm not sure I remember exactly where we walked yesterday."

Analisa leaned right, peering around his wide shoulders. "Just go up a ways. You'll see the elk trail before long. They migrate up from the low pastures each summer."

"You must have had an early warm spell."

"We did. Very early. It's unusual to have tall grass so soon, but I'm going to take advantage of it to get an extra cutting."

They rode in silence for several strides. Analisa became more accustomed to her mare's gait.

"I never thought about what people did before there were hay balers and tractors," David said, his tone contemplative. "Cutting by hand seems like such hard work."

She shrugged. "I don't have any choice. Jurgen and Papa used to handle such things, but now that they're gone, I must make sure we have feed for the animals this winter."

"In my time, we buy the big round bales or smaller square ones and have them delivered. The same with feed. It comes in fifty-pound sacks from somewhere else, maybe Kansas or Nebraska. I'm not sure. We can get feed year 'round, unless there's a pretty severe blizzard and the roads are blocked.''

She remembered milder winters and roads, neighbors to visit and mercantiles where all manner of items could be bought. The Ohio of her childhood had no doubt changed, although it probably wasn't as advanced as David's era. "That sounds wonderful. I worry that the animals might not have enough with only me to feed them.''

"I'll help.''

She thought about his quick, unthinking response. How could she depend on him when he might be gone tomorrow? Once he accepted the fact that the rainbow was his way home, all he had to do was fly away. And she knew he would. He missed his world, the conveniences she couldn't imagine, and, most of all, his daughter.

And that woman named Holly.

There was no time like the present to ask.

"You mentioned that Holly didn't believe in women's work,'' Analisa remarked as casually as possible. "What did you mean by that?''

"She's what you call a liberated woman,'' David replied with a chuckle. "I gave Jamie a Barbie doll last Christmas and I thought Holly was going to go through the roof.''

"What do you mean?''

"Barbie is a very girlish doll. She's got long legs and big—never mind. Let's just say that she doesn't look like most real women. Holly also objects to the way Barbie is often portrayed in traditional female roles.''

"What traditional roles?''

"Let's see. Well, the outfits she wears look like she's going on a date all the time. And I think you can buy uniforms like a nurse or something.'' He shrugged. "I'm not sure. I'm not really into dolls.''

Analisa could believe that. "What do you mean by going on a date?''

"It's a ritual, like courtship, only not so serious. If you lived in my time and I asked you out on a date, for example, I'd drive to your house, maybe bring you some flowers. We'd go to dinner at your favorite restaurant, then maybe take in a movie.''

"What's a movie?''

"It's . . . Well, it's kind of hard to describe. I suppose the best explanation is that it's a series of photographs shown so fast that it looks like the people or animals in the photograph are moving.''

"Really?''

"And now, with computers, they can create all kinds of special effects and . . . But I'm getting away from the subject.''

"So dates involve going to eat in a restaurant, seeing one of these movies, and then what?''

"Conversation. We'd talk a lot, about our jobs and hobbies. Families. Anything and everything.''

"And then?''

"I'd take you home and tell you what a great time I had.''

"Did you have a great time?'' she asked softly.

He turned back to look at her, his eyes smiling. "Yes. I had a very good time.''

Analisa's heart beat a little faster. Would she ever become used to the way this man affected her? "And that is the end of the date?'' she said, hoping her tone sounded light.

"No,'' he said slowly, turning back around. "I'd probably kiss you good night.''

"Really?" Her squeaky reply slipped out before she could stop herself.

"Really," he said firmly, all trace of laughter gone.

"And that wouldn't be a good idea," Analisa finished.

"That's right." He shifted in the saddle, as though he was uncomfortable. "Let's change the subject."

There was only one other subject she wanted to discuss.

"What about your wife?"

"My wife?"

"Yes. Did you go on dates with her?"

He was silent for so long that Analisa suspected he wouldn't answer. He nudged Tommelise into a faster walk, maneuvering onto the trail.

"Yes," he said in a voice devoid of emotion, "we went on dates."

Analisa sagged, but caught herself before she touched David's broad, solid back. So he was a married man, not a widower. She'd practically thrown herself at him, offering him more than hospitality.

She turned her head away, shamed by her forward actions. She'd known—she'd always known—that he was married. He'd spoken so sweetly of his daughter but never was clear about a wife. And to have a daughter, he had to have a wife.

The problem was that he didn't behave like a married man. At least, not the way she expected a married man to act.

She tried to summon anger at his behavior, but her sense of loss eclipsed all other emotions. Loss of a new friend. Loss of the one man she'd wanted to kiss her . . . and more. If she hadn't been riding behind David, she would have stopped Tommelise and rested in the cool forest. Crying didn't accomplish anything, but it might make her feel better. At the very least, the burning sensation in her eyes would ease. She didn't know how much longer she could tolerate being so close to his body.

Analisa sniffed, refusing to let any tears fall in front of him. Later, she'd chastise him for not being honest. All she felt right now, as they rode near the edge of the forest, was sadness.

"What's wrong?"

His voice cut into her thoughts like the thrust of a knife. She straightened abruptly, blinking at the brightness of the day. In that instant, she lost her balance.

David reached around back and grabbed her arm, hauling her against him with startling speed. She gasped, grabbing him before she tumbled from Tommelise's back. The mare danced forward, taking them into the shadows of the pines.

"What the hell were you doing back there?" he asked as he brought their mount under control, his voice revealing equal measures of anger and concern.

"Nothing!" she replied, jerking her arm from his firm hold. She was tired of being manhandled and manipulated. Tired of being deceived by a womanizing bully.

"What's wrong with you?"

"Nothing!" she cried again. "Just leave me alone, David Terrell."

He pulled Tommelise to a halt. "No way. I'd like to know what set you off. We weren't even arguing!"

"Well, maybe we should!" Analisa replied in a huff. Before David could stop her, she swung her leg over the mare's rump and slid to the ground.

She struggled to retain her balance on the uneven ground, fought against the tall tufts of grass that threatened to trip her. All the while, she backed away from him.

"Analisa, stop!"

"Don't tell me what to do," she yelled. She'd walk back to the cabin if she wanted. It wasn't that far. But then she'd have to leave her only horse, her best friend, in David's clutches. And Tommelise didn't seem too happy to be under his control, fighting the bit, her legs pumping like the pistons of the locomotive that had brought her family west.

No, she wouldn't leave Tommelise. "Get off my horse."

He stared at her as though she'd gone berserk. "For God's sake, would you please just tell me what this is all about?"

She walked to Tommelise's head and grasped the bridle on both sides. "I want you off my horse." The mare rolled her eyes, pranced, and tried to pull away. Tommelise wasn't used to arguments, or to other people trying to control her.

"All right, if that's what you want. I thought we'd already settled the argument about walking versus riding to the meadow."

"This isn't about walking or riding, it's about—"

She felt her eyes widen, and sucked in the breath she was about to expel.

"What?" David's frantic question startled her to action.

"Behind you!"

"What the hell?" he whispered as he looked toward the trees.

He froze for only a second, then turned back for an instant and pinned her with an intense gaze. Then he jerked Tommelise from her grasp, kicked the mare forward, and reached toward Analisa with surprising speed.

The breath left her body in a loud *whoosh* as she slammed into David's knee and the saddle. She dangled

from the side of the horse as Tommelise sprang forward.
Trying to focus on the sight behind them, all she could
see was a mountain of brown fur, menacing teeth, and
claws, growling in outrage, running toward them.

David put his heel to the mare, reining her to the wide
section of grassland at the same time that he held on to
Analisa with all his strength. She was a big girl, and he
had a precarious hold across her back, under her arm,
with only one hand. Thankfully, she clutched him
tightly, as frightened by the bear as he was.

The mare ran straight, probably spooked by the scent.
Hell, she'd probably been spooked before the bear stood
up on its hind legs and growled at them. If he hadn't
been so distracted by Analisa's odd behavior, he would
have noticed the mare's nervousness. But he hadn't noticed, and he'd put Analisa's life in danger.

He kicked free of the stirrup. "Put your foot in here.
See if you can swing up," he ordered, slowing the horse
only slightly.

She struggled against him, finally managing to slip her
foot in. She tugged on him, and, unbalanced by her
weight and leaning to the other side, he nearly lost his
grip on the mare. He slowed her even more. Finally,
Analisa managed to get her leg over and wrapped her
arms around him tightly.

He would have enjoyed the feeling if he hadn't been
so shaken.

Now that he was more in control of Analisa and the
horse, he turned back to look at the bear. It had stopped
running after them, it's nose pointed in the air, sniffing
and growling some thirty yards away. Not enough distance to satisfy him. He turned back and nudged the
mare with his heels.

He felt Analisa look at the bear. "It's hard to believe they're so fast," she said breathlessly.

"Good thing it's a black bear and not a grizzly. They can run as fast as a horse."

He felt Analisa shudder.

"We must have spooked it," he continued, trying to reassure her. "And it's probably hungry and in a bad mood after coming out of hibernation. I'm sure bears aren't all that common this low in the mountains." At least, in 1997 he rarely saw one in this area. Of course, in his time this was close to civilization. Close to his own house.

"It's probably a female. She could have a cub nearby," Analisa said.

He felt her turn to look behind them. "If so, that's one lucky cub. If I had a rifle with me, I would have shot his momma."

"It's not her fault!" Analisa said indignantly, sitting straight behind him again. "She's just defending her family."

"You don't know that. She might be a he. And he might just be in a bad mood."

"*People* get in bad moods," she replied.

She almost raised her nose in the air when she made that pronouncement.

"Animals act naturally," she added, as if that put the stamp of approval on anything they did.

"You're the animal expert." He looked back once more and saw that the bear had lost interest in them and was lumbering back toward the woods, so he slowed the mare to a walk.

From his experience in the area and flying backpackers into the wilderness, he knew most bears didn't want to attack people; unfortunately, campers and hikers sometimes got in their way. That was why paying attention was so important—something he'd completely forgotten earlier.

"I'm no expert, but I don't believe in killing unnecessarily," she said defensively.

"Neither do I," he admitted. "If I *had* shot the bear, it would have been a gut reaction." All he could think about at the time was that Analisa was on the ground, vulnerable, and could have fought him, stumbled, or fallen from the horse. And the bear didn't care that Analisa hadn't harmed it. Or that she had a heart of gold.

"Then I suppose it's a good thing we didn't bring the gun."

"You have one?"

"Yes," she said, almost reluctantly. "It was Papa's. He had it with him when . . ." Her voice trailed off to a whisper. The silence of her pain descended. Only the sound of her mare's hooves, brushing against the grass, and the chirps of birds interrupted the hush of the foothills. When she spoke again, her voice was steady but without the energy that poured from her so naturally. "The men who found him brought it to me, along with Jurgen's knife. But they didn't bring their bodies back. They're buried up there," she said softly, a catch in her voice.

David felt her pivot behind him. He turned to see where she was looking. Her finger pointed due west, toward Mount Meek.

"There's a pass up there. They were trying to cross the mountains, but the snow came . . . They shouldn't have been there."

He looked at the mountains he knew so well. He'd flown over them dozens of times, landed on narrow strips of land, taken off when the winds were too strong for safety. As many risks as he'd taken in the past, he'd never really understood what danger might mean to an-

other person until Catherine. Until she'd risked everything and lost.

"I know the place," he said softly. "Meek Pass."

"Is that what it's called? I never knew."

She was silent for a moment, then whispered, "They
shouldn't have gone."

"People make mistakes," he said gently.

"But they died. A mistake is leaving the bread in the
oven too long. Forgetting to feed the chickens. Not trying to cross a pass in the winter."

Her pain was raw, so new to her that she still felt
betrayed and fought the anger that threatened to smother
the love she felt for her father and brother. David knew
the feelings well, but his were dulled by four years of
coming to terms with Catherine's death, some family
counseling, and most of all, the knowledge that he had
to be strong for Jamie's sake. Analisa had no one—to
talk to or to love.

"They didn't mean to hurt you," he said, knowing
that she'd have to deal with the feelings in her own way,
in her own time.

"They didn't think of me at all," she whispered.

He had no answer. After all, hadn't he come to the
same conclusion after Catherine's accident?

After a few moments, Analisa relaxed against him. He
wished he could see her face, take her in his arms and
just hold her. Until she'd let some of her anger escape,
he hadn't realized how much she suffered from her family's death, and how very lonely she was.

But he had no right to hold her, and he wasn't the
man to ease her grief. Soon, he'd find his way back
home, leaving Analisa alone once more. Maybe not the
same as her father and brother, but close enough.

As she settled more closely against him, her even
breath teasing his spine and her soft breasts pressing be-

92

low his shoulder blades, he told himself again that he wasn't the person Analisa needed. She should have a counselor, a friend, to talk to. She shouldn't be isolated here in the wilds of the Tetons, subjected to hardship and danger. But she was—and there wasn't a damned thing he could do about it.

With a keen sense of sadness, he guided the mare back toward the cabin. There would be time enough to cut hay tomorrow. He wasn't going anywhere. Not yet.

Analisa jolted awake, her cheek damp from resting on David's back, her arms holding his waist even in sleep. The bleating of her goat and the quacking of the two ducks greeted her. And then the bray of a donkey broke the usual sounds of homecoming.

But they were supposed to be cutting hay. Why were they back at the cabin? The answer came immediately— the bear. David must have assumed they'd need to return and, in all fairness, she hadn't told him any differently. She'd been happy to relax into his strength and ignore the danger and the pain.

But the donkey?

She grasped David's shoulders, looking around his back at the cabin. Sure enough, Sweet Sue was tied to the fence, a mouthful of grass hanging from her muzzle, her long ears twitching. And that meant that Red Weasel Charlie was inside, down from the mountains for the summer.

"Whose donkey?" David asked, pulling Tommelise to a halt.

"A friend," Analisa replied. "I want to get down."

He barely had time to give her his hand as she swung her leg over and jumped to the ground. As soon as she touched the dirt, she turned and ran toward the door.

"Charlie!"

The door opened a crack, then wider, as a gnarled hand and wrinkled face came into view.

"Charlie!" she called again, so happy to see her oldest friend.

She towered over him now, so she bent low and hugged him. His bones seemed even more pronounced, but she thought that every year when he made the circuit to visit. And he never really changed. *She'd* grown taller and stronger.

"Fer the love o' Pete, Annie-girl, yer goin' to break my bones," he gasped in his raspy voice.

As a child she'd told him his voice was rusty, and he'd agreed. "No need to talk, 'cept to Sue," he'd said with a little laugh. And obviously he hadn't been practicing enough.

"I'm so glad to see you," she said, easing away from his equally rusty hug.

"Ya don't look all that lonesome to me," he replied, raising one reddish-gray eyebrow and giving a nod toward the yard.

"Oh, him," she said, glancing over her shoulder.

"Ya gone and taken yerself a man?"

"No! He's a . . . a visitor."

"He's a'ridin' yer horse," Charlie commented, raising his eyebrow again.

"I know. We were going to cut hay, but a bear spooked us."

Charlie shook his balding head. "Not good. I thought I taught ya better."

"You did. But I wasn't watching." She hugged him again to get him off the subject. "I'm just so glad to see you."

"Ee-nough of that, girl. Darn females are too 'fectionate for their own good," he growled.

94

"I know we are," Analisa said, smiling as she stepped back.

She knew when David walked up behind her, although his boots barely made a sound in the dirt. She seemed to have some strange sense of him, something she'd never experienced before.

"David, this is Red Weasel Charlie. He's my oldest friend."

"David Terrell," he said, holding out his hand.

Charlie shook it, his elbow pumping. "Where ya visitin' from?" he asked abruptly.

David looked taken aback. What kind of answer could he give? But he recovered quickly, answering Charlie after extracting his hand from the mountain man's grip. "Texas," he said.

"That's a fer piece. Been there once. Too hot." Charlie frowned, his leathery skin wrinkling even more than usual.

"Yes, it is," David replied, looking to her as though he wanted some help.

"Did you fix yourself some supper, Charlie?" Analisa asked, knowing that he had no problem helping himself to whatever might be simmering on the stove or stored in the cold room.

"Naw, I jus' got here. Ain't even made Sue comfor'ble yet."

"What about Little Red?"

"Asleep in the woodpile inside," he said with a chuckle.

Analisa smiled. "Why don't I take Sue to the barn with Tommelise? That will give them time to get acquainted again."

"I'll talk to yer man here," Charlie announced, jerking his thumb toward David.

Analisa felt herself blush. "I told you he's not my man."

"Well, he's a man and he's with ya. I don't see no other woman hangin' on," Charlie observed with his usual bluntness.

Analisa drew in a deep breath. She'd almost forgotten—again. "His wife is back at his home, Charlie." She turned to look at David, trying her best to ignore the pain those words caused. "In *Texas.*"

"What?" she heard David ask, but she was already walking toward the donkey, willing to ignore him for once. She didn't want to discuss Holly in front of Charlie—not at the moment. Maybe later, when she got her emotions under control, she could again face the fact that David was married. And absolutely not "her man."

Chapter Six

"I brung her them ducks to fatten up fer Chris'mas dinner," Charlie said, leaning back in the chair near the fireplace, "and she done gone and made 'em pets."

"They are a nuisance," David agreed, smiling both at the older man's speech and the story he told. "But I doubt she'd have the heart to kill anything out there," he continued, gesturing toward the yard. "At least, I haven't seen any evidence of meat other than stringy elk."

"Must've been an old one if she kilt it."

"You've got that right," David replied, still smiling. He walked to the shelf of clay figures. "How long has she been sculpting?"

"Whatcha call that?"

"Sculpting. Making these figures."

"Oh, them things. She started when her mama died. Them's the fairies and goblins from those books. Her daddy was big on readin' an' writin'." Charlie pushed out of the chair and sauntered across the room. He squinted up at the trolls and beasts. "This one here is me," he said, a grin splitting his weathered face.

David stared at the elfish figure. He could see Charlie's face in the finely molded, heavy eyebrows, the nose with the bump in the middle, the folded-up chin and scrawny neck. "Not the ears, though," David commented. "Those aren't yours."

" 'Course not," Charlie scoffed. "Girl has imag'nation."

At that moment, the "girl" walked through the door, dusting her hands on her thighs, covered in heavy cotton. David vividly recalled the feel of her strong legs pressed alongside his as they rode together. Another image popped into his mind, unprovoked and, at the moment, unwanted. Of Analisa's firm, pale thighs pressed close around his waist, her head thrown back, her hair wild and free.

He suppressed a groan as he turned to face the wall, hiding his body's reaction by examining the sculptures in great detail.

"Sue gettin' 'long with the mare?"

"They're fine. You know how they have to snort and fuss at first. Now they're rubbing necks and talking like old friends."

Charlie chuckled. "Always the same."

David heard Analisa move around the cabin as he got his body under control. Or as much control as he seemed to possess around her. Placing a particularly grotesque monster back on the shelf, he faced the room.

"Do you come often?" he asked the older man.

"Twice a year," he replied, hitching up his pants and walking back toward the chair, a pipe in his hand. "Reg'lar as clockwork."

"Charlie comes on his way south from the mountains

with his pelts," Analisa added. "And then again at the end of the summer, on his way back up."

"Gots to get my grub fer the winter," Charlie explained, "and some trinkets to trade with the Injuns."

"Trinkets?" David asked.

"Odd and ends. Ribbons and lace sometimes. Harness and tack are good, aren't they, Charlie?" Analisa asked.

"Yep, but ain't much stuff to trade since the mountain men are all gone."

"You're still here," she reminded him.

"Yeah, but in my pappy's day, they'd rendezvous for a couple 'r weeks down in the valley."

"The Jackson Rendezvous. I've heard of it," David said. "That's how Jackson started."

"Started what?" Charlie asked.

David glanced from the older man to Analisa. "Started . . ." She gave him a look that told him she knew he'd slipped up. Hiding the truth was harder than he'd imagined. Not that he'd even considered how careful he'd have to be around others. According to what Analisa had said earlier, he hadn't expected to face any other residents of the 1880s for some time.

"Started getting famous," David answered, hoping Charlie didn't question him further, since he was playing this by ear. He strolled across the room toward Analisa. "Is that our lunch?" he asked, pointing to the pouch she'd brought in.

"Yes. I packed it for the meadow, but . . ." She took a deep breath and busied herself with unfolding the cloth. When she spoke again, her tone was different, more businesslike. "Are you hungry?"

He imagined she was remembering the bear incident and might still be shaken. Or perhaps the conversation about her father and brother had caused her new pain.

"I am. How about you, Charlie?" David asked, turning toward the mountain man.

"I could eat a bit."

David walked to the sink, where he'd stacked the dishes that morning. "I'll set the table," he offered, grabbing the enameled plates.

"Don't be silly," Analisa said, reaching for the tinware, her fingers brushing his. She sucked in her breath, as though he'd shocked her.

"I told you I want to help." He held on to the plates, wondering at her change of mood.

She tugged on the plates. "Why? So *Holly* won't be angry?" She spat out his sister's name as though it were venom. "Would you please give me those?"

"What do you have against Holly?"

"Nothing!"

"Well, something has you spitting mad. You're acting just like you did when we were riding up the trail. And then we weren't even talking about her."

"Of course we were talking about her. Except you don't talk about her at all. You act like she doesn't even exist until you want to tell me about dolls or women's work or some such nonsense." She pulled at the plates again. "And let me set the table!"

David shook his head. "I know I'm a guest here, but I've got to tell you that you're not making any sense."

"What doesn't make sense is why a man who is married to a woman he admires, who quotes his wife and finds her admirable, would act as though he's not even married!" Her voice rose until she was nearly shouting across the corner of the table.

"I'm not married!" he roared back. "I was, but I'm not now."

"You divorced your poor wife?" she asked incredulously.

"No!" He ran a hand through his hair, more confused by the second. Then suddenly the whole thing made sense. He'd spent so much time wondering at Analisa's reaction that he hadn't listened closely enough to what she was saying. And he'd forgotten, until now, her parting words as she'd hurried to the barn earlier—that his wife was home in Texas.

"You think Holly is my wife, don't you?"

"Of course Holly is your wife!"

"She's my sister."

"Wait jus' a danged minute," Charlie spoke up. "Yer married to yer sister?"

David hadn't even heard the man walk up. Apparently Analisa hadn't either, because she stopped tugging on the plates.

"No, I'm not married to my sister," David explained with as much patience as he could muster. "Holly is my sister. Catherine was my wife."

"Holly's not your wife?" Analisa asked, confusion causing a line to appear between her eyes.

"No. I never said she was."

"So where's yer wife?" Charlie asked bluntly, "And whatcha doin' at this here cabin, alone with Annie?"

As he tipped his head to the side and squinted up at him, David thought the older man looked very much like the elf Analisa had created.

"She's dead," David said quietly. "In an accident in the mountains, four years ago." His gaze sought Analisa's as his words seemed to finally sink in. "I'm not a married man. Not anymore."

Analisa fell into a chair. The sensation of her bottom hitting the seat wasn't nearly as shocking as David's news. He was a widower! And after all the recriminations she'd suffered from believing she'd kissed a married man. Why, he was a . . . a toad!

As soon as her anger surfaced, raising her from the chair with a sharp retort on her lips, she realized she was being unfair. He was a widower, separated from his young daughter.

She remembered earlier in the day, when she'd asked him about dates—if he and his wife had gone to dinner and movies. And he'd become very silent and eventually said yes. He must have loved her very much to still feel such pain over her death. Analisa didn't like to think about the loss of her loved ones because it hurt too much. Although their deaths were more recent, David had lost his *wife,* the mother of his child.

She felt his eyes on her even before she raised her head and met his dark gaze. He looked at her steadily, deeply, until the rest of the world fell away and the two of them were the only people anywhere. She wanted to tell him that she was sorry, that she knew what he was going through, but her feelings were too confused. Memories of passion and pain swirled through her, until the two became one. She imagined that David had kissed her because he was lonely and sad, and she had desired him for the same reason. And that if they were left alone, they would do the same thing, again and again, until the pain went away.

"Sorry 'bout the wife," Charlie said in his rusty voice.

Analisa blinked, then glanced around the room. The rest of the world was still there, as always. A shaft of sunshine slanted through the window, and the smells of milk and rennet permeated the kitchen.

She looked at David in time to see him nod to Charlie in acknowledgment, then place the plates on the table and walk away. His tall, muscular body blocked the sun for a moment as he passed by the window, then he opened the door and strode outside.

She rose from the chair, taking a step in his direction before she stopped herself. He would be back. He had nowhere else to go, and he wasn't angry. She knew from experience that sometimes men needed to be alone. She turned back to the table in time to see Charlie's contemplative look.

"Not yer man, hmm," he said, his gaze also following David's retreating form.

"He's not going to stay," Analisa tried to explain. "He's just here until . . . until he can find his way home."

"Maybe he is home," Charlie said. "Ever think of that?"

"No." Analisa grasped the plates, their edges still warm from David's hands. "No, I don't think about that. He has a daughter and a life where he's from." *And a sister,* she silently added. "He wants to go back."

"Then go with him, girl," Charlie said, as if that was the most simple solution to the problem.

"I . . . I can't."

"Why not?"

She shook her head. "I can't go where he's going." She blinked away the sting of tears at the thought of being alone now that she'd met David. "It's impossible."

"Pshaw," Charlie spat. "Ain't nothin' impossible if yer of a mind."

"Believe me, Charlie, this is." Analisa set each plate very carefully on the well-used wood. "Impossible," she whispered as she continued to set the table.

Later that night, after a supper of rabbit that Charlie had killed, skinned, and fried, David sat in the shadows and watched as Analisa settled on a stool near the hearth. In her lap frolicked a bundle of red and white fur, Charlie's namesake, Little Red. David had to admit that the red weasel was cute. Holly would have loved to play with the energetic animal. He could imagine his daughter and Analisa sharing such an experience, but in front of his fireplace, in his home, in 1997.

The expression on Analisa's face, combined with thoughts of his daughter, reminded him that his hostess was way too young; the setting reminded him that she was not of his time. In every regard, they were worlds apart.

But he still wanted her.

Charlie smoked his pipe, clearly enjoying the tobacco that had belonged to Analisa's father. On the rough-hewn table beside the chair, a single candle burned with a clear yellow flame. Apparently, Analisa didn't have a large supply of candles; David remembered thinking last night that the interior of the cabin was way too dark. The lack of a store or even a way to trade brought home the isolation of this place even more than the log structure or the genuine mountain man.

"She looks like a baby," Analisa said with a laugh. "And her teeth are still so sharp."

"She's no baby," Charlie replied. "I figure she's 'bout two now."

"I think you're right. The first time you brought her with you, I wanted to keep her."

"You want to keep all them danged animals," Charlie scoffed.

David smiled in the darkness. "Like ducks for Christmas dinner?"

"He knew those ducks would never make it to the table," Analisa replied in a knowing tone. "If he'd

104

wanted to eat duck, he would have brought them to the cabin with their necks wrung.''

"Why, that's not true!" Charlie protested, cradling the pipe in one hand. "I was jus' keepin' them ducks fresh.''

"All the way from the wagons in a wooden crate with their own supply of corn? In September? I don't think so.''

David chuckled. "Sounds like Analisa isn't the only animal lover around here.''

Charlie stuck the pipe in his mouth and made some scoffing sound.

"That's right. He might trap for a living, but he has a soft spot in his heart for animals.''

"I'm not goin' to sit here and listen to this," Charlie grumbled. "I'm headin' to sleep.''

"Take the bed," David said, rising from his chair.

"Nope. Never get used to sleepin' so high offa the ground. I'll sack out with Sue, jus' like always.''

"Don't be silly," David insisted. "At least stay here, inside the house. There's no reason to sleep in the barn.''

"Yes, Charlie," Analisa added, looking up with pleading eyes. "Stay here.''

The older man looked back and forth between them. "So I'm s'posed to be yer nanny?" His laugh sounded more like a cackle. "Yer full grown. I ain't playing the part of a bundle in yer bed.''

"Charlie!"

He cackled again in answer, scratching his pet weasel behind the ears before heading toward the door.

"I've a good mind to take back that tobacco and pipe," Analisa said, frowning at Charlie's back.

"Don't cut yer nose to spite yer face," he said before closing the door behind him.

"Darned man," she said in his general direction, placing the weasel on the floor. It scampered to the door and sniffed at the air coming in through the bottom crack.

"What's a bundle?" David asked, walking toward the chair Charlie had vacated.

Analisa pivoted and paced the floor, her hands hugging her arms. "It's just a custom," she said, apparently still irritated by Charlie's departure.

"What kind of custom?"

"I'm not exactly sure, but I've heard that back east, sometimes courting couples might have to share the same bed."

"Have to?" David asked, amused by this archaic practice. Or was it a thing of the past? "Maybe they *wanted* to share a bed."

"No!" she said quickly. "They kept all their clothes on. And a roll of blankets or pillows was placed between them."

"As if that would keep them from—"

"Please! This is a real custom."

"My era has some customs too. Like sharing a bed without a roll of blankets between them," David said, smiling at her flustered expression.

"I'm sure you do! Now, if you'll excuse me, I need to pack the cheese for the cold room."

"Need some help?" he called after her.

"No, thank you," she replied primly from the kitchen. "This is definitely women's work."

David grinned and reached for the weasel, who was sniffing at his boots. "Well, at least you didn't run off and leave me," he said, cradling the small animal next to his chest.

For the next few minutes, he played with Little Red, amused by the animal's boundless energy. Eventually, Red wandered off and David's eyes grew heavy as he settled into the chair. The flickering flame grew blurry when he gave up his fight to stay awake.

Analisa hunkered down beside the chair where David slumped, his head rolled to the side. He would be uncomfortable when he awoke, but better now than later, when he'd have a real crick in his neck.

At least he was sleepy; he must not have slept any more than she last night. Unfortunately, despite tossing and turning after their encounter by the hearth, and the excitement of the day, she still felt restless and full of energy.

Had only one full day passed since David had found her sitting by the hearth, had tempted her with feelings she'd never experienced before? Within one day, she'd been kissed for the first time, experienced the heights of joy and re-lived the depths of sorrow. All because of this man from the future, who had a family that missed him and a life to return to.

But no wife. She sighed, knowing that she should have just asked him if he was married when she'd first thought of it. Or he should have made his status clear to her. But that wasn't fair. She didn't go around announcing that her father and brother were dead, or that she was unmarried. And with the strange occurrence of David's arrival into the past, he probably didn't realize that she'd jumped to the conclusion that he was married to Holly, His sister.

Analisa sighed. Placing a hand on David's forearm, she shook him slightly.

"What?" he asked, his eyes snapping open.

"I thought you might want to take your bed. The hour is late."

"I dozed off." He passed a hand over his face, rubbing his eyes. "It usually takes 'The Tonight Show' to make me fall asleep in my chair."

"What's 'The Tonight Show?' " she asked softly.

"It's on television. Kind of like movies, only in your home, and smaller." He gestured with his hands, making a square less than a yard wide and tall.

She shook her head, wondering at all these odd forms of entertainment. "I don't understand, but I believe you."

He smiled in a lazy, sleepy way that made her heart beat faster. In his dark eyes, she saw the flicker of the candle and the flare of desire.

Her mind screamed *danger,* but her body leaned closer, craving his touch like a deer at a salt lick or a bear in a berry patch.

"Analisa," he whispered in a sleepy voice.

"Yes?"

"You're doing it again."

She frowned. "What?"

"Encouraging me to kiss you. I thought we agreed that wasn't a good idea."

She sat back on her heels, teetering precariously. David grabbed her arm.

"Don't fall. I didn't mean you were in imminent danger of being molested."

"I wasn't thinking that at all," she replied, pushing to her feet. She brushed the wrinkles from her skirt, which she'd donned earlier in honor of Charlie's visit.

Smoothing her hair back into the braid she wore around the cabin, she struggled to ignore the effect of David Terrell's sleep-rumpled appearance—especially when he stretched and pushed himself up from the chair. His shirt pulled tight across his chest and his denim pants, too snug to be acceptable, accented his manhood in a way she'd never noticed before.

"You'll need some extra clothes," she said in a high, tight voice that nearly caused her to moan in embarrassment. Why couldn't she control herself?

"You're right," he replied, glancing down at himself. "Is there someplace to buy clothes out here?"

She shook her head. "You can use Jurgen's. He was a bit broader than you, but I'm sure I can make them fit."

"I don't want to be any more trouble."

"You're not," she said, her voice still unsteady. "You can pay me back with some chores."

"I'd love to," he said, his voice smooth.

When she saw the gleam in his eyes, she took another step back just to be certain she wasn't tempting him.

"You don't look sleepy," he observed, his gaze a light caress from the top of her head to the wrinkles on her skirt.

"I . . . I'm not. I may do a little more work. Or perhaps I'll go check on the animals."

"You've done enough work today," David said. "And the animals are fine. Charlie is out there with them, remember?"

"Yes, but I'll just lie abed and stare at the ceiling. I might as well do some mending, or melt the candle stubs, or—"

"What makes you sleepy?" he asked abruptly.

She frowned, trying to remember a time when she'd had trouble falling asleep. Usually, she was tired from the day's labor. As long as she didn't let herself remember the past, she could watch the embers of the fire and drift off easily.

But a long time ago, when they'd moved west, she hadn't been able to rest easily. The sounds of the forest and mountain meadows had frightened her, along with the isolation and the endless blue sky. Her mother had held her close, her gentle voice recounting her beloved folk tales, even without the precious books they'd carried from Ohio.

"A long time ago, my mother read to me," Analisa said softly, her gaze resting on the rough-hewn shelves her father had built to hold the German and English books they'd brought with them to Wyoming "But I was only a child then," she added quickly. "I haven't had cause to worry about falling asleep."

"I could read to you," David offered.

"No, that's not necessary," she said, her heart beating fast again as she imagined David holding her close to his warm, hard body as his soothing voice vibrated through her.

"I don't mind. You can take the chair," he offered. "Or better still, get ready for bed and I'll stay in here and read aloud. I'll bet that after a few minutes, you'll be ready to sleep just to escape my boring voice."

Analisa smiled. "I don't think you have a boring voice. But you don't have to read to me. I'm not accustomed to such a thing."

"Maybe you should be," David said with a twist to his mouth. "Besides, I read to my daughter Jamie every night. I miss it."

Analisa took a step backward. "I'd feel odd."

"You'll feel sleepy," David insisted. "Go get ready for bed. I'll pick out a book."

She hurried out the door before she changed her mind and barricaded herself in her room. Reading to a grown woman! Who'd heard of such a thing? Charlie would no doubt laugh himself silly if he discovered David reading a fairy tale.

But Charlie need never know. By the light of a half moon, Analisa ran to the outhouse, her heart considerably lighter.

*   *   *

David stared at the book in his hands, appalled by some of the horror stories that the Brothers Grimm had passed off as fairy tales. What awful images to leave in the minds of children! How did parents read this stuff to their kids? If Jamie heard these tales, she'd have nightmares for years to come.

He finally chose a story with the same name as Analisa's horse, Tommelise. At least this one didn't feature fathers who slit the throats of their children as they slept, or monsters who tore people limb from limb, or young women who died because they dared to defy their oppressive parents.

Analisa had slipped inside moments ago. He heard her in the kitchen, washing her face, brushing her teeth. As he settled in the chair and opened the book, he saw her from the corner of his eye. Her white nightgown covered with a shawl or a blanket, she walked quickly to her room. Even from this far away, he imagined that a becoming blush stained her cheeks. "I'm ready," she called out a few seconds later.

"You all settled in bed?"

"Yes."

"Covers up to your chin?"

He heard a giggle. "Yes."

"Did you say your prayers?"

"No, I forgot." Her voice reflected that cross between amusement and contriteness he'd heard before.

He smiled. How many times had Jamie said the same thing to him? Then they'd kneel together beside her bed and ask God to watch over Mommy in heaven, Aunt Holly, and various and assorted friends—both real and fictitious.

"Well, say them now. I'll wait," he answered.

Moments of soft, comfortable sounds followed. In the

woodpile near the fireplace, David heard the weasel settle down for the night. The fire popped and flared, then dimmed to a red-gold glow.

"I'm ready." Analisa's voice drifted out of her bedroom, blending with the night, the cabin, the mountains. She was a part of this place, as much as the pine trees and wildlife, the golden sun and the deep blue sky.

He knew this land, but not with this cabin or clearing. In his time, nothing remained of Analisa Ludke, her family, or her friends. No descendants that he knew of, no photos he'd seen, and no record of her name on the property deed.

When he returned, he'd remember the beautiful girl with the soft heart who'd nearly stolen his own. He'd remember, in case anyone ever asked who had lived on the land before him.

"Okay then," he said, settling into the chair by the fireplace. His voice sounded nearly as rusty as Charlie's, but needed to be strong and clear to carry across the cabin into Analisa's room. Entering her room in the dead of night, with only a candle as a chaperone, was not a good idea for either of them.

David took a deep, calming breath, then tilted the book toward the meager candlelight. "Here we go. Once upon a time . . ."

Chapter Seven

Charlie, Little Red, and Sue stayed for two more days, then packed up for the one-day trek to Jackson's Hole, across the twisting river. Although no rendezvous or outpost existed now, a few homesteaders traded staple items, clothes, or trinkets for Charlie's furs. When he finished trading, he'd return, Sue laden with all manner of goods to see them through the winter and to barter with the Indians.

"Take care of Little Red," Analisa said as she gave the weasel one more stroke, then handed her to Charlie.

"Always do," he replied before tucking his pet into a specially made saddlebag. Sue's swaying walk kept Little Red sound asleep for most of the day. "And ya better take care of yer man," Charlie added, jerking his thumb back to indicate David, " 'cause he might up and get restless for Texas."

"He's not my man, Charlie," Analisa corrected him, "and I think he misses his home a lot."

113

"Ain't nothin' there that he don't have here."

Oh, if you only knew, Analisa wanted to say. But she couldn't tell Charlie about David's true home, more than a hundred years distant, or of the airplane hidden in the meadow. "There's his daughter," she said simply, reminding herself as much as her friend that David had a future elsewhere.

"Shoot, the lil' one can come on up. Ain't no better place to raise a child than these here wide open spaces."

Analisa smiled, remembering her own childhood among the farm families in Ohio. Granted, her parents hadn't owned the land, and they didn't have many frills, but at least she'd grown up with other children, friends she'd never see again. After fourteen years, she couldn't clearly remember their family names, but their faces—browned by the summer sun, smiling with strawberry jam grins, spitting seeds through missing teeth—were burned into her memory like initials carved into a tree.

David had brought all those memories back by reading her to sleep with fairy tales. Memories of her mother's voice, childhood fears, friends in Ohio. Darn him for making her miss them all over again. Until he'd flown into her life, she'd done so well to forget the people she'd never see again.

Shaking her head, she brought herself back to the present. "I don't think it's possible for him to bring his daughter here, Charlie."

"He's a good man, Annie. You'd best be thinkin' 'bout yer future."

She nodded, knowing that the future was something she'd never take for granted again. Who knew if she'd even be alive this time next summer? Or if Charlie would survive another winter in the frigid, unforgiving mountains?

Thoughts of disaster and death, along with memories

of the past, filled her eyes with tears. She blinked, then hugged Charlie to hide her watery eyes. "You take care of yourself. I'll see you in a few weeks."

"Don't go gettin' all mushy on me," he complained, giving her arm an awkward pat. "I'll bring ya back somethin' purty."

"I don't need anything," she said, thinking of how wonderful a new dress might be. One not too tight or too short. Or something for David.

She pushed away from Charlie's wiry frame. "Do you think you could take a couple of my figurines? Maybe you could trade them."

"Jus' pack 'em with the rabbit pelts. Whatcha need?"

Analisa turned back to look at David, who was busy splitting wood beside the cabin. "David?"

He looked up, his face a bit flushed, his forearms bulging with thick, long muscles as he placed the ax on the tree stub they used as a block. "Yes?"

"Charlie's ready to leave. Can he try to get anything for you?"

David wiped a hand across his sweating brow. "What's available?"

Analisa shrugged. "It's hard to tell. Whatever the new settlers might have, or some goods from back east."

"Well, if he can find any coffee, he'll have my eternal gratitude."

Analisa nodded.

"Charlie, see what you can do. I forgot how much Papa missed coffee. Almost as much as tobacco."

"Iffen anyone has some, I'll try to get yer man a ration or two."

"He's not my man."

"Go get them figurines, girl. Sue's stomping to go."

Analisa raised her eyebrow. Sue was dozing in the

115

dappled sunlight of the swaying pines. "I'll get you a few. And he's not my man."

She heard Charlie snort his response as she hurried into the cabin. Looking over the shelf, she chose a wizened old hag, a grinning troll, and a giant with one eye in the middle of his forehead. She strode quickly outside and secured the clay figures into the leather pouch of soft, white fur, her fingers lingering for just a moment.

She thought of all the frightened little snowshoe hares that left their odd tracks in the snow; that huddled near the ground when an eagle screeched and soared through the sky; that scattered into the brush at the smallest sound. She didn't want to count the number that had died to provide such soft fur for someone's collar or cuff.

"Trappin' keeps the number down," Charlie reminded her, reading her mind as he closed the pouch. "They'd starve iffen they kept on havin' litters."

"I know, but I wonder how many we can kill before there aren't enough left."

"Well, now, I et these rabbits, so don't go denyin' my dinner."

Analisa smiled sadly. "I'm not, Charlie. Sometimes I just think about the animals more than I do the people."

"Um-hmm," he said, pulling Sue's lead rope free from the fence. "You should be thinkin' 'bout that man who's splittin' yer wood. Leave the trappin' to me."

"Don't you ever get tired of it, Charlie? All the cold and the loneliness? It's hard work, and you're not getting any younger."

"Don't go buryin' me 'fore my time," he grumbled. "An' trappin's all I know. My daddy trapped back when the rendezvous was goin' on in the thirties and forties. It's what I know, an' I 'spect I'll keep on 'til the animals or my time runs out."

"You could stay here," Analisa offered. "I could use some help this winter, and you'd have a warm place for Sue. She's not young anymore, either."

"This here's yer home."

"It was my father's home too, and Jurgen's, but they're gone."

"He's here," Charlie said, jerking his thumb toward David.

"Not forever."

Charlie frowned. "I'll think on it."

"Good," Analisa smiled as Charlie wrapped the lead rope once around his fist. She looked back at David. "Charlie's leaving," she announced.

David imbedded the ax in the stump with a heave, then wiped his forehead. With alarm, she noticed that not only were his sleeves rolled up, but his shirt was now unbuttoned and hanging open. She felt her eyes widen as his gaze met hers.

He smiled slightly as he fastened the two buttons in the middle, as though he had remembered her admonitions about his unclothed condition that first night, by the hearth. With a sharp intake of breath, she tore her gaze from him and back to Charlie . . . who was whistling as he looked up into the trees.

Darned man. He thought he knew everything. He was as bad as the matchmaking old biddy from the Lutheran church they'd attended in Ohio, always claiming this girl and this young man were a perfect match. She was wrong more than half the time, Analisa's mother had confided once.

"Good-bye, Charlie," David said as he walked up. He held out his hand. "Take care."

The two men shook hands.

"Charlie will be back in a week or two," Analisa said quickly. "He's going trading."

David nodded. "I'd pay for some coffee, but I'm afraid I don't have any money with me."

"It's taken care of," Charlie advised, walking to Sue's head. "Jus' be decent to Annie, ya hear? I don't wanna have to take a strap to a grown man."

"Don't worry," David replied easily, smiling despite Charlie's warning. "I'll do my best to take care of her."

"I can take care of myself, thank you very much," Analisa said, narrowing her eyes at the two men. "I don't appreciate you talking about me as though I wasn't standing right here."

"Don't get yer feathers in a ruff," Charlie said. "Come on, Sue."

"My feathers are not in a ruff," Analisa replied. "And you're the one who should take care of yourself. I know the rheumatism in your knees acts up, and that you don't eat enough vegetables."

Charlie chortled as he tugged on Sue's lead. "Come on, gal. We'd best be gettin' out of here 'fore Annie straps a bonnet to yer head and puts me in a pair of short pants."

David laughed.

Analisa turned and walked toward the cabin. Tears burned in her eyes again, but this time for two very different reasons: her anger at Charlie and David's teasing, and her fear that her friend might not return someday from his rounds in the valley or the mountains.

Just like her father and Jurgen.

"Alone at last," David teased as they sat down to dinner.

"What?" Analisa looked up from the pan-fried trout he'd fixed over her protest that cooking was women's work. Of course, she'd used the same argument when Charlie brought in the lifeless rabbit, except that her response had been more automatic than genuine. Even though she was a great cook, Analisa was a woman made for eating in restaurants—preferably vegetarian ones—or fixing frozen meals.

"It's a joke. You seemed distracted." He pushed around the remainder of his filet. A wedge of lemon would be great—and totally unattainable. "Did Charlie's leaving upset you?"

The early evening sunlight caressed her face in misty shades of gold. For once David was grateful that she had few candles, and no electricity. Nothing could compare to Analisa's clear, fresh beauty in natural light.

Except that a frown worried her forehead and her eyes appeared troubled.

"I'm used to Charlie coming and going. Twice a year he shows up: as soon as the snow melts and the streams go down from the run-off, and then again when he finishes his trading and tires of the settlers in the valley. But this year . . ."

"This year what?" David prompted, leaning forward on the table.

She toyed with her food. "This year is different. Papa's not here to sit and smoke with Charlie, and Jurgen can't go with him on his rounds to visit and talk to newcomers and passers-through."

"But he still came to see you. And he'll be back."

She shifted in her chair. "But what about next year? What if something happens? What if he doesn't—"

She stopped abruptly, looking away from her plate, from him, as though she wanted to see beyond the everyday and into the future.

"There's no way to know what will happen, Analisa, but Charlie has been living in these mountains all his life. Surely he's as safe as anyone could be."

"Pardon me if that's not very reassuring. I thought

Papa and Jurgen knew their way, but they didn't.''

"They made a mistake."

"So could Charlie."

"But your father and brother hadn't lived for forty or so years in these mountains. Surely Charlie knows more than they did."

She shrugged. "But he's getting older."

"And maybe wiser." David reached across the table and took her cool hand in his. "What do you want to do, lock him up? You've got to have some faith in him," he said gently.

She looked down at their clasped hands. "I do have faith in him," she whispered, "but that doesn't keep me from worrying."

"Have you always worried so much about him?"

She shook her head, not meeting his eyes.

"Then this probably has more to do with your father and brother, right?" When she remained silent, he continued. "Analisa, you can't save the world."

"Save the world?" She looked up then, more troubled and unsure than he'd seen her before. "I'm not trying to save the world. I'm trying to help Charlie."

"I know, honey, but he's a grown man." The endearment slipped out before he even knew it, but it sounded so right. In the last few days, as he'd worked around the cabin and learned to cope in this frontier environment, his respect for and attraction to Analisa had grown stronger. Too strong, he imagined.

Usually, she didn't even realize that he watched her, or thought about her almost constantly. But was she aware tonight? He doubted she noticed the endearment he'd used . . . until she raised wide, questioning eyes to his.

"What did you say?"

He shrugged, embarrassed that she'd picked up on his

sign of affection. He felt like a teenager caught necking in the high-school parking lot. He wasn't ready to explain how he felt, especially when he was still coping with his trip to the past.

"It just slipped out," he said as casually as possible. "I say things like that all the time."

She pulled her hand out of his grasp. "Of course. I didn't mean to . . . I shouldn't have said anything."

He closed his eyes, but he could still see the uncertainty on Analisa's face. For the sake of his pride, he'd hurt her by claiming he used endearments often, when that wasn't the case at all. He just hadn't realized how callous his words might sound to her sensitive ears. He might not have led a perfect life, but he'd always been honest with the women he'd dated, never letting them believe that they were special to him if they weren't.

"I'm sorry," he said, opening his eyes and watching her across the table. "I lied. I never call anyone 'honey' or 'sweetheart' or anything like that. At least I haven't in a long, long time."

She frowned and tipped her head to the side. "Then why?"

"Because that's the way I feel about you," he stated simply, holding her hand again. "Surely you know I care."

"No . . . I just know what you told me about kissing you and . . . things." Her eyes strayed to his lips and he felt a rush of heat to his groin. His hand tightened around hers.

"How I feel about you is more complicated than that," he tried to explain. "I want you, yes. But I also admire you. I know it sounds corny as hell, but I respect you."

"I don't know what you mean by corny, but I think the other is a compliment."

121

He smiled. "Yes, it is. There's a saying—a joke, really—about a guy telling a girl that he'll respect her in the morning, just so he can get her in bed." At her wide eyes and shocked expression, he continued, "But that's not what I meant. I'm talking about the way you work, the way you take care of all these animals, Charlie, me. If it weren't for you, I'd probably starve to death or get eaten by a wild animal."

She shook her head. "No, you wouldn't."

"Analisa, I know how to take campers into the mountain. I can catch trout and fry them, fix breakfast, set a broken leg, apply a tourniquet, navigate by instruments, and read a hell of a bedtime story. But I know next to nothing about surviving in your time. Believe me, when I camp, it's with a tent, a supply of freeze-dried food, and a sleeping bag rated to sixty below."

"I don't do that much. I don't do that well."

"Yes, you do. Don't you know how special that is? How many women could cope with what you've been through?"

She looked at him steadily, blinking only once. "Women do it all the time. When their husbands go off to work in mines or mountains, when they're widowed, when they have to. And I'm not doing it well," she whispered, breaking eye contact.

"What do you mean?" he asked gently, sweeping their plates aside with his free hand, clasping both of hers. "You're doing great. We got the hay cut, despite the bear. You've made cheese and churned butter. Your animals are fat and happy. I'm well fed. How is it you're not doing well?"

She was silent, looking down at the table, at their hands, anywhere but his eyes.

"Talk to me, honey. Tell me what's wrong."

She paused, as if fighting her need to confide in him,

but she lost the battle with the reserved part of herself—that part that kept her feelings in check at any cost. "I'm not frightened for Charlie. I know he can take of himself, that he's been safe in the mountains for years. That's just an excuse." A catch in her voice stopped her, but then she looked up for just a moment and continued. "I'm scared for me," she said finally in a small voice that reminded him how young she was, and how much of a burden rested on her strong but fragile shoulders. She bowed her head, as though she was ashamed to meet his eyes.

And then he felt the plop of a tear on his hand and his heart melted. "Oh, damn, honey. I didn't mean to make you cry."

With that, he pushed out of the chair, walked around the table in two swift strides, and pulled her into his arms.

She tried to push away in a token protest, but he ignored her, holding her tightly against him. She let her emotions go in a shuddering sigh, melting into his embrace, her fingers curled into his chest like a clinging kitten.

"It's okay to be scared," he whispered into her cornsilk hair. "It's okay, honey."

He swayed and she followed, her quiet sobs muffled against his chest. When she stopped crying, he reached down, looped an arm beneath her knees, and picked her up.

"What are you doing?" she asked, her body stiffening in surprise.

"Carrying you across the room," he answered, marveling at how substantial and right she felt in his arms.

"I'm too big to carry!"

"You're a big girl, all right," he agreed, "but not too heavy for me."

123

"David, put me down."

"In a second," he said, easing into the chair next to the hearth. It groaned beneath their combined weight.

"Why are you doing this?"

"Because you need someone to remind you how competent and special you are," he explained, settling back more comfortably, "and because I need to hold you."

"I didn't mean . . . I don't know why I told you that."

"Maybe you needed to tell someone how you felt."

She shook her head. "That's silly. I've never needed to tell someone everything before."

"Well, I'd say losing your family and having the responsibility for yourself and these animals is enough stress to make you a bit emotional. It's not a crime to admit it, you know."

"I shouldn't have said anything about Charlie."

"Of course you should. We're friends, aren't we? And friends talk about how they're feeling."

She folded her hands against her stomach. "I had friends back in Ohio. I remembered them earlier today, and how we used to play and laugh. I hadn't thought about them in a long time. I hadn't thought about a lot of things until you came."

His heart seemed to skip a beat at her quiet, heart-felt admission. He wished he knew whether dredging up the past was good or bad. All he had to go on were his instincts, and they told him that Analisa's pain couldn't be buried forever. "I'm no psychologist, but I think you're lonely. You need to have someone around. A friend."

"Like Charlie."

"Or like me."

She looked up at him. "But how long will you be here?"

"I wish I knew."

"But I know," she said simply, blinking her misty, sky-blue eyes. "You'll be here until you realize that your way home is across another rainbow."

Analisa woke abruptly but didn't know why. No sounds came from David's bedroom or outside. The cabin was dark—so dark she couldn't see the bedcovers or the doorway. She held her breath and imagined that this was what a tomb felt like—cold, silent, dark.

She sucked in air in a rush. The idea of being inside a tomb caused a sense of panic, making her heart beat faster and her breathing uneven. She reminded herself that this was her home. Light would eventually shine through the window; morning would awaken the animals in the barn, the birds in the trees, and the insects that buzzed from flower to flower in the meadow.

She had a lifetime ahead of her, not behind her. But she wondered if she'd encased her emotions in a tomb, far away from the light of day. Before David's arrival, she'd tried very hard to construct walls around her feelings so she didn't hurt so much. After all, what good did crying do? She might rave against fate all she wanted, but alone, with no one to hear, did it do any good? No, she didn't believe so. All it accomplished was to make her want her family back more than ever, and that wasn't going to happen. The safest and best way to go on was to pack the feelings away in a chest, along with the physical reminders that Momma, Papa, and Jurgen were gone.

Talking to David last night had opened the door to her entombed emotions just a little wider. She shouldn't have given in to the needs he raised in her, but she had. Now she didn't know if she'd ever be able to shut the door again. When he left, would she forever crave the special closeness they'd shared on a lonely night? She suspected she would.

Friends, he'd said. Yes, she was beginning to think of him that way, but not the same kind of friend as Charlie or her childhood playmates. With David she craved the physical closeness as well, a woman-and-man closeness she'd never felt before. Charlie barely tolerated a hug when he arrived and left twice a year.

Analisa knew she'd always want to touch David, and although she'd protested his method, she'd felt a rush of excitement when he'd picked her up and carried her across the floor. Papa had often picked her up as a small child, carried her on his shoulders when she ran into the fields at the end of the day, or when they went to the yearly harvest fair in their small Ohio community. She'd liked the feeling of being a special little girl, but David's arms felt totally different. She'd wanted to snuggle against him, melt into him by the fire, become as close as possible to his warmth and caring . . . and to his body.

She rolled to her side, feeling the heat of a blush across her cheeks. When David left, she'd have another painful memory to pack away. If she wasn't careful with her feelings, this one might be too heartbreaking to ever forget.

David didn't sleep well that night. Knowing that Analisa lay in another bed, just steps away, tormented him, especially since he'd held her in his arms, mixing his desire with a deep-felt need to comfort her and chase away her doubts and fears. He tried to tell himself that she wasn't his responsibility, but that was the cold, hard, logical part of his brain. In his heart, he felt responsible, even though he couldn't imagine a more star-crossed pair of would-be lovers.

Concentrating on Jamie and his life in 1997 didn't

help. He knew Holly was taking care of his daughter, but he missed her like crazy. She was due to start first grade in the fall. Would he be there to walk hand-in-hand to her room, meet her teacher, see which desk was hers? Would he be there to play tooth fairy, to place a shiny silver dollar under her pillow for the next tooth she lost, or would Holly take his place? He wished he knew, but only if the answer was yes. If he wasn't going back, he'd have to rebuild his life here, with Analisa, and try not to dwell on the daughter he'd never tuck into bed again, or watch graduate from high school, or walk down the aisle when she married. And he didn't know how he'd bear it.

He was torturing himself, he knew, but that seemed to be his modus operandi lately. Reading bedtime stories to Analisa was another combination of pleasure and pain he'd welcomed with open arms and a heavy heart. Every time he began to read, he saw Jamie's little pixie face, smiling up with wide-eyed interest, even though she'd heard the story a hundred times before.

And as he continued to read these unfamiliar tales to Analisa, a different, darker image formed, of a young woman ready to indulge her own fantasies, with desires and needs she didn't understand, who lay alone in bed and perhaps dreamed of him. Did she fashion herself the tiny, lost young woman named Tommelise, who wanted to escape the amorous intent of an aging mole? Or the sleeping princess, ready to be awakened with a kiss?

With a groan of frustration, he rolled off the feather mattress. Cool, damp wood greeted his bare feet as he padded across the floor and retrieved his freshly laundered shirt. Pulling it on over his briefs, he eased through the half-open doorway and walked to the window. Dawn had yet to light the sky, but from the grayness of the light, he could tell the sun would be up in another half hour.

He stretched his arms high and grasped the frame as he stared out into the near-morning darkness. A brisk wind swayed the trees and scattered leaves across the hard-packed soil in front of the cabin. Dark gray clouds, tinged with pink, streaked across the indigo sky. No creature stirred this early; even the infernal ducks and the goat, which, three days ago he'd realized wasn't just fat, but very pregnant.

If he'd been at home, he would have turned on an all-news station, or at least watched the weather reports for flying conditions later in the day. He tried to recall how many days he'd been here—was it four or five? Had he missed any major jobs? Probably. The calendar he'd carefully updated after each reservation or phone call was a fuzzy blur in his memory.

Holly, are you okay? he wanted to ask. *Have they searched for me and found no trace? Did you hire another pilot to take the charters we'd booked?* God, he hoped so. Without the income from his business, she and Jamie would be in a world of hurt. If he was declared lost, seven years had to pass before he could be pronounced legally dead. Seven years before they could collect the life insurance money he'd made sure would be available if he couldn't care for them.

In seven years Jamie would be a teenager, Holly would have probably lost the air charter service, and who knew where they'd be living. He couldn't imagine his little girl as a teenager, not when she dressed like a boy half the time and had two front teeth missing. By then she'd be wearing bras, and lipstick, at least out of sight of the house, and he'd be cautioning her to stay with her group of friends and not be late.

His hands clenched on the rough wood as frustrated

rage pounded through his body. God, he couldn't stand this uncertainty! He had to get back to his own time, to the family that needed him. He'd gotten into the past by humoring Jamie and flying across the rainbow, the optical illusion she'd called "the one." Well, to get back he might just have to fly across the rainbow that Analisa decided was his way home. His only way home.

Chapter Eight

"Aunt Holly, come here quick. I can't see Daddy's plane no more."

"*Any* more."

"I can't see it any more." Jamie grabbed the binoculars from the desk and looked real hard at the sky. The rainbow disappeared, and she put down the binoculars and blinked. No, it was still there. She looked through them again.

"I can't see him or the rainbow through these darned things!" she said.

"Watch your language," Aunt Holly warned in her grown-up voice. "Let me see."

Aunt Holly stood beside her and took the binoculars.

"He was just there. The radio got all staticky for a minute, and then I couldn't see him no—any—more."

"It's probably just the angle of his plane and the sunlight. It's a trick of light."

"That's what Daddy says about the rainbow, but I

know better. And I think that maybe he really did get lost. I can always find Daddy's plane."

"Let's try to get him on the radio again."

"Okay." Jamie grasped the radio in both hands and pressed down on the button. "Daddy, this is Jamie. Where are you?"

She didn't hear anything, even static. She got really scared. "Aunt Holly, my daddy's gone!"

"He can't be gone, Jamie. We were just talking to him."

"But I can't find him!"

Aunt Holly looked worried too, even though she said Daddy wasn't gone. But what did she know about magic rainbows? Not any more than Daddy, that was for sure!

"I've got to wish him back," Jamie whispered. She sat the radio down on the desk, slid off the stool, and ran toward the door. The rainbow didn't look too good. Kind of pale. She could barely see the pretty purple color on the bottom.

"Jamie, wait!"

She heard Aunt Holly, but she didn't want to stop. She ran away from the building and kept on looking at the sky. When she got out far enough, she stopped. "Daddy, you get back down here!" she yelled, shaking her fist at the rainbow. "Get back down here right now with the princess!"

She heard Aunt Holly run up behind her and put a hand on her shoulder. "He'll be back in a minute or two, honey." Aunt Holly sounded out of breath. "He probably made a wide bank to the right that we couldn't see. As soon as he levels out and starts his descent, we'll be able to see his plane."

"Well, he'd better get back here soon. That rainbow isn't very pretty anymore, and rainbows have to be pretty to work magic."

"He'll be back," Aunt Holly said with one of those smiles she used whenever she wanted her to be very brave or good. "Your daddy would never go off and leave you."

Jamie folded her arms over her favorite T-shirt. "I'm gonna wait right here for him."

"Okay. I'll go in and check the radio. Don't you move, young lady. I want to keep you in sight."

"I'm not going anywhere until my daddy gets back!"

Chapter Nine

Analisa hurried to make an oatmeal porridge for breakfast while David attended to chores outside. He had been up and dressed when she rose from bed, later than usual due to the dark clouds that hid the sun. She suspected they'd get a storm before the day was through, and she never welcomed the wind and heavy rain. Not when the roof of the cabin sometimes leaked where it joined the slant of the hill, or the yard flooded, creating mud that lasted for days.

She sprinkled in the oats, stirring the boiling water as she thought of the way she'd confessed her fears to David last night. She shouldn't have burdened him with her doubts about the coming winter. And she shouldn't have allowed him to carry her from the kitchen to the hearth, or sat in his lap as he listened to her childish ramblings.

Since David's arrival, she thought less of what she *needed* to do and more of what she *wanted* to do.

133

The image of her nuzzling his chest, clutching him, breathing in his scent, caused her blood to turn as hot as the boiling porridge. And his kiss . . . She could almost hear her growing passion for him, a steamy sizzle that threatened to erupt at any moment.

The smell of scorched oatmeal made her jump in surprise. Porridge boiled over the sides of the pot, flowing into the flames beneath. She grabbed a towel, wrapped it around the handle, then pulled the pot off the heat. As she fanned the smell away from the confines of the kitchen, the front door opened and David entered the cabin.

"Leave it open," she said, stirring with one hand and fanning with the other. "I've let the porridge boil over."

"There's a brisk, cool wind," he said, walking toward her. "The smell should clear out in a minute." He stopped beside her, looking at the mess. "You must have been napping," he observed in a friendly, non-accusatory tone.

Even though he couldn't possibly read her errant thoughts, Analisa felt her cheeks grow even warmer. "I was . . . thinking," she said, looking away from his wind-tossed hair and pink cheeks. Darn, but the man looked good no matter what, night or day.

He smiled. "Glad to hear it. Can I do anything to help?" he asked, nodding toward the stove.

"No thank you." She wet a towel and scraped some of the oatmeal off the blackened stovetop. "But if you'd like, you can put the spoons and butter on the table."

"Sure."

He reached for the items, so close that his arm nearly brushed hers. Her heart began to thud despite the fact that they were merely preparing breakfast together.

"I'm glad you've decided I can help out around here. I don't want to be a burden."

"You're not."

"I'm eating your food, causing you extra work. I'd say that's a burden."

"But you're also helping me with the animals. And if you'd like, I'll show you a few other chores that need to be done in the summer to prepare the cabin for winter. We need to add sod to the hill above the roof, and repair some chinking in the barn, and . . ."

Her voice trailed off as she realized what she'd implied—that he'd be here to work beside her throughout the summer. She should have remembered, after their conversation last night, that his visit to her time was only temporary. He would be gone before the first snow, she knew, because he couldn't stand being apart from his daughter.

As he looked at her, his smile gone and the spark in his eyes dimmed to the luster of the blackened stovetop, she regretted reminding him—and herself—that he wouldn't be in her life forever.

She glanced away, finished with the cleaning for now. Without a word, she dished porridge into the bowls, then set them on the table. David took his seat across from her and, silently, they ate breakfast.

The deluge came in earnest later that morning, descending from the mountain peaks like the proverbial flood, soaking the yard until it appeared they were adrift on a gunmetal gray sea. Sheets of rain blocked the sight of the pines and muted the point where the equally gray sky met the earth.

All in all, it was a pretty miserable day, David thought as he again stood at the window and stared outside.

Analisa worked quietly on some mending, sitting near a single candle as she made tiny stitches in a white garment that might be a shirt or a nightgown. She'd barely spoken since breakfast, preferring the solitude of her thoughts, he supposed, rather than anything he might say.

And what could he say? That he'd work around the cabin, fix the barn, and wait for the next magical rainbow? Even he was having a hard time with that one in this rather dim light of day.

He looked through Analisa's supply of books, finding a few fairly new editions that were now considered classics. *Huckleberry Finn*, with a copyright date of 1884, had a crisp spine and no dog-eared pages, but David clearly remembered the story from his own childhood—not to mention a few movies featuring popular child stars Jamie said were really "hot."

He finally chose a book he hadn't read before, Helen Hunt Jackson's *A Century of Dishonor*, about government policy toward the Indians. He was surprised that, 115 years after the book was published, some views stayed the same. If she'd written the book in the 1990s, she would have referred to "indigenous people" or "Native Americans," rather than "Indians," but other than that, he found her arguments to be very similar to those expressed today. Strange; he'd assumed that the views of his generation's activists were fairly original.

He was so absorbed in the book that he didn't realize the hour was late until he glanced up and saw Analisa flinging an oilskin around her head and shoulders.

"Where are you going?" he asked.

"To feed. The rain seems to be slowing down, so I'm going to the barn."

"I'll go," he volunteered.

"I'd like to get out. Besides, I need to check on Daisy. She's due to drop her kid any day now."

He had to think a minute to realize she was talking

about the pregnant goat. "Okay. But if you need me, call."

"I will."

When she opened the door, a gust of cool, damp wind swirled inside, gutting the candle. The room settled into semidarkness as she closed the heavy wood door behind her. It was quiet, so darned quiet. Without a television or radio, set into the side of a hill, the cabin seemed as silent as a tomb in the isolated mountains.

How did Analisa stand the quiet? Now that he was no longer reading, the lack of noise, the loneliness, was about to drive him crazy.

He rose from the chair and stretched, his muscles cramped from several hours of reading. Analisa's chairs were hardly recliners, and the dampness seemed to seep into his bones.

The rain had slacked up a little, he saw as he stood at the window, but it looked as though it might continue for another hour or so. With a sigh of frustration, David walked quickly into the bedroom and searched the pegs on the wall for some old clothes that would be suitable to the rain and mud.

He chose pants, a frayed shirt, and an oiled slicker. Glancing down at his boots—his favorite, expensive Luceses—he searched the corner for some old and battered footwear. He found them, along with some hand-knit socks, when he retrieved and re-lit the candle stub. After discarding his twentieth-century apparel, David donned Jurgen's clothes and headed outside.

He found Analisa in the barn, throwing a saddle she claimed she rarely used on the back of her mare.

"What are you doing?"

She jumped, nearly dropping the heavy saddle. "You scared me." She squinted against the meager light coming in through the door. Her eyes widened as she took in each article of clothing.

"I'm sorry. I should have asked if—"

"No, that's all right. I was just surprised. I meant for you to use Jurgen's clothes." She went back to her task with unusual haste.

David went around to the other side of Tommelise and adjusted the saddle blanket, then handed Analisa the girth underneath the mare's belly. "Why are you going out in this rain?"

"Daisy broke through the fence," she replied, her voice rushed and strained with worry. "I didn't realize the water would rise so high in her pen, but even the ground beneath her shed was wet. Her time must be near, so she's trying to find a safe place."

"Are you sure that's what she'd do? I mean, how will you know where to look?"

"She's not stupid. She'll go up the hill and try to find some shelter. I've got to find her before dark. If she gives birth, the smell of blood will bring wolves or coyotes, maybe even a bear." He saw her shudder as she said the last word and knew she was remembering their fright of a few days ago.

"I'm going with you," he announced. "Do I need to get anything from the house?"

"You don't need to go. I know the land. I should be able to find her."

"Then what? You can't pick her up if she's injured or having the baby—I mean kid."

"No, but I can stay with her. I'll take the gun."

"I'm going. There's no way I'm letting you go alone."

"I don't remember asking for your permission to care for my animals."

"No, you didn't. And I probably shouldn't be so

138

damned chauvinistic, but I can't seem to help myself. The two of us will have a better chance. We can fan out just a little, if you'd like, as long as we're within sight.''

She shook her head. ''I know this land. I can go faster alone.''

''Analisa, I know this land too.''

She stopped pulling on the girth and stared at him over the mare's back. ''What do you mean?''

''This place where the cabin is— it's on my land.''

''Your land?''

''I bought my property in 1989, when Catherine and I married and we moved to Jackson. The area where your cabin is located is on the northeast corner of my land.''

He could tell she had questions, but she didn't ask them, shaking her head instead. ''I can't talk right now. I need to find Daisy.''

''*We* need to find Daisy,'' he corrected her. ''Why don't you go get the gun and the ammo? I'll finish up here.''

She opened her mouth as if to argue, then must have thought better of it. Setting her mouth in a straight, firm line, she pivoted and marched out the barn door.

Analisa guided Tommelise through the cold rain, watching for any sign of Daisy. She couldn't see a trail because any tracks would have been covered by flowing water or wind-battered grass. Once before the goat had escaped from the pen. She'd followed a similar path and Analisa had tracked her, certain the silly animal was headed into the mountains. She hoped that Daisy remembered that earlier flight, because there wasn't anything to go on except instincts, and Analisa's told her to keep riding higher, toward the grassy meadow.

The feel of David riding behind her was a comfort

and a curse. She welcomed his strength and support, despite her arguments earlier to keep him at the cabin. Involving him in her problems hardly seemed fair; if he wasn't here, she'd still go after Daisy. And he might try to keep her from going out in the storm, even though the wind and rain had lessened and no more lightning streaked the sky.

When she'd first realized the goat was missing, she hadn't considered telling him. Then she thought about his reaction when he couldn't find her, so she planned to saddle Tommelise first, get everything prepared, and tell him before riding off. He couldn't have followed on foot.

But he would have been angry. Very angry, if she'd tried to pull that escape. For some reason, he felt extremely protective of her, as though she hadn't taken care of herself for the past five months—and many more before that, when Papa and Jurgen took off on one of their expeditions.

"There's a stand of trees up here that looks encouraging," he said, leaning closer to her ear.

She felt his warm breath and the press of his chest against her shoulder blades as she concentrated on guiding Tommelise closer to the woods. "I know. Let's try it."

"I hope the bear's moved on," David added, almost too casually.

"I imagine she's found her den in this weather."

"I expect you're right. This isn't fit weather for man or beast—or goat."

The mare didn't balk at entering the treeline, but soon the aspens and pines grew too close, some of their limbs bowed low with water. "We need to get off. I'll lead Tommelise," Analisa said, looking back over her shoulder at David.

He leaned forward again, so quickly that she had to turn away or risk brushing her lips against his—accidentally, of course.

"I'll get the gun and the rope," he offered as she pulled her horse to a halt.

Within seconds they were walking beneath the canopy of trees.

"If you cut straight through here," David said, pointing over Tommelise's left ear, "you're about a hundred and fifty yards from the plane."

"I didn't realize we were so close." Between the rain, the premature darkness, and the trees, there was no way she could see the great white bird, as she still preferred to think of the plane. That sounded much more romantic and appealing than calling it a machine.

If he didn't have the plane, he couldn't fly away. The thought popped into her head, so unexpected that she stumbled over a rotting limb.

"Be careful," David admonished, catching her arm to steady her.

"Sorry," she mumbled, frowning at the turn of her thoughts. David, forever in her time, living with her in the cabin, helping her care for the animals and making the chores less demanding. Her settling in his lap beside the fire on cold evenings, sitting across from him at the table each meal. The pictures kept coming, until they caused an ache in her heart she couldn't endure.

She stopped, pressing her hand to her eyes to try to block the images.

"What's wrong?"

Everything, she longed to say. But how could she admit to David that after all her other confessions of self-doubt, fear, and loneliness, she'd even consider keeping him in her time?

"Nothing," she said. "I suppose there's just something in my eye."

He faced her, framed her face with his hands, and looked into her eyes with the concentration of a skilled doctor. She blinked, hoping he couldn't tell she'd lied, that nothing irritated her except her selfish thoughts.

"I can't see anything."

"The rain must have washed it out. I feel fine now."

He released her face but smoothed his hands down her shoulders in a comforting gesture. "Good, then let's find that damned goat and get out of this rain. Your brother's boots weren't made for trekking over the mountains."

"You're right; they weren't. His other boots were on him when he . . ."

In an instant, David hugged her to him. "I'm sorry. I wasn't thinking. How could I be so cruel?"

"It's not your fault. You were just observing that the boots weren't comfortable," she muttered into the oilcloth slicker.

"I wasn't thinking," he repeated, his strength and warmth welcome as he held her tight.

"David, it's all right. I've come to terms with—" She stopped, listening for the sound that had barely registered.

"What?" he asked, releasing her.

"I thought I heard Daisy." She put her finger to her lips and listened for a repeat of the faint bleating sound. When it didn't come again, she turned from David, cupped her hands around her mouth, and called, "Daisy!"

Repeating the call in all directions, she welcomed the diversion from David's arms—and his guilt over bringing up the subject of Jurgen's death. She didn't want David to suffer any recriminations over an innocent slip when she was imagining what it would be like to keep him here forever.

"Do you hear anything?" she whispered.

"I thought I did." David stood very still. Even Tommelise cooperated, patiently waiting with her head down low, looking miserably wet.

From the right, the sound came again, this time more clearly. "It's her!" Analisa started in that direction, tugging the mare's reins.

"Give me the gun and let me go first," David insisted, catching hold of her arm.

"Why?"

"In case she's in trouble," he said, looking ahead at the tangle of bushes on the other edge of the wooded area.

"I can handle it."

"You can't stand the sight of a skinned rabbit. What if Daisy's hurt?"

"I can handle it," she insisted, raising her chin a notch. "Believe it or not, I actually did a fine job of living before you arrived." She tugged on Tommelise's reins, continuing toward the undergrowth.

There. That should show him she wasn't depending on him to save her from the realities of life. She wasn't asking for his help. She'd be perfectly fine when he left for his home, his family, his time.

She heard David curse beneath his breath as he followed her.

After tying the reins to a low branch, Analisa called out again. "Daisy? Where are you, girl?" She crouched low, peering into the thicket of gooseberry bushes. She could just see a patch of white amid the green of the leaves and the dark shadows caused by the dreary day and the thick growth.

"I'm coming, girl," Analisa said as reassuringly as

possible as she searched for an opening large enough to squeeze through without scratching herself on the prickly bushes.

"Since you're so damned independent, I don't suppose you want my help," David said in a cool voice from behind her.

"Not unless you have an ax to cut away this undergrowth," she replied, still looking for a clearing as she alternately crouched and walked on the edge of the gooseberry bushes. To her left, she spotted a possibility. Yes, there were several broken twigs, as though Daisy had used this same spot.

She dropped to her knees, ready to crawl through the opening. Suddenly she was gripped from behind, strong hands closing around her waist. "What are you doing?"

"Keeping you from rushing into something dangerous," David growled as he hauled her backward.

"Let go of me!"

"No, not this time."

"What are you talking about? She twisted, breaking his hold for just a moment. But David bent over her, his hands hauling her off the wet ground, his expression intense.

"I'm talking about putting yourself in danger for no good reason. I'm talking about looking before you leap. I'm talking about having some common sense!" His voice rose with each word until he was yelling.

"Stop it! I'm just trying to help Daisy. I can see her through the bushes—her, not anything else. Now let . . . me . . . go," she said, accenting each word with a shove against his hard chest.

He released her. She stumbled backward, catching herself before she landed on her bottom. Putting a little more distance between her and this raving, lunatic version of David, she grabbed the gun and the rope. "I don't know what's wrong with you, but I hope you get over it soon.''

He wiped a hand over his face, his eyes closed as though he were in pain. "I know." He rubbed his forehead, frowning. "I'm sorry. I thought . . . never mind what I thought. Just call if you need me."

Turning away from her with a droop to his shoulders, David looked as lost and alone as she'd often felt. Under different circumstances, she'd go to him, offer comfort, but not now. She felt too confused, and besides, she had to get to Daisy. A few pitiful bleats had her scrambling through the opening.

"I'm coming, girl, I'm coming," she crooned as she crawled beneath the gooseberry bushes. Thorns snagged at her jacket and pants, but she ignored them. Water seeped through the knees of her pants, and she now felt the dampness from falling on the ground—being dragged to the ground—by David.

"Darn man," she muttered beneath her breath as she made her way toward Daisy.

Lying in the small clearing was her rain-soaked, no-longer-pregnant goat.

"Oh, Daisy, you certainly picked a fine day and an equally fine place for this," Analisa groaned as she took in the two kids, as wet as their mother, who tried to lick them dry. "Not in this weather," Analisa advised, then realized that the rain had stopped. Only a few stray drops from the trees above filtered down to land on them.

"David, we're going to need that ax," she called out, hoping he hadn't wandered off.

"Are you okay?"

"I'm fine, but Daisy has produced two kids, and they're all soaking wet. I could use some rags, too, and maybe an old blanket."

"Will you be safe there?"

145

"Of course. Nothing is coming in here except through that opening, and I have the gun."

He was silent for a moment. "All right. I'll be back as quickly as possible."

"You know where the ax is. There's an old blanket at the foot of the bed in Jurgen's room. And there are rags in the kitchen."

"I'll find them." She heard one muffled, soggy footstep before he stopped. "Analisa?"

"Yes?"

"I'm sorry for yelling. Just be careful, okay?"

"I will. I'm not going anywhere."

She listened as his footsteps faded away. The faint creak of saddle leather, followed by the sound of Tommelise's large hooves sinking into the wet ground, gradually faded away as well. Then all was quiet.

Turning her attention back to Daisy, Analisa tried to get comfortable in the small space. She placed the gun at her right side, facing the narrow tunnel, and stroked the goat's long ears with one hand. David was gone, at least for the moment, and the forest was waking up again. High overhead, birds began chirping to celebrate the clear skies. A slight breeze bent branches soaked with moisture, depositing drops on her head, arms, and legs. Inside the clearing, Daisy continued her task of cleaning her babies.

"It's just you and me, Daisy," Analisa whispered to the new mother as she gently picked up one of the small, wet kids and cradled it in her lap. "He'll be back soon, but you can't get used to him, you hear? He's not going to stay forever, and we may as well accept it."

She listened to the sounds of the forest and tried not to think of David, his protective nature, his claims that this was his land—more than a hundred years in the future—or the great white bird that rested a short distance away, ready to carry him back to his own time.

David rode as fast as he dared on the wet ground, bringing the items Analisa had requested, plus a few more he'd thrown in for good measure. Tommelise's large hooves pounded into the soft earth as they cantered around the stand of pines and aspens, coming close to the other side of the spot where the gooseberry bushes provided shelter for one eccentric goat and her stubborn owner.

He knew, as soon as he'd done it, that he'd over reacted. He should never have hauled her out of the brambles, much less yelled at her for being concerned about a member of her zoo. But she'd charged in, so sure that she couldn't be harmed, that there was nothing inside that tangle of bushes that was dangerous.

He'd literally seen red—blood red. He'd imagined a predator lurking inside, attacking the foolish goat, attacking Analisa as she tried to rescue her precious animal. And he'd grabbed her, pulled her back from danger the only way he knew how.

If he'd been able to do the same thing to Catherine, she'd be alive today. Jamie would not have grown up without a mother. He wouldn't have been a widower. Holly wouldn't be strapped with the responsibility of being a twenty-seven-year old aunt and surrogate mother to an active six-year-old.

Guilt, raw and unresolved, ate at his gut. He knew it, but had never resolved that issue. Trying to protect Analisa from every danger wasn't going to resolve it either, but keeping her from harm made him feel like he was *doing* something.

He hadn't done anything to save Catherine except ask her to be careful before she hiked into the mountains, the gleam of discovery and excitement in her eyes. If only he'd told her one more time how he worried about her, how much Jamie needed her, how they'd miss her if anything happened to her, perhaps she wouldn't have taken the unnecessary risk and fallen to her death.

But he couldn't change the past—at least not his recent past with Catherine. He had to get over her death and get on with his life.

As if some unseen force had heard his thoughts and agreed, the clouds parted and sunshine flooded the meadow. He pulled Tommelise to a halt, staring at the fresh-washed wonder of the mountains in summer. Grass so green and shiny it nearly blinded him, sky so blue he had to squint to see the white clouds scatter in the high winds off the mountain peaks. A sprinkling of wildflowers dotted the tall grass, and as he watched, they seemed to unfurl and embrace the sunlight.

All the colors of the rainbow. He could almost hear Jamie say that very thing. Maybe he had heard her say it. To Jamie, almost anything could be related, in some, often obscure way, to a rainbow.

He shook his head, knowing he had to get back to his baby. The thought of never seeing her again was intolerable. He must return to his own time.

And again, as if some unseen force heard his thoughts, as he swung his leg over the mare's broad back, a rainbow began to form in the east. Just a faint glimmer of color between the fleeing clouds. He dropped to the ground and stared, a rush of feeling coursing through his body. Excitement. Hope. Fear that he could be losing his mind because he was thinking that this rainbow might just be the way home.

Tommelise snorted loudly, stamping her foot. From inside the wooded area, Analisa called out, "David?"

"I'm here." He watched as the clouds swallowed up

the rainbow, then turned away, grabbing the bundle of rags and the ax, wrapped in the old blanket. "I'm coming."

But I'm coming home to you someday, Jamie, he silently vowed. *Don't give up on Daddy.*

He wrapped the mare's reins around a limb, then walked quickly toward the gooseberry bushes. Within a minute, he'd removed the ax from the bundle and begun hacking away at the undergrowth.

Chapter Ten

"Aren't they adorable?" Analisa asked as she handed one of the kids to David. "Daisy outdid herself."

He grasped the wiggling, tan-and-white baby with a look of slight distaste on his face. "It certainly has sharp little feet."

"Hooves," she corrected. "And they're about its only weapons." She held her own kid firmly as she walked out of the gooseberry patch with David at her heels. Daisy trotted beside her, looking up at her offspring and bleating sadly.

"Is she going to do that all the way home?" David asked.

"Probably. Does it really bother you?"

"Yes."

"I'm sorry, but there's nothing I can do."

"I know it. I'm still mad at her for getting out," he grumbled. "This afternoon I'm going to build the strongest fence that damned goat has ever seen."

"That's a good idea," she said. "I'd appreciate not having to chase her around the territory."

They reached Tommelise. David had found the prospector's pack harness that had been in the back of the barn for years.

"I wasn't sure what these were or whether they'd work, but I thought we'd make better time if the little guys didn't try to walk home," he said as he lifted the dusty item for her to see.

"That's a great idea." Analisa tested the leather straps for dry rot. They appeared to be strong enough to hold two squirming kids, one on each side of Tommelise. "It was Papa's. When we first moved out here, he heard about gold in a stream that came out of Death Canyon. He and Jurgen used to go there, prospecting for gold."

"Did they ever find any?"

"Just some nuggets. Not very much."

"I've never heard of any big gold strikes near Jackson."

"Even if they'd found gold, what would we do with it? There are no stores, no place to buy much of anything. People out here want to trade for goods, not gold. Papa gave the prospector—the one who gave up searching for a fortune—three chickens and Momma's good shoes for that pack, because he could take those shoes and trade them for flour or cornmeal. You can't eat gold in the winter."

"That's a good way to look at it. We don't have that problem any more, unless someone is stranded in the wilderness. In those rare cases, I'm sure they'd trade all their cash for warm clothes and hearty food."

She took David's kid from him and placed it inside one of the pockets, along with some rags for padding. Its small head peered out from beneath the flap, calling for its mother. "In the winter, I get so tired of eating

151

meat and beans," she said. "Sometimes I sit in the cabin and want a fresh, crisp apple so badly that my mouth waters and I can smell it."

"If I could, I'd send you a hundred bushels of apples," David said, standing close and placing his hand over hers. "I'm sorry your life is so hard. Would you like to move somewhere else? I could help you go back to Ohio, if you'd like. Perhaps your friends are still there. Or do you have any relatives?"

She gently removed her hand from his warm touch and shook her head. "No relatives. And I'm not sure how to find my friends. I tried the other night . . . and I can't remember their names." She turned away from his concerned, dark eyes. The newborn goats gave her plenty of excuses not to pursue this conversation. There was no point in tormenting herself with what could never be. "We'd better get them home. I'm sure Daisy could use some rest and grain."

"Look, Analisa, I hate to see you like this. I keep thinking about how rough things are here, and I can't stand the idea of you staying here alone in the winter, even if you do have enough meat and beans—or apples, for that matter. We've got to find a way to work this out. I know you think you can handle living alone, but—"

"This isn't the time to talk of it, David," she said, still not looking at him. She busied herself placing a few more rags for padding. "Why don't you let Tommelise sniff the babies so they don't frighten her? Then you can put the saddlebag over her back."

She heard David sigh, but he did as she asked. Tommelise pricked up her ears, flared her nostrils, and breathed in the scent of the kids. Then she bobbed her head up and down, as if giving her approval to Daisy's offspring.

152

When he carefully placed the bundle over the mare's back, Analisa turned to watch. She was so glad that the sky had cleared. The water would soak in or run off quickly, and then they could . . .

In the eastern sky a rainbow appeared, starting as a pale glow and growing brighter and brighter. She stood there, staring at the arch of colors, the bright blue above it, the lighter blue inside, and wondered if David felt it too.

"Do you see?" she whispered.

"I saw it earlier too, but it faded away."

She watched him look into the sky, an expression of rapt attention on his face. His strong jaw appeared clenched and tight. His lips thinned to a straight line. His eyes squinted against the sunlight.

"You can go home," she said softly.

He shook his head.

"Yes, you can. This is your way home," she said, grasping his forearm. "All you have to do is clear the brush off your plane, fly up into the sky, and go back to your life. To your daughter."

He turned to her, his expression still intense. "And leave you here alone, with these animals, the leaking roof, the fences that need repair? Go off and never know if you had enough food to make it though the winter? If Charlie came back to stay with you, or died in the mountains? Do you really expect me to do that?"

She stared at him until her eyes filled with tears. She clenched her own jaw, swallowing hard. She didn't know if she'd be able to speak. She didn't know what to say. Life without David would never be the same. Whenever she entered the cabin, she knew she'd expect to look up and see him there. But that wasn't to be. He had to go back to his own time and continue his life there. He didn't belong here in the wilds any more than she did, but at least she was in her own time, her own era.

Finally, she whispered, "Yes."

"You can't be serious."

"Yes, I am. This is your way home. Do you expect me to stop you from going to your daughter?" She turned away, battling tears as she busied herself with the damned goat.

"Dammit, Analisa, I can't." He'd thought about it. He'd let himself believe, for just one instant, that he could fly off into that rainbow and be back in 1997 with Jamie and Holly. He'd even imagined what it would feel like to bank his plane and find Jackson Airport below, along with the roads, the power lines, the houses—all back where they were supposed to be.

But how could he go off and leave Analisa, when she had nothing except an occasional visit from an old mountain man, and carried the responsibility for herself and every other living thing that she came in contact with? At least he knew Jamie was being well cared for by Holly.

"There'll be other times," he said, as gently as possible. "Other rainbows."

"You don't know that. Summers can be very dry. We may not get rain for weeks."

"Then I'll wait," he said with a shrug. "Eventually, another rainbow will appear. Maybe that will be the right time."

"How will you know?" she asked, looking at him again. "I'm still going to be here, living in the cabin, caring for my animals. Are you going to change your opinion of my living alone?"

"Charlie could decide to stay. When he comes back, I'll talk to him."

"And if he doesn't?"

"Dammit, Analisa, I don't know, okay?" He ran a hand through his hair, closing his eyes. She wanted answers he couldn't give, reassurances that were beyond his control.

"I didn't mean to make you angry," she said, untying the mare's reins and leading her away from the trees.

"You didn't make me angry. The situation made me mad. There has to be a way . . ."

"For you to leave and know that I'm safe and sound for all time? I don't think so."

Why hadn't he thought of the solution before? "I'll take you with me."

"What?"

"When I leave, you'll go with me. You can start a new life. You'll love my time. Hell, we're almost to a new century. You'll have the chance to live in three separate centuries. How many people can make that claim?"

"Not many, I'm sure, but that's not the point." She stopped the mare and placed a hand on his arm, looking up into his eyes. "I don't belong in your time, David. I'm supposed to live here, in my time, just like you're supposed to live in yours. Isn't that what you told me before when you explained time travel? Think about all the horrible consequences of that action! That's why you'll go back—to be where you belong."

"You don't know that. I was telling you theories of writers in Hollywood—the place where they make the movies I told you about. What if the reason I came here was to bring you back with me?"

She shook her head. "I think you came here because your daughter believes in rainbows and fairy tales, and you needed to believe in them too. This made you see that there are powers we don't understand. Sometimes you have to believe in things you can't see or touch."

"Okay, I'll admit I didn't believe Jamie when she told me about the rainbow. Hell, I'm still a little skeptical. But that doesn't mean you can't go back with me."

"Don't you see? I wouldn't be going back. I'd be going forward, to a place that doesn't exist for me. Your time, David, not mine. This is where I live," she said emphatically, sweeping her hand from the ground to the sky. "On this dirt and beneath these mountains in the year 1886."

"The dirt's the same. The mountains are still there in 1997."

"But *I'm* not there. I'm not even sure I could go where you're going."

"We could try."

"And what if we fail? What if you couldn't go back because I was with you, or if something happened and I . . . No, I just can't believe it would work."

"Now who doesn't have faith in what she can't see or touch?" he asked, trying to keep the sarcasm out of his voice. "You can't base your life on theories expressed in movies. Who knows anything about time travel? About the rules or restrictions?"

She'd wanted an answer and he'd supplied one. But she didn't like the conclusion he'd reached. Why couldn't she just admit it was the best solution?

"I believe that you need to go back," she said with a patience he found annoying. "That's the best I can do. Please don't ask for more." She turned her back on him and started walking down the hill, leading her horse, the bleating goat trotting alongside her.

"Dammit," he muttered under his breath. Just when he thought he'd found the answer, she had to balk. He took one more look into the eastern sky, in time to see the once magnificent rainbow fade away.

*   *   *

She made a conscious decision to stay away from David for the rest of the day, spending time with Daisy and the two kids, catching up on the chores in the barn. She turned the stacks of hay they'd cut three days ago, added manure to the compost heap, measured the remaining grain so she'd know how much they'd need when she went to trade.

The other settlers should be ready to trade within a month, and she had to get provisions to last the rest of the year. She hadn't figured what she'd need without Papa and Jurgen, and she had more animals now than last winter. Hopefully, the two gold nuggets she had left, plus the eggs, butter, cheese, and chickens, would be enough to trade for wheat, corn, and oats.

At least she didn't have to worry about feeding David, she convinced herself. He'd wanted to go today; she'd seen the look in his eyes as he'd watched the rainbow grow brighter, stronger. If Charlie had been there, if she'd never mentioned to David that she worried about the coming season, he might have gone today.

Flown out of her life, just as he'd flown in. The reality of his leaving had slapped her in the face, at a moment when she was physically and emotionally tired. Her defenses were down; otherwise, she would have done a better job of assuring him she was fine. That she knew just what to do. That she'd convince Charlie to stay the winter and help out. With his trapping and her household management, they'd be snug and healthy all winter long.

She had to be stronger for the next time. She had to convince him that she was no weak woman who needed a man to take care of her. And starting today, she'd do just that. By the time the next rainbow appeared, David would be able to fly away without any regrets.

She heard hammering as she retrieved the bucket to get fresh water from the stream. It would be muddy, she knew, from the rain run-off that swelled against the banks, but the silt would settle and the animals wouldn't mind.

She, on the other hand, hated the muddy water. She'd have to let a lot settle; she needed a bath after today's mud and muck.

Bathing had never been a problem; she'd send Papa and Jurgen outside, or hang a sheet across the opening to the kitchen, and place her tub in there beside the stove. But getting rid of David would be more difficult. Just admitting why she wanted him to leave would be embarrassing.

But she'd do it. She'd quit simpering and stammering, stop acting weak around him. He'd know, without a doubt, that she was her own woman.

She marched past Daisy's pen on her way to the creek. The afternoon sun beat down, making the air heavy with moisture and warm without a breeze. The sky seemed so quiet, as though the storm had wrung all the life out of the wind, the clouds, and the air. And, as promised, David hammered away on the fence—without his shirt.

She nearly stumbled, banging the wooden bucket against her leg. She bit down on her lip to keep from moaning over the sudden pain; she'd have a bruise there tomorrow. But apparently David hadn't seen her blunder. He worked on, adding a rail so Daisy and the new kids couldn't climb through. His bronzed muscles gleamed with sweat. He'd tied one of Jurgen's bandannas around his head to keep moisture and hair out of his eyes.

Mercy, he was a good-looking man. She could stay there all day and watch. In fact, she probably would have stopped if she hadn't made her new resolution. But not any more. She wasn't going to succumb to temptation any longer. Wanting him as a woman wants a man would be an enormous mistake, because she knew, with some feminine instinct she couldn't even name, that then she'd never let him go.

How could she? He was everything she could ever want in a man—in a husband. And that type of thinking was far too dangerous to indulge.

So she broke her gaze away from his half-naked body and continued walking toward the rain-swollen stream, where red-brown water flowed swiftly down the hills. And she forced herself to figure the pints, quarts, gallons, and barrels of grain and meal in her head, just to keep her mind so busy she couldn't recall how impressive David Terrell looked without a shirt.

She was avoiding him. David knew it as well as he knew his own name. She'd barely talked during dinner, just answered his few questions or comments with polite, one-word replies. He'd finally given up, cleaning his plate and retiring outside, just in time to see the last of the sunset. Cooling air swept gently off the mountains, moving the high pink and purple clouds toward the east.

Toward the place where the rainbow had arched across the sky.

He stepped farther from the cabin, wishing he had a cup of coffee to sip while he watched the sky change from orange to indigo. Wishing he knew what had happened earlier today when he'd seen the second rainbow, the bright one that had given him hope that he could go home again.

He hadn't wanted to believe, but when he'd stared up into the sky, he'd known, somehow, that the rainbow *could* take him home. Analisa had known. From the first, she'd insisted that the rainbow was the way back for

159

him. Whatever her reason—a mother who read her fairy tales, a father who chased dreams from Ohio to Wyoming—she had a rare faith in things that couldn't be seen.

When Catherine had gone into the mountains for the last time, he hadn't doubted her ability to take care of herself. But he'd known that accidents could happen to even the most experienced camper or woodsman. Several times in his years as a pilot, he'd flown the bodies of victims out of the mountains. Mangled by falls down shale and granite cliffs, smothered by tons of snow in an avalanche, exposed to the freezing temperatures of unexpected blizzards, nothing mattered except that they were dead.

And when he'd flown Catherine out of the mountains for the last time, she'd joined them in death. The rangers had suggested she'd climbed a cliff, set up a makeshift camp on a ledge, and waited for the eagles to accept her presence. From where she'd sat, she could use the telephoto lens to capture the adults in flight, landing on the nest, or feeding their offspring. But to view the young, she'd had to shimmy up a lodgepole pine, hold on while shooting and loading, and climb down to her narrow ledge again. No one knew what had happened; she might have lost her grip, missed her step on the ledge, or been attacked by the eagles. In the end, the reason hadn't mattered, because she'd fallen forty or fifty feet to the rocks below her perch.

She'd died instantly, the coroner had told him. That piece of information had been the only consolation to his grief and anger. Catherine hadn't suffered, but her family had—for days, weeks, months. As the acute suffering had turned to a dull pain, he and Jamie had gone on. Holly had arrived to help temporarily but stayed on permanently. Without her, he couldn't have continued his business and raised his daughter. And even though Jamie didn't remember her mother, he did.

He'd never forgiven Catherine for putting herself in danger. Did the world need another picture of eagles more than Jamie needed a mother? He didn't think so. Could someone else have provided those photos? Surely. Someone who didn't have a husband and child waiting for her at home.

He leaned against the fence as the sky darkened, merging with the shadowy mountain peaks as night descended. On the other side of the barrier, Analisa's giant pig waddled over, its big pink head bowed low, as if it were commiserating with him. When it stopped on the other side of the fence, it looked up at him with tiny eyes and let out several chortling grunts.

"Yeah, me too," David replied. Coarse-looking white hair covered the pig's head and neck. A smile seemed to lift the corners of the wide mouth.

"I guess you're a female pig, hmm?" As a matter of fact, all the animals around here seemed to be females, except for that damned duck. "At least you didn't run off and get stuck somewhere. I suppose you don't mind a little water and mud."

"She doesn't."

Analisa's soft voice charged the peaceful night with a jolt of electricity David felt all the way to his toes. He looked at her over his shoulder. "I didn't hear you come up."

"The ground is soft." She hugged a blanket closer around her shoulders. "I just wanted to tell you that I was going to be in the barn for a few minutes. Then I'll be preparing a bath in the kitchen. I'd appreciate it if you'd stay outside until I finish."

"Am I still invited inside to sleep, or should I find somewhere else?"

161

"Of course you're welcome. I just wanted to let you know my plans." She looked away, hugged the blanket even higher on her arms, and walked toward the barn.

"Analisa, wait."

She stopped but didn't look at him.

"We should talk about what happened."

"Not now, David."

"Then when?"

"I'm not sure." She started walking again. "There are some things I need to do. I'll see you later."

"I can't help that I care about you."

She didn't say anything, didn't even acknowledge that she'd heard him except by a slight hesitation in her steps.

He let her go. He'd never been one to force an issue unless it was absolutely necessary. Most of the time, patience paid off. Hadn't he told Jamie that a hundred times? But his own patience wouldn't last, he predicted, if he were around this new, subdued Analisa for long.

Especially if he envisioned her in a tub, naked, with warm water and soap bubbles caressing her pale skin.

David waited until he saw the dim glow of candlelight from the half-open door of the barn. From the sounds inside the barn, he could tell she was feeding Daisy. The bleats of the newborn kids told him that the mother goat was ignoring them in favor of the feed trough. Analisa's voiced drifted through the night. A hoof stomped, hay rustled, and then silence settled once again over the homestead.

On the other side of the fence, the pig snorted.

"I don't suppose you have any advice, do you?" he asked the sow.

Even though the light from the cabin and barn was very dim, he saw her raise an eyebrow as she squinted up at him.

162

"Whatever that means," he said, frowning into the night.

He had to find a way to bridge the gap the rainbow had caused. His first instinct was to take Analisa into his arms, convince her to trust him—who she could see and feel and touch—as much as she trusted in things outside the realm of science. But he knew that although he could make her forget her fears and arguments, they'd come back. She would never hide her head in the sand and pretend that nothing could harm her. She'd confront her fears with the same strength she used to face the hardships of life.

Patience, he told himself. Follow his own advice. The only problem was that he didn't have all the time in the world—not with Jamie wondering where her daddy was, what had happened to him when he flew across the rainbow. He had to get home *and* make sure that Analisa was safe—with him or in her own time.

But deep inside, he knew that the only way he'd ever be sure was if she was with him—the beautiful princess Jamie had said he'd bring home.

Chapter Eleven

Analisa awoke early the next morning. The embers of the fire had long since burned out, and no dawn light filtered across the floor of the main room. The cabin was as dark as could be, with no sounds except her own breathing. And nothing to occupy her mind but her own thoughts. This was the time of day she dreaded most—along with the evening hours, before she went to sleep—because until David had flown into her life, she'd been alone.

He'd exposed her vulnerability yesterday; how could anyone know whether she'd survive the winter? If her mother had succumbed to lung fever despite the family to care for her, if her Papa and Jurgen had died in a blizzard despite knowing the mountains . . .

All the memories . . . she couldn't face them when she was here alone, so she'd pushed them from her mind. But with David here, the feelings came flooding back like the swollen streams that rushed from the mountains each spring. The emotions overran the banks, swelled into the flat, calm meadows of her life until she could no longer ignore their presence. She felt like that now, like she was wading in a mire of unfamiliar sensations. Somehow, she had to get herself back on solid ground. Only then would she be able to figure out what she had to do, how she could convince David that she didn't need him in her future to survive and be happy.

He wanted to be certain she wouldn't be alone. Only two scenarios presented themselves, given that she was here in the Wyoming territory rather than somewhere else; she could convince Charlie to stay with her, or she could marry someone who would provide protection and companionship.

But not love. The thought flashed through her mind as quickly as a leaping trout. No, she couldn't expect love to grow from such an arrangement with a local man. In her dreams, she'd hoped for someone magical and special to swoop down on a white horse, to carry her off to an enchanted land where life was easy and happiness was expected.

Someone just like David, her own prince.

But although he was real, he wasn't *her* prince. The days of her childhood were behind her; she was an adult now, not ruled by fairy tales of handsome princes and magical lands. Before David's arrival, she'd been able to separate the fantasy of her younger years from the reality of life. She'd always believed that princes and enchanted lands were the stuff of dreams, and no matter how much one wished they were real, they weren't. But how did one separate the two when magic happened right in front of one's eyes?

She flopped to her side, punching the pillow in frustration. There were no answers. All she knew was that she had to release David to go back to his own time, and to do that she had to convince him that she was safe.

She could begin her trading early, traveling to the other cabins to see if they had any extra grain. Perhaps someone new had moved in, bringing with him supplies to trade. There were more settlers in the valley now, as well as along the river.

Maybe one of them had a son looking for a wife.

She shifted to her back, a shudder passing through her as she tried to imagine marrying a stranger. Bringing him into her snug cabin . . . into her bed. Somehow she couldn't imagine that intimate part of married life unless she placed David in the picture. His heated kisses, the strength of his body, the glow in his dark eyes, all made a very vivid image of what sharing that most personal act might involve. Just remembering how she felt whenever he was near made her blood warm, her skin become sensitive to the fabric of her nightgown and the weight of the blanket. She shifted her legs, trying to ignore the throb of her heartbeat, deep within her body, but she wasn't successful. She wanted David as a bride wants her husband, and no arguments about her time or his, no logical plans to marry a stranger, could change how much.

With a strength born of frustration, she threw back the covers, letting the cool air rush over her skin. Her twisted nightgown exposed her legs and bound her body, so she stood, shaking the cotton fabric until it again flowed loosely around her.

Except on her breasts. She didn't need light to know that her nipples were hard and sensitive. *It's the cold,* she told herself, but inside she knew that thoughts of David had caused the reaction. That only his touch would soothe the ache there, and lower, where she still felt the heavy pulse of her heartbeat in a place she'd been taught to ignore.

She'd pushed aside her feelings before; she'd do it again, she vowed silently. She'd pack up her supplies and make the rounds early, looking for new settlers with sons of marrying age. Or widowers, perhaps, who needed a wife. Yes, that was her new goal, and one she would pursue as soon as the sun came up.

Until then, she'd start her day as she always did. She'd push aside these sensations by concentrating on the routine of cooking breakfast, feeding the animals, and preparing for the coming evening meal. Just as she'd decided yesterday, she'd treat David politely but not melt at his slightest glance, or stammer over his remarks. She'd behaved properly last night, hadn't she? She could continue to do so until she was safely committed to another man or sure that Charlie would stay the winter.

And then David would be free to leave, go back to his own time, where he belonged, with his young daughter and the magic of his era. She'd have a life, with a husband and possibly children of her own, or she'd continue on with Charlie, raising her animals and enjoying the peaceful pace of life. Or she could decide not to marry after David was gone. Once he was safely back in his time, she wouldn't be bound to enter into a relationship she couldn't tolerate.

Whichever option she chose, David would be gone. Years from now, he'd be a memory to place on her shelf beside the trolls and goblins of her fairy-tale books, and whenever she thought of him, she'd remember him as a prince who'd visited from a far-off land and returned to his family after a grand adventure.

Perhaps she'd even write a fairy tale of her own someday.

* * *

"What are you doing?" David asked, amazed at the quantity of food Analisa had assembled on the table.

"Measuring my cheese and butter. I need to trade for provisions I don't produce."

"I thought Charlie was the one who traded."

"He does—for himself. I do my own. Or at least, I do now," she said with a slight frown. "Papa and Jurgen used to, but now it's my responsibility."

"Who do you trade with?"

"The other settlers. Perhaps there'll be some new ones this year."

"You said there wasn't anyone very close. How far away do you have to go?"

"I'll cross the river and go to Jackson Hole. The circuit will take a few days." She shrugged, as if the idea of going off in a fairly unpopulated area was of no concern to her.

"I'll go with you."

"No, I'm sorry, you can't," she said, folding cloth back around a block of cheese.

"What?" Surely she didn't think he'd allow her to go off on her own after what had already happened.

"These may not be close neighbors, but they are the only ones I have. I've heard that more people are moving in each summer. If they believe I'm living in this cabin with you, they'll think the worst. No one will trade with me then, and it's possible no one will allow my stock to be bred, or even want me in the area."

She took in a deep breath. "I must go alone to trade."

"Analisa, be reasonable. You can't go off on your own. What if you're attacked by another wild animal, or Indians? What if a settler decides to take your trade goods just because he's stronger than you? How are you going to stop any of that from happening?"

She shrugged. "How is having you along going to

168

help?'' She picked up the cheese and carried it back to the cold room through a small door into the side of the hill, right off the kitchen.

"How?" he asked incredulously. "Because I'm a man. I'll be there to defend you."

"I could have ridden away from that bear on my own, David. And I doubt if a hunting party of thirty braves cares whether there are two of us or only one. And as for the settlers, that doesn't happen. Not out here. We all depend on each other to survive."

She straightened, pressed a hand to her back, and closed the door.

"I can't believe you'd think I wouldn't be a help!"

Analisa turned to look him in the eye. "The fact is that you're a stranger to this area. We're not a married couple, and people won't trust you. I'm not going to ruin my reputation so that you'll feel more like a man."

With that, she turned and walked back through the kitchen.

"Wait a minute," he said, catching up with her and placing his hand on her arm. "This isn't about me. This is about you and the foolish risk you'd be taking by going off on your own. There's no reason to take such a risk."

"I've already told you the reasons. You're the one having a hard time believing the truth."

"Your arguments for why I shouldn't accompany you are far outweighed by the risks."

"I don't think so."

"You . . ." He wiped a hand across his face. "Look, this is crazy. I can't believe we're arguing."

"I can't either." She pulled her arm away from his grasp. "I have a lot more to do."

"When did you plan to leave?"

"Tomorrow, if it doesn't rain again."

"Fine. I'll be ready whenever you are."

She faced him squarely, her hands on her hips. "You misunderstood me, David. I meant I couldn't believe *you* were arguing. I'm going alone, and that's final. This is my cabin, my trade goods, and my life. If you don't like it, then that's just too darn bad."

She pivoted and walked, nearly ran, toward the door but hadn't taken two steps before she stopped and turned back toward him. "Oh, and I hope you'll repay my hospitality by taking care of my animals while I'm gone. That's the only thing I require from you."

She continued her trek toward freedom, away from the cabin. He stood there and watched, knowing that if she turned, she'd see an expression of anger and disbelief on his face. But she wasn't about to turn around and look. She was dead set on trading alone.

He'd have to find a way to go without her knowledge. He wasn't going to stay here in the cabin, slinging grain to chickens and getting chased by that damned duck, while Analisa traipsed around the countryside alone.

Or, he thought, a slow smile spreading across his face, he'd have to find a way to keep her at the cabin.

Analisa was proud of the way she'd held her ground that morning. She'd firmly stated her intention to go trading, countered David's arguments, and left before getting angry enough to do or say something foolish. At last, he'd have to take her seriously and bow to her wishes.

Yes, she thought, as she placed a meal of minced elk fritters and dandelion salad on the table, she'd taken a big step today toward her goal. If all went well, David would be free of his imagined obligation to keep her safe before long. He'd be able to fly away to his own life, and she could decide what to do with hers.

Marry a settler's son or a widower, convince Charlie to stay with her this winter, or make her way alone. She felt more confident about her abilities now, no matter what choice she made about her future.

"Dinner is ready," she announced to David, who'd worked on the roof after finishing reinforcements to Daisy's fence.

"I'll be right there," he said from inside the bedroom. She looked up just in time to see him pull on a shirt. His bronzed chest looked even darker in the fading light of day, and his eyes took on a mysterious shine as he walked toward her, working each button through its hole very slowly.

"I hope I'm not late," he said with a slight smile.

"No . . . no, you're not," she said, her voice breathless despite her best intentions to be strong. She broke her gaze away from the vee of his chest, revealed by the unbuttoned shirt. Darn the man! He knew what he did to her and yet he'd decided to flaunt himself again. She strengthened her resolve, tipped up her chin, and said, "When you're dressed, we can eat dinner."

She stayed busy pouring a glass of beer for David and some milk for herself. Finally, she heard the scrape of a chair on the floor and turned around.

"This is some of my father's brew. It's been in the cold room, so I believe it's still fresh."

"Thanks," David said, taking the glass from her, lightly brushing the tips of his fingers against hers.

She released the glass quickly and sat down, tucking her tingling fingers into her apron pocket. "After dinner, I'd like to go over the chores that need to be done while I'm gone. As I said earlier, I shouldn't be away for long."

"Gee, I wish we'd had time to discuss this before you stormed out this morning. I just remembered that I have some very important maintenance that must be performed on my airplane engine.''

''Maintenance?''

''You know—labor that keeps it working. I need to make sure the engine will start and run properly when the time is right.''

She felt as if the air had left her lungs. ''Surely this can be done when I get back.''

David shook his head, his expression one of sadness. She wasn't fooled for an instant. ''I'm sorry, but it has to be done on time, every week. I'd just finished the maintenance before I flew the last time, so it's due now again.''

''But you won't be flying for days, maybe weeks. Why do you need to do this ... maintenance ... right now?''

''The oil in the engine will become gunked if I don't. It's a technical term for the deposit of carbon-based material on the pistons of the engine.'' He shook his head again. ''No, I'm sorry, but flying or not, I have to do the work.''

''Can't it be done during the day? You should have enough time to walk to the plane after the morning feeding and be back by nightfall.''

''It's difficult to say,'' he replied, rubbing his chin. ''I may have to stay at the plane for a couple of days to complete the de-gunking process. I've never had to do it under such primitive conditions, without all my tools.''

She narrowed her eyes and stared at him across the table. ''You're doing this to force me to stay, aren't you?''

''Why, Analisa, how could you think such a thing? Do you think I'd stoop so low as to manipulate you into changing your plans?''

"That's exactly what I think," she said, throwing her napkin on the table. "You made yourself perfectly clear this morning. Well, forget it, David Terrell. Go de-gunk your plane if you must. You won't keep me away from trading forever. As soon as Charlie returns, I'll be gone."

She pushed away from the table, taking her plate with her. "And I hope you and your plane are very happy together for the next few days. I wouldn't want to keep you away from such important . . . de-gunking."

With that last heated remark echoing in the air, Analisa marched out of the cabin with her dinner. She should have known! He was intelligent and crafty; he was bound to think of a way to join her or keep her home.

Why he couldn't accept her need to take care of herself and her animals was beyond her comprehension. But whatever his reason, she'd show him a thing or two as soon as Charlie returned. She'd be away from this cabin so fast he wouldn't have time to follow, she vowed as she marched toward the creek.

"Not without a horse," she whispered as she settled on a boulder beside the stream. The thought that she had the only mount around filled her with a kind of malicious happiness. Let him try to keep up on foot; Tommelise could carry her and all the trade goods and still outdistance a man on foot.

As she closed her eyes, bit into the elk fritter, and envisioned David's frowning face, she smiled. She'd started out with the best of intentions, willing to sacrifice her pride and freedom for his way back home. He'd turned her campaign into a war, winning the first battle tonight. But he wouldn't win the war. She'd outsmart him yet, and by the time the next rainbow came around, David Terrell would run to his plane to get back home.

She had a few battle strategies of her own. And he wasn't going to find any peace in 1886.

After dinner, David settled into the chair, lit the candle stub, and picked up the volume he'd started the other night. Analisa was still outside, probably messing with the newborns or doing some sort of "maintenance" on her animals. He smiled as he remembered the word he'd come up with to explain the fictitious process of degunking.

A stroke of genius, if he did say so himself. At least she'd have to stay around the cabin for several more days while he was supposedly in the meadow with the plane. Of course, that wasn't where he would be. He'd become aware of a distinct disadvantage regarding transportation in this era; a man without a horse was about as useful as a fish with a bicycle.

With any luck, he'd correct that problem before Charlie returned. Then they could proceed to the next step of this unscripted play—chasing Analisa around the valley.

About the time he opened the book and found his place, Analisa entered the room, carrying with her the smells of the animals and hay. While he'd never considered those scents either appealing or unappealing, on her they seemed so natural that he couldn't imagine her otherwise.

He watched her walk across the room and wondered what type of perfume she'd prefer when they made a trip to Salt Lake City or Denver. Something light and floral, no doubt. Something that reminded him of mountain meadows and sunshine.

"What's wrong?"

He blinked, realizing he must have been staring. "Sorry. My mind was a hundred miles—or years—

away," he said with a smile. He knew he was going to win. He'd return to his own time, to Jamie and Holly, and bring Analisa back with him. Jamie would be so excited that the fairy princess was real.

She took a seat in the rocking chair on the other side of the fireplace. "You must be homesick."

"Not really, except for Jamie."

"But there must be a great many things that you have in your own time that you don't have here. I know you mentioned food when you first came. What are some of the other things?" She pushed the chair with her toe and appeared very casual. The only thing giving her away was that Analisa never pried into his life *and* tried to look casual at the same time.

But he'd be glad to play her game. "Okay. I suppose I miss my truck. It's black, with an extended cab and four-wheel drive. A real gas guzzler, but it will get up and go."

"What is a truck?"

"It's like a wagon, only with an engine in front instead of horses. Actually, the power of the engine is measured in horses, which is kind of funny, isn't it?" She didn't laugh, so he continued. "Anyway, I think mine has the equivalent of about three hundred horses under the hood."

"Three hundred horses! You must be joking!"

"No, I'm not, but I can see how that would be amazing to you, considering the covered wagons were pulled by four horses or mules, or six ox, or something like that. But if you think about how powerful the engine on a train is, for example, you'll have a better idea about trucks."

She nodded, her eyes wide. "I can see how you would miss something that exciting. And you ride in this truck like you would a wagon?"

"Actually, I drive the truck like I would a wagon, but yes, I sit on a seat and steer. There's a wheel that turns right or left, and pedals on the floor to use to accelerate or stop. It's a lot like my plane, really. Did I ever show you that?"

He knew darn well he hadn't.

"No, you were trying to hide the plane with brush, if I remember correctly."

"Oh. Well, after I finish the de-gunking process, perhaps you'd like to take a look inside. We might even take it for a little spin to see whether it's running okay."

"A spin?"

"Up in the air," he said with a swoop of his hand to indicate a takeoff. Analisa's eyes widened as she followed the course.

"With me?"

"Sure. You're not afraid of flying, are you?"

She sat back in the rocker and looked at him across the hearth. "I don't know. I've never thought about such a thing."

"Why don't you think about it? Then, if you'd like and if I have enough gas, we can take it up for just a short flight."

"I . . . I'll think about it."

David nodded and sat back in his chair, smiling.

"What else?" Analisa asked, pushing off with her foot again.

"What else what?"

"What do you miss beside your . . . truck?" she asked, forcing out the new word like she was puckering up to kiss a toad.

"Let's see . . . I'm not missing television much. We already talked about food. I think maybe I miss telephones. I never thought I'd admit it, because I complain if I have to talk too long, but I miss being able to pick up the phone and call someone for information or just to say hi.''

"I know about telephones," Analisa said, her tone more animated. "I've never talked on one, but I read about them in a newspaper once. Back east they're becoming more common. I read that wires are strung everywhere in New York City, from building to building, across the streets. There was a photograph in the newspaper."

"Really? That's interesting. In my time, the wires are either underground or strung from T-shaped poles that go from the main line to individual houses. They really aren't that noticeable, or maybe it's just that we're used to them.

"Electricity is handled the same way—transmitted through wires from poles. Now that's something I miss. Electric lights, air conditioning, modern stoves and ovens. You'd love electricity."

"What's air conditioning?"

"It's a machine that cools the air inside buildings. The cooled air is blown through vents into each room."

"Doesn't the hot air come in from outside?"

"No. You have to keep all the windows and doors shut to keep the cool air in and the hot air out."

"Really? You can't even open a window?"

"Well, you could, but it wouldn't be very efficient."

"I'd miss the fresh air," she said with a sigh.

"You don't have to use air conditioning that much, especially up here. It's just for the hottest days. Businesses use it all the time in the summer, but that's because they can't open their windows."

"That sounds odd. Do they have no windows?"

"Some of them just have a wall of glass that doesn't open up. We use lots of glass in my time."

"I suppose you miss that," she said wistfully.

He shrugged. "I suppose. In my house, I have a glass up high on one wall just so I can see the sky and the mountains. I have a great view."

"You mentioned before that my cabin is on your land. Where is your house?"

"About halfway between here and the meadow where my plane is parked. It faces southeast, and you can see the Tetons from my bedroom upstairs."

"Really? What kind of materials were used to build your house?"

"Wood, mostly. I have lots of wood beams and paneling inside. Outside, it's natural rock and wood so it blends into the landscape. I didn't want anything that looked out of place here in the foothills."

"I understand that. My father said the same thing when my mother complained that we couldn't have a white clapboard house here like back in Ohio."

"Your cabin is snug and well built," David remarked. He'd seen evidence of the good construction when he'd been on the roof earlier.

"We had some help—some settlers who wanted to go back east. Papa traded them the team and wagon we bought in Green River City when we got off the train, and they helped finish the cabin that first summer."

"I've seen some photographs of early buildings. Most of them look as though a good wind would blow them over. Bare wood planks, sitting out in the middle of a field," he said, shaking his head. "I couldn't imagine why they were built that way."

"I suppose it depends on where their land is. Most people want the flatlands so they can build fences and farm." She shrugged. "Papa wasn't interested in farming, although we always had a vegetable patch."

"Farming never did take off in Wyoming. Cattle have been our biggest success, but even then, you need lots of acreage to support a herd, and you lose many head during a bad winter."

He watched a shudder pass through her as she paused in her rocking.

"You don't like the blizzards, do you?" he asked gently.

"No, not much," she said with a twisted smile. "I dread the winter because of the snow and wind that goes on for days. I get so tired of the sound and the whiteness. And I know the animals suffer."

"They still do, but not as much. We've built shelters and windbreaks for the cattle, and there's an elk reserve where the wild herds are fed. As for the pets . . . well, they live better than most people do now, I'd bet."

"But the blizzards still come."

"Yes, although we have stronger, larger homes, and we can drive in all but the most severe storms in our cars and trucks, so people aren't stuck in one place when a blizzard hits. Still, we have to be careful. Snow can pile up faster than the snowplows can clear it from the roads, and snowdrifts stop trains sometimes."

"That sounds like an improvement."

"It is. I think you wouldn't mind them as much in my time," he said tentatively.

She stopped rocking again. "Is that what you're trying to do? Convince me that I'd be better off in your time than in mine?"

He shrugged and tried to appear casual. "That's my opinion, yes. We have a lot of advantages, like our homes, medicine for most illnesses, improved communication, and better transportation."

"You can't tempt me to come with you by offering to take me into the sky in your plane, or telling me that I wouldn't mind the blizzards as much."

"I'm not trying to talk you into doing anything you don't want to do."

"It sounds to me like you are."

"Really? And you're saying that you weren't trying to make me homesick for my time by asking about what I miss?" There. He had her now.

"I . . . How could you ask such a thing?" She adopted an expression of outrage, but he read the subtle signs that her very creative and active brain was trying to find a way out of this without admitting a thing. When all else failed, she tipped up her chin.

If he were a true gentleman, he'd allow her a graceful exit. However, at the moment, he wasn't feeling all that gentlemanly. Not in the middle of yet another, albeit rather enjoyable and mild, battle.

"Just a wild guess," he said

"Well, you're wrong. I was simply making conversation."

"If you say so, but it sounded like you wanted me to get homesick."

"That's a terrible accusation," she said, launching herself from the rocker.

"I call it like I see it." He pushed out of the chair and faced her across the rag rug in front of the hearth.

"You must have a terrible opinion of me to think such a thing."

"On the contrary," he said, taking a step toward her. "I have a lot of respect for you. You're trying to forward your own agenda—convince me to fly off and leave you here alone. For what reason, I have no idea, but that's another argument."

"You need to get back to your daughter and—"

He placed a finger on her lips. "That's another argument," he repeated softly.

"Don't do that!" she demanded, stepping back.

"I admitted before that I wasn't very good at keeping my hands off you."

"This is different. You're trying to win by . . . Never mind how. Just don't try to make me be quiet by touching me."

He couldn't resist pushing her just a little more, so he stepped closer, boxing her in between the chair and the fireplace. "I'd encourage you to be anything but quiet when I touch you," he said in a low, soft voice. He watched her eyes widen, then turn as smoky as green wood lapped by flame.

"You don't fight fair," she whispered.

"I know. Did I say I would?"

"The subject never came up."

"It's definitely up now," he said with an irony he knew she wouldn't understand.

Maybe not, but she must have recognized the change in his tone or the way he was looking at her. She scooted around him like he was a red-hot poker. Which, come to think of it, was very close. Thank God he was wearing Jurgen's heavy, loose trousers.

"I'm going to say good night now," she said in a shaky voice. "I think we've talked enough about your time."

"I think you're right." He faced the rock wall, his hands in his pockets so he wouldn't cross the space separating them and take her into his arms. "Sleep tight, Analisa. We can continue our battles tomorrow."

He heard her rapid footsteps across the floor, and then the soft closing of her bedroom door. After a minute, he headed outside for a breath of fresh air. A cold shower would have been helpful, too.

He stopped at the fence, leaning against the same spot where he'd stood last night. In a moment, the sow wandered over and greeted him with a few grunts.

181

"More woman trouble," he announced before reaching down and scratching the coarse white hair and thick, pink skin.

He realized, as he stood there and scratched the friendly pig, that Analisa had accomplished one thing tonight: He had become homesick for a few things from his time. His king-size bed—with Analisa sprawled in the center. His bubbling hot tub—with Analisa naked against him and the snow falling on their wet heads. Blizzards roaring down from the mountains—with Analisa snug beside him on the couch and Jamie playing on the thick rug in front of a blazing fire.

Tomorrow he would leave on the fictitious de-gunking mission. If he was successful in his quest, he'd be able to thwart Analisa's reckless, independent streak.

Too bad there wasn't a Chevy dealer just down the hill. A four-wheel drive with a big V-8 would go a long way toward keeping up with the industrious, independent, and innocent young woman who had captured his heart.

Chapter Twelve

After breakfast, David gathered an extra set of clothing, his borrowed personal items, a blanket, and some food that Analisa reluctantly packed for him.

"I hope you're being testy because you don't want me to go," he joked as he stuffed the items into a leather saddlebag that she'd let him borrow.

"You're right; I don't want you to go. I'd much rather you stay here and tend the animals so I can go trading."

"You can still go trading . . . later. Surely Charlie will be back soon."

"Maybe. He's unpredictable. If he meets an old friend, he may summer in another place."

"He'll be back soon," David predicted. "Charlie isn't too sure about me. He's not about to leave you alone for long. He'll be back in a few days, mark my words, just to see that I haven't ravished your body or taken you off to my home . . . the one in Texas," he added with a chuckle.

Analisa's expression didn't change, but she seemed to be considering his words. "Maybe you're right. Charlie's like an uncle to me. I'm sure he had his doubts about you."

"He'd have even more if we told him where I was really from."

She shrugged. "He might surprise you. He's seen a lot in his time. A few years ago, he told me a story he'd heard from near the Wind River country of a woman who appeared one day at a ranch, stayed for about a month, and then disappeared."

"I'm sure there are many people who pass through the area on their way west, or come out here and decide they can't handle the isolation, the heat, or the cold."

"No, I mean she really disappeared, right in front of some people after a shooting. One minute she was there, and the next she was gone. The man who told Charlie swears it's true. His boss was the one doing the shooting."

"Well, there are always far-fetched tales. If you saw some of the magic tricks that are done in my day, you'd be astonished. A few years ago a magician named David Copperfield made the Statue of Liberty disappear."

"Really? The one in New York?"

"The very same. Like you said, one minute it was there, the next it was gone. And this was on national television."

"I'd like to see something like that. My mother always believed in magic."

"I'll make a prediction," David said, resting his hands lightly on Analisa's shoulders. "One day soon you'll have the chance to see all the magic you want." And with those words resting between them, he leaned closer and kissed her quickly, but with enough pressure to get her attention.

He wasn't disappointed. The minute he released her lips, she stepped back and raised her hand to her mouth, her eyes wide. "You shouldn't have done that."

"I just wanted to say good-bye properly. I'll see you tomorrow, I hope."

"You don't know?"

"As I explained, the de-gunking process is a little unpredictable under these conditions. I'll be back as soon as I can. You'll be okay, won't you?"

"Yes, I'll be fine." Irritation slipped through her polite reply. "Impatient to go trading, but fine."

David laughed. "I don't suppose you'd like to loan me that fine horse of yours."

Analisa folded her arms across her chest. "I doubt Tommelise can help you work on your plane."

He laughed again. "You're right. I'm just trying to save myself a long walk."

"It's not that far."

It is where I'm going. But of course he couldn't tell her that. "I'll see you in a few days. Be careful while I'm gone." With a heave, he threw the saddlebag over his shoulder.

"I'm a careful person," she said, narrowing her eyes. "My father didn't raise me to be a fool, David Terrell."

"I know that." He smiled, then turned and started walking away from the cabin. Before he reached the end of the fence that enclosed the friendly sow, he turned around and paused. "Think of me while I'm gone," he called, sending her a heated look he knew she recognized. Lord knows, he could certainly tell when she sent him one.

She drew in a deep breath, pushing her breasts against the soft, faded plaid shirt. With one finger, she touched her lips, then turned and walked into the cabin.

David smiled and continued on his journey. He hadn't

reached the turn in the path when he heard Analisa call out, "You be careful too, David Terrell. If you're not back in two days, I'm coming after you." She stood outside the cabin, fists on her hips, looking none too pleased.

"I'll look forward to it," he said with a laugh, waving as he watched her spin around and become swallowed up by the shadows, closing the door with an enthusiastic push.

Things are definitely looking up, he said to himself as he walked quickly up the slope. She cared about him, just as he cared for her, though she was too stubborn to admit it. Hell, she might not even realize what was happening between them. But one thing was certain; when he returned, they'd continue their skirmishes and battles. Based on her response last night and this morning, he was more confident than ever that when the time came, he'd bring his princess home.

Analisa felt like a pouting child but couldn't seem to lighten her mood. The rooms seemed empty and dark without David. Her food tasted bland and unappealing, even though she'd taken special care to fix a dish of creamed, smoked meat that she usually enjoyed. And when the sun set and she closed the door for the night, the cabin felt especially lonely.

She might as well admit it; *she* was lonely.

In the days that he'd stayed with her, she'd grown accustomed to his quiet presence and quick wit. She'd known his sympathy and shared his sorrow. And his passion. Yes, there was that, too.

What was she going to do? Each day she grew more fond of him, yet she'd decided to seek a husband, if she must, to allow David to leave. But could she actually go through with her plan? The thought of acting interested in another man after knowing David was . . . distasteful. She couldn't stop the way her nose and lips turned up at the thought, and she wondered if she'd have the same response when actually faced with the situation.

That would give a prospective groom a good image of her, wouldn't it? A bride who couldn't bear to be around her husband? Analisa threw down her sewing and paced the cabin, frustrated at the dilemma she'd created. Save David by sacrificing herself, or keep him here with her, denying him the daughter he loved?

Or, she thought, easing into the chair he sat in each night, she could just leave with him. Forget her fears and fly off into the unknown future—perhaps. What if she couldn't leave her own time? David's presentation of his theories on time travel had made so much sense, and yet even he had to admit that no one knew how it worked for sure.

After the rainbow the other day, he'd tried to convince her that she *could* go back with him. What if she couldn't go forward and held him back when they flew across the rainbow? Would they end up somewhere else in time, perhaps back in her own past? There was no way to tell.

She was scared, she admitted. Afraid of the great unknown of the future, of a time where people flew in the sky, where the power of three hundred horses existed inside the space of a wagon, where air was cooled or heated to keep people comfortable all the time. These inventions sounded so appealing, but they were frightening in their scope. What else existed in David's time that seemed normal and right to him, yet would appear foreign and wrong to her?

With a sigh, she rested her head against the back of the chair and breathed in his scent. She didn't want to lose David, of that she was certain. But could she risk leaving her time to travel to his? She didn't know. Her last thought before her eyes drifted shut was that she wished she had a telephone that would let her talk to him tonight. To hear his voice before she drifted off to sleep . . .

The trek to the plane didn't take too long, since David was now familiar with the tree and grass patterns, slightly different than in his own time. In the hundred years or so that separated his time from this one, there had no doubt been fires and blizzards, perhaps even some logging or attempts to clear the land for grazing or farming. The trees where Daisy had decided to give birth weren't there in his time. Instead, the meadow was wider and longer, rich with wildflowers and summer insects.

He cleared the brush away from the cockpit and opened the door. The familiar scent of his favorite plane comforted him as he inhaled deeply. Strange, he thought, smiling to himself, but he hadn't realized that plastic and synthetic fibers could have such a distinctive smell.

He looked around, seeing evidence that he'd flown recently. His sunglasses, flung casually on the passenger seat, reminded him that he'd removed them upon landing when he was still in denial of what had happened. After the second landing, he hadn't picked them up again.

His favorite cap—black and tan canvas, sporting a discreet Looney Tunes logo—had been given to him by Jamie on his birthday. It had apparently fallen to the floor during the rough landing. David picked it up and put it on the seat beside his sunglasses.

On the partition behind his seat, his flight records hung, just waiting to be updated. *14:30. Take-off from Jackson Hole Airport, ascended to 8400 feet, banked right. 14:50. Landed in remote region, 1886.* That would look great for the FAA investigators. His license would be pulled before he could say *nutcase.*

He moved his sunglasses and cap, then stowed his saddlebag on the passenger seat before hefting himself into the plane. He flipped on the power, checking the electrical equipment to make sure the battery was still charged. Good. At least that was working. He was fairly sure he couldn't get a jump start in 1886.

He shut down the power, then wedged himself between the seats and bent over, reaching toward the rear cargo door. There was an emergency pack stowed there, along with a first-aid kit. He located the gear, looking through the contents for the dried food and utensils. Holding up a packet of instant coffee, he smiled broadly, then kissed the square with the kind of reverence usually reserved for religious artifacts.

"Thank you," he said with a look skyward. He knew how he was going to start his morning. He looked through more of the food, finding dehydrated eggs and milk. After about a week of Analisa's cooking—with just-laid eggs and fresh, whole, unpasteurized milk—those particular packets didn't look too appealing. He tossed them back into the emergency kit anyway; they might come in handy later.

After a few minutes of rummaging around, he made his way to the front of the plane. He grabbed both his packs—the emergency one and the saddlebag—and his cap and sunglasses, then exited the plane. At the last minute, he decided to leave a note, just in case Analisa rode up to check on him. He located a pencil and paper in the pack, wrote about hearing an unusual noise and going to investigate, then stuck the note in the door handle.

It didn't take long to replace the brush that hid the

plane. Unless someone looked closely, they wouldn't recognize the shape of the Cessna. Not that someone in 1886 would recognize an airplane anyway.

He settled his sunglasses on the bridge of his nose, adjusted his cap, then set off west to pick up the route of Valley Trail. The actual hiking trail probably didn't exist now, but the land should be similar, and he knew the terrain. He'd walk south-southwest to where the ranger station was in 1997, then cut down the slope toward Phelps Lake. Analisa had mentioned a family over the ridge, by a lake. They probably wouldn't think it odd that a man on foot wanted to trade for a horse.

The afternoon sun beat down as he stared at the lake from atop the ridge. Sure enough, there was a house or cabin—hard to tell from this distance. The settlers appeared to have cultivated some land, and he saw two white or gray ox, which they probably used for plowing. No horses, though.

He made his way to the cabin, wishing he had some hiking boots instead of the cowboy boots he wore around the hangar. He felt a blister forming on his heel, and his feet were damp with perspiration. Hell, his whole body was damp. Despite bathing in the creek and wearing freshly laundered clothes, he probably smelled like a mountain man by now. What he wouldn't give for a hot shower, real shaving cream, and some deodorant.

As he neared the dwelling, he saw a man and a boy working in the field, clearing weeds from the tilled soil.

"Hello!" David called out the greeting when he was still a good fifty yards away, hoping he wouldn't alarm the folks. He remembered his sunglasses at the last minute and removed them, certain that bronze aviator glasses weren't common in this era.

The man looked up, resting his arm on his hoe as he whispered something to the boy, who ran toward the house. As soon as the boy left, the man motioned him closer.

David trudged in the furrows of the sandy soil, keeping away from the tiny green shoots that formed each row. He couldn't tell what crop they were attempting, but he knew they'd ultimately fail. This part of the country wasn't good for growing much of anything but cattle, and sometimes that was unpredictable.

"What's your business?" the balding farmer asked when David neared.

"I'm looking for a trade," he said. "I need a horse."

"Whatcha trading?" The man swiped a bandanna across his high forehead, then shoved it back into the pocket of his loose-fitting pants.

"A watch," David said. Actually, a Seiko two-toned kinetic that he'd received from Holly last Christmas. "It's the latest style, from back east, to wear on your wrist."

"I don't have much need to know the time," the man said, as if that were painfully obvious.

David hadn't thought of that. He'd assumed that nineteenth-century residents would be fascinated by the workings of a twentieth-century timepiece. Now he remembered Analisa's comment: you can't eat gold. He guessed that applied to watches, as well.

"I have a good leather wallet," he said, hoping that might be of interest, "and a compass. Or you could tell me what you need. Maybe I have it."

"I'm in need of a hat," the farmer said, swiping his gnarled hand over his shiny head. "What's that you're wearing?"

"This?" Damn, he didn't want to trade for his cap. Jamie would be disappointed when he came back without it. But he might not have any choice. He really needed a horse—and he would be bringing back a princess. "It's called a cap, but I'm pretty attached to it. I'd like to see the horse first."

The man nodded, then stepped over the rows and walked toward the planked-board house. As they neared the dwelling, David could tell that the boards had been part of a wagon once. The back of the house was a standard chinked log design. Apparently the family had tried to put a civilized touch on their home with the milled boards.

A thin, middle-aged woman stood in the doorway, her arm around the boy's shoulders. David touched the bill of his cap and dipped his head, hoping for a believable gesture. "Good day, ma'am," he said.

The woman nodded as he passed by, following the man to the side of the house. Hobbled nearby stood a gelding of indeterminate years, a roan, David hoped. Otherwise it was a chestnut who was turning gray.

The horse wasn't wearing a halter, but it didn't object when the man approached and slid a rope around his neck. The farmer fashioned a halter by slipping a loop around the gelding's nose, then untied the hobbles.

"He's not too spirited, but he's sound," the man said, leading over the heavy-legged animal. "You want to try him out?"

"Sure." David decided that almost anything was better than walking. He dropped his packs to the ground, then revised the farmer's halter, using the rest of the rope to make some reins. After talking to the gelding in a low voice, letting him get his scent, David grabbed a handful of mane and swung onto the horse's back.

He'd half-expected a buck or two, or at least some token protest. But the horse just stood there, waiting for instructions. David touched his heels to the animal's sides and clucked him forward. The gelding had a nice, smooth walk. Urging him faster, David discovered the most bone-jarring trot he'd ever encountered. Deciding the horse must be sound to hit the ground so hard, he slowed him and turned back to the farmer.

"That'll shake up your insides," he said as he dismounted.

The man shrugged. "Only got the one horse. Can't part with my ox. Let's see that hat."

David pulled off the birthday present, took one last look at Daffy Duck, Porky Pig, and Taz, and handed it to the farmer. While the man examined the cap, frowning in confusion at the colorful cartoon characters, David checked the teeth, hooves, and legs of the gelding. He was sound. Not pretty or graceful, but sound. And he had enough teeth to chew.

"You got anything else in that pack?" the farmer— now sporting a fairly new Looney Tunes cap—asked.

"Some food and clothes." David opened the emergency rations kit and removed the packets of dehydrated food, remembering what Analisa had said about eating. "These are good for emergencies—like if you're trapped in a blizzard or run out of food. All you have to do is mix them with hot water and you have a meal."

"There's food inside this? the man asked in a confused voice, turning the package of dehydrated eggs over and over.

"Yes, but don't open it until you're ready to eat. It's a powder, so it can spill. Also, it will lose it's flavor and might get spoiled if you open it before you're going to use it. The instructions are printed on the back." He hoped the man could read.

The farmer squinted. *Great*, David thought. Packaged food with twentieth-century instructions for illiterate settlers. Of course this won't work.

"What's this mean . . . Expiration date November 24, 1998?"

"Oh, that." *Think fast, Terrell.* "That must be a misprint. It means 1898. That means you need to use the package before November of 1898 or it starts to lose some of its flavor and nutritional value."

"Well, I'll be damned. What'll they think of next?" the man said in a voice filled with awe. "How much of this kind of food do you have?"

Knowing he'd made the sale, David dug around until he found chicken soup, more eggs, beef broth, and several kinds of bean dishes. He made a mound of the items on the grass. "I'll throw in the compass if you have a bridle and a saddle for the horse."

The man shook his head. "I've got a bridle, but no saddle."

"Okay, the bridle then. I'll give you the cap, the food, and the compass."

"Let's see the compass," the farmer said.

Within fifteen minutes, David rode away from the modest home of Ezekial Welsh and his family, who now owned the most extensive supply of twentieth-century items this side of Valley Trail. He turned and waved to the farmer, who looked pretty silly in the Looney Tunes cap, sweat-stained calico shirt, and baggy twill pants.

He just hoped he hadn't altered history by leaving a modern trademark cap with a nineteenth-century settler. At least he'd torn out the label first.

The time for regrets or second guesses was gone. He'd parted with the modern items and was now the somewhat proud owner of a docile roan gelding. He'd accomplished his first task with time to spare. He'd be back at the plane before the sun went down, fix himself some dinner, and sleep snug and sound inside the plane tonight. Tomorrow he'd get a little oil under his nails— just to give credence to his "de-gunking" activities— then ride back to the cabin.

Or maybe he'd stay away one extra night, just to make sure Charlie had enough time to get back. If Analisa took it in her head to go off trading on her own, then David knew he wouldn't have another excuse not to stay and feed the animals. And as much as he hated to admit it, someone really did need to mind the zoo while the head zookeeper was wandering around the countryside.

He'd bet his last packet of freeze-dried stew that Charlie was already at the cabin. The older man might want to see Analisa "get herself a man," but he'd also want to see that she was safe and happy. David felt like he and Charlie had an understanding of sorts, but that didn't mean the older man would forget "Annie" entirely.

Staying away would be hard to do but was probably the best approach. Besides, Analisa would be glad to see him, he told himself as the gelding plodded slowly, steadily, up the hill. The question was, would she be glad to see his mighty stead?

Chapter Thirteen

Analisa had never been as happy to see anyone as she was to see Charlie, walking up to the barn. Sitting cross-legged on the floor, playing with Daisy's twins, she had to stop herself from jumping up and hugging him.

"Charlie! You came back early." She placed the kids on the ground, where they frolicked to their mother.

"Ain't nothin' new comin' into the valley 'cept a bunch of settlers who don't have a need fer pelts and the like." He spat on the ground, as if showing his disgust. "Damned dirt farmers."

"Now, Charlie, you know they're necessary. And I think you managed to trade for a bit of tobacco, didn't you?" She pushed herself off the dusty floor, brushing hay and powdery clay off her pants.

" 'Bout all I could get," he said, unloading the packs from Sue's back. "Had to trade hard to get it, too. Damned dirt farmers," he repeated with contempt in his raspy voice.

Analisa stifled a laugh at Charlie's vehemence toward the settlers. He'd probably never get used to the idea that the area would change over time, from the fur-trading days of his father to the . . . well, to David's time.

"Tell me about the new settlers," she said. "How many are there and where are they living?"

"Three families pitched tents in the valley between them two buttes, not far. They're cuttin' timber and buildin' cabins like beavers in springtime."

"What kind of families? I mean, are there children, or younger married couples?"

"Hell, Annie, I don't know. I talked to the menfolk, not the babies."

"Of course you did," she replied, disappointed that Charlie hadn't volunteered any information on men of marrying age. She'd just have to look for herself, but first, it wouldn't hurt to try one more time. "Any others?"

"A new cabin near the marsh, down in the hole. Didn't see no women folks, but two men brung in a few cows."

"Good. We could use some new stock. Maybe they have a bull."

"Don't know 'bout that. They're from Minnesota, they said. Big yella-haired men."

"Really?" That was interesting news. If they were blond, they probably weren't too old. Perhaps one of them was looking for a wife. Or at least she could make David believe that she was interested in becoming the man's wife.

The more she thought about it, the more she decided she'd rather stay a spinster than marry a man just so she'd have someone around. Besides, men didn't stay around, did they? They went off whenever they got the urge—whether to look for gold or fur, or to de-gunk the engine of a big white bird.

"I got yer man some coffee, though," Charlie said, plucking a cloth bag from the pack and grinning like he'd found a big treasure.

"I'm sure he'll appreciate it." At least a dozen times today, she'd wondered what David was doing up in the meadow. Was he working on his plane, or just staying away? Or was he injured? He could have hurt himself and not been able to walk back down the hill.

Or was he just being contrary?

"As a matter of fact, I think I'll go find him and tell him you're back with the coffee."

"And where'd he be off to?" Charlie asked, looking around as though he'd just realized David was nowhere to be seen.

"He went . . ." Darn, she hadn't thought of a good excuse. She couldn't tell Charlie that David was working on a machine that hadn't been invented yet. "He went exploring."

"Explorin'?" he repeated with a disbelieving snort. "What's he need to explore?"

"He just wanted to see more of the area," she lied, keeping her fingers crossed behind her back. With any luck, he wouldn't fly his plane into the sky where Charlie could see him. That just wouldn't do.

"He been treatin' you all right?"

"Yes, we're fine. Actually, he stayed in . . . he stayed out last night, wherever he is."

"Then how in the heck are you goin' to find him and tell him 'bout the coffee?"

"Well, I . . . He said he'd be in the meadow today."

Charlie shook his head. "If that don't beat all. I've seen some odd things in my time, but the two of you done taken the cake."

"Why? What's wrong with us?"

"Ain't neither one of you thinkin' with a clear head. He's out runnin' 'round the hills, explorin' for God knows what. You're thinkin' ya can just go up to the meadow and find the man. And the both of ya, thinkin' there ain't nothin' goin' on between ya." Charlie shook his head again. "Why don't ya just admit that the two of ya are sweet on each other and do somethin' 'bout it?"

"Like what?"

"Like get hitched. Jump the broom. Tie the knot."

"Charlie! I told you he's not my man. I'm not taking him for a husband when I'm not sure he's staying. As a matter of fact, I'm sure he'll be leaving soon."

Charlie made a rude noise and led Sue outside, then opened the gate to the small pasture where Tommelise grazed. He'd made his point, Analisa knew, and he wouldn't say any more on the subject . . . for now. She just hoped he didn't say anything to David.

Silently, she walked toward the cabin, the two ducks trailing her. She'd fix a meal for Charlie, who probably hadn't eaten well since getting a supply of tobacco. She hated the stuff because it killed his appetite, and Charlie needed all the good food he could get. But he loved his "chaw," as he called the slimy brown stuff, which was rare in these parts. She supposed she should be grateful that few settlers brought enough to trade.

Charlie fell into step beside her, dodging a well-aimed peck from Louie. "Durn duck," he murmured.

"After the meal, I'm going to ride up to the meadow, just in case David is there," she said as she entered the cabin.

Charlie followed, heading toward the hearth. "Whatever ya want to do," he said, putting Little Red's pack on the chair and opening the flap. A small head with white-tipped ears and black, inquisitive eyes popped up.

"Hello, Little Red," Analisa crooned, reaching in and picking up the weasel. "Did you have a good trip? I think you would have had a better time staying here with me. Charlie is as grumpy as an old bear."

"Hmpf," was the only reply she got as Charlie reached into the other pack and pulled out the one-eyed giant. "Didn't need this one to trade. Maybe next time."

"Thanks." She put Red down on the floor and watched her explore the cabin. "I'll get the food."

Charlie settled into the chair—the one Analisa now thought of as David's. At least with Charlie here, she wouldn't sit in the chair and breath in the scent of David's hair on the cloth, or remember what is was like to settle in his lap and accept the comfort he freely offered. No, she'd be better off not thinking that way at all.

David walked the roan gelding away from the plane so he wouldn't be spooked by the smell of the oil, or by the sound of metal on metal. Not that he really thought anything would spook the horse, who stood calmly as David looped the hobbles around his legs.

Without doubt, he was the most calm animal David had ever seen—either that or the horse just didn't care what was going on. He hadn't minded walking away from Welsh's dwelling, or following the ridge to the meadow, or grazing alone the rest of the day with a stranger for company.

They'd shared a silent late afternoon in the sunny meadow. For dinner last night, David had combined the food Analisa had given him with some dried fruit and a cup of hot tea. As the sun eased behind Prospector's Mountain, he'd sat in front of a small fire, savored a Snickers bar, and hummed Jamie's favorite song, "The Rainbow Connection." The tea had warmed him, the candy had soothed him, and his memories had brought a sad smile to his face.

The evening had been so similar to the time he'd taken Jamie camping last summer up in Yellowstone. She'd taken to the outdoors like a trooper, just like her mother, he'd thought. Even though Jamie didn't remember Catherine, they shared some common traits: light hair, a creative mind, and a fondness for nature. His responsibility was to make sure Jamie didn't take the type of unnecessary risks that had taken her mother's life.

He'd shaken off the melancholy thoughts last night, and he did so again now. Catherine was gone, but Jamie was alive and well—in 1997. He needed to get back to her, and the sooner the better. His obligation as a father required it; his love for her demanded it.

Jamie was probably trying to be brave about his disappearance but wanted to cry so bad her eyes hurt; Holly was no doubt trying to come up with a logical explanation but, at the same time, comforting Jamie. Together, they would get through the ordeal. Jamie couldn't be in better hands. He just hoped they'd believe where he'd been when he returned and explained everything to them. Of course, if he came back with Analisa, Jamie would be convinced. The princess would be in the plane.

David smiled, thinking of the reunion. The happy picture he envisioned of himself, Jamie, and Analisa.

First, though, he had to convince her to go with him. As much as he loved his daughter, he couldn't fly off and leave Analisa, alone and struggling. Not and still call himself a man. There had to be a way to ensure her safety and happiness, and he was going to find it before he left. Charlie would be one solution, but for how long?

He wasn't a young man, although he seemed fairly healthy.

If she wanted to stay here because she didn't care enough for him to travel to his time, he supposed he could accept that. But if she was just frightened, either of flying or of the future, he needed to calm her fears. When he'd mentioned time-travel theories, he hadn't anticipated any such complications. He could kick himself now, though. If he'd never put those thoughts in her head, she wouldn't be afraid of going. As a matter of fact, he knew she'd love the twentieth century—as soon as she understood it. He'd be her teacher and more, if she wanted him.

But first he needed to give Charlie time to get back to the cabin. Then, if Analisa was still intent on traveling around the area—against his advice, David added to himself—he'd follow her on his own horse. He gave the animal one last pat on the shoulder before heading back to his time-travel machine.

After he cleared the brush away from the plane, he checked the engine for any possible damage caused by the elements or animals. Everything looked fine, if a little dusty. In the hangar, he kept his planes as spotless as possible, from the pistons to the carpet. His clients expected the best, whether he was taking a senior citizen to a medical specialist in Salt Lake City or a celebrity's guests to a mountain retreat.

Retrieving his tools from inside the Cessna, David began a thorough cleaning and checking of the engine. He'd get the oil under his nails the honest way, he decided with a smile. If Analisa showed up, he'd explain all about "de-gunking." If she didn't . . . well, at least he'd have a flight-ready plane.

Just in case there was another rainbow—and Analisa decided to chance a trip to his century.

*   *   *

Analisa rode Tommelise into the meadow at a slow gallop, hoping David would hear her coming and not be surprised. After all, she'd told him she would check on him if he didn't come back to the cabin. He shouldn't be surprised. She was only being friendly, and hadn't he said they were friends?

She heard an unusual, loud noise and gripped Tommelise's sides as the mare missed a stride, throwing her head and fighting the bit. Analisa slowed the mare to a prancing walk, continuing toward the airplane. The source of a noise was hard to determine in the hills, especially on a flat meadow like this one, where sounds seemed to come from all directions. However, she believed David was working on the plane, making the unusual noise as part of that de-gunking he'd talked so much about.

As though she might understand the importance of working on a mechanical engine that was as powerful as hundreds of horses. She had trouble keeping her own mare under control.

"David!" she called out as she neared the pile of brush that had been pushed back from his great white bird. "Are you there?"

A muffled answer came back to her. Tommelise pricked her ears forward and shifted nervously. In just a moment, David appeared from beneath a door of white metal, wiping his hands on a cloth.

"So, you decided to come and see me," he said with a smile. "I thought you might."

"Charlie came back," Analisa answered in what she hoped was a normal, even voice, when, in fact, the sight of David's bare chest and low-slung pants made her heart race faster than Tommelise's panting breaths. He was hot, she saw from the glistening sweat on his golden-brown muscles and forehead. As she watched, he swiped a forearm across his face, leaving a dark smudge that made him look like a drawing of an Indian she'd seen once in a newspaper, painted for battle.

Only David didn't look ready for a battle. He looked . . . she didn't have a word in her vocabulary for his appeal at that moment.

"I was just finishing up," he said.

"You have something on your forehead," she said, pointing, as though he didn't know where his forehead was. She almost groaned at her bumbling nature whenever they were alone together—especially when one of them was only partially clothed. To hide her embarrassment, she slid off Tommelise's back and looped the reins around a nearby branch.

She drew in a deep breath, turned, and almost collided with his chest. "Oh!"

"Why don't you wipe it off for me? I don't have a mirror." He made the request in such a reasonable tone that she couldn't very well refuse. And, after all, she was the one who'd brought the smudge to his attention.

He placed a clean corner of the cloth in her hand, his fingers warm on hers. She hoped he couldn't see the rise and fall of her breasts beneath the soft, faded cotton of her shirt.

"Go ahead. I promise not to bite." He smiled, and her attention was drawn to his mouth, where a row of white teeth showed beneath his finely sculpted lips.

She drew in another breath and leaned forward. He did the same, until his face was so close that she felt the heat of his skin. She focused on the dark smudge instead of his eyes or his mouth, hoping she could get her reaction to him under control. How could she hope to let him go back to his own time when all she wanted to do was crawl inside his skin and never let him go?

"Hold still," she whispered.

"I'm not moving," he replied in a low, deep voice that sent tingles down her spine and caused her hands to shake.

She pressed the cloth against the spot and rubbed until the blackness was on the white cloth. And then she found another, smaller spot, and cleaned that one too. And she used another corner of the rag to blot the sweat from his brow.

"There," she said in a shaky voice. "I'm finished."

"But I'm not," he whispered. He grasped her hand, plucked the cloth from her fingers, and dropped it to the ground. His other hand reached for her, grasped her around the waist, and pulled her toward him.

They collided with a shared gasp. Her breasts flattened into his chest. Each breath he took pressed her closer as his hand tightened on her back. His other hand guided her arm around his neck. She felt her heartbeat, thudding wildly inside, and was sure he felt it too. The thought that she should run flashed in her mind, but her legs wouldn't move.

She didn't want to run. She wanted to sink into him, with him, to the carpet of grass below. Her legs felt weak, but David held her so tight that she could feel his tense muscles through the fabric of his trousers and hers. And also a solid, hard ridge pressing into her belly.

She groaned as she realized how quickly their desire had built. She instinctively knew what that swelled ridge meant. The knowledge should have frightened her, but instead, almost against her will, she pressed her lips against his.

David moaned as if in pain, then closed his eyes and took her mouth in a hard, demanding kiss. The shock of his possession froze her in place for just a moment, then she parted her lips and melted into his arms, molding her body to his. Never before had she wanted this passion so intensely.

His hands slid lower to cup her bottom and bring her tighter against him. His tongue teased and plundered, and she learned to follow his lead, tasting him, using her lips and teeth as he did to increase the pleasure. With her eyes tightly closed, she knew nothing outside his arms, felt only their kiss, on and on to eternity.

When she saw twinkling stars and felt herself slip into a darkness deeper than night, she heard David whisper against her lips, ''Breathe.'' She did, opening her eyes to see his, dark and simmering, above her. The stars went back to the heavens and she went back to their kiss, breathing in the smell of him to join with the other senses.

He broke the kiss. She moaned in protest until she felt his mouth on her neck, below her ear. His tongue and teeth traced a path around her throat until she closed her eyes again. Her legs buckled at the same time he brought her up hard against him, until he was pressed between the cradle of her thighs so tightly she felt the heat and dampness all the way to her soul.

''David,'' she whispered as she felt him lower her to the ground. His hands slid up her back as he followed her down, still kissing her neck, his breath hot and fast against her throat. Then she was lying on her back and he was on her, his weight crushing her into the cool, green grass.

He kissed his way back to her lips, his body moving against her until he was once again pressed tightly to that very private place. She barely stilled her hips from rocking against him, because she wanted to so badly yet didn't know if that would be right. But then, as if he read her mind, his own hips rocked forward, making her arch toward him, her head curled back against the ground and her eyes tightly shut. The stars returned, dancing in front of her eyes, entering her body and tingling all her nerves.

"Yes, that's it," he whispered against her ear. "You do want me."

"Yes," was all she could say as the pressure increased. "Yes."

He slid a hand up her body, cupping her breast with a firm grip before finding her hard nipple and teasing it with his fingers. She felt the sensation race through her, like a bowstring that went from her breast to the place between her thighs. She snapped tight, gasping for air.

"What are you doing to me?" she whispered in wonder as he repeated that wonderful caress.

"Making love to you," he said against her cheek. "Next time, we'll be making love together."

"Next time," she repeated, her mind refusing to consider anything beyond this moment.

"You'll stay with me, won't you, Analisa?" he asked softly as he rolled her nipple between his fingers. "We'll have this magic forever."

Something wasn't right, but she couldn't think what could be wrong. All she knew was that if he stopped, she'd die. Her heart surely couldn't beat without matching his rhythm. Her breath would surely stop unless mingled with his. They had to share the same air, the same space, the same feelings.

The same century. The answer brought a gasp to her lips as David kissed her jawline. The throbbing pressure between her legs continued, but she tried to ignore the urgency. Her breast rested within his grasp, but she put aside the tingling sensation for a moment. Long enough to think. To remember why this wasn't possible.

"No," she whispered.

"No, you don't want to make love?" he asked, his own body still, poised above her.

"We can't."

"I have protection in the plane. I'll get it in a minute." He lowered his mouth to her neck again, his tongue like a brand of fire.

"Protection?"

"So you won't get pregnant. Nothing else. I'm safe, and I know you are." His words scorched her throat with puffs of moist heat. "Don't worry, honey. I'll take care of you."

"No," she said again, this time pushing against his shoulders.

"No, you don't want to use protection?"

"No, I don't want you to take care of me. No, we shouldn't be doing this." She pushed again, until he rolled off of her. The shock of air against her damp flesh, even through the layers of clothing, made her remember how tightly they'd fit. How right, yet how wrong.

"Analisa, what's the matter?"

"I told you I can't think when we . . ." She ran a hand through her tangled, grass-matted hair, then scooted away on elbows and heels. "You're doing this for a reason."

"Yeah, and the reason is that it feels so good. So right. Don't try to tell me you didn't feel it too," he demanded in a low, raspy voice.

"What I felt doesn't matter!"

"It damn well does to me!"

"This is wrong. You want to bind me to you, so I'll go with you when you leave. Well, I can't! I just can't!"

She pushed to her feet, tears streaming down her hot cheeks. David lay on his side, propped up on one arm, glaring at her as though she'd grown another head. "Don't do this to me."

"Don't do this to *us*," he said softly, his eyes narrowed, his expression grim.

"There can never be an *us*," she whispered, then turned and ran to Tommelise.

"Analisa, no," she heard David say, but she didn't stop running until she'd untied the reins and led the mare away from where she'd almost surrendered body, heart, and soul to David Terrell. She found a fallen tree, used it to mount, and kicked Tommelise in the sides.

They raced down the hill, away from David, from all that he represented. Freedom from this place, but at what price? To trade what she'd gained in independence for an easier life? Or perhaps no life at all, if others were right about traveling through time.

She didn't belong with him, she knew, as the wind dried her cheeks almost as quickly as her tears fell, and she didn't belong in his century. They were from two different worlds, two times that should never have met except for a young girl and her belief in rainbows and happily ever after endings.

This story would not have that kind of ending. Because as much as she didn't belong in David's world, she didn't belong *to* him.

David heard the pounding hoofbeats of Analisa's mare as they raced away. He flopped on his back, shutting out the sun dappled leaves overhead with his arm. His body throbbed and ached as it had when he was sixteen and had to stop making out with Mandy Sue Parker in the back seat of his father's Oldsmobile. Only this time, the pain went far deeper, because Analisa had touched his heart in a way that Mandy never had.

He groaned as he heard the birds begin singing again, as the hoofbeats died away. He wished he could cry right now, but his eyes were as dry as his arms were empty.

Analisa had once again showed him a glimpse of heaven, only to close the door.

Why? What had he said that had triggered such a response? Was she upset that he didn't want her to get pregnant? No, that wasn't it, although he vaguely remembered her surprise. Was she afraid of making love? He didn't think so, because she wanted him badly—as badly as he wanted her, his still-throbbing body told him.

"I don't want you to take care of me." Her words echoed in his mind, giving him the answer he needed. He'd meant that he'd take care of her sexually—and otherwise, of course. He *did* care for her. Different from the way he'd felt for Catherine, but deeply.

With his wife, he'd felt comfortable. They had their own careers to pursue, and they had Jamie between them. They'd loved quiet evenings together, eating a pizza in town and then watching a movie at home. When she left on an assignment, he hadn't missed her physically as much as he worried about her safety. Catherine could be totally focused on her goals, so much so that she forgot everything, including him and Jamie.

The guilt still haunted him, even as he desired another woman. He should have worried more. He should have tried to talk to Catherine one more time about weighing risks. But he hadn't, because he'd told himself that she was an adult and he didn't have the right to interfere in her life.

He'd been wrong. He should have warned her, again and again, even if it meant being called a male chauvinist pig.

Analisa didn't know about the feminist movement or male chauvinists—at least, not enough to give them a name. She just knew she'd been on her own and had succeeded, despite her fears. He admired her for that, but she'd proved herself. She didn't need to keep trying, not when he could make her life so much easier. Not when he wanted her in his bed and in his life.

Once they were back in his own time, they could see how far the relationship could go. He didn't want to trap her into marrying a man when she'd never known any others. That wouldn't be fair to Analisa, even though the idea of her dating someone else made him clench his fists and grind his teeth. She didn't need another man; she needed him. But she had to see that for herself.

He'd thought he'd done an admirable job of convincing her this afternoon, until she'd jumped up and raced away.

He couldn't face her right now. He still wanted her, and if he saw her, he'd take her in his arms and start up where they'd left off. Never had anything felt so right as Analisa tight against him, returning his kisses, offering her sweet, innocent passion.

He had to quit thinking of her that way and get through the night alone. Tomorrow, in the light of a new day, he'd be in control once again. For now, he had to ignore the part of him that wanted to follow her like a divining wand, down the hill. A cold shower wasn't available, but a small pond on the other side of the meadow would do the trick.

Minutes later, he plunged into the cold mountain water, buck naked, gasping when he came up for air. In a rare show of interest, the roan watched him with pricked ears.

"You wouldn't understand," he told the gelding between shivers that threatened to crack his teeth together. "You just wouldn't understand."

Chapter Fourteen

"What do you mean, she's gone?" David bellowed, leaning toward Charlie as panic seized his heart.

"Went tradin'," the older man replied, scratching his neck with a gnarled hand. "Left jus' after dawn."

David had the irrational urge to lift Charlie by his shirtfront and shake him like a terrier on a rat. "And you let her go, a woman alone, off to who knows where?"

"Couldn'ave stopped her. She's a right bit stubborn at times."

"Dammit, old man, if anything happens to her—"

"Now how's anythin' gonna happen to her with ya trailin' after her like a lovesick puppy?"

"A lovesick puppy? You don't know what you're talking about."

"Ha! The both'a ya—crazy as magpies."

David turned away before he let his anger get away from him. He should have come back last night, fol-

lowed Analisa down the hill, talked to her about what
had happened between them. She'd jumped to all kinds
of wild conclusions thus far, so he should have anticipated this latest development. But instead, all he'd
thought about was how much he'd wanted to finish what
they'd started, and how that wasn't going to happen.

"Dammit," he repeated again. He turned back to face
Charlie, who'd begun to repair a trap mechanism. "Do
you know where she went?"

"She asked a bunch'a questions 'bout new settlers.
Said she wanted to trade." The older man shrugged. "I
'spect she's gonna cross the river, then cut over by
where them two buttes nearly come together. Ya know
the place?"

"If you mean where the Snake River and the Gros
Ventre join, I do. There are two buttes with a valley
between them, and a creek."

"That there's the place." Charlie narrowed his eyes.
"Fer a man from Texas, ya shore do know this place."

"I know it very well, and I didn't say I'd been in
Texas all these years. Now, is there somewhere else she
might have gone?"

"I tol' her 'bout two men from Minnesota with a few
cows off by the marshy land, next to that small butte
east of the other ones."

"Miller Butte. I know the place."

"Didn't know it had a name."

"Maybe it doesn't. That's what we call it now," David said distractedly. "And she'd go up to those two
strange men to trade?"

"Ain't nothin' particular strange 'bout em, 'cept
they're big, yella-haired men."

"Great." David's mind conjured up a picture of Analisa ogling those twin bodybuilders/models/actors who
posed for a calendar that Holly had up on her wall.

Tanned, godlike hunks. That's all he needed—competition from two blond male bimbos.

He rubbed the space between his eyes where a headache was forming. "I suppose she has some other neighbors too. Some regulars she trades with?"

"Yep, I 'spose she does, but I don't know all the folks. Some of 'em see me comin' and close their doors." He cackled, as if that were a funny tale. "Some of 'em don't want no hides or Injun trade goods. Now, they all want Annie's cheese and butter." He cackled again.

"She can't cart that cheese and butter all over the place. She'll probably trade as much as she can for it first. That will slow her down," he said, mostly to himself.

"Well, can't rightly say which direction she'd be travelin', but she was powerful interested in the new folks. I 'spect she'll get to them as soon as she can."

"Okay, then that's where I'll head. Is there a crossing on the Snake?"

"The river?"

"Yes. Where can I get across?"

"Down the valley, then cut back nor'east until yer right smack across from that single butte. The ferry's there where the river don't have as many forks as the devil's tail."

"I know the place." Menor's Ferry still existed on some maps. Now two roads came together just before the bridge over the Snake River, directly south of where the ferry had operated in the late 1800s.

David strode inside the barn, looking for another saddle. All he found was a wooden-framed pack saddle and some leather straps that looked dry-rotted.

He went back outside and looked at the bare back of

his trusty stead. "I don't suppose there's another saddle around, is there?"

"Nope. Annie took the only one."

"Great." He put his hands on his hips, wondering if there was anything in the cabin that he could take with him for food, since he'd traded most of his emergency rations to Farmer Welsh. Surely she'd kept some of that cheese. He headed inside, then rummaged through the cold room. Within a few minutes he'd put together some items that should see him through a day or two. He'd find Analisa by then—and bring her home.

Charlie was waiting for him outside the door. "Don't you be gettin' on Annie fer tradin'. She's jus' doin' what she knows she's got to do. Ain't nobody bringin' her supplies up here iffen she don't go tradin'."

"I know she's doing what she thinks she needs to do, but there's no reason for her to go alone. It's too dangerous. I imagine there are Indians around, and who knows what kind of men. She's too naive to survive on her own."

"She's been survivin' since her pappy died," Charlie reminded him. "And 'fore that, she was here alone." He shook his head. "Girl's been alone too much, iffen ya ask me." He spat on the ground.

"I agree with you, Charlie." David stowed his food in the saddlebag he'd borrowed from Analisa before he'd gone up to the meadow. "And look, I'm not angry at you. Not really. I'm just frustrated because I didn't expect her to do this after . . . well, she surprised me, that's all."

"Women can be damned surprisin' at times," Charlie agreed, "an' usually when ya'd jus' as soon they surprised ya, they do what ya don't want."

"I suppose. I . . . I haven't had that kind of problem before. Other kinds, but not that one."

"Never married," Charlie offered. "Ain't no woman what wants to travel in these here mountains, up and down, all year."

"I can't imagine why many men would either. Have you thought about staying?"

"I'm athinkin' on it," Charlie said gruffly. "Ya'd best be goin' iffen ya want to catch her before the day's gone."

"Okay, I'm out of here." David positioned his sunglasses on his nose, then swung the saddlebags over the gelding's back.

"What're those?" Charlie asked, pointing to the sunglasses.

"Oh, these." David had forgotten that people of this century didn't wear colored glasses to shade their eyes. Why, he had no idea. The concept seemed so simple. "Colored glass. They cut the glare of the sun. Want to try?" He handed the aviator-style sunglasses to Charlie.

He held them up to his eyes and looked around. "Well, if that don't beat all! Where'd ya get these?"

How did he explain a sunglass store to a nineteenth-century mountain man? "Just a small store down in Denver."

"I need to get me a pair of those," Charlie said with amusement in his voice. "Sure beats gettin' all squinty-eyed."

"Yeah, it does." Charlie reluctantly handed the glasses back. "You're going to be here, aren't you, to take care of the animals?"

"Told Annie I would."

"You have everything you need?"

"Sure do, granny. Now get yerself on down the hole and find Annie. I ain't that happy 'bout her goin' off on her own, either."

"We'll be back soon."

"I'll be here. Ain't got nowhere better to go."

"Okay." David swung onto the gelding's back.

"Where'd ya get that horse?"

"From a farmer on the other side of the ridge, by the lake." He gathered the reins while the roan continued to ignore his presence.

"Dirt poor farmer with two white ox?"

"That's him."

"Ain't heard of him tradin' 'fore," Charlie said with a frown.

"He needed a hat," David said simply, adjusting the saddlebag on the horse's bare back. "And I knew I'd need a horse to keep up with Analisa." He paused, looking at the older man. "Thanks, Charlie, for taking care of Analisa's animals. I'll bring her home."

"Ya do that. Now get goin' 'fore I'm tempted to look myself."

David put his heels to the roan, deciding he should give the animal a name. Or maybe he'd wait until he found Analisa and let her do it. That might take her mind off the fact that he was dragging her home.

And that they had some unfinished business between them.

Analisa smiled to herself as she rode away from the Shepherd place, her second stop of the day. They'd deliver corn at the end of the summer, and she'd gotten rid of most of the butter and cheese that had weighed down the saddlebags. Besides trading, she'd spent the noon meal with them, laughing at the antics of their three children. The youngest was learning to eat on his own and made a big mess of his dinner. Analisa had to clean a spot of buttered toast and jelly off her good calico shirt before traveling on, but she didn't mind. She

217

enjoyed playing with children, something she didn't get to do often.

Anything to keep from thinking about yesterday—especially the comment that David had made about protection from pregnancy. She hadn't even thought about that possibility, but now, watching the children, she couldn't seem to think of anything else.

To distract herself, she'd volunteered to help Mrs. Shepherd hang the laundry on the line after the meal. But the good-natured woman had declined the help, enlisting the aid of the eldest girl instead, and sending Analisa on her way with an admonition to be careful and stay with a good family this evening.

Analisa had smiled and said she would. She hoped she could find a good, familiar family. Sometimes, after a harsh winter, families packed up and left, unable to stand another season of hardship. After her father and brother's deaths, she'd thought about finding such a family and going with them. She'd lose the homestead, of course, and the animals . . . what would happen to Daisy and Rose and the ducks if she wasn't there to care for them? They'd end up in a stew pot or hanging in a smokehouse, that's what.

She crossed the river at Menor's Ferry, nervous as always on the wide, wooden raft. Tommelise wasn't much better, and Mr. Menor offered to blindfold her. But the mare quieted when they moved away from the swaying cottonwood trees and into the current without mishap. Soon the raft pulled up on the eastern shore, the bump against the bank and the groan of the wood causing another protest from Tommelise as her hooves beat a marching rhythm against the solid planks.

Analissa paid in coin, which she kept for this purpose. Other than Mr. Menor, no one else was interested in accepting money, which was good, because coin wasn't easy to come by.

After adjusting the saddlebags and remounting Tommelise, Analisa headed south toward the settlement between the buttes. She felt a growing excitement over meeting new people and making trades on her own. She just hoped that the newcomers to the valley were upstanding people who were willing to stay and build a future here. She'd seen too many families leave after one year in Wyoming, mainly because the land had been misrepresented to them.

She'd read some of the articles and brochures that had urged people to settle here; writers had described this as good farmland with plenty of water and a moderate temperature. Nothing could be further from the truth. Rainfall was scarce and undependable; snows were heavy on the plains and in the mountains, but less harsh in the hills. Sometimes the lakes and rivers flooded when spring came and the snowcap melted. Other years, there wasn't enough snowfall to fill the streams.

She headed south on the flats toward the other river, the Gros Ventre. More of a stream really; a ferry wasn't necessary to cross the water because it was shallow, except during snowmelt. The flats rippled with tall grass, the tips going to seed already due to the warm, early temperatures. Closer to the river, cottonwoods grew tall and swayed gently in the summer breeze, but here, only the light blue sage broke the wide expanse of green.

At first she thought she'd startled a small group of antelope, but then she saw the wagons, moving like ships with white sails through the sea of grass. Only the heads and upper bodies of the oxen were visible. She pulled Tommelise to a halt and shielded her eyes with her hand, trying to see how many settlers occupied the wagons.

And they were settlers. She saw women on the wagon seats, and two children riding on the back of a mule. Several men rode horseback, but a few more walked. This was a good-size group, and Analisa hoped they planned to settle close by.

She urged Tommelise into a trot, waving as they drew closer to the lead wagon. One of the men rode out to meet her.

"Hello," Analisa called out as the man reined his bay to a halt. She noticed immediately that he was dressed for the trail, in heavy denim pants, a shirt bleached nearly white from sun and washings, and gloves that had seen many miles of wear.

"Afternoon," he replied, tipping his felt hat. "You live around these parts?"

"Not far." Analisa pivoted in the saddle and pointed west. "On the other side of the river, in the foothills." She turned back to the man. "Are you settling here?"

"Near Jenny Lake. My brother-in-law was with the Hayden party back in seventy-two and wants to lay claim to the land. We came out with him."

"My family is from Ohio."

The man shook his head. "We're from Missouri."

She didn't really expect them to be from the same area, but after talking about it to David the other day, she'd begun to think more about neighbors and friends. The urge to socialize with the people who lived around her had become stronger every day, until she knew that when David left, she'd keep closer touch with the families nearby. Perhaps she could even hold a school for the children during part of the summer. She liked children, even though she hadn't been around them very much.

"I have some butter and cheese for trading, if you have any staples."

"Come on back. You can talk to the women about that."

The man wheeled his horse and trotted back to the wagons. Analisa followed, glad that he was willing to stop for a while and trade. She'd love to get some sugar for baking.

She met the two married women, a young orphaned niece, and the children, who ranged in age from just under two to twelve years. After much sorting through inventory and discussing how much they'd need for the winter, the women parted with two pounds of sugar for four pounds of butter and cheese, and Analisa traded one of her clay figures for a new pipe for Charlie. The man threw in some pipe tobacco for a dozen eggs Analisa had carefully wrapped that morning.

As she handed the youngest child back to his mother, he sneezed on her, making her chuckle at his wrinkled-up expression. She wiped his nose with her handkerchief, then gave him a final hug. There was something so special about a baby—even one with a case of sniffles—something she'd never noticed before. Perhaps someday she would have a baby of her own.

But not with David. He would be long gone before she married and gave birth. The knowledge that her baby wouldn't have his dark, dark hair or flashing eyes, or know about the amazing inventions and stories from the future, made her sad as she rode away from the wagons.

She'd go to see the new settlers before the first snowfall, she vowed, to see that they'd winter well. Some folks just didn't realize how brutal the winters could be.

As she continued south, she pushed thoughts of wagons, babies, and David from her mind. She'd lost nearly an hour in socializing, and she wanted to be safe with a family she knew before nightfall. She could camp out alone but didn't relish the idea.

Crossing the Gros Ventre was easy; rainfall from the last storm had long since run off, and Tommelise was only belly deep in water in the middle of the stream. The midafternoon sun made her shade her eyes and squint against the brightness, reminding her that the day was passing quickly. Yet despite the necessity of finding a place to stay tonight, she felt an urgency to find the cabin of the two men from Minnesota.

She needed to discover what her reaction would be to a young, unmarried man other than David. Would a stranger send her senses reeling? Or would she see them as she did Charlie?

No matter what David said, she knew they weren't friends. She and Charlie were *friends*. She and David had almost become lovers.

She headed south along the side of the eastern butte, right up against the marshy land where spring-fed creeks and ponds mingled with tall grasses and willows along the banks. A moose cow and her calf waded into the water, pulling up water plants and chewing slowly as they watched her from a distance. Her passage startled a nearby pair of herons, who took off clumsily from one of the small ponds and spread their wide wings in lazy flight. A family of geese nested on a mound in the middle of another pond, their long necks searching for a sign of danger from her.

She kept Tommelise to a walk, enjoying the freedom to observe this very different area. She'd been this way a few times before with Papa, but that was several years ago. If she could convince Charlie to stay, she could come this way more often, perhaps make some new friends among the settlers. David had said that there was a town called Jackson, and she'd like to see that. Thinking of a large group of buildings here, of more people in one place than now lived in the entire area, was nearly unbelievable.

She sighed as her thoughts kept turning to David. She wanted to forget about him, at least for now, and think of the other men she might meet. This plan she'd come up with . . . well, she had to convince him that she would be fine on her own. David was remarkably single-minded about her safety.

Turning east at the end of the marsh, the partially completed cabins soon came into view. Two tents also shared the area, along with some corrals containing horses. Her heart beat faster as she rode toward the small settlement. In just a few minutes, she'd see how she reacted to meeting new men.

And maybe she'd find a bull to freshen Lucy. Her milk would dry up soon if she wasn't bred to produce another calf. Analisa sighed. Another calf meant another animal to feed, because she was sure she'd never be able to butcher her friendly cow's calf.

She pulled her mare to a halt, then checked her braid, smoothing back the curling shorter tendrils that always escaped control. She wiped the corner of her handkerchief over her face to remove any dust, straightened her clothes, and settled herself firmly in the saddle. Taking a deep breath, she touched her heels to Tommelise, urging her forward.

They hadn't gone but a few steps when she heard hoofbeats. Riding toward her was someone with dark hair and tanned skin, a plaid shirt that had once belonged to Jurgen, and tight denim pants. Oh, how she knew those denim pants. The memory caused her heart to pound and her cheeks to heat even more than the summer sun. His eyes were hidden behind the dark glasses, but she knew him anyway.

David. How had he found her, and why? And where in the world had he gotten that . . . horse?

His first urge was to shake her silly; his second was to kiss her senseless. But, he reminded himself, she didn't need any help being senseless, because anyone— especially any woman—who'd head out alone in this wilderness full of desperate men, dangerous animals, and the hostile tribes was already lacking in common sense.

He kicked his gelding to a slightly faster trot, the limit of the horse's speed. The gait jarred his teeth and made him wonder if he'd be able to father any other children, but he needed to get to Analisa before she took it in her head to run off.

There was no way he could catch her, except maybe if both of them were on foot. And he didn't intend to run in these boots.

He pulled the roan to a halt, but before he could say a word, she asked, "What are you doing here?"

"Chasing you around the countryside," he answered, folding his hands over the horse's withers and giving her a look that he hoped conveyed the seriousness of the situation. "Are you totally lacking in common sense, or is this some tactic designed to drive me crazy?"

She stuck her chin in the air. "I'm only doing what's done every year. And besides, it's none of your business."

"I'm making it my business," he growled. "Do you have any idea how worried I was? I'm thinking of locking you inside the cabin."

"You wouldn't dare!"

"I might. Don't tempt me."

"You, Mr. David Terrell, can go straight to . . . to hell!" She put her heels to Tommelise, but he reached out just in time to grab the bridle. The mare squealed in protest as she spun her hindquarters around. Analisa nearly lost her seat, grabbing the pommel as the saddle-bags flew out from the horse's sides like square, brown wings.

The moment her mare stopped moving, Analisa jumped from her back and started running.

David cursed long and hard under his breath while dismounting. He tugged both horses to a sage brush and wrapped the reins around a branch before taking off after her. Sure enough, his boots weren't meant for running.

She had a long stride, hampered only by the fact she was also wearing boots. His muscles, unaccustomed to riding bareback all day, rebelled against this further abuse, cramping just as he reached Analisa. He made a lunging grab for her waist, pulling her down to the sandy soil as he absorbed the impact.

They rolled once. She landed across his middle, knocking the air from his lungs. His shoulder ached from the fall, his leg muscles were still cramping, and now he couldn't breathe. Great. Hadn't someone warned him about he dangers of younger women? He thought they'd meant an entirely different type of physical exhaustion.

She recovered first, squirming across him in a way that at another time he would have truly appreciated. But not at the moment. Especially not after her knee connected with his already-damaged male anatomy.

"Ouch!"

"Tell me what I did so I can do it again," she muttered as she tried to dislodge his hands. "Let go of me!"

"No way. I'm not up to chasing you at the moment, even if we were both on hands and knees. I'm too old for this."

"You're not old, but you *are* a bully," she complained, giving him an elbow to his ribs.

He rolled to the side, wrapping his arms around her

more securely and resting spoon-fashion until he regained his breath—and the feeling in the lower half of his body. "Why in the hell did you run away?"

"Because I didn't want to talk to you, listen to you, or see you any more."

"That's pretty definitive. Anything else?"

"Yes. I think you're a bully."

"You already said that."

"It bears repeating. Now would you let me up?"

"Not even if you promise not to run away."

"We are not going to stay this way all afternoon. And it will be dusk soon. I've got to make this stop and find a family around the butte to spend the night."

"No way. I'm not letting you go off by yourself again."

"I wasn't aware that I asked your permission."

"You didn't, which is too bad. A simple *no* from me would have avoided all this running about."

"You expected me to ask your permission? And you expected me to obey your dictates?" she asked in an incredulous voice. "Who do you think you are? My father?"

"No, I don't have any fatherly feelings for you at all, not even when you act like a headstrong child. No, and not your brother, either. Almost your lover, though. Doesn't that count for something?"

"No, it doesn't. You tricked me into . . . into what we did yesterday. And you only did it to get me to say I'd go with you."

"I did not. It just happened."

"I doubt that. You plan things too well."

"Think whatever you want, but I didn't plan to seduce you to get your compliance. Not for something as important as where you're going to spend the rest of your life," he answered honestly.

"I'm glad to know that you believe it's a serious decision. And I'd like to point out that it's *my* decision, not yours."

"It's your decision as long as you don't screw it up."

"You . . . I can't believe you are so . . ."

"Thoughtful?" he offered, knowing that would irritate her all over again but unable to resist. She obviously didn't take this subject lightly and saw no humor in their situation. His own sense of the absurd was coming back, along with the feeling in his legs and other parts of his body.

"No!"

"Look, I know you're mad at me. I really can't blame you. If someone was keeping me from doing something I wanted to do, I'd be angry too."

"Then why are you doing this? Why are you trying to make me live by your rules?"

He hesitated only slightly before answering, knowing he owed her an explanation. "Because once I didn't make any rules, and I lost someone I loved. I don't ever want to go through that again." He rubbed her arms where he'd held her so tightly. "I don't want to lose you through my own carelessness."

"You're not careless," she said, confused. "Are you talking about your wife?" She wiggled away from him and turned around so they were face-to-face.

"Yes. If I'd stressed to her how reckless she'd become— how much Jamie and I needed her, then perhaps she wouldn't have gone into the mountains that last time.

"Would you have told her she couldn't go?" Analisa's voice snapped him back to the present.

"Catherine? Are you serious? She would have laughed in my face and told me that I was crazy."

"Then how would you have stopped her? And why

do you think you can stop me from doing what I have to do to get supplies?''

"For one thing, I could have been more forceful, reminding her that she didn't have to take this assignment, that she had a daughter and a husband at home who needed her. But I didn't say those things, and now she's dead.''

"You don't know what might have happened,'' she said gently.

"No, but I'll always believe that I should have done more to show her how much we cared for her.''

"Did you love her?'' Analisa asked in a small, barely audible voice.

"Yes, I did. She was intelligent and clever, so full of life. You couldn't help but love Catherine. I'm just sorry that Jamie doesn't remember her. She was only two when—''

"Then that's all the more reason you need to get back to your daughter. Her mother will always be alive in your heart, and it's up to you to tell her all the good things,'' Analisa replied quickly, then pushed to her feet. She shook off the grass and dirt from her pants and shirt.

He knew she was right—about Catherine being alive in his heart *and* about getting back to Jamie. But he realized something else too; his heart had more room than he'd ever thought possible. Enough for Catherine's memory, for Jamie, and even enough for Analisa.

As she walked back toward the horses, he rested his head between his bent knees, his fingers woven together behind his thick skull. The swish of her footsteps through the knee-high grass gradually faded away, just like his anger at her for putting herself in jeopardy.

Analisa might think he was too hard on her about this one issue, but she was also pretty good at focusing on one thing—his trip back to his own time. And she was right; he did need to go back to Jamie, but he really believed he'd found a way to have his cake and eat it too. By the time the next rainbow showed up, he planned to have Analisa convinced that she belonged far away from the danger and hardship of this century.

With any luck at all—and some cooperation from the weather gods—by this time next month Analisa would be living in Jackson Hole, Wyoming, 1997.

Chapter Fifteen

She did her best to repair her appearance, combing the snags from her hair with difficulty. Visiting the two men from Minnesota with grass stains on her shirt and leaves in her hair wouldn't do. Darn David Terrell, chasing her down like that, handling her as though she were nothing more than a barnyard animal. Tears threatened as she tugged on her hair. He was going to ruin everything.

"Let me help."

His voice startled her. She hadn't heard him approach, but she shouldn't be surprised. She'd been unusually bound up in her own thoughts lately, and now, with David's latest admissions about his wife's death and his feelings for her, she had even more to think about.

"I can manage," she replied, hoping to discourage him from touching her again. She couldn't think clearly when he was too close.

"I'm good at this," he admitted as his fingers closed over her hand and drew the comb from her grasp. She resisted, but he was just as firm and demanding in this small task as he was about her going to the future with him.

Without the comb to hold, she had nothing to do with her hands, so she turned to Tommelise and held on to the saddle, dropping her head forward so all she saw was the grass and wildflowers beneath her feet. And David's shadow, merging with hers as the afternoon sun distorted their images. Her legs and his, so long and close as he stood behind her. His arm, rising and falling as he gathered her hair in his hands and pulled the comb through the tangled strands.

"You're tense," he said, his voice little more than a whisper in the stillness of the afternoon.

"For good reason," she said defensively. "There is a certain man who is driving me to the madhouse."

"That's not my intention," he said, the back of his hand brushing against her lower back as he worked another snag from her hair.

"I won't ask any more about your intentions. I think they're clear."

"How would you know? I'm not sure myself at times. At least, I'm not sure the extent of my intentions."

She tensed even more. She didn't want to hear any more about his feelings or plans.

"Ah, you're doing it again. You're acting like a frightened deer. Relax. No one is threatening you."

If only he knew how threatened she felt. But she had no intention of admitting—again—how he affected her. Then his fingers threaded through her hair to her scalp, rubbing lightly over skin that felt stretched too tight. He massaged her gently, slowly, until she moaned and dropped her forehead to the saddle.

"Isn't that better?" he asked softly. "I didn't mean to make you tense, or mess up your clothes. I was just so worried about you, Analisa.'' His voice was as much a caress as his fingers, working magic to relax her until she wanted to snuggle close and accept the protection he offered.

Not protection against the dangers of wild animals, the weather, or other people. The safety she craved from David was for the loneliness of her soul, for that special connection she'd felt just briefly when they'd kissed and held each other. For those few minutes, she hadn't been alone. He'd understood her without words, without any barriers. And although she still didn't understand all the complexities of his wants and needs, she knew he craved a special bond as much as he needed to forgive himself for his wife's death.

He stepped closer, his chest warmer against her back than the sunlight. But the memory of their recent conversation made her pull away, both physically and mentally. David had loved his wife; he might never love another woman the same way. And his guilt caused him to be so domineering that she doubted anyone could accept his restrictions.

Analisa knew she couldn't, no matter how much she craved his affections, or how much she wanted to help him forgive himself. She felt no guilt for her father and brother's deaths, but she knew the despair that came from that kind of loss. She could only imagine how much more devastating the pain would be if someone blamed himself.

She had to stay with her plan of allowing David to go back to his daughter and sister. He would never be whole in the past, living without everything he'd loved so much before the fateful day he'd flown across the rainbow.

She slipped away. He let her go, her hair flowing through his fingers as she walked to Tommelise's head and turned to face David. The look of such stark need on his face caused her breath to catch in her throat and her heart to drop as fast as a sled on a snow-covered hill.

Fortunately, he gained control of his own emotions, shoving his fingers through his hair. She barely restrained herself from walking to him, sinking her hands in his hair, pulling his head to her chest, rubbing away all his sorrow and longing. Her own fingers clenched into fists as she stood her ground.

"I need to visit these new settlers," she said, forcing the words past a throat suddenly grown tight. "This is something I need to do alone."

He nodded. "Go ahead, but know that I'm close by. I won't interfere, but I won't let you get into trouble either."

"Fair enough," she said, glad that there would be no further arguments.

"Let me braid you hair," David offered. "You don't want to go to the house looking like that." He pointed to her loose hair, streaming across her shoulders and chest.

"I can"

"I'm good at this, remember?" he said with a slight smile. "I've braided hair, parted hair, put up ponytails and puppy dog ears."

"For Jamie?" she asked, turning around and offering a ribbon over her shoulder.

His fingers worked quickly to separate her hair into three parts, then begin braiding. "Yes, and a few times for Holly when we were younger. She decided that she had to have a French braid every morning when she was in junior high school, but she never was any good at it. I was drafted to be her hairdresser," he confessed with a chuckle. "I've never admitted that to anyone else."

233

"Why?"

"It's not a very 'manly' thing for a high-school senior to do," he explained. "Especially not for your baby sister."

"I think your help was nice."

"Thanks, but when I was seventeen or eighteen, being nice to my sister wasn't my main concern."

"What was?"

"Don't ask," he said sternly, tying the ribbon around the end of her braid.

She turned around, concerned that she'd brought up another bad memory, but saw that he was still smiling. Apparently this was another answer that only men understood.

"I'll be waiting, listening. Go ahead and make your trades, but if they do anything threatening, I'm coming in."

"You don't have a gun."

"Good point. Give me the rifle."

"No!"

"Analisa, you don't know these people. If they try something, there's no way you can pull your weapon and fire first. Now just give me the damn rifle and quit arguing with everything I say."

She frowned and pulled the rifle from the scabbard. "I'm giving you the gun, but only because what you said makes sense. *Not* because you ordered me to."

"Fair enough. But has it ever occurred to you that I wouldn't ask if it didn't make sense?"

"You didn't ask," she replied angrily, "you demanded." She placed her foot in the stirrup and hauled herself onto Tommelise's back. "And don't interfere unless someone comes after me with a weapon. These are my new neighbors, not yours."

"They're strangers," he answered, his eyes hidden behind the colored glasses.

Not for long, she wanted to say, but she bit back the words, putting her heel to her mare's sides and trotting away from David. She didn't look back, but focused instead on the cabins and tents, and the men who might give her a reason to stay in the past—and David a reason to go back to his time.

"Hello the house!"

Analisa waited for someone to emerge from the open doorway of the tent, but no one did. At least there didn't seem to be any women or children about. That was a sign these were unmarried men. The cabin was nearly complete, with the logs and part of the roof in place. The chinking between the logs seemed to be progressing well too. This would be a secure cabin for the winter.

But not as good as hers, she thought with a feeling of pride. She had protection from the snows that the butte to the northeast couldn't provide, and here there was a danger of flooding if the snowmelt filled the creeks and ran into the spring-fed marsh. She had to admit, however, that the new settlers would never suffer from a water shortage such as her family had occasionally faced, when the winter snows were not plentiful and didn't provide enough summer melt to fill the creek.

She guided Tommelise around to the side so she could see the barn, which was complete. Wide doors stood open to the south, and she could see the shadowed shapes of people inside, as well as hear their indistinct voices.

"Hello the barn!" she called out.

This time they heard her, stopping their tasks and walking to the doorway.

My goodness, they certainly are large. The two men—

235

who seemed to be twins in size and appearance—filled the doorway of the barn. Just as Charlie had reported, they had blond hair and Scandinavian good looks. She'd known some Swedish immigrants in Ohio, and these men looked very much like them, from their height to their pale complexions.

"Hello," one of the men replied, walking forward with a wide smile on his face. The other one followed, his expression more cautious.

"I've come to welcome you to the valley," she said, forcing a smile despite her nervousness over meeting the two men—and the fact that she'd just caught a glimpse of a rider behind the barn, hidden by the large rocks.

"And a fine welcome it is," the smiling man said, stopping beside Tommelise. "Bjorn Olafson," he said, extending his hand in a very forward manner.

She accepted the greeting with a slight, unsteady smile. "Analisa Ludke," she replied, hoping her fingers weren't crushed in his bearlike grip.

"It's been a good long time since we've had such a lovely visitor, isn't that right, Thor?" he asked, turning back to the other man.

"That's right," the less friendly blond giant replied. "A good long time." He offered a handshake. "Thorburn Olafson. This one's brother."

"Pleased to meet you," Analisa responded from lessons her mother had stressed so many years ago but she'd had little practice using. She tightened her grip on the reins as Tommelise pranced and threw her head.

"My mare's a little nervous from being around strangers," she explained.

"Then come down and sit a spell. We won't be strangers long."

The way he made the remark made her feel as uneasy as Tommelise, but she didn't know why, except that the men—or at least the one man—seemed more friendly than most folks she'd met. Like the people in the wagons, she thought. They'd been grateful that she'd brought goods to trade and could talk about the area, but they hadn't overwhelmed her.

Perhaps it's because they're bachelors, she thought. *Maybe you are responding to them as a woman to men.* She'd never know until she tried to be more friendly herself.

"My mare and I would both appreciate a drink of water," she said, walking Tommelise in a circle and stopping her near the more friendly man—Bjorn Olafson, she remembered.

"Certainly." He sauntered to the shade of the house, where a barrel contained a supply of water, then filled a wooden bucket and a dipper.

"Why don't you get down from the saddle and rest a bit? There's shade, and we can get to know each other better."

"Of course," she replied, easing her leg across Tommelise's broad back. She risked a glance toward the base of the butte and saw David's head, craning to get a better view of what she was doing. He was no doubt cursing the fact that he'd agreed to let her go the homestead alone, since he couldn't get close himself. Too bad. He'd have to suffer in silence, because these men didn't appear to harbor any thoughts of harming her. If anything, they'd keep her too long with their need to visit.

She led Tommelise to the bucket Mr. Olafson provided, then accepted the dipper of water from his huge, bearlike hand. She had the sudden image of that hand pawing at her, and it made her shudder in distaste. His hands were nothing like David's—large but gentle, long-fingered and sensitive. She shook away the picture. She

237

wasn't here to think of *him,* but to try to establish a future for herself.

She should have worn something more feminine, she realized, if she was trying to be more than just neighborly to these two men. But the idea of riding all day in a too-tight, too-short dress wasn't appealing in the least. Her pants were much more practical, and if the Olafson brothers didn't like them, then . . . then she just didn't care. She didn't have the money or the time to sew herself some full riding skirts, as she'd seen a woman wearing in a photograph from a newspaper Charlie had brought back last year.

"Are you alone?" Thorburn Olafson said suddenly, snapping her out of her musings.

"I'm . . . I'm alone at the moment," she hedged, feeling a prick of unease at the abrupt question. Just like when David had first come to the cabin, she was reluctant to tell these men that she had no male family members—or that David was hiding in the rocks behind the barn.

"My . . . uncle is expecting me back at the cabin," she lied, although she did think of Charlie as a member of the family, and he was expecting her back—tomorrow.

"Thor, don't frighten the lady off," Bjorn said jovially. "She'll think we're rude barbarians. Come," he gestured with a sweep of his hand, "sit a spell and tell us how you came to visit us today."

A series of tree stumps provided stools for them to sit. She chose one facing the butte, so she could see if David made any sudden moves. Bjorn Olafson hoisted his stump closer to hers, leaned forward, and appeared ready to soak up each word she said. Thorburn, on the other hand, sat more stiffly, watching her with hooded eyes that she couldn't read.

"Charlie told me some new families had moved into the area. I came to visit and to trade, although most of my cheese and butter is gone, and I traded all my eggs earlier today to several families traveling north by wagon."

"They overnighted nearby," Bjorn said, still smiling. "Is Charlie your uncle?"

"Yes, he is," she lied again. "He's small, with reddish gray hair. He travels with a donkey."

"We saw him," Thorburn said, "last week. He didn't say anything about a niece."

"He probably didn't realize I'd set out so soon to trade. I usually wait until later, but with the new families, I decided to go now."

"And we're glad you did," Bjorn said easily, leaning even closer. Analisa had the urge to sit back even straighter.

"I wondered if you had a bull," she said quickly, wanting to keep the conversation moving, since they didn't mention trading.

"We do," Thorburn replied. "We're raising beef cattle."

"Oh. Well, I have a cow that needs to be freshened. Perhaps we could discuss a trade for your bull's services."

"I'm sure we can work something out," Bjorn said, his smile beginning to irritate her. "When did you say your uncle was expecting you back?"

"I . . . I didn't," she said, standing abruptly. His presence seemed to overwhelm her, but not in the same way David's did. This man made her want to run, fast and far, from some threat she didn't understand but could sense with every feminine instinct she possessed.

"Don't leave," Bjorn said. "Do you know how long it's been since we've seen a beautiful young woman?

Surely you wouldn't deny us the pleasure of your company for just a little longer." His bearlike hand reached toward her arm.

Analisa stepped back, not realizing her mistake until she felt another set of hands on her arms. She looked over her shoulder at the same time she tried to break away and saw Thorburn Olafson's unreadable expression.

"Let me go," she said clearly, loudly.

"Not yet. We'd really like to get to know you . . . much, much better."

His hand came toward her chest. She watched in horror as the implication set in; these men *did* want to harm her, and in the worst way.

"Let me go," she repeated, twisting in the firm grasp of Thorburn. "How could you think of such a thing? I was only being neighborly!"

"We'd like to be neighborly too," Bjorn said, grinning. "Like I said, we haven't seen a good-looking woman like you in months. This won't take very long, and we'll even let you bring your cow by. We all aim to be of service," he ended with a laugh.

She tried to kick him, but he evaded her booted feet with a smile and a gleam in his eyes that told her he was enjoying her attempts to fight them off. Just as she felt herself being lifted by the arms, as she thought she was going to be thrown to the ground, she heard the deadly click of a cartridge sliding into a chamber.

"Let her go." David's steely, angry voice cut through the summer day like a knife through butter. The homestead went silent; even the birds ceased their chatter.

She looked at him, sitting statue-still on his gelding's back, the rifle pointed squarely at Bjorn Olafson's chest. Never had he appeared more the princely rescuer; never had she been more relieved to see him.

Thorburn's hands finally eased. She lurched from his grasp, then swung around and kicked with all her might. He cursed as he grabbed his shin, and while he was distracted, she sent her knee hard into his groin.

Thorburn Olafson collapsed on the ground like a wounded elk, thrashing and moaning. She felt a burst of satisfaction as she turned to his brother.

"I'll tie him up if you'd like to castrate him," David offered calmly, still pointing the rifle.

"I wouldn't want to get that close to him," she said with a sneer. "But I think he should have to pay for what he planned to do."

"Come here and hold the rifle on him then," David ordered.

"I don't need you to fight my battles," she spat back. "Just shoot him if he moves."

"Analisa, he's not going to stand still while you vent your anger."

"He'd better."

"Cowards never take their medicine like men. No, for this one, I think we're going to have to work together."

David dismounted, then handed her the rifle, which she pointed at Bjorn's chest, all the while keeping an eye on Thorburn. He was still on the ground, still moaning and clutching his privates.

David walked to the tent, bent down, and jerked on the knot that held the canvas to the stake. He untied several lengths of rope, then returned to where Thorburn lay groaning. The tent collapsed in the summer breeze.

Within seconds, he'd bound the brother's hands behind his back, then secured his feet. He rose from his crouch and advanced on Bjorn.

"We were just having some fun. We wouldn't have hurt her," the blond giant offered.

"I should cut you myself," she heard David growl,

''for frightening her. No one messes with her while I'm around.''

''Who are you?'' Bjorn asked, holding up his hands and backing away.

''Stay where you are!'' Analisa shouted, ready to shoot him if he made a move toward David.

''I'm her man,'' David replied softly. ''You won't forget it.''

''No! I won't. Just ride on out of here and—''

''Not yet.'' While Bjorn's eyes flashed with fear and his hands stayed high in the air, David's arm shot forward so fast that Analisa barely saw the punch.

Bjorn fell, his body crashing to the sandy soil like an ancient lodgepole pine. He tried to raise his head but appeared dazed. David used his boot to roll the Swede over—none too gently, either. He used the same technique he'd applied to Thorburn, binding the brother most effectively.

''Where did you learn to tie that quickly?'' Analisa asked.

''Rodeo—4-H senior bull-dogging champion in Jefferson County, Colorado,'' David said, dusting his hands on his thighs. He walked toward her, his stride fast and steady, and Analisa felt her heartbeat leap in awareness.

Without a word or a warning, he reached out one hand, held the back of her head, and kissed her hard. This was no gentle persuasion, but a possession of the most elementary kind. *My woman,* he'd said, and the hard, breath-stealing kiss proved his point.

He broke off the kiss as abruptly as he'd started it, his eyes burning with an inner fire she'd never seen before. He dropped his hand and she swayed slightly before catching herself. Her heart raced so fast she thought it might leap from her chest. Her lips felt bruised and swollen, and despite the violence she'd just witnessed, she had the irrational urge to throw herself at David and kiss him back.

"Let's get out of here," he said softly, but with an underlying edge she found nearly as exciting as the hot look he sent her.

"What about them?" she asked as she walked on shaky legs to Tommelise.

"They'll be able to get untied soon enough," David replied, giving the brothers another glance. Both still appeared slightly dazed. "And if they can't, the wolves will have a good feast tonight."

"David!"

"Just wishful thinking," he said, jumping up, then swinging his leg over the bare back of his gelding.

"You're some kind of murdering half-breed, aren't you?" Bjorn said, glaring through one bruised, swollen eye. "You going to finish the job?" he taunted. "You and your Indian-loving whore!"

"Only about one-fourth, on my mother's side," David answered easily, urging his gelding closer until he stood high above the felled Swede. "And don't tempt me to finish you off. I haven't taken a blond scalp in a long time."

"You—"

"And Analisa is *mine*. If you so much as mention her name to anyone in this valley, I'll come after you . . . if there's anything left for me. She's a favorite around here, you see. Everyone loves her because she's good and generous to a fault. So I'd be real careful what you say. Your cattle might just find their way to a dozen tables this winter, and you'll freeze your asses off alone."

He nudged his roan closer, so the gelding's hooves rested against Bjorn's exposed stomach. "Be careful what you say," David said softly, leaning over his

243

horse's neck. "Because if they don't get you, I will."

He walked the roan over Bjorn's still body. Analisa heard the man's whimpers as he lay, vulnerable and tied, on the ground.

"If I have to come back, you won't like the outcome, I promise you." With those final words, David rammed his heels into the gelding's sides, sending the horse over Bjorn with a squeal. She couldn't tell if it came from man or animal.

She followed David from the homestead, the curses of the brothers—urgent requests to come back and loosen the ropes—following them around the butte.

She wasn't sure where David was heading, but she didn't care. Her heart still raced, her skin tingled, and she knew that he was right. No matter the consequences, no matter how foolish, she was his woman.

As if he could read her thoughts, he slowed the gelding and looked at her with those burning eyes. *Half-breed,* the Swede had called David. She hadn't thought about his ancestry, nor had she cared. But the knowledge that his black hair, dark eyes, and red-gold skin came from the blood of Indian ancestors made her heart beat even faster.

She didn't know if his possessive nature came from that blood, or if the savage threat she'd witnessed was a product of it. All she knew was that David excited her as no other man could. She wanted him, because of who he was, in spite of where he was from.

She returned his heated gaze, breathing deeply as her eyelids drifted shut and her thighs tightened involuntarily. *Tonight,* she thought. Tonight she would become his woman.

He had loved his wife, but Catherine was gone. He might never love anyone again, but then, life didn't hold any certainties except death.

Analisa needed to know the power of David's passion for one night—or maybe for many more. For once, she didn't want to plan for the future. She just wanted to live . . . and love.

Chapter Sixteen

There would be no stopping at a settler's cabin tonight. As they skirted Miller Butte and turned north around the marsh, he acknowledged that their relationship had reached a crisis. Only two possibilities existed—and one of those was unacceptable.

He would not leave her. Not now, not ever.

He also knew that he'd spoken from his heart, from feelings long buried, primal, and brutally honest; she was his woman. Across more than a hundred years, despite their differences, they were meant for each other.

And so when late afternoon clouds slid over the Tetons and turned the sky dark with the promise of a summer shower, he pushed them harder toward the shelter of Blacktail Butte. The rugged terrain produced some rock overhangs where they could stay warm and dry, and the trees cut the wind and rain. With any luck, they'd finally talk through their differences, although talk wasn't all that he wanted from Analisa now.

He'd known before, at the meadow, that making love to her was wrong. That he was going to leave. That she hadn't committed to going with him. And yet, he would have gladly lost himself in her willing, passionate body like a teenager who lacked self-control. At least he'd thought of protection; fortunately, there was always some in the emergency kit on the plane in case a client forgot, or if previously unexpected circumstances presented themselves.

Like traveling back in time and meeting a woman like no other.

The first drops of rain landed with fat plops on his nose and cheek as they crossed the Snake River near the Gros Ventre campground. If only the structures existed now . . .

But they didn't. As he and Analisa rode out of the water into the tall grasses along the bank, he pushed the gelding into a trot. They crossed the meadow as fast as his game little horse would carry him, the butte in clear sight. Lighting flashed across the sky to the west, a dramatic, ragged slash against the dark clouds.

"We'll make shelter in a few minutes," he shouted to Analisa. One glance in her direction made him all the more anxious to be safe and dry, since the fat drops of rain had plastered her shirt to her chest, outlining her breasts and hardened nipples in vivid detail.

"It's okay," she shouted back. "A little water won't hurt us."

Perhaps not, but the way his body was heating up, he'd soon be producing steam.

As they reached the base of the butte and started the ascent, the horses slipped on the loose rock and gravel.

"We'll need to walk them from here," he said, pointing to an overhang about thirty feet ahead. Douglas firs grew thick to the side of the rocky ledge, and Aspens

247

formed a natural barrier in front. The horses would have protection from wind and rain in the heavy forest area.

They hurried up the slope, not needing to speak. Analisa jumped down from her mare's back and began unsaddling her immediately.

"I'll do that. Why don't you see if you can clear off a place for us? Do you have something to start a fire?"

"If we can find some dry kindling." The rain came down harder now, wetting her hair and making him doubt they'd find any wood untouched by dampness.

She grabbed his saddlebags and hers, then hurried to the rocks while he hobbled both horses in the shelter of the firs and removed their bridles. Beneath the heavy, low boughs, he found dry kindling and pine needles, and he bundled them together, sheltering them with his body as he sprinted toward Analisa.

"I found branches, but no . . ." Her voice trailed off as she spotted the kindling. "Thanks. Put it here," she said, smiling as she pointed to a spot barely covered by the sheltering rocks. "I'll have a fire going before long."

"I can do that if you'd like."

"No, but you could clear away some of the larger rocks to give us more room. We could use them to contain the fire."

"You've got it."

They wouldn't need much room, he thought as he heaved some of the irregular-shaped reddish-brown stones toward the fire. Enough to snuggle together. Enough to lay side by side, skin-to-skin, while the rain and wind serenaded them, and the firelight caressed them to a golden glow.

David smiled, thinking how poetic he'd become since claiming Analisa as his own. Tonight, he'd make that claim a reality.

He paused after positioning the saddlebags near the back of their rocky suite. God, how he loved to watch her, he thought as she arranged the broken branches only a few feet away. If not for the jagged rocks and gravelly soil, he'd pull her to him now, kiss her breathless, and make love to her until all thoughts of rain, fire, and poetry flew from his head. Until she became everything in his world, and he became the only thing in hers.

She struck the tinder, and the shaved bark and pine needles burst into flame. Leaning back, she watched the dry sticks catch fire, then turned to him.

"Are you . . ." Her voice trailed off as her gaze locked with his. Desire must have shown in his eyes, because she answered his passion with a flash in her blue eyes that had nothing to do with the flames, and everything to do with her own emotions.

". . . finished?"

"Come here," he said, knowing that if he didn't kiss her in the next ten seconds, he would die. Explode. Combust.

She crawled across the floor of their tiny shelter. He met her halfway, folding his arms around her and pulling her close until they were chest-to-chest, heart-to-heart. Her lips were cool under his; he silently vowed to warm them.

She melted into his arms as she always did, as though she'd been made exactly for him. When he touched his tongue to her lips, she opened for him. The fire inside him flared to life, shattering the control he'd tried so hard to maintain all afternoon, ever since he'd seen Analisa manhandled by that blond Neanderthal. David knew he would have hurt the man far worse if Analisa hadn't been there to temper his anger.

She was his. The knowledge spread through him like wildfire, fueled by the winds of fear and anger. The kiss deepened, returned by the tentative thrust of her tongue, the nibbling demands of her lips. A primitive urge, unlike anything he'd experienced before, resurfaced. He needed to claim her, to show her that they belonged together.

He broke away, breathing hard. Behind her, the fire cast a golden halo of light and heat, yet she shivered.

"You're wet. Let me help you with those clothes," he said, his unsteady hands going to the buttons of her shirt. He slid each from its hole, then pulled the shirttails from her pants as she watched, wide-eyed and breathing just as heavily.

"You can tell me no now," he explained, spreading the edges of her shirt apart to reveal a modest camisole. He trailed his fingers along the white cotton, watching her face as he neared the peak of her breast. She appeared even more surprised, and gasped when he stroked her nipple through the thin fabric.

"Are you going to tell me no, Analisa?" he asked, fighting the urge to make love fast and hard. He wanted to savor each moment, but the desire to claim her was nearly overwhelming, and he fought the darkness by watching her innocent, sensual response.

"No," she breathed, the whisper of sound blending with the sizzle and snap of the fire.

"No, you're not going to tell me no, or no, you don't want me to make love to you?"

She frowned at his question, and instead of answering, lifted her hands and placed them over his, squeezing her breasts, urging him to caress her again and again.

"Yes," she whispered when he complied, teasing each peak until she gasped and let her hands drop away. They came to rest on his shoulders, pulling him closer.

"I want to be your woman," she whispered near his

lips. "I want to make love with you. I want to know, David. I need to know . . ."

"This isn't about one afternoon in a storm, Analisa. This is about you and me and happily-ever-after endings."

He slid his hands to her back and jerked her closer. "I'm not going to leave you after this. When I go back, you're going with me. I realize now that *you* are why I flew across the rainbow that day. Not Jamie. You."

"Oh, David," she sighed, her hands mimicking his as she held him tightly. "I want to go with you. Really, I do. And I think I understand now . . ."

He kissed her again, because their future was sealed, their fate entwined. As united as their hearts, as joined as their bodies would soon be.

He pushed the damp shirt from her arms. She shivered as the cool air touched her chilled skin, so he warmed her with caresses to every exposed inch of flesh. Against her back, he felt the heat of the fire. Around them, the rain fell and the air grew cooler.

"The blankets," she whispered against his neck.

He broke away long enough to find his, folded in one side of the saddlebag, and hers, rolled with a slicker she hadn't donned. With a flick of his wrists, first one, then the second, blanket settled over the sandy ground.

When he turned back to Analisa, she'd knelt in front of the fire, her shirt open. She'd unbraided her hair and finger-combed the strands so the warmth could dry them. In the darkness of the late afternoon storm, she appeared as a golden goddess worshipping the flames.

"In my time, we have an invention called a blow dryer," he said, crouching behind her and letting the golden silk fall across his callused palms, "but if we were back inside my house, I'd dry your hair by brushing it before the fireplace. Then I'd lay you down on a

251

soft, fluffy rug, spread your hair around you like a halo, and make love with you until we were both damp with sweat and hot enough to start our own blaze.''

''Then do that here,'' she whispered urgently, her lips nearly touching the back of his hand. ''Make love to me until we don't care where we are—in your time or mine, outside or within your house. Just make me yours.''

''You are,'' he whispered against her hair, his throat tight with love—the one word he hadn't said to a woman in four years. ''You are.''

He lowered his head and moved her hair aside, then placed his lips against her neck and kissed her as though she nourished something hungry and hollow inside him.

Exquisite sensations shot from Analisa's head to her toes. She arched into the kiss, leaning her head back on his shoulder as his lips continued a path down her throat. His hands pulled the shirt from her arms, exposing her to the night air. Her nipples tightened against the camisole, aching for David's touch. But he didn't satisfy that craving. Instead, his fingers dipped beneath the waistband of her pants, working the buttons loose.

She sucked in her stomach, pressing her back more fully against his chest. He was nearly as hot as the fire, scorching her with a wonderful heat like she'd experienced only once before, in the meadow beside his plane. She shivered as he slid each button from its hole, spreading the front of her pants open until she felt the heat of the fire on the thin cotton of her drawers.

''You respond so naturally,'' he whispered into her ear. ''So honest in your passion that you take my breath away.''

She didn't know what he meant by responding naturally and being honest. She knew nothing of what he wanted, so she followed her own feelings and desires.

Someday she'd ask, but not now. Not when whatever she was doing pleased him so very much.

His fingers dipped lower, pushing her pants down her hips in a slow, steady motion. She should probably be shocked but couldn't find that sentiment inside. All she knew was that each moment was a wonderful new experience, one that she intended to savor.

Her pants caught at her knees. David solved the problem by hauling her back with him until she sat across his lap on the blankets. She could finally see his face, and the passion in his eyes stunned her anew. "You want me," she said softly, touching his cheek with trembling fingertips.

"Like I've never wanted anyone," he said fiercely.

"Not even—"

"No one. Ever." He stopped her question by taking her fingers into his mouth and sucking on each tip until she closed her eyes and swallowed a moan. When she opened her eyes, she watched in fascination as he traced the palm of her hand with his tongue, then kissed the center, hard.

She felt herself grow damp in that private place between her thighs. An ache was building there, one that throbbed with an intensity she'd never felt before. David built that passion with each glance, each action. Now, as he slipped off her boots and socks, then pulled the pants down her legs, she wondered if the ache would be appeased soon, or if it would ever go away.

"Will this longing ever stop?" she asked. Her voice sounded soft and husky, as though she'd just awakened from a long sleep.

"God, I hope not," he said, his gaze roaming over her like a feather.

"But I feel so . . . I don't know how to describe the way I feel. I want something, but I don't know what."

"Don't worry—I do," he said, his dark eyes shining brightly, his lips smiling ever so slightly. She broke her gaze away when she felt his hand come to rest on her stomach. Looking down at his tanned fingers, fanned across her white camisole, she sucked in her breath and waited . . . and watched.

He stroked upward, to the rise of her breast, to the peak that tightened even more. The ache there mirrored the one between her thighs, which tensed as he stroked her through the thin cotton. She closed her eyes and let her head roll back against his arm, unable to stop herself from moaning.

"It's okay," he said gently. "You can moan. You can move. You can do whatever you want, to yourself or to me. Just let go, Analisa. You're so good at this. So natural."

"Touch me," she entreated, her voice as faint and whispy as the smoke from their fire.

"Like this?" He pushed up the camisole, his hand hot on her skin. But it wasn't enough . . .

"More," she demanded, and he complied, taking her breast in his hand, catching the nipple between his fingers and applying such sweet pressure that she cried out.

"Too much?" he asked, his hand resting lightly on her sensitive flesh.

"No!" She felt light-headed, damp with longing. "More."

When David moaned, she opened her eyes and glimpsed his intense expression for only a moment before he dipped his head and placed his mouth over her breast. The pressure! Oh, the sweet, hard ache as he kissed her there.

She arched from his arms, pressing herself against his mouth, her heart racing so fast she thought she might die. His hands seemed everywhere, kneading, stroking, teasing. And then he removed his mouth, only to do the same thing to her other breast while his fingers pushed down her cotton drawers and sank between her tensed legs.

"Oh!" Her eyes flew open to see his dark head, bent across her chest, and his wide shoulders, blocking her view of the magic he performed below.

"You're so wet," he said, his breath hot against her damp skin.

"I'm sorry. I can't help—"

"No, that's good," he said, raising his head until their gazes locked. "That means you're ready for me, that you want me inside you." He nuzzled her breast as he watched her, then took her nipple into his mouth.

She moaned and closed her eyes, the sight of David taking her into his mouth, the thought that a part of him would be inside of her. Too much! Oh, it was all too much. And yet he didn't stop . . .

Her legs tensed as he delved deeper, stroking her, making the ache so much worse. His mouth suckled, stroked, nipped at her breasts. She couldn't stand this torture . . . yet if it ceased for one second, she knew she would die from need.

"David," she whispered, "please . . ." She rolled her head back, watched the red shadows and dancing firelight on the roof of their shelter, and felt herself fly into a million golden stars.

He watched her for as long as he could, until holding back was so painful that he felt as though he might explode. His arousal threatened the zipper of his jeans, his hands longed to explore her more completely, with no barriers of clothing. His skin burned to be next to hers— dark gold against the palest white. Hot against soft. Damp.

Victoria Chancellor

He eased his fingers from her tight, wet passage, still clenching around him. Without opening her eyes, she arched against him. Even half-conscious, she wanted him.

He couldn't resist another stroke, feeling her natural, uninhibited response. The smell of arousal and the knowledge that he'd made her ache that badly nearly sent him over the edge. He removed his hand, resting it on her flat stomach between her wide hipbones.

She's a born mother. The instinct spoke from deep inside. *With love enough for everyone and everything. She won't desert you . . .*

He shook off the direction of his thoughts. Tonight, nothing would come between them except a thin, latex barrier. Pregnancy was not the way to bind her to him. She had to come with him based on a willing heart, not because she had no other option.

"Wake up, my princess," he whispered into her ear. "Your prince has decreed that the night is not yet over."

She smiled, then stirred, turning toward him like a sleepy, trusting kitten.

"I want to see all of you," he said, even though he knew she was still dazed. "I want our skin to touch. I want to feast on you with my eyes, as well as my lips, and all the rest of me."

He eased his legs from beneath her, realizing that part of him was just as asleep as she'd been a moment ago. Needles and pins pricked him as the blood returned to his thighs and calves. His knees felt as though he'd played four quarters with the Broncos. A moan brought Analisa's eyes open at last.

"What's wrong?"

"Nothing to worry about. My legs went to sleep while we were . . . while you recovered," he said with a smile, laying her back on the blankets.

"Is that all?" she asked, a line creased in the middle of her forehead.

"Yes, that's all. I'll be fine in a second."

"Oh." She seemed even more confused. "I thought there would be more."

He realized suddenly what she meant and couldn't stop a chuckle. "There's more," he assured her. "Much more. But first, I thought we might get the rest of our clothes off."

The line disappeared. She smiled, her eyes alight with interest. "I'd like that," she said simply, reaching for the buttons of his shirt. "May I?"

"Yes, you may," he said, watching her expression as she carefully undid each closure and pushed aside his shirt. Her hands, cool against his hot skin, roamed tentatively over his chest. He'd always known she was fascinated by him, and the knowledge had acted as a time-release aphrodisiac.

He held his cuffs up for her to unbutton. As soon as she finished, he asked, "Would you like to take it off me?"

She nodded, her hands stripping him so fast that he felt the rush of cool air. His shirt landed on the other side of their shelter—probably close to hers. Her pants, he vaguely remembered, were on the opposite end.

"May I . . . kiss you?" she asked shyly, her hand resting right above his heart.

"You," he said, stretching out beside her and propping his head up with one hand, "may do anything you want to me, as long as it doesn't involve ropes or whips."

"Why would I want to use them?"

"No reason," he said, smiling as she leaned her head to one side. "Just a little joke."

She seemed to dismiss his remarks, her eyes straying

to his chest. So intent was she that he lay back, allowing her hands to roam as freely as her gaze, and soon felt the touch of her lips against his pectorals.

The dart of her tongue as she tasted him. The heat of her lips as she kissed him . . . lower, as he'd kissed her. He tensed, made fists, and promised not to disgrace himself before they'd barely begun. But it was hard—oh, yes, it was definitely hard.

"Wait," he said, as her enthusiasm increased. She'd thrown one leg over his and was firmly pressed against his side. "How about my jeans?" he suggested.

"Jeans?"

"My pants. Would you like to take those off me as well?"

"May I?"

"Oh, yeah," he growled. "Just be careful with the zipper."

She slipped the button from the top hole, then let her hand rest over the tip of his erection, beneath two layers of fabric that seemed to disappear.

"On second thought, you'd better let me. I have a little more experience with zippers than you do."

"Show me," she said, fire dancing in her eyes.

He smiled slowly as he drew her hand inside the placket. "Right there. Feel it? Yes, that's right. Now ease it down gently." The feel of her against that most sensitive flesh made him ache so badly he couldn't stop a grimace.

"Did I hurt you?" she asked, alarm in her voice, on her face.

"No, but when a man wants to make love to a woman as much as I want to make love to you, he . . . swells, and then waits for the release. It's a wonderful kind of pain."

"I know," she said seriously as she continued to slide

the zipper down slowly. "I think I had the same feeling. I thought I might die if you didn't stop the ache."

"And did I stop it?" he asked, touching her bottom lip, wondering how he could tease her when every nerve ending in his body was screaming in delicious longing.

"Yes," she whispered, her voice dreamy. "But only for awhile. I'm aching again."

The zipper finally ran out of track and stopped. His briefs threatened to rip at the seams.

"Release? Is that what you call it?" she asked, touching him with innocent fascination through his cotton underwear. Good thing he wasn't wearing anything too revealing, or she'd have a handful of raw, excited male.

"Among other things," he managed to say. "Climax is another word. And then there are the technical terms and the slang, but we'll talk about that later. As a matter of fact, we'll talk about a lot of things later. But right now, if I don't make love to you, I really am going to explode."

Her hand tightened briefly before she lay back on the blankets. "I never knew I could feel this way. It's so amazing to learn what our bodies are capable of."

Oh, God, don't say anything else. Let me get out of these boots and socks and jeans and . . . damn, why am I wearing so many clothes? But he didn't ask her that question. He squelched his impatience as much as possible and thought about watching her face as he eased into her tight passage. "Yes, it is amazing. I hope you're ready for the next lesson."

"I'm ready," she said quickly. "Especially if it has anything to do with aches and releases and more."

He flung the last of his clothes aside, missing the fire, hoping he missed the rain as well. "Oh, it does. It definitely does."

With a sweep, he lifted her hips and pulled off her

baggy, shapeless white underwear. When they got home, he'd take her to Victoria's Secret and buy her two dozen pair of silk panties. Better still, he'd keep her at home, naked in his bed, and order them through Holly's catalog.

So intent was he on the task of undressing her that he missed her startled look until she gasped, then swallowed. Her eyes wide, she stared at his erection, licked her lips, and swallowed again.

"Oh, God," he groaned again. "Analisa, you're going to be the death of me yet," he said as he leaned over, pulled the camisole from beneath her, and swept it over her head.

"But . . ." she said, never finishing the thought, her eyes staring at that part of him that needed no further encouragement.

"Don't worry," he assured her. "This will work." And as he raised himself up, let his eyes see her lush breasts and all her glory, bathed in red-gold firelight, he knew he was telling the truth. For once in his life, things were going to work out perfectly.

He tilted up her chin, met her gaze, and eased against her, chest to toe. The feeling was exquisite, like nothing else he'd ever known. He kissed her deeply, until she parted her thighs and arched against him. And after making sure there would be no unexpected consequences, he made her his woman. Nothing had ever been so right. So very, very perfect.

Chapter Seventeen

Analisa woke just before dawn, the gray sky slashed by lines of straight, dark clouds, and just a touch of pink above the hills to the east. She felt warm, too warm, and suddenly realized the heat came from behind her, where David's large, firm body pressed against her back . . . and her hips, and her legs.

A rush of sensation passed through her. She barely suppressed a shudder of reaction when the memories from yesterday flooded her. All the things she'd done . . . he'd done. The things she'd told him. The praise he'd heaped on her. She'd felt like a much-loved guest at Christmas dinner, plate piled high with all the sinfully rich food imaginable—rich morsels that would be savored and remembered until the next holiday meal.

David had heaped her plate very high last night.

She felt her cheeks warm and knew she blushed. She should be thankful he couldn't see the tell-tale color on her face and chest, where she always showed embarrassment. He would no doubt tease her unmercifully.

"Ready to wake up?" his honey-smooth voice rumbled against her neck.

She drew in a deep breath and shivered from the sensations racing along her nerves. Surely making love had the most incredible effect on her. She still felt lightheaded and warm.

"Aren't you talking to me?" he asked, his hand stroking her arm where it lay outside the blanket.

"I was just thinking," she answered, feeling a trickle of sweat where her hair was trapped between them. She hadn't remembered a morning being so warm, but then, she'd never awakened with David before. He'd certainly been warm last night, she recalled with a smile.

"About what?"

"About you . . . and last night . . . and waking up this morning."

"Any regrets?" he asked, his hand resting on her arm, his body motionless behind her.

"No," she answered quickly, certain that she didn't. Yesterday had been her turning point. She was a woman now—David's woman. They needed to talk about certain things, like the way he'd worried so much. But she'd think about all that later. For now, she just wanted to savor the memories of making love.

But he didn't say he loved you, she reminded herself. He only said they were making love. Still, he'd made it clear that he'd claimed her for his own, and although David had been possessive and tyrannical before, she was sure now that he knew her feelings, he would trust her.

Thankfully, he didn't know about her plans—*former* plans—to find a husband—or at least appear to find one. She didn't think he'd care for that course of action, especially considering the disastrous visit to the Olafson brothers yesterday. The memory of them made her feel slightly ill.

"I need to get up," she said, uncertain how she'd accomplish that task when she was completely naked beneath the blanket. So was David, she knew very well. She felt his warm skin next to hers even as she tried to think of a way to find her clothes and dress without him watching her every move.

"Do you want me to leave?" he asked, as though he sensed her dilemma.

"I . . . well, I don't know how to . . ." She felt her cheeks warm again as she imagined David's amusement.

He kissed her neck, just behind her ear. "You're awfully warm. Are you sure you're okay?"

"I suppose. I do feel hot, but I thought that was because . . . because of you," she finished in a small voice. She wasn't a shy person usually, but David seemed to bring that part of her nature to light.

"I think maybe it's us together," he whispered, his breath hot against her damp skin. She felt him pull away, and some of the heat went with him. "Just wrap the blanket around you," he suggested. "I don't need it. Memories of the afternoon—not to mention last night—are enough to keep me plenty warm."

"I'll get your clothes," she offered, pulling the scratchy blanket around her as she pushed herself up from their makeshift bed. Her arms and legs felt heavy, as though she was sunk deeply into the sand.

"Don't bother. I'll get them in a few minutes. You go do what you need to do. There's a very small stream that should have some run-off from the rain."

"I won't be long," she said, sitting up. She felt David shift behind her, and looked at him for the first time. He lay on his stomach, appearing very rumpled, with a shadow of a beard. She knew how that felt when it rubbed against her sensitive skin. His black hair fell over his forehead. He looked very male, very powerful, and yet seemed to possess the charm of a small boy.

Except there was nothing—nothing—small about David.

"Is that a blush?" he asked, trailing his fingers along her cheek.

"Maybe," she said, looking away from the teasing glint in his eyes, only to find herself staring at his muscled back and round, firm buttocks.

"Oh, my," she whispered.

"I could turn over," he offered. "I'm trying my best to keep from revealing exactly how much I'd like to roll around on this bed some more. I just assumed you might be a little too . . . tired to start over this morning."

"No, I . . . well, I am . . . tired."

His expression sobered. "Sore?"

Her cheeks felt even hotter. "I suppose. I'll be fine."

"I know, but I just hoped that we hadn't gotten too enthusiastic last night. It was your first time . . . and your second, and—"

"I'm fine," she broke in, her embarrassment growing.

"Okay, but if I can do anything to help, let me know. I may have some salve or something in my emergency kit."

She knelt on their bed and gathered the blanket around her chest. Beads of perspiration formed between her breasts as she tucked in the tail. The feeling of light-headedness returned, but she pushed it aside. She wasn't used to what they'd done yesterday afternoon—and several times last night.

The last thing she wanted was David's help to attend to the call of nature. Plus, the thought of cleansing herself in the cool water of a stream sounded way too heavenly to ignore.

She had trouble getting to her feet. David's hands clasped her upper arms, steadying her as the horizon seemed to dip and move in a very odd way.

"I think you should rest. Let me get you something to eat before you try to—"

"No, I need to . . . I'm just stiff and maybe tired. Don't worry."

"I'll always worry, love. But I'll try not to be too bossy. I know I've got to watch that."

Love. He'd called her *love.* That endearment alone was enough to cause a rush of heat and dizziness.

She smiled at him, forgetting he was naked and standing close. She looked at him quickly, unable to stop herself. And swayed closer.

"You'd better stop that or you're going to be even more stiff and tired. And we might not get back to the cabin before next week."

"We don't have that much food."

"Who needs food? Haven't you heard of living on love?"

"No. Is that what we're doing?" she whispered.

"I think so. Don't you?"

"I . . . maybe." She looked away. The horizon appeared steady once more, the dawn breaking in magnificent colors of pink, purple, and rose.

"Think about it," he said softly. "And don't be gone long. I miss you already."

She smiled and gathered the blanket around her. "I'll be back soon. Maybe you can find something for breakfast."

"I'll do my best. Now go before I change my mind and see whether your body looks pink and alabaster all over in the morning light."

She smiled at his teasing, making her way slowly down the slope toward the trickle of water she heard to her left. Several times she had to stop and steady herself when the world seemed to tilt. Making love certainly had a strange effect on a body, she thought. Did this happen every time, or was it because she'd been a virgin? She wished there was someone to ask, but there wasn't. As open as David was about the subject, she couldn't imagine asking him about womanly subjects.

Yesterday afternoon you didn't have any trouble asking questions, she reminded herself. *You asked, touched, tasted . . .*

She had been bold, but how could she not? David had encouraged her, complimented her, when she'd touched his smooth chest, explored his body, kissed his tight skin. All the things she'd craved to do since the first time she'd seen him standing near the hearth.

She shook the thoughts from her head. She needed a cool drink of water for her tight throat, then she could relieve herself and wash up. They needed to get back to the cabin, if for no other reason than to tell Charlie he was right about her feelings for David.

She crouched beside the tiny, fast-running stream and took several gulps of water from her cupped hands. The cool water trickled down her chin, but it felt so good that she splashed more on her face. She shouldn't be so hot. Not away from David, away from the confines of the shelter.

She stumbled to her feet and into the cover of the firs. In a moment, she made her way back to the stream. More water. That's what she needed.

As she stood looking down at the silvery water, her vision blurred. The world was moving again, swaying away from her. Why? What was happening? She seemed to be tangled in the blanket, so she let it slip away. Better. Yes, she was better now.

The last thing she felt before falling to the rocky

ground was the cool morning air against her hot, hot skin.

She should have been back by now, David thought as he built up the embers of the fire from last night. He was going to surprise her with a cup of coffee, courtesy of the freeze-dried packets from the plane, but breakfast would wait until he was sure she was well. She'd said that she was okay, but she had seemed unusually flushed and unbalanced after standing up.

He wanted to attribute her behavior and appearance to an afternoon and night spent exploring each other's bodies, but instinct told him that wasn't the only cause. And he didn't think she was upset, despite the fact that intimacy was new to her. She seemed shy, but charmingly so. So that left some kind of illness as the cause of her hot skin and dizziness.

Damn, if they were in his time, he'd just run her by the doctor's office. But what was he to do here, with only the emergency first-aid kit from the plane? He could set a broken arm or apply a tourniquet, but he wasn't trained to diagnose infections or allergies or whatever might be bothering Analisa.

Hell, when Jamie's fever had risen to 101 degrees last New Year's Eve, he'd rushed her to the emergency room because Holly was out of town. He could never remember whether 101 was dangerous, or what the other signs of serious illness were, or if antibiotics were effective against the flu or a cold.

He should have paid more attention, he thought as he slid down the rock-strewn hillside at an angle, toward the little stream.

"Analisa!" He called her name when he didn't see her bathing or standing nearby. Had she wandered off into the woods? She'd better not have done anything reckless. The fright she'd given him yesterday at the homestead of those felonious Scandinavians was enough to last a lifetime.

"Analisa!" he called again, looking into the thick trees. Where could she be?

He nearly stumbled over her, catching himself at the last minute and throwing himself to the ground. She lay, naked and unconscious, at an awkward angle between mossy rocks and sandy dirt, her arm stretched out into the clumpy grass. The blanket that she'd so carefully arranged around her breasts was half beneath her, half over her, as though it had come undone.

Or someone had stripped it from her. God, no. Surely not so quickly.

He ran his hands over her arms, her ribs, then her neck and scalp. Other than a scrape where she'd hit her head against a rock, probably when she fell, there were no signs of injury. She was burning up with fever, though. Two round pink spots stained her cheeks; her chest echoed the color.

Was this measles, an infection, the flu? "Analisa, sweetheart, wake up. I have to ask you something."

His answer was a weak moan and an attempt to move her head.

"That's it, love. Listen to me. I need to know what's wrong with you. Can you tell me?"

She looked as though she wanted to speak, but her lips made what Jamie would describe as baby bird motions, and only a whimper of sound came out.

He placed his hand on her forehead, trying to judge the level of fever. Was it high enough to cause delusions, unconsciousness? God, where was that great instant thermometer Holly had given him after the last time he'd gone ballistic over fever? *Home,* he answered himself, in the medicine cabinet. Not in 1886 Wyoming territory.

"Analisa, baby, wake up," he said, hearing an edge of panic in his voice. "Tell me what's wrong. I don't know what to do."

"Hot," she muttered. "Too hot."

"I know, love, I know. You're burning up with fever." What to do? *Cool her,* his instincts said. He remembered an episode of some TV show where they'd cooled the patient with ice.

All he had was an icy stream.

He scooped Analisa gently into his arms, then staggered to his feet, nearly dropping her as he hurried across the uneven ground toward the water. He found a spot where he could place her mostly in the stream and lean her back against the rocks.

As soon as her legs and bottom touched the cold water, she flinched in protest, thrashing her head and moaning. Was it too cold? He had no idea but kept thinking of the patient with the ice cubes. So he lowered her naked body into the shallow depression, scooping and splashing the frigid water over her shoulders and chest.

She quit fighting him suddenly, going limp against his arm. He used the opportunity to bathe her cheeks and forehead, getting her hair wet but not caring at this point whether she ended up with a snarled mess. All he cared about was getting her well.

She grabbed his shirtfront, her eyes open and staring.

"Analisa?"

"Don't let them get me," she demanded. "They're after me."

"No they aren't, love. No one is after you. No one is going to harm you," he said steadily, softly.

"Bears!"

"Bears are after you?" Had she built that fantasy in her mind, or had she really seen a bear in the trees?

Damn, he should have stayed with her. He should have insisted she stay safe.

She never answered him, slipping again into unconsciousness.

His arm felt frozen; he didn't know if he'd be able to lift her from the stream if he stayed in there any longer. With great effort, he pulled her from the water and close to his trembling body.

"Hang in there," he whispered against her hair. He couldn't get her back to 1997 right now, but it was possible he could find something to help in the medical kit. And to do that, he needed to get her back to the cabin.

Charlie would help care for her. He might even know some home remedies that would help. He must know more than a pilot from the next century.

"Babies," she muttered against his shirt.

"You want babies? We'll have them—as many as you want. Just keep fighting."

"Babies . . . wagon babies."

Wagon babies? What the hell were wagon babies? "What is it, love? Can you tell me more about these wagon babies.?"

She lapsed into unconsciousness again, her head resting against his shoulder, soaking his shirt. He didn't care. All he knew was that he had to get her back to the cabin. Back to her home.

He lay her on the blankets, then kicked out the fire, covered it with sand, and stuffed the rest of their belongings into the saddlebags. He scooped the trash—four used foil packets and as many spent condoms—and buried it in the dirt. For good measure, he placed a rock over it.

Hopefully, latex and foil would degrade in a hundred years or so. If not, he prayed whoever found the evidence of time travel didn't know what he'd discovered.

The horses hadn't wandered far, just a little way into the sunlit meadow for better grass. He slipped Tommelise's bridle over her head, fighting the nervous animal every step of the way. It was as though she knew something was wrong, but then, David realized, he was sending all kinds of signals out to alert the mare. His own gelding, on the other hand, stood calmly and allowed himself to be bridled without a fuss.

He made quick work of the hobbles, then led the animals closer to the rock overhang. They didn't like the smoke in the air, but he tugged harder and talked to them in as calm a tone as he could muster.

After throwing the packs over his gelding's back, he carried Analisa toward her mare. Tommelise shied away, rolling her eyes at Analisa's prone, lifeless form.

"Shh, girl. It's okay. We've got to get her home."

The mare would have none of it. Frustrated, David lay Analisa back down, suddenly realizing that she was still naked. With a curse, he pulled out her drawers, pants, and shirt, and dressed her quickly.

She awoke as he slipped the socks on her feet, instantly fighting him. "Don't let them get close," she begged him. "They're coming."

"The wagon babies?" he asked distractedly.

"Bears!" she said again.

"No bears, honey, no bears." He stroked her hair off her hot forehead, gathered the blankets, and carried her toward the horses. She was quiet while he talked, so he commented on the trees, the rocks, the sky. What did it matter, when Analisa was so ill that she didn't even know what he was saying?

Tommelise threatened to break her reins, arching her thick, gray neck and rolling her eyes as David tried to approach. She wasn't going to let both of them ride her.

271

"Okay, I get the picture," he muttered.

With a curse, he lay Analisa down in the grass, then transferred all the pack materials back to Tommelise. To hell with a saddle, to hell with riding the stronger horse. All he needed was a mount; the cabin was four or five miles from the ferry, and they were maybe five miles from Menor's. He'd have Analisa tucked into her own bed by lunchtime.

He guided the steady little roan beside a flat-topped boulder, then eased onto the horse's back with Analisa cradled against his chest. Picking up the reins, he urged the gelding close to Tommelise and snagged her reins too. Then they were off, slow and steady, his heart pounding much faster than their pace.

He didn't care. All he wanted was to find out what was wrong with Analisa—and make her better.

She stirred in his arms and began to mutter about bears. Big bears. Mean bears. He did what he would have done if this were Jamie, restless in his arms; he told her a story.

"Once upon a time there were three bears: Momma Bear, Poppa Bear, and Baby Bear. And they lived in a nice little house in the woods. One day Momma Bear fixed porridge, but it was too hot. . . ."

And so they went, slowly toward the only medical help around for hundreds of miles. Unfortunately, the emergency kit was designed for injuries, not illness. Too bad there wasn't a manual for survival in another time, another place, where medical help wasn't a phone call or ambulance ride away.

David smoothed the golden hair back from Analisa's forehead, alarmed at her high fever and lifeless state. Dammit, he needed a doctor! "I'll do my best," he whispered, placing his lips against her hot, dry skin.

He looked toward the river, where the ferry awaited.

And his throat clenched tight when he thought of how little he knew, and how much he cared.

"Charlie!" David yelled as he pulled the gelding to a halt near the cabin door. He dropped Tommelise's reins, not caring at the moment if she wandered off or not. All he could think of was getting Analisa into her bed, then lowering her fever.

"Charlie!"

The old mountain man shuffled quickly out of the barn, wiping his hands on a tattered bandanna. The two ducks followed, the bigger one quacking and nipping at his pants' leg. "What's the ruckus?" he asked gruffly before looking up and catching sight of Analisa lying limply in David's arms.

"She's sick—really sick."

Charlie held the roan's head as David carefully dismounted. "I'll need some cool water and cloths. She's burning up with fever. I don't know what's wrong. She was fine yesterday."

His throat tightened as he remembered how very fine she'd been as they'd taken shelter from the rain. He'd always known that she possessed a loving, generous heart, but she'd shown him a depth of passion that had taken his breath away. They'd loved the night away, and then she'd become so ill, so fast.

He pushed through the door, Charlie right behind him. Across the room, he saw a streak of red fur head for the firewood stack. Outside, the now familiar sounds of Analisa's barnyard greeted him, but he felt no joy at such a homecoming. Not when she was sick.

Was getting wet, then hot, enough to bring on such an illness? He knew enough to realize that she had to have been exposed to some sort of bacteria or virus to get sick, but he also knew that many people claimed that going without a hat, or getting their feet wet, or any number of other exposures, could bring on a cold or the flu.

"Pull back the quilt," he said to Charlie. Carefully, David lowered her to the cool sheets. She seemed to sigh in relief and sink deeper into the mattress.

Where had she picked up the bug? From the two blond jerks? From other settlers? Where had she been before he'd met up with her? If he knew, he could send Charlie to find out what illness had struck them.

The idea that he could also get sick sent a wave of fear through him. He had to stay well to take care of Analisa. He wouldn't even consider another possibility, he decided, clenching his jaw.

"Goldilocks," she murmured, surprising him with the softly spoken word—one he was sure she hadn't heard before.

"You want me to tell you about Goldilocks again?" he asked softly.

Charlie peered over David's shoulder. "Who's this Goldilocks?"

"Just a children's tale," David said, taking Analisa's hand in his. "Just something I told her to keep her quiet on the ride back."

"Hmpf. I'll git the water and them towels."

David stroked her hand and began the tale again, encouraged that she seemed quieter now that they were home.

Home. Funny how the word just seemed to fit. But could he ever really call this home when he had left Jamie and Holly back in 1997? He didn't know. He just prayed that Analisa would be better soon, so they could both go to his real home, where he didn't feel so damned helpless.

Chapter Eighteen

After he bathed Analisa in the cool cloths, she seemed to sleep peacefully. This was a good time to get his supplies—everything he could carry with him from the plane—anything that might make her more comfortable or help her recover.

"I'm going to my . . . I'm going up to the meadow," he told Charlie, who was in the kitchen preparing some broth. Chicken broth, if the trail of white feathers was any indication. Analisa's little flock was missing one member.

"Goin' to the meadow? Have ya lost yer ever-lovin' mind? This ain't no time to be gallivantin' 'round the countryside," Charlie advised, brandishing a spoon. "Yer gal is sicker 'n a dog!"

"I have some supplies up there that might help Analisa," David said, realizing that what he brought back would look awfully strange to a man born in the mid-1800s. "I don't have time to explain everything right

275

now, Charlie, but I promise we'll talk as soon as she's better.''

"Go on with ya, then. I'll take care of the gal. She's likely got ague, 'cept I ain't seen it around these parts lately. Or she coulda come down with miasma iffen she was around that marsh.''

Ague? Miasma? What did that mean in twentieth-century medical terms? "I don't know those conditions. Are they serious? Do you know how to treat them?''

"Don't know the ague?'' Charlie shook his head. "Iffen we had some quinine, that might help. Maybe some laudanum. She might have a bottle of that 'round the cabin.''

"Laudanum—isn't that made out of morphine or opium or something?'' David wondered aloud. "I don't see how that's going to help.''

"Don't know what's in it, jus' know that folks use it some.''

Great. Not even Charlie was well-versed in nine-teenth-century healing. "Okay, just stay with her. I'll take her mare and be back soon.''

"I put the animals up. Gave that little roan some grain. He was plum tuckered out.''

"I'm not surprised. He carried us both from the butte across the river to the cabin. I'm lucky I found him.''

"Yep. Well, git to ridin'. I'll have this here broth ready when Annie wakes up. I'll take good care of her.''

"Thanks, Charlie.'' David turned, ignoring his own hunger. How long had it been since he'd eaten? A day? They'd barely taken time to snack last night, and only then to keep up their strength so they could make love again.

God, he'd taken poor care of her.

He saddled Tommelise over her objections. He wasn't in any mood to take lip from a horse—especially one who'd made his life difficult. As soon as they cleared the yard, he put his heels to her and galloped all the way to the plane.

He loaded up the medical kit, a few magazines he'd found in a bin, along with a woman's cosmetic bag that had been left on board during a recent flight. And the rest of the emergency supplies. There was so little, yet it would have to be enough.

He raced down the hill, each of Tommelise's strides bringing him closer to the woman he loved.

He tensed in the saddle, slowing the mare until he realized he'd tightened his grip on the reins. Yes, he could finally admit it. He loved her. The knowledge rocked him, yet eased inside his soul until he couldn't wait to whisper the words in her ear. *I love you, Analisa,* he repeated over and over in his mind. He urged the mare into a mile-eating rhythm again.

Love you, love you, love you, he silently chanted in time to the strong, steady hoofbeats, all the way home.

David forced aspirin past Analisa's lips, coaxed her to swallow the unfamiliar tablets with promises of sweet tea, then spoon-fed Charlie's broth to her long into the night. He told her stories— all he could remember— when he could barely talk himself. She developed a cough, a dry raspy one that bothered him more than he wanted to admit.

He remembered that she'd told him that her mother had died after they moved out here from a lung fever. Is that what Analisa had? God, what was he supposed to do about infection? The only antibiotic he had in the medical kit was topical, not oral.

When she slept he lay beside her and dozed, only to awaken when she began to murmur about wagons and babies and big yellow bears.

He had a suspicion the bears were really the Olafson brothers, and that she'd made them bears in her fever dreams because they'd frightened her—and because they'd acted like the lowest form of animal. He had a strong urge to ride back to their cabin and inflict a little more damage. But he wouldn't. Analisa was too ill to leave.

He lay beside her now, exhausted but worried that her fever, although it seemed somewhat lower, showed no signs of breaking. Her skin was hot and dry to the touch. He bathed her with cool water, pushing aside the nightgown he'd dressed her in after coming back from the plane. When she coughed, he tried to soothe her with a lemony sports drink mix he'd found in the emergency kit.

"David?" she said suddenly, her voice weak.

"Yes, love. I'm here." He smoothed his hand across her brow and prayed that she was coming out of her nearly unconscious state.

"I'm sorry," she said, her eyes still closed. "You need to go home now."

"I'm not going anywhere. Not yet. And not without you. Don't you remember that we decided to be together?" he reminded her gently. "I'm not leaving you."

"Go home," she repeated.

"Not until you're well," he said softly, smiling at her insistence. "When you're feeling better, we'll find the next rainbow and fly off together. We'll live happily ever after—you and me and Jamie—just like in the fairy tales."

"I tried," she said weakly.

"Tried what, sweetheart?"

"Tried to find a husband."

"A what? Why did you try to find a husband?" Had

he heard her right? Was she hallucinating again?

Her head drifted to one side and she began to breath evenly.

No, now is not the time to sleep, he wanted to shout. But she needed to rest more than he needed to know why in the hell she was talking about husbands.

"How's she doin'?" Charlie whispered from the open doorway.

David pushed himself off the bed carefully, then joined the older man. "She seemed to be aware for just a minute, but then she said something odd and drifted back to sleep again."

"Ya need more broth?"

"No, not now. She's taken quite a bit. I worry that I don't have any cough syrup or something to soothe her throat."

"I kin fix her up some syrup," Charlie offered.

"Really? Out of what? None of the laudanum. That stuff is dangerous."

"Naw, jus' a little honey and whiskey. I gots some whiskey I keep fer the gripe."

"Gripe?"

"That's right," the older man said with a nod. "I'll be fixin' the syrup up."

"You should get some sleep," David said, worried that Analisa's illness might be hard on Charlie too.

"Don't need too much sleep. Plenty of time to rest in the winter."

"Really?"

"Yep. I reckon I'll be stayin' on at the cabin, iffen Annie still wants the company." Charlie squinted up at him. "She said you'd be leavin'."

"I'm going to take her with me."

"She said she couldn't be goin' with ya."

"She changed her mind."

"Hmpf." Charlie turned and walked out of the bedroom, toward the kitchen. He stopped before he'd gone very many steps. "That's some odd-lookin' gear ya brung back."

"I know. I'll explain it to you later."

The older man nodded, then continued to the kitchen.

David returned to the bed and stared down at Analisa. What was going on inside her head right now? What dreams entertained her, plagued her? He'd thought he knew her well, after yesterday.

He ran a hand through his hair. That wasn't yesterday; it was the day before. He was losing track of time. He only hoped he wasn't running out of it.

Analisa moaned and turned her head from side to side. He sat beside her, lifting her hand from the sheet and stroking the back with his thumb. "Tell me about husbands, love. Tell me what you meant."

She remained silent, but then, he hadn't expected her to answer. In a moment, Charlie returned with a batch of homemade cough syrup.

"She went back to sleep," David explained. "Just put it on the table and I'll give her some later."

He heard the sound of the bottle being placed on the wooden surface, but Charlie didn't leave. "One year she found a half-growed fox with a bullet in its hind-end. She brung it back here, fixed it up real good, and then she had this here half-wild, full-growed fox. That durn thing chased her chickens and ate them eggs, and Annie knew she had to get rid of it, but she worried 'bout the durn thing all the same."

"That sounds like her."

"Yeah, it sure 'nuff does. But ya know what she did? She chased it off. She wouldn't feed it, wouldn't let it stay 'round. It durn near broke her heart. She'd come in, jus' a-cryin', but she done it anyhow."

"Your point?"

"Jus' think 'bout it. Annie-girl'll do the right thing, even if it breaks her heart."

"The right thing is for her to go with me."

"Well, I guess you're right 'bout that. Thing is, she thinks more 'bout the chickens and the fox than she does 'bout her own self."

Charlie walked out of the room, his shuffling footsteps fading away as David frowned and studied Analisa's face. Somehow, this all fit together, but he didn't want to jump to conclusions. He wanted to talk to her about her feelings and her reasoning. Was he just another wild fox? Maybe he'd been —he didn't know. But not after they'd made love. Everything had changed.

Something he'd heard a long time ago echoed in his head, but he didn't want to heed the advice: Making love doesn't solve any problems, but it can create new ones. Is that what they'd done?

No, they hadn't. He loved her. That's why they'd made love.

But she'd never said she loved him. Not in all the hours they'd spent together, not after giving herself, body and soul. Had she held back her heart?

He didn't want to believe that about Analisa. She was sweet and generous, a woman with a great capacity to love. And he believed she loved him. Maybe she didn't realize it yet, maybe she didn't want to admit it, but she did.

He clung to that belief through the remainder of the night.

Analisa knew she wasn't really awake, but she thought she heard voices. Soft, faint voices. Where was she? She moved her fingers to feel a texture. A sheet. Was she home? She didn't know. Where had she been?

She knew she'd been somewhere—maybe with David?

She sighed as an image formed in her mind. David's shoulders in the firelight, his muscles flexing as he . . . what was he doing?

Her whole body felt odd. Had she been this hot before? She thought so. She remembered something else, something that made her frown. Cold water—being naked in cold water. And David. He'd put her in that cold water.

"No," she murmured, "no more cold water." Her throat hurt. Her chest burned. Why did David do that?

"Analisa?"

She tried to open her eyes, but they felt so heavy. That was David's voice, though. "Why?" she said hoarsely.

"Why what, love?"

"Why did you . . . put me . . . in cold water?"

She heard him chuckle and wished she could get her eyes open.

"You remembered that, did you?" He put his hand on her forehead. "I think your fever might be down a little. That's good. You've been very sick. Do you know what's wrong with you? Do you know where you caught this?"

"Caught?"

"Were you around anyone who was sick?"

She tried to think, but she didn't know where she'd been. "Am I home?" she asked.

"Yes, you're home. I carried you here on my horse."

"Why?" She felt more and more confused. Where had they been? She remembered firelight and cold water . . . and David, but was he wearing no clothes?

"It's okay, sweetheart. Let me get you some of Charlie's cough syrup for your throat."

"Charlie's here?"

"Yes. He took care of the animals while you were gone."

"I was gone," she said, frowning. She still didn't know where.

"It's okay. Don't think about it right now. I'm just so glad that you're awake."

"I feel so tired. And hot."

"I know. That's because of the fever."

He put his arm around her and lifted her shoulders from the bed. She felt the press of metal on her lower lip and opened her mouth. The taste of whiskey and honey rolled across her tongue and she swallowed. Memories of her mother, giving her the same medicine for a sore throat, rushed through her, bringing tears to her eyes.

"Momma," she whispered.

"Oh, sweetheart," she heard David whisper against her hair. "I'm here with you. I'll take care of you."

She sniffed back the tears and turned toward David. Something else was bothering her, but she couldn't remember what. As the heady whiskey seeped into her blood, she decided that it could wait. She was too tired to think. . . .

After Analisa went to sleep, David walked into the main room. To his surprise, sunlight streamed through the window. He hadn't realized—he'd thought it was still night. But then, day and night had run together for the last forty-eight hours or so.

He stopped, sniffing. He must be as out of it as Analisa, because he could swear he smelled coffee. Rich, strong coffee.

Charlie walked out of the kitchen. "Got ya this. Annie said ya had a hankerin' for a cup."

"You have no idea," he said, cradling the heavy, hot

mug in his hands. He inhaled deeply, exhaustion evaporating like the fragrant steam. "Charlie, I may kiss you."

"I wouldn't try it, iffen I were you," the older man said with a chuckle.

David took a sip and nearly scalded his tongue. Well, it wasn't French Roast, but it was coffee. He blew on the top and glanced at Charlie, who carried his own mug. Now was probably a good time to explain things to him.

"Annie doin' better?"

"I think. We actually talked. She made sense, for a few sentences, at least." David shrugged. "Her fever is down a little."

Charlie nodded. "Ya wanna tell me 'bout this stuff ya brung down the hill?"

"Sure." David took another sip of his coffee. "Actually, it might be easier to show you." He reached for the saddlebag and the medical kit, which lay out on the table where he'd left it yesterday. "Did you look inside the saddlebag?" he asked Charlie.

"Nope. Ain't my nature to go through a body's belongin's."

"I understand. I just couldn't remember if I left it out or not. I haven't been thinking too clearly myself."

Charlie nodded. "Whatcha got in there?"

"Things from my home." He pulled out two magazines; one featured a photo of a smiling Julia Roberts, while the other was one of his subscriptions, a monthly aviation journal. "This will give you an idea where I really come from."

"Annie tol' me it weren't Texas."

"No, it's not." He handed the glossy, full-color magazines to Charlie, certain there was nothing remotely similar to this in 1886.

"I'll be damned," Charlie said slowly, his voice reflecting the shock that showed on his lined face. "How'd they do this?" He touched the slick surface with reverence.

"With a camera, a printing press, a computer."

"A what?"

"A computer. It's something that hasn't been invented yet. I think the first one was made in around the middle of the twentieth century."

"The . . . what are ya talkin' 'bout?"

"Look at the date on the magazines," David instructed, pointing to the upper corner. "I know this sounds odd, Charlie, but believe me, it's the truth: I'm from the future."

"The future? But . . . how did ya git here?"

"I'm not really sure, but I'll tell you what happened." David thumbed through the aviation journal until he found a photo and article on a Cessna similar to his plane. "I fly airplanes. See this one? I have one almost like it, hidden in the meadow. That's where I landed."

Charlie studied the magazine with interest. His eyes widened as he saw photos of a plane in flight, with the terrain below clearly visible. "You fly in the sky? Like some big bird?"

David chuckled. "Actually, the plane flies. I just control it. But that's what Analisa thought my plane was. She called it a big white bird."

Charlie shook his head. "If that don't beat all. Who thought of such a thing—flyin' in the sky?"

"The Wright Brothers, in Kitty Hawk, North Carolina, on December 17th, 1903. It's an important date for pilots."

"Pilots?"

"That's what people who fly airplanes are called."

Charlie shook his head again. "In 1903, ya say? Damn, that's only . . . how many years away is that?"

"Seventeen," David answered, smiling at the older man's bewildered look. "That's not very long, is it?"

"Naw. Damn, I might just live to see that happen."

"You sure might."

"So what year would you be from?" Charlie peered at the magazine cover again.

"When I flew up into the sky, it was the summer of 1997."

"Damn! 1997. That's more 'an a hundred years from now!"

"I know. Believe me, no one was more surprised than I to learn what had happened."

He got a refill of coffee for both of them, then told Charlie the story of Jamie and her belief in rainbows. He took a break to check on Analisa, and when he came back, Charlie was looking through the women's magazine.

"This what the ladies look like in yer time?"

David chuckled. "Well, not all of them. But a few in Hollywood and New York. They're called models, and they're paid large sums of money to look beautiful."

"Damn," Charlie said again. That must be his new favorite word. Of course, if someone landed at Jackson Airport and claimed to be from the year 2097, he'd be a little speechless himself.

While Charlie was occupied looking at "girlie" pictures and reading articles and ads on nineties relationships, AIDS, feminine hygiene, and diet fads, David bathed Analisa again. At least she was resting peacefully now. Good. The best thing for her was sleep, he imagined, as long as her temperature was going down and she was breathing normally.

As he ran the cloth over her chest and stomach, he remembered their one and only night together—so far. When she was well again . . . There would be plenty of nights in the future, plenty of opportunities to bathe her in his big whirlpool tub, with a soft sponge and lots of fragrant bubbles.

He'd better not think of that at the moment. First, he needed to get her over this illness.

He supposed it was some kind of virus. He'd thought about it, and remembered that flu was caused by a virus, and there were all kinds of flu. Maybe that's what she had. Now, if he could just keep her from getting a complication like pneumonia or strep throat.

She opened her eyes then, looked at him directly, and said, "You're not going to put me in the cold water again, are you?"

He grinned, resting the palm of his hand on her cheek. "No, love. I won't dunk you in the cold water any more."

"Am I better?"

"Yes, I think you are. Do you feel better?"

She frowned. "I don't know. Maybe. I don't feel so hot."

"You're not. Your fever is coming down."

She blinked, then looked around the room. "It's morning?"

"Nearly noon. You've been ill for two and a half days."

"I don't remember much, but I feel like I've been lying in this bed for weeks. I'm so sore and tired." She looked around, then down at her body. And stiffened. "What are you doing?" she shrieked.

"Bathing you," he said calmly, pulling the edges of her nightgown closed.

"David!"

Charlie burst into the room, glossy magazine in hand. "What's the ruckus? Annie, are you feelin' okay?"

"Charlie! Yes, I'm much better. I was just . . . surprised." She gave David an incredulous look that said *I don't know what you thought you were doing, but I'm terribly offended.*

"That's odd. I wasn't surprised at all," David replied, so relieved that she was awake and coherent that he wanted to raise her off the bed and kiss her senseless.

"Not surprised! What do you mean?"

He shrugged. "I suppose you don't remember the little trip we took," he suggested softly. "And the rain. And the rock overhang. Anything sound familiar yet?"

Her eyes widened, her mouth formed a perfect *o,* and her cheeks became flushed all over again.

Chapter Nineteen

Analisa felt well enough to take the evening meal with Charlie and David. Chicken stew, with Charlie's chewy-as-leather biscuits. She'd tried to show him once how to blend in lard to make them flaky, but he swore he liked them this way.

David bit into one, wrestled with it, and began to chew.

"Sticks to yer ribs," Charlie said, brandishing a spoon.

David raised his eyebrows and nodded.

Analisa pretended to yawn so she could stifle a giggle behind her hand. She felt absolutely, sincerely happy for the first time in longer than she could remember. Sitting at her small table, watching the man she loved eat a meal cooked by the second-dearest man alive . . . well, she just couldn't think of anything better.

David finally swallowed the doughy mass. "Are you tired?"

"No, I'm fine. Getting out of the bed feels good. I feel like I've been lying down forever." As soon as she finished speaking, an image of lying on a blanket in their makeshift cave, David naked above her, his shoulders gleaming with firelight as he moved within her, flashed in her mind. Her cheeks flamed.

David smiled at her across the table, his eyes dark and heavy-lidded.

"Annie, yer lookin' a mite flushed. Ya better get some vittles in yer stomach 'fore ya get sick again."

She ignored Charlie's observation as she returned David's smile and swallowed a bubble of joy. She wanted to shout that she was in love, that she didn't need food or sleep or anything but David, but she didn't. Charlie probably wouldn't appreciate her outburst, or understand the overwhelming feelings that fed her soul.

"Charlie's right. You need to get your strength back up," David said softly. "We have a lot to do."

She breathed deeply, knowing what she wanted to do. And he was right; she needed her strength for that kind of activity. *Making love.* How wonderful those words sounded. How marvelous the experience.

Taking a bite of stew, she leaned toward the table, unable to take her eyes off David. She even loved his name. So strong, so simple.

"I ain't never seen such a lovesick look on the face of any critter since Sue went and got herself in-fat-u-ated with Possum Pete's big ol' mule," Charlie said in mock disgust. He shook his head. "I done tol' ya both what was goin' on, but did ya believe me? Nooo."

"You were right," Analisa said softly, breaking her gaze from David's heated eyes.

"Yeah, you were right," David said, amusement in his voice.

"So, the two of ya goin' to fly up in the sky in that

airplane of yers?'' Charlie asked, wagging a biscuit in David's direction.

"As soon as we find the right rainbow."

"We'll need to get the homestead settled for winter," Analisa added. When she'd said she wanted to go with David, she hadn't thought of all the things they'd have to accomplish first. If Charlie was going to stay here, he needed food for the animals and himself, firewood stacked to the roof beside the house, and repairs to the chinking and the barn.

"No problem. I'll work on that while you get to feeling better."

"Charlie, are you sure you want to stay?"

"Yep. Ain't no reason to trap these days. Folks ain't buyin' fur 'round these parts. I s'pect I'll make a tolerable good farmer," he added with a chuckle. "I even hear tell of men comin' in the mountains to hunt. Rich men what need guides. I might jus' give it a try. 'Course, I'd have to get me a helper to take care of yer place, but I'm gonna see about relievin' some of them there rich folks of their money."

"I think you'll be a great farmer or guide," she said, placing her hand over the top of his. "I'm just so glad that you'll be able to take care of the animals when I leave. I don't know what I'd do if you weren't here."

"One thing we're not doing is taking your zoo with us," David warned, his tone teasing. "I'd never be able to get up to air speed with those hay-burners on board, even if I could get them through the door."

"I can just imagine trying to lead Tommelise into ..." She blinked, suddenly realizing what going with David would mean. Leaving Charlie and everything behind. Tommelise, Daisy and her new twins, Rose, Sweet Sue, Little Red, and all the rest. Never to see them again. When she arrived in David's time, Charlie would be long gone—dead for many, many years. And Tommelise, who had been the most steady friend anyone could ask for, would be lost to her forever.

Tears filled her eyes as sorrow flooded her heart. She pushed back from the table, her hands shaking and legs weak. "I need to . . . please excuse me."

"Analisa!"

She heard the scrape of David's chair on the floor as she hurried toward her bedroom. She walked faster, needing to be alone . . . to think about the decision she'd made.

But she was so weak. She watched the doorway to her bedroom ripple like the echo of a pebble across the surface of a pond. Before her legs buckled, David's arms closed around her, scooping her off the floor and against his chest. Her head spun as he continued into her bedroom and deposited her gently on the bed.

"What's wrong?" he asked, easing his hands from beneath her. "Did you feel sick? Dizzy?"

She shook her head, but that made the room spin even more. "Yes, dizzy. I . . . I don't feel like talking right now."

He placed his palm on her forehead. "You don't feel very feverish."

"I'm fine," she said, closing her eyes. "I just need to rest."

"Can I get you some water? Some of Charlie's cough syrup?"

"No!" She immediately regretted her outburst. David had taken care of her for days; he was only trying to make her more comfortable. "I'm sorry," she said, looking up at his concerned face. "I'd like to rest now. Maybe we could talk later, or in the morning."

He smoothed her hair from her face. "Okay. Get

some rest. I'm just worried that you might have a relapse."

"A what?"

"A relapse. That means you might get sick again."

"Oh. No, I think I'll be fine."

"You didn't eat much."

"David, please," she entreated. Would the man always talk so much when she needed to be alone?

"Okay, I'm leaving." He removed her slippers, then pulled the sheet up to her chest. "Call me if you need anything."

"I will. Thank you."

She listened to his footsteps as he walked back into the kitchen. The indistinct sound of Charlie's voice, followed by David's answering murmur, seeped through the cabin. An ache that had nothing to do with her lingering illness filled her with sadness. Could she leave this cabin, knowing every inch so well, seeing her parents and brother in each room? When she saw the table by the hearth, she thought of Papa filling the bowl of his pipe, then settling in his chair. She could recall sitting cross-legged on the floor on the other side of the wide fireplace, working on an embroidery sampler while her mother read the story of Tommelise, the tiny flower girl, from *Fairy Tales* by Hans Christian Andersen, the book with beautiful color illustrations they'd bought before leaving Ohio.

Shortly afterwards, Papa had traded for a gangly gray filly, and Analisa had been allowed to name her. From that day forward, she'd never been separated from her horse, who was still with her when everyone else was gone. Tommelise had listened to her complain about Jurgen's childhood pranks, cry for her mother, and agonize over her sudden burst of growth at age sixteen.

If Jurgen had had his way, he and Papa would have

taken Tommelise into the mountains as a pack animal, but Analisa's protests had prevailed and the two men had gone off alone—to their deaths.

She turned her head toward the wall, covering her mouth with her fist. She would not let David or Charlie know how much she dreaded leaving all she knew behind. As much as she wanted to be with David, she wouldn't have the rest of the things she loved around her. And would Charlie be able to care for them, year after year? He wasn't a young man. The idea of Tommelise or any of the animals suffering, starving, made her ill.

She rolled to her side, clutching her stomach. The few bites of stew felt as leaden as Charlie's biscuits.

Closing her eyes, she tried to blank her mind, to shut out the images of her animals with no one to care for them during the long, cold winter. A tear rolled down her cheek, but she didn't wipe it away. All she could do was curl up and wonder if she'd be able to leave the place she'd lived for so long and go somewhere unknown, with nothing but the clothes she wore and her love for David.

If only she felt better, perhaps she could understand how the idea had seemed so right just minutes ago and so very wrong now. But her head hurt and her stomach churned. All she wanted to do was lie alone in the dark and shut out the demands of the world—her very real and confusing world.

David spent the morning chopping wood, letting Charlie fix Analisa a breakfast of porridge with cream and honey. Invalid's food, the older man had called it, swearing he knew what she needed. In truth, David was glad to let Charlie take over the duties for a while. Analisa had been quiet and uncommunicative this morning, and he suspected she'd cried last night after he'd left her alone.

What was bothering her? She'd looked so happy when they'd sat down to eat. Smiling, blushing, flirting with her eyes. He'd half-expected to feel one of her feet trace a path up his leg under the table—a particular fantasy of his where she was concerned. But then they'd started talking about the fact that she was leaving with him as soon as they could, and she'd seemed so glad that Charlie was there. Her abrupt change of demeanor, then her rush from the table, was as unexpected as her illness.

With a sigh, he rested his chin on the ax handle and tried to remember the last thing he'd said—some joke, he believed. But he couldn't remember the exact words, just a jest about all her animals and how they wouldn't fit in the plane.

Surely that hadn't upset her. She *knew* the animals wouldn't fit in the plane. He felt certain she'd considered that when she'd committed to him in the cave. Their conversation at the table had reinforced the fact that she was going with him. After all, she'd asked Charlie to stay on, she'd talked about leaving, and she was well aware that the plane was necessary to transport them into the future.

He positioned another piece, then swung the ax again, splitting a length of pine into firewood. Charlie needed a bunch. David planned to put up enough kindling and logs to last the old man through the winter. Maybe next summer, Charlie could hire one of the young men in the area to clear trees and limbs felled by ice and wind during the winter and cut them into firewood. With the chickens for eggs and the cow for milk and butter, there should be plenty to sell or trade.

David wiped his face and neck on the shirt, then flicked wood chips off his chest, where they clung to his sweaty skin. He remembered how Analisa had loved to touch his chest, running her fingers lightly over him, caressing him with her palms, clinging to him with her short nails.

Thank God she didn't sport those long, lethal red ones. With her strength and enthusiasm, she could do a lot of damage, he thought with a chuckle.

But now was not the time to be thinking about their one night together, he knew as he heaved the ax again. As much as he wanted to walk into her bedroom and take her into his arms—if only to comfort and support her—he knew she wasn't ready for anything like the passion they'd shared. And he knew from experience how quickly an innocent touch or gesture could turn to desire by either or both of them.

Sex was *not* going to be a problem area for them, he theorized as he took another swing at a large chunk of seasoned pine.

Remembering how compatible they'd been when they made love led him to think about how long he planned to be with Analisa. The only answer that came to mind was *forever*. Destiny had intervened, sending him to the one woman who needed him as much as he needed her. As soon as she felt a little stronger, he had to confirm that she wanted the same thing—which he was certain she'd expressed the other night at the butte.

He looked up into the wide, blue sky, the feathery white clouds following the jet stream east. In the years since Catherine's death, he doubted that he'd spent much time looking at clouds or skies for any reason other than to evaluate weather patterns. He'd believed in physics, not psychics.

So how he'd come to the past, to land in Analisa's meadow at the exact time she was there cutting hay, he didn't know. Through some miraculous means, Jamie had known there was magic waiting for him beyond that rainbow. "I think it's the one, Daddy," she'd announced with the exuberance only children possessed. She'd been right.

He placed another cross-section of pine on the chopping block. The exercise felt good; the sun was as welcome as the clean, warm air sweeping up the slopes from the south. After lunch, he'd see if Analisa was up to a talk. This was as good a time as any to discuss a future that included Jamie, home, hearth, and family—and a wedding with all the trimmings.

Analisa dressed, for the first time since her illness, for the noon meal. Charlie had cooked again, this time beans and salt pork. The aroma wafted through the cabin, along with the distinctive smell of scorched biscuits. Where had Charlie gotten salt pork?

She had a strong urge to go outside and make sure her sow still safely munched on winter turnips and meal scraps.

Her muscles ached as she pulled stockings up nearly to her knees. The illness had left her tired and sore, but at least she no longer felt feverish. The heaviness in her chest had lifted somewhat, and she wasn't coughing as much today. Hopefully, she'd have her strength back soon. There were so many chores to be done during the short summer months.

She wondered what types of chores were necessary in David's time.

With a sigh, she slid slowly to her feet; she'd learned to get her balance before taking off across the floor. She'd practically fallen on her face late last night, searching for the chamber pot Charlie had thoughtfully provided. David didn't seem to realize the importance of having that convenience inside the house, although she supposed something similar existed in the future.

She didn't want to think of how he'd attended to her needs for two long days. Although they'd been . . . intimate, he'd no doubt been forced to cross the boundaries of propriety.

To David's credit, he never brought up such embarrassing topics, never teased her about anything that he knew would offend. He was such a caring man . . . sometimes a little too caring.

They hadn't really discussed his need to protect those he loved. Although he'd admitted he probably couldn't have stopped his wife from doing what he considered reckless, he seemed determined to enforce his ideas about riding out alone, trading with neighbors, and saving pregnant goats. While he seemed genuinely outraged, Analisa couldn't figure out what he found objectionable most of the time. And she worried that her life would be a constant struggle for independence against his stifling rules.

She did understand how his wife's death had made him cautious, but she didn't care for the way he'd decided that his mission in life was to protect everyone from illness, injury, or acts of nature.

Or acts of men, she thought, shuddering as the Olafson brothers' behavior reminded her that every now and then David was right.

Charlie was putting plates on the table, looking out of place in the kitchen, but at the same time, wearing an expression she'd never seen before. Pride, perhaps? Was he enjoying his newfound duties of cook and sometimes nursemaid?

"I smelled the beans and salt pork," Analisa said, taking a chair at the table. "I suppose my sow is still enjoying good health?"

"Fit as a fiddle," Charlie said, turning back to the

stove and stirring the enameled pot. "I ain't got no plans to add that overgrown pig to the menu, lessen she get as mean as that drake. I'm a-thinkin' that roast duck would be mighty tasty come the first frost."

"Don't even joke about that. You know he's just showing off for his lady."

"This mornin', he showed off to the tune of pullin' loose the back pocket of my pants when I weren't lookin'," Charlie said gruffly. "Ain't no duck gonna tear up my clothes and live to brag about it to his durn lady-friend."

"He isn't just being mean to you, Charlie. He's like that to everyone."

"He'd best watch his tailfeathers," Charlie said with the dull clang of the wooden spoon against the metal pot. "That's all I've got to say on the subject."

"I'm sure we can work something out. Maybe he needs to be penned all the time," she said with another sigh, adding that to her mental list of things for David to do.

Charlie sat down across from her. "Ya look a bit down, Annie girl. What's eaten at ya?"

She ran her fingers along the rim of the plate. "I'm just worried, Charlie."

" 'Bout what?"

She forced a weak smile. "The idea of leaving you, all my animals, and everything I know so I can fly in David's plane into the future. And I'm not sure what that future will be like. Maybe it's an awful place I wouldn't like. Or maybe there are strange customs that will confuse me." She shrugged, feeling the soreness more now than before. Or perhaps she was tense from worrying. Her emotions had taken a beating since making love to David, getting ill, deciding to go with him, then worrying about her ability to leave her world behind. She'd gone through so much recently that she didn't trust her judgment any longer.

"Ain't nobody knows what's gonna happen to 'em," Charlie advised.

"I know, but I'm afraid David's century will be far different from the kind of life I lead. Maybe as different as Wyoming territory is from our town in Ohio."

"Why, I reckon it is!" Charlie said with a great deal of enthusiasm. "There's strange and wonderful things a-goin' on in David's time."

"Really? How do you know this?" Surely David hadn't told Charlie more than he'd told her.

"Yer man brung me a magazine from his airplane. Well, he brung two of 'em, but the one's got mostly pictures and writin' 'bout flying airplanes up in the sky. I reckon you'd like the other one. It's got pictures of ladies like I never seen afore."

"A magazine? Like *Godey's* or *The Saturday Evening Post*?" They occasionally received a copy of those publications from passing travelers or settlers who had read them many times, cover to cover.

"Better'n either one. This one's got pictures in color—and I don't mean that weak-lookin' paintin' neither." His eyes lit up. "Wait right there, Annie-girl, and I'll fetch the magazine. It's truly amazin', I'll tell you that," he said with a chuckle.

He hurried back in just a moment with the most amazing thing she'd seen—except for David and his plane. Her fingertips traced the shiny image of a woman with a big smile and perfect teeth. She looked so real, every color vivid and perfect. And the writing! So much of it, all over the cover, in bright pink and dark blue, red and a blue-green that was as bright as the pink. When she read the words, she was shocked by the subjects. Sex! They came right out and wrote that word on the cover of a magazine for one and all to see? Other articles seemed to be about food and cooking, and then not eating much of either.

Analisa shook her head. "This is amazing, Charlie."

"David said there're hundreds of these here magazines in the stores. All kinds of people can buy a magazine 'bout anything."

"What else did he say?"

Charlie shrugged. "We had a fair 'mount of time to chew the fat whilst you were sick."

"I'm surprised he told you the truth about where he was from."

"Well, when he brung that stuff from the plane, I knowed something was up. I ain't never seen the like of boxes and packages."

"Have you seen the plane?"

"Nope, but I plan to see it. Can't quite imagine it."

"You should have seen it swoop down from the sky, Charlie. I was so scared because I thought it was a giant bird. First, though, I heard a noise like a thousand angry bees, then a roar like I'd never heard before. When David opened the door and stepped out, I nearly got up on Tommelise and raced away. But I couldn't. I wanted to know what type of man could fly in the sky."

"Yep, I do too," Charlie said with an emphatic nod. "David tol' me about the first time men flew—December 17, 1903, in Kitty Hawk, North Carolina. Annie-girl, I'd give my left arm to be standin' there when those Wright Brothers fly in the air—and me knowin' it was 'bout to happen!"

"That would be exciting, Charlie." North Carolina was thousands of miles away, though, and she didn't think there was any way for him to make the trip.

"It's only seventeen years. Think of it, Annie! Here we are tryin' to get a wagonload of supplies to keep us from starvin' in the winter, and somewhere else, men are tryin' to make a machine that flies in the sky.''

"That is strange, when you put it that way. I always told you that the east was more civilized, though, didn't I? We had lots of conveniences in Ohio that we'll probably never have here.''

"Maybe. Can't never tell." Charlie laughed aloud and slapped his knee. " 'Course ya can! All ya have to do is ask David." He pushed away from the table and went back to stirring his pot of beans.

Analisa sat at the table for a few more moments, then clutched the magazine to her chest and stood. "I think I'm going to get some fresh air, Charlie. I won't be gone long.''

"We'll be eatin' directly," he reminded her.

"I know. I'd just like to feel the sun on my face and look over this amazing magazine.''

She opened the door and walked outside, blinking at the brightness. No wonder David wore those colored glasses to shield his eyes. She saw where he'd been chopping wood, but he wasn't around at the moment. Heading for the fence, she was relieved to see Rose, who trotted toward her with grunted greetings.

"I'm happy to see you too," she said, reaching over the fence and scratching her ears. "Have you missed me? I've been sick, but I'm better now," she explained to the pig.

Thankfully, Louie and Marie didn't notice her, and the chickens seemed quiet as well. She was able to walk away from the cabin without generating a parade.

Wildflowers beckoned just beyond the yard, so she continued her walk. The sun seemed to give her strength, but she reminded herself that her legs could get weak with little warning. She was less sore than she'd been earlier, so she supposed the mild exercise was good for her.

Not far away, a boulder nestled among the wildflowers. That was her goal, one she achieved just as she began to tire. The sun-warmed rock felt good against her bottom and legs, and she settled as comfortably as possible with the magazine. She'd just read an article or two, and look at more of the pictures. She'd hear Charlie when he called her for lunch, although she wasn't particularly hungry.

She opened the magazine and was immediately drawn to the images of smiling, beautiful women. Her hand strayed to her own hair, pulled back in her usual braid, then traced the features of her face. Anyone could see that these women put paint on to enhance their eyes, lips, and cheeks. Was that what David was used to— women with short, curling hair and painted faces? If so, she feared she fell far short of the standards of his time. She'd stand out like a duck among chickens.

She continued turning the pages, reading about the problems of raising children, having relationships with friends, and breaking up with lovers. The more she read, the more strange his time seemed. How was she ever going to fit in there?

A headache pounded between her eyes. She rubbed her forehead, then put the magazine down beside her on the boulder. Would she ever feel good about leaving everything she knew and venturing into a strange future? Was knowing David enough to make her happy in a strange time where she didn't belong?

The agonizing thoughts kept swirling through her head. She wished she felt stronger . . . she wished she knew the right answer.

With a sigh, she curled up on the sun-warmed rock and closed her eyes. Perhaps if she just rested for a moment, this pounding headache would go away so she could think more clearly.

David finished washing in the cold water of the creek, then donned the change of clothes Charlie had washed for him yesterday. The shirt was stiff and wrinkled, but hell, David didn't plan on entering any fashion contests. Jurgen's pants did fit a little better now after one washing by Charlie, who probably boiled them with lye soap.

Beggars can't be choosers, he reminded himself. Grateful that Charlie knew how to do the chores David took for granted, he bundled up the sweaty clothes, soap, and shaving supplies. His stomach growled, reminding him that it was time for lunch. And he hoped to see Analisa feeling better so they could have a talk after the meal. He needed to tell her how much he loved her, and ask her to marry him. He'd been wrong to avoid the subject this far; he should have asked her before they made love.

As he left the gentle roar of the stream behind, he heard Charlie's voice, calling to Analisa. Had she gone out earlier? He must have missed her, or already been washing in the stream.

He picked up his pace, listening to Charlie's tone of voice. Was there a thread of panic? David thought so; he broke into a run.

"What's wrong?" he asked as he rounded the corner of the cabin and stopped in front of Charlie.

"Annie took that magazine ya gave me and went outside fer a spell. Said she weren't goin' far, but she ain't comin' when I call."

David scanned the area. "When was this?"

"Not long ago. I done set the table and finished with my beans since she left."

"Stay here in case she shows up. I'll look for her."

He tossed his clothes, soap, and razor to the ground and strode away, cupping his hands around his mouth and calling, "Analisa!"

No answer. His pulse began to race and he wiped his damp palms against his thighs. *She's fine,* he told himself. *She's only been gone a few minutes.*

But that bear attack had taken mere seconds. Or she could have gotten weak, fallen, and hit her head in the space of a heartbeat.

He cupped his hands and called again. "Analisa!"

Only the distant sounds of chirping birds answered him.

With a feeling of dread eating away like acid in his stomach, he started running.

Chapter Twenty

She wasn't sure how long she'd been sleeping when she heard the sound of her name being called. She rose slowly to a sitting position, her head feeling as though it were stuffed with cotton wool. Why was someone calling her?

She looked around the meadow at the brilliant yellows, reds, and purples of the wildflowers and remembered the magazine she'd been reading. She was just going to glance at it before Charlie prepared the noon meal . . .

"Analisa!"

David's voice, cutting through the peaceful day, brought her fully awake. She'd probably missed lunch, or caused them to delay their meal.

"David?" Her voice came out raspy and hoarse. She carefully stood up, cleared her throat, and tried again. "David!"

She saw him running toward her and waved. Perhaps

they'd have some time together after the meal. She needed to explain why she'd gotten up from the table and wouldn't talk to him the night before.

As he drew closer, though, she noticed the frown lines in the middle of his forehead, above the dark glasses. His mouth was set in an unsmiling slash across his clenched jaw. He did not look as though he were happy to see her, or that he wanted to talk.

"What's wrong?" she asked as soon as he came within earshot.

"What's wrong? I'll tell you what's wrong," he said angrily. "I've been out of my head with worry, thinking you'd been injured or . . . and then I find you standing in the meadow, clearly within hearing distance, and you ask me what's wrong?"

He ended with almost a shout. If his hands hadn't come out to grasp her shoulders, she would have backed away. She wanted to. This wasn't the kind, gentle man who'd cared for her the past few days. Who'd made love to her so sweetly that very special night.

"I was asleep," she explained as calmly as possible. "I didn't know you were looking for me."

"What were you doing out here anyway? You should be home, resting, eating lunch and getting your strength back."

"I needed some fresh air, and besides, I've done little but rest in bed for days. I thought the sun would do me good."

"Well, it doesn't do me good to have a heart attack over your disappearance," he returned, his fingers holding her tighter.

"Let go. You're hurting me," she said, twisting from his grip. "It's not my fault that you assumed something was wrong. All I did was walk outside."

"You were totally insensitive to Charlie and me. He's as worried as I was."

"I doubt that. I can't imagine anyone being as worried—or should I say angry—as you," she shot back, becoming more and more irritated by his attitude. "I fell asleep. That's not a crime—at least not in my day and age!"

"What's that supposed to mean?"

"Just that I can't understand why you act like you do. Why you get angry at me when you reach the wrong conclusion. I can't live like this, David," she said with passion, then softened her tone. "I won't live like this." She walked away from the boulder and rubbed her arms.

"What are you saying?" As she glanced back, he advanced on her like a mountain lion on prey.

She whirled and faced him. "You expect me to give up everything I know and travel with you to the future. But what kind of future? One where I don't know anyone but you? One where you'll constantly be yelling at me when I do something you consider dangerous? No, I can't live that way. And you shouldn't expect me to."

"I'm only angry because I care!"

"You care more about your own fear than you do my happiness, David! That's what you care about. Don't try to put the responsibility for your behavior back on *my* shoulders. *I* simply fell asleep near my house on a beautiful, calm summer day. *You* ran out like a madman, yelling at me for nothing. Nothing, David!"

She turned and walked back toward the cabin, willing herself to stay strong enough to make it when inside she was coming apart. All her newfound happiness vanished in one instant of anger. Not her anger, but his.

She stumbled over an exposed rock but kept on walking, stomping wildflowers beneath her feet, ignoring the beauty of the day and the warmth of the sun. What did those things matter when her chance of happiness lay crushed and bleeding in the dirt?

When she got to the cabin, she ignored Charlie's questions, brushing past him with a rudeness she'd apologize for later. At the moment, she didn't trust herself to speak. She walked into her bedroom and shut the door, sliding home the bolt for the first time since David had arrived in the past.

She'd never truly felt threatened by him until now, because she'd never risked her heart before. She'd risked it—and lost. There would be no future filled with flying machines and wide glass windows. No competition with other women who painted their faces and wore scandalously short skirts and bare arms. No meeting with a motherless little girl who loved fairy tales and rainbows.

No, just the comfort of her animals, her homestead, and Charlie. The quiet days of winter and the busy activity of summer. The years of drought and the times of floods. But this was the life she knew and trusted. She'd been foolish to think there was anything else out there for her, any special man who would come and rescue her from this place.

She no longer wanted to be rescued, she decided with as much bravado as she could muster. Let David fly back to his home and his life; she could never be the kind of woman he wanted, and she didn't care to try.

Besides, she realized, her chin sinking in exhaustion, he hadn't asked her to stay with him forever. He'd never proposed—a commitment she would have expected from any other man. He'd talked of desire and happily-ever-after endings, but he'd never actually asked her to . . . She didn't even want to think the word.

And perhaps he'd say that he'd come across the rainbow for her only because he felt it was his duty to save her. Not because they were truly meant to be together forever.

Maybe his idea of happily-ever-after wasn't the same as hers.

Three loud raps sounded on her door, followed by David's muffled voice. "Analisa, open up."

She shook her head, blinking back tears. "No," she whispered, half expecting him to take the ax to the wood and chop his way through to get what he wanted.

But he didn't. In a moment, all was quiet again. She curled up on the bed, in the darkness, and clutched her stomach. Despite the summer day and the two men who waited just outside, she felt cold and alone. With only a sliver of light coming under the door, her room seemed a prison she could never escape.

But I don't want to escape, she thought as she closed her eyes. The lingering illness and her flight from the meadow had sapped the last of her strength. All she wanted was peace . . . the kind of peace she'd known before David had flown into her life . . . the kind of peace she feared she'd never know again.

He'd blown it. As the night sounds swirled around him and the dampness of the earth seeped through the seat of his pants, he took another sip of beer and faced the fact that he'd stepped over the line of caring concern and into the realm of manic obsession.

He didn't blame Analisa for running away in fear. Hell, he'd had nearly the same reaction when he'd come to his senses. He only hoped she'd feel more like listening to him later.

Charlie had taken her a meal that afternoon, waking her from sleep. She didn't have a fever, the older man had reported, but was "powerful sad." That pretty well summed up the atmosphere of everyone in the cabin.

That's one reason he'd retreated outside—to listen to her animals settle in for the night and try to find some peace within himself.

He set the beer mug down on the ground and leaned back on his hands, staring up into a sky peppered with a million stars. With no lights to interfere, they covered the heavens like a glittering, sequined blanket. He'd dreamed of lying in a chaise longue on his balcony, looking at these same stars, Analisa snug and safe in his arms. In his dream, they'd put Jamie to bed together, then retreated to their own private world where nothing would intrude.

Where she was safe.

He sat up slowly, knowing that he was onto something important. Something that had to do with how he wanted things to be. And then it hit him like a ton of bricks. He'd tried to create a world away from everything and everyone, isolate his family from the reality of life. His home contained every comfort available. In the winter, they didn't have to leave for weeks. In the summer, he flew them wherever they wanted to visit, or drove to nearby sites or towns. But never did he consider the fact that someone he loved might need a life outside the boundaries of *his* home, *his* life.

Which was fine, when his family consisted of a six-year-old who had an independent streak a mile wide and needed guidance. But he'd tried to put Analisa into that same mold, make her a grown-up version of a child who needed protecting and nurturing.

Analisa didn't need his protection; she needed his love. And love didn't smother or restrict. Love was supposed to provide an environment in which to grow together, to feel free and happy. When had he lost sight of that important concept? After Catherine's death? Before? Was she rebelling when she took those risky assignments, or was she just expressing herself?

He'd probably never know, he realized with a pang of sorrow. Catherine had seemed happy. She'd laughed when he'd told her to be careful, and she'd loved her photography. He hadn't stifled her, had he? No, he didn't think she could have been preserved and pampered, put into a nice, safe place.

Her love of life had attracted him to her in the first place. He hadn't wanted to protect her then; he'd simply wanted to start a life together, each with their own dreams, but with enough shared ones to make a family together. After Jamie was born, he probably did change, maybe more than Catherine. He'd taken one look at his daughter and every protective instinct man had ever possessed had come rushing out.

Had he ever asked Analisa about her dreams, her hopes and fears? Not really. When she was upset, he'd encouraged her to talk about what was bothering her, but that was mainly as a friend. He hadn't fallen in love with her then. And the stronger his feelings for her had grown, the more insistent his urge to protect her had become.

Until he'd stepped over the line today.

Of all the things he knew about Analisa, he figured her own instincts to protect and nurture were her strongest traits. Didn't she take in animals destined for table or trap? Didn't she feel an obligation to save everyone who crossed her path? So maybe if he could explain his own feelings and fears in relation to hers, she'd understand.

But did that mean she'd forgive him, or believe he wouldn't do it again? *Would* he try to control her again? How could he be sure?

For the first time, he considered the faith in him and the courage she'd need to leave her world behind. To him, this was a territory with no modern amenities—an inconvenience, but nothing he hadn't dealt with before during camping or wilderness treks. To Analisa, the future was a huge, blank canvas. All she knew was the tidbits he'd told her, and the information she might have gleaned from the magazine he'd found on that boulder. Had the images, so unlike everything she knew, frightened her? Probably. He couldn't imagine traveling into the future with nothing but a sketchy profile provided by someone who was obviously prejudiced toward that era.

And then there was the issue of leaving behind everything she cared about. Her parents and brother were dead. She cared for Charlie, nearly like a blood relative, and worried about his health and the risks he took living in the mountains. Then there were the animals—the whole menagerie that any other nineteenth-century, struggling homesteader would consider nothing more than protein on the hoof—or wing, as the case might be. Not Analisa. These were her friends, her responsibility. A decision to leave them would be heartbreaking for her.

Suddenly, the conversation at dinner last night made sense. As soon as they'd started talking about leaving and Charlie staying there to take care of the homestead and the animals, she'd changed. He recalled his joke about not taking the animals on the plane, and realized that she hadn't truly considered what going away would mean.

Leaving everyone and everything behind must have hit her right then, and she'd run away the only way she knew how. He knew from previous experience that she kept her feelings inside, because there usually wasn't anyone to talk to here. She hadn't come to him with her problem because he was part of it. How could she confess her doubts and fears without invoking the same in him?

He knew what it felt like to leave everything behind. Hadn't he panicked when he realized Jamie was watching for his plane, waiting for her daddy to return, only to have him vanish before her eyes? God, he hoped she didn't harbor any feelings of guilt because it was her idea that he fly across the rainbow. He knew Holly would comfort her, but still, a child could be devastated by such an event.

As though these kinds of events happened . . . ever.

He sighed, looking once more toward the stars. If it weren't for Jamie—and, to a lesser degree, Holly—he'd stay right here with Analisa, build a new life with his own two hands and her at his side. They'd expand the cabin for the children they'd create, struggle through everything that nature could throw at them, and live to see the dawning of the twentieth century, prohibition, the suffrage movement, and the first world war. He knew all of those things would happen, but he'd see them first-hand.

He couldn't allow himself to stay, though. Jamie needed him. He firmly believed that a parent had an obligation to his child, first and foremost over his own desire.

He would go back as soon as possible, to tell his fantasy-loving daughter the kind of story that no adult would ever believe. Only one question remained: Would Analisa be on the plane with him when he flew back to 1997?

For the first time, he realized the decision was hers alone.

She ventured outside her room after she heard David and Charlie leave for the meadow. She was so thankful for some time alone that she'd given Charlie permission to take Tommelise. Besides, he was as excited to see the plane as a child on Christmas Day.

The effects of her illness were fading. Today she'd been well enough to stand on her side of the bedroom door and listen to the two men discuss their plans. She hadn't felt weak, even though the sound of David's voice cut through her soul like a knife. How she could still want him when she knew they could never be happy together was a mystery to her. Despite her best efforts, her mind and her heart didn't seem to be communicating with each other. As often as she told herself that she was much better off living alone, or with Charlie, she still longed to be held in his arms one more time.

This obsession with David was hopeless. Perhaps when he was gone from her life, she'd no longer think of him so often, or so deeply. Perhaps, in time, the memories of their night together in the firelight and rain would fade away.

With a sigh, she took another step into the room, and realized that her memories of David would never fade, just as she still recalled her mother's voice and laughter, and her papa's deep chuckles, and Jurgen's snappy remarks, his good-natured teasing. She would never forget David, but she would go on. She'd endured separation from those she loved before, and time was as solid a barrier as death.

She used the men's absence to prepare a simple dinner of hard-boiled eggs and venison sausage. Apples would have gone well with the meal, but she had none. Perhaps later a wagon would come through with fresh fruit.

When she finished cooking, she took a book outside and sat with Daisy and the twins, which she had decided to name Bernard and Beatrice. They were now frolicking as though they'd never been wobbly, wet creatures who needed help standing to nurse from their mother. They ignored her, but Daisy seemed to enjoy her company.

As she turned the pages and searched for a story she hadn't read in some time, Marie waddled up, followed closely by Louie. The female wanted her head scratched, and the male was equally adamant that he didn't want anyone else touching his mate.

"You should talk to David," she said to the drake as she shooed him away. "He's just as demanding and bossy as you are."

Analisa read aloud from "The Princess and the Pea," about a prince who wanted to marry, but only a real princess would do. The story of a poor, bedraggled princess finding her way to the castle of a handsome prince, only to be chosen by him as his bride, had been romantic when she was younger. Or even last month. Now, she resented the prince's attitude that the princess should have to prove herself to him, as though he were some great prize and any woman other than a princess was inferior.

The more she thought about his attitude, the more irritated she became. Perhaps the writings from David's time had influenced her, or perhaps just her understanding the nature of men a little better now made her feel this way. Whatever the reason, she suddenly found that she had no patience for the prince's mother's trick of putting a pea under all those mattresses. Or the prince for being so weak-willed and dominated by her.

Analisa had no respect for weak-willed men, she realized. At the same time, living with a strong-willed one was extremely difficult. Was there no way to be happy with a man?

She slammed the book shut. "That's all for today," she announced. "I'm going for a walk."

Inside the cabin, she placed her book of fairy tales

back on the shelf, realizing with a sense of regret that she'd never feel quite the same way about some of the stories again. She'd thought she was very mature, but now she realized that until she'd met and fallen in love with David, she hadn't really grown into a woman. Making love had changed her forever. Hadn't David told her there was no turning back? She hadn't known what he'd meant then; now she did.

Or perhaps it wasn't that act, but what had followed—her realization that loving someone wasn't always enough. They should have waited until they'd discussed David's possessive and dictatorial nature, or her inability to let go of the past. But they hadn't. The high emotion, the rain, the fire—everything had seemed so right. She'd naively believed that their problems would be burned away by the heat of their passion. She'd been wrong.

Because she didn't want to worry Charlie, or send David into another useless search fueled by anger, she wrote a note and left it on the table. Grabbing a hunk of cheese and a few biscuits that weren't too burned, she set off for a small, weaving path that led gently uphill from the stream.

David pulled Tommelise to a halt near the barn, automatically searching for Analisa. She wasn't outside; he'd hoped she would be. He didn't want his presence to confine her to her room. If he thought that was the case, he'd stay at the plane until they had a chance to talk. The last thing he wanted to do was drive her farther away, especially after the way he'd treated her yesterday.

"I jus' can't believe I gots to ride in a airplane," Charlie said as he dismounted. "I ain't never goin' to ferget what it felt like to be up in the sky," he added, excitement still lighting up his eyes.

"I'm glad you enjoyed it. Like I said, I needed to get the plane out anyway for a test run." David took the reins of both mounts. "I'll put the horses up. Why don't you see if Analisa is around? She'd probably rather see you at the moment."

"Ya really done gone and pissed her off," Charlie said with such succinct accuracy that David couldn't argue the point.

"Yes, I did. I'm going to try to fix it."

"Don't be sittin' on yer hands when ya should be down on yer knees," Charlie advised him with a wag of his finger.

David laughed. "That's good advice. I'll remember that."

After Charlie went to the cabin, David removed the bridles and turned the horses into the small pen attached to the barn. He carried water from the stream and filled their buckets, washed the bits, and hung the bridles in the barn. What the cabin needed was a well, he thought, so they wouldn't have to carry water for every task. But he had no idea how wells were dug in this century, and he was certain he had no tools to accomplish the task.

The weight of his limitations pressed down on him. He felt ineffective—not his usual state of mind. If he were in his own time, he'd know exactly how to get a well dug, or install electrical lighting in the cabin. But here, he could only do the most basic tasks, ones involving physical strength or persistence.

Charlie met him at the door. "She left ya a note."

David took the note from Charlie's hand and read Analisa's neat, precise script. "She's gone for a walk, up the hill behind the cabin."

"Ya goin' after her?"

David squelched his urge to reply, "Yes." He remembered the way he'd chased her down yesterday, accusing her of intentionally ignoring him. He'd been wrong yesterday, he'd be equally wrong to follow her today. She was a grown woman and deserved some time alone.

"No, I'm going to see if I can find a way to divert part of the stream closer to the barn to create a natural trough for the animals. At least that way we won't have to carry so much water."

"*You* ain't gonna carry the water," Charlie reminded him.

"You're right," David admitted. "I've got to go back to my own time."

"Sounds to me like ya want to go back."

David nodded. "I admit I miss my own time, but mostly I have to get back to my daughter Jamie. She needs me. Her mother died when she was just two years old."

"Annie needs ya too."

"Yes, but needing and wanting are two different things, I've learned. And right now, she doesn't really want to be around me."

"Ah, she'll come around."

"I hope you're right, but I really overstepped my bounds yesterday. I don't blame her for being angry with me."

"All the more reason to say yer sorry, and say it fast."

"I'm not going after her. She's got to understand that I can give her the freedom she needs."

"All this talk about women's rights and men's rights and relationships that you twentieth-century folks write about . . . well, it seems like a bunch of nonsense to me. Just give her a peck on the cheek and tell her yer sorry."

David had to smile at the simplistic way Charlie approached the problem. Somehow, a "peck on the cheek'' didn't seem sufficient to make up for his over-bearing attitude. He also had to wonder how much experience Charlie had with women. ''I'll take your advice under consideration,'' he said with as much sincerity as he could project.

He folded the note and placed it in his pocket, then unbuttoned and removed his shirt and draped it over the nearest fencepost. He'd seen a shovel and a pick in the barn. He'd need both to dig the trough.

An hour later, dirty, sweaty and tired, he paused in his digging. Had he heard something? He looked around and found Analisa standing about ten feet away, her lips parted in surprise, her hand resting just above her breasts. She was breathing hard, and he had to wonder if she'd overexerted herself.

But she gave him a perusal that was the equal of any he'd ever received, and decided that her rapid breathing wasn't totally caused by her hike. She looked healthy again, with color in her cheeks and lips, and life back in her eyes.

''Hello, Analisa,'' he said quietly. His own pulse speeded up in response to her nearness.

''I heard the plane,'' she said breathlessly. ''I thought you'd left.''

''I took Charlie for a ride.''

''That was kind of you.'' She seemed to compose herself as she took a deep breath.

David shrugged. ''It was the least I could do.''

She glanced down at the muddy mess. ''What are you doing?''

''I'm digging a trench that will divert water from the stream to the animals. That should make life easier for Charlie.''

''And me,'' she said, dropping her eyes.

''We should talk about that,'' he suggested.

"I think we've already talked."

"No, I yelled. I apologize for that."

"Very well, I accept your apology." She started to walk away. "I need to finish dinner."

"Analisa."

She stopped, still not meeting his eyes. "What?"

"I know I've been a fool and a bully. I'm trying to tell you I'm sorry, and that it won't happen again."

She raised her eyes and looked at him directly, her expression unreadable. "I'd have a difficult time believing that, David, when you've been so consistent."

"I was wrong."

She shook her head. He thought he saw a sheen of tears. "Yes, you were, but that doesn't mean you'll change."

"At least let me explain," he said, rushing on before she walked away again. He had a horrible feeling that this time she wouldn't be back.

"I need to tell you what I've learned about myself these last few days. It all started when Catherine got an assignment to photograph eagles in the park—Yellowstone. It's a national park north of your cabin, which is on land called Teton National Park. Anyway, the land is very rugged. I flew her into the closest drop-off point and she hiked the rest of the way. I asked her to be careful. . . .

"She gave me a look that said, 'I've heard all this before,' and she kissed my cheek. 'Don't worry. I'll be careful,' she said with a laugh. That was the last time I saw her alive."

"So what has changed, David? Do you still feel as though you could have stopped her?"

"No, I don't. I realize now that part of what everyone loved about Catherine was her commitment to her goal. She loved animals, just like you, but not to own them herself. She wanted to preserve them for Jamie, and Jamie's children, by showing them in their natural environment.''

''That seems to be a very good goal. Why didn't you agree with her?''

''I did! My concerns weren't about her goals, just about how she went after achieving them. And the fact that she assumed she was the only photographer who could do that particular assignment.''

''Was she?''

''No, but she honestly believed that she could do a better job than anyone else. That perhaps one special picture might touch someone's heart and make all the difference in saving our natural resources.''

Before Analisa could comment, he rushed on. ''I didn't realize that then, however. I was only able to separate my reaction to Catherine's decisions from my own anger and guilt after I yelled at you the other day. You made me realize that there's a big difference between loving someone completely and loving things about them.''

''I don't know what you mean.''

''I'm trying to say that I've learned there's a big difference between love and acceptance. I think you must have both to really *be* in love with someone. I didn't know that before. I didn't know how to love her and still let her go.''

Analisa watched him with a mixture of confusion and doubt etched on her clear, young face.

''Look, I hadn't planned to talk at this moment.'' He held out his dirt-streaked arms. ''Let me get cleaned up and we'll sit down together. I promise I won't yell. I need to explain why I felt the need to protect you. If you'll just listen—''

''I'm sorry, but I can't risk my . . . I can't risk everything on your word that you've suddenly changed. Forgive me, David, but I can't . . . I just can't.''

She whirled away and ran back to the cabin.

Inside, Charlie was playing with Little Red, snaking a length of rope across the floor. The weasel grabbed the knot at the end and shook it fiercely, then let loose and jumped around the now-limp toy.

''How're ya feelin', Annie-girl?''

''Better,'' she said, knowing her voice sounded lifeless.

''Yeah, yer soundin' really good,'' he said sarcastically.

''Well, I was feeling better before I saw David,'' she said, sinking to the floor and playing with Little Red.

''Ya have another spat?''

''Charlie, we're not 'spatting.' Again and again, David has proven he doesn't trust me out of his sight. He yelled and accused me of intentionally not answering his calls yesterday, as though I was a child who needed a swatting. I'm sure that if he'd found the note instead of you, he would have come up the mountain after me.''

''Annie, he did see that note. I showed it to him. And I think ya oughta give the man a chance. He's awful sorry, and he loves ya powerful much.''

Chapter Twenty-one

For the next few days, David worked like a man possessed, because he knew a rainbow would appear sooner or later. He rose early and came back to the cabin only when twilight tinged the sky. Charlie served him meals; Analisa avoided him, busying herself with cheese-making, cleaning, and preserving the meat that Charlie brought home on two different occasions.

She stayed busy so she wouldn't have time to think, because whenever she did, emotions and arguments tangled with the wild impulses that she resisted. She couldn't forget the look on David's face as he stood before her, dirt-splattered and sweating, hair hanging over his forehead and eyes shining with sincerity.

She'd told him she couldn't believe him. She'd told herself the same thing. But her heart wouldn't listen. Instead, she found herself wanting to believe that he would give her the freedom she needed to survive. That he not only respected her, as he'd said before, but trusted her ability to make decisions . . . and even mistakes. She wanted to look into the eyes of the man who'd said he was wrong and find out if he'd really changed.

If she could trust her heart . . . Her pulse increased with the idea that perhaps her heart was all she *could* trust.

Even if she did believe David and trust her heart, could she leave her world behind? She found herself standing in the yard, or in a room, looking at nothing and yet everything, soaking in the feeling of things around her. Smells, sounds, and sights she'd never noticed before flooded her senses.

On the morning of the fifth day, after David had left for the meadow to scythe more hay for the winter, she stood at the fence and watched Charlie at Daisy's pen. The goat bleated for his attention, angling her head and sticking her velvety soft nose through the slats. He talked to her, then reached into his pocket and handed her a piece of something—Analisa suspected it was a bread crust or biscuit.

And it hit her, as she watched, that all she'd ever really wanted for these animals was a safe place to live. They'd become her friends, the neighbors she'd didn't have, the friends she'd left behind in Ohio. They were her family, too, listening to her when she had to talk, letting her cry against their shoulders when she felt overcome with loneliness or doubt.

All she wanted was for them to be safe . . . and Charlie could provide a home for them as well as she could. They didn't need *her;* she'd needed them.

Tears filled her eyes as her world blurred around her. She could go away and leave Daisy, Rose, and Lucy. They would be fine. But when she thought about leaving Tommelise, she wavered. Her horse, David, and her world; which one could she live without? She'd thought that she couldn't live with him; now she wondered if she could live without him.

She had to find out. Now. She'd put off talking to him, pushing him away. All her instincts had told her to listen to him, but she hadn't wanted to hear words when she'd seen his actions. Now she had to find the truth. Before it was too late . . .

"He's not leaving, is he?" she asked, still sniffling. "You don't mean he's up there right now—"

"Oh, he's up there, all right, just waitin' for the right rainbow. Looks like rain later too."

"No!"

"Ya got to decide, Annie. Not too many folks live the life they want. Most of 'em play the cards they're dealt, but ya got a chance to decide," Charlie said, uncharacteristic passion in his gravely voice. "Whatcha goin' to do with that chance?"

"I'm going to find out," she said firmly. "I'm going to the meadow and look him in the eye. I'm going to listen to him, Charlie, and—"

"Ah, Annie, jus' get on up there and look inside yer heart. Ya done gone and started thinkin' too much."

She laughed despite the tears. But when she turned back to Tommelise, the laughter died. She lay her hand on the mare's soft muzzle.

She ran from the barn, sad but filled with an excitement she'd never felt before. The emotions warring inside her upset her stomach and made her hands tremble as she pulled out a small chest containing her treasured family items. Her mother's Bible, a photograph taken by Jackson of their family after her mother's death, and a painted miniature of Papa's mother from Germany. To the chest she added two of her favorite clay figures, wrapped in her best dress, which was as short as her other one. But she couldn't go into David's time dressed only in a calico shirt and rough men's pants, held up by one of Jurgen's belts, that she'd cut down to fit.

Charlie walked into the room. "Whatcha want me to do, Annie?"

"I don't know, Charlie! I can't think."

"Jus' calm down. David won't be goin' off without his good-byes."

She took several deep breaths, but her head still spun. "This is David's land in his time, Charlie. Did you know that?"

"Yep. He mentioned it."

"Then maybe, if you hid something for me, I could get it when I arrive in his time."

"Might be. I could pack it away in the cold room. Even if somethin' happened to the cabin, the room'd still be there."

"You're right! That's a great idea. When it's time . . . Oh, Charlie, I wish you could go too."

"Annie, I ain't a-goin' into another time. I've a hankerin' to see that first flight in North Caroliny now that I've been up there myself. I'm gonna find a way, too."

"Oh, Charlie. I hope you do get to go. I hope you see that first flight and smile and think to yourself that you've already done more than they have."

He nodded, a sly smile on his face. "That's what I'm a thinkin' too."

Little Red came out from behind the woodpile, stretching and yawning. Analisa gathered her in her arms. "I'll miss you, too, little one. You take good care of the house, you hear? Keep the mice and snakes away."

She handed the weasel to Charlie and pushed herself from the floor. "I can't believe I just decided to leave."

"Ya haven't gone yet."

"I know, but I feel that I'm going. I want to believe him, Charlie."

"Then get on up there. I'll go get the horses iffen I see the plane fly into the sky."

"The rainbow might not come."

"I think this might be the lucky day."

"David said his daughter knew the rainbow was a special one."

Charlie nodded. "I saddled yer mare. Let's get these things on her."

Analisa stood and turned in a circle, looking all around the cabin that had been her home for so many years. There were good memories here, and some sad ones too. But the memories weren't in these rooms, but inside her mind and her heart. As long as she remembered, the cabin would still be there. She could go back and visit whenever she wanted.

She walked through the rooms and touched the things she'd used each day and never considered before. She ran her hand over the quilt on the bed in Jurgen's room, and over the wooden pegs her papa had carved to hang her clothes on in her room. When she reached the front window, she trailed her fingers over the curtains she'd helped her mother sew that first winter.

All the memories were alive inside her.

She walked outside, past the new trench David had finished, to the marker beneath the pines where her mother was buried. She knelt and touched the wooden cross where Papa had carved leaves and vines from the engravings in one of her mother's fairy-tale books. "Good-bye, Momma," Analisa whispered. "I'll still come and visit you. I'll remember, Momma."

With tears blurring her vision once more, she ran back to the house, said a quick good-bye to Rose, Daisy and the kids, Sweet Sue, and Lucy. The chickens scattered across the yard as she hurried out of the barn, but the two ducks ran with her, as though they didn't want her to go.

"I've got to try," she said to Marie.

Charlie carried her chest out of the house and tied it to Tommelise's saddle. Louie waddled over and pecked his leg.

"Ouch! I swear, that durn duck is goin' to end up on my table yet!"

"No!" She couldn't let Louie get himself killed because he was ill-mannered. "I'll take him with me," she said instinctively.

"Yer man ain't gonna want this mean-tempered ol' drake."

"Well, if he absolutely refuses, then I'll just turn Louie loose at the pond, along with Marie. Maybe a few days in the wild will make him appreciate you more. Will you go check on him soon? If I leave them, I'll put the crate beside the pond."

"Oh, all right. I'll go get the durn thing, and I'll give him a second chance to behave himself."

Analisa retrieved the crate that Charlie had used to bring the two ducks to her last fall. Charlie had already caught the angry drake and was holding him around the wings and bill.

Within a few seconds, she'd stuffed both Marie and Louie into the crate and Charlie had tied it to the other side of Tommelise. "David is going to be very surprised when I show up."

"'Specially with them ducks."

Analisa smiled. "I'm really going to do this, aren't I?"

"I reckon ya are," he said, his own eyes sparkling. "I'll miss ya, Annie-girl," he said softly, his voice hoarse.

329

She wrapped him in her arms, hugged his bony but solid shoulders until she thought he'd object. But he didn't. He patted her back and let her hold him tight until she could finally let go.

"Don't ya worry none 'bout me," he said, fighting back a sniffle. "I'm goin' to do jus' fine. And I'll take care of all yer critters, and I'll be hidin' somethin' for ya. I'll put it in somethin' nice and tight, and bury it good inside the cold room."

"You do that," she said softly. "And I'll find it, too. And I'll laugh and cry, and I won't be sad."

"Get on outta here, now. I'll come get them horses and the ducks, iffen they be there. Ya go with yer man. It's where ya belong, Annie-girl. I knowed it from the first."

He turned and walked into the cabin, not looking back.

Within seconds, she'd mounted and urged Tommelise into a gallop. The future awaited just ahead, around the next bend of the trail . . . across the next rainbow.

David heard the pounding of hooves as he pulled away the last of the brush from the plane. Charlie, maybe? Perhaps something was wrong at the cabin. But even as the thought formed, he tamped it down. He'd learned from his mistake, and he wasn't going to jump to conclusions—especially by automatically thinking the worst.

He removed his sunglasses, then ran his forearm across his brow. The threat of rain made him think of rainbows . . . and of going home.

Without Analisa? He'd come to the conclusion that she might not go with him, that he might have to make the trip alone and never know what had happened to her, Charlie, and the homestead. After all, no indication of a homestead at that location existed on his land. Even the wide stone fireplace, which should have withstood the ravages of time and the elements, didn't exist.

He'd begun to believe that he'd dreamed all this.

The hoofbeats grew louder. He threw aside the last branch and walked into the meadow. Riding toward him was Analisa, looking more beautiful than he remembered, very much as she'd looked that first day when he'd stepped out of his plane.

When he saw the chest attached to one side of the saddle, his heart began to pound. She was either bringing him the last of his belongings, all neatly packed, or she had another reason to be here. One that required her to work her horse into a lather.

God, please, let it be what I'm thinking, he silently prayed. *Don't make me choose between Jamie and Analisa.*

She pulled Tommelise to a halt at the last minute, sending the mare's head bobbing and her eyes rolling. Analisa didn't seem to notice; her eyes focused on him, only him. He forced himself to stand very still, to let her make the next move.

But when she didn't, when he couldn't stand the wait, he walked toward her with long strides and held out his arms.

She seemed to soften before his eyes, a small cry escaping her lips as she threw her leg over the mare's back to dismount. David couldn't wait. He grasped her under her arms, slid her down his body in a rush of sensation that made him gasp with pleasure . . . and with relief. As she melted into his embrace, he gave silent thanks to God, or the leprechauns, or the elves in charge of rainbows. Whoever had granted his wish for someone to love—someone who needed him as much as he needed her.

"I was afraid you wouldn't come," he whispered into her hair, "or that you'd come to say good-bye. And I didn't know if I could leave you. Not now, not ever."

"I know," she said softly against his neck. "I didn't know if I could say good-bye to my life here. But when I thought about never seeing you again, I knew I had to come to you. To see if what you said was true—that you've changed and you know that love can't survive in a cage, no matter how beautiful the confinement. That I couldn't be the woman you wanted me to be."

"I'll never want you to be anyone except who you are," he said, pulling away enough to look into the shimmering blue depths of her eyes. "I don't want you to change, ever. Not for me. I want you to be happy, and I want to be a part of your life."

He ran his hands up her arms until they rested lightly on her shoulders. "But Analisa, I understand now that I can never be all of it. I can't make someone else happy; I can only do my best to let them find their own happiness."

She blinked, then smiled at him with a radiance he'd never seen before. "I love you, David. And I'll do my best to help you find your happiness too."

"Oh, love, I have found mine. I found it the moment I stepped from my plane into your world. And I pray that you'll feel the same way when you step into mine."

He pulled her to him, kissed her long and hard, until both worlds fell away and there was nothing but the two of them. And when the barrier of clothes became too much, they undressed each other in haste, beneath the fleeting clouds of afternoon that sent shadows racing across the meadow. The gentle breeze caressed their bodies as they sank to the meadow floor.

Analisa knew that she'd remember this moment always. This time, so full of love and hope, filled her with a joy she couldn't express any other way except through her hands, her lips, her body. She memorized the way his skin felt, sleek and slightly damp, stretched over muscles and bone that moved and flexed above her. She opened her eyes and watched his blue-black hair fall across his forehead as he bent to kiss her once more. She smelled the grass he'd cut in the meadow, the lingering sunshine, and the promise of rain. And she closed her eyes when his rough palms caressed her breasts, when he slid down her body and tasted her, and when at last he moved inside her.

She cried his name, arching from the meadow floor, holding him for all eternity. In the distance, she heard his answering cry, and then he shuddered and held her so tightly that they had to breathe together or not at all. Daylight faded and their two worlds merged into one for that brief, magical moment.

She felt the first drops of rain against her hands, still holding David close. He didn't seem to notice. His head rested beside hers, on a pillow of her hair.

"It's raining," she whispered.

"I know. I just don't want to leave you, even for an instant."

She turned her head and looked to the west. This was only a brief, light shower; already, the sun shone brightly against the peaks of the Tetons. Sunshine and rain . . . and rainbows.

"We have to get up," she said, pushing against his shoulders.

"Why?"

"The rainbow! We have to be ready."

"Right now?"

"Yes! David, this is it. I know it is."

"You're sure?"

"Yes! I know there will be a rainbow."

"No, I mean are you absolutely sure about going with me? Leaving your world behind? Because if you do, there will be no turning back."

"David," she said gently, laying her hand against his cheek, "there never was any turning back. Not once I gave my heart to you. I just didn't realize it at first. I'm yours, and I want to go forward . . . with you, together."

He framed her face with his hands. "I love you," he said, then kissed her hard and fast, his body reacting even as he pulled away.

"We'll continue this later tonight, at my house," he said with a smile. Leaping to his feet, totally unconcerned with his impressive nakedness, he held out his hand. "I thought you were in a hurry."

She laughed and let him pull her to her feet. "I am. I have to get my chest and . . . one other thing."

Chapter Twenty-two

He grabbed his denim pants and pulled them on. "What other thing? I'm afraid we won't have much time, once the rainbow forms."

"Don't worry. The other thing is here."

He looked toward Tommelise, who grazed in the meadow nearby. "What? Analisa, I know how much you love that horse, but she won't fit on the plane."

"I know," she said, a shaft of pain going through her heart when she thought of leaving her best friend behind. "I'm going to leave her here for Charlie. He's going to come to the meadow for the horses after we fly into the sky. And I've already said good-bye to everyone else—Daisy, Little Red, Rose—"

"Then what are you talking about?"

"The ducks, David. I'm afraid to leave them with Charlie. He hates Louie, and I know that sooner or later Louie will push him too far and end up as Sunday dinner. And then Marie would be very unhappy, because even though he's mean to us, she loves him, so—''

"Okay, you can bring the damn ducks," he said in a resigned tone, shaking his head. However, she noticed there was a slight smile on his face.

"Thank you," she said, infused with happiness. Wearing only her camisole and drawers, she ran to Tommelise.

"Aren't you forgetting something?" he asked.

She whirled around. He was holding up her pants and shirt.

"No. I don't want to go dressed like that. I want to wear my dress. It's here, in the chest."

He walked toward her, helping her untie the chest and the crate of ducks, who were indignant about being caged for so long. Louie bobbed his head up and down and quacked his displeasure.

"Hush, now. You're getting to go with me. I don't want to hear any complaints, or I'll leave you for Charlie and that nice sharp ax."

A loud quack was his answer. Analisa laughed, so happy she could barely contain herself. She wanted to run through the meadow, twirl around in David's arms, and laugh for joy. But they didn't have time. She'd do that later, as David had said, back in his time, in this same meadow.

She stepped into the blue dress with the embroidery of white flowers on the collar and cuffs. "Button me up?" she asked, presenting her back.

David made quick work of the pearl buttons and she made one twirl, shaking out the wrinkles as much as possible.

"You look like a fairy princess," he said, his eyes shining with love.

"I do?"

"Yes, silly. Of course you do. Jamie asked me if I

was going to bring back the fairy princess to be my wife and her new mother, and I told her I wasn't. That if there was going to be a fairy princess, she'd have to show up later because I wasn't going to land my plane. After we land, she'll be saying 'I told you so' for months."

"Her new mother?"

"Of course. We are going to be married, aren't we?"

"I . . . I don't know. You haven't asked," she said, suddenly shy.

"I haven't asked? Damn, I am so stupid sometimes." He took her hands in his and looked into her eyes. "Analisa, would you be my wife? Would you come back with me and be my fairy princess, and take on the responsibility of helping me raise my rather precocious child? We promise that we'll love you forever."

"Both of you?" She smiled, then laughed. "Yes, yes, I will."

"Great. Now we'd better hurry. I think I see the first sign of our ticket back home."

She glanced to the east, ready to hurry toward the plane with her belongings, but then she remembered something David had said before he proposed.

"David, I hope your daughter isn't disappointed," Analisa said, putting her hand on his arm. "I think fairy princesses are small and dainty, with beautiful faces and lovely gowns."

"You happen to be from the land of tall fairy princesses," he said, smiling in that way that made her insides melt. "And you are the most beautiful princess I've ever seen, even without a fancy gown."

"You think I'm beautiful?"

"I know you're beautiful. Don't you think you are?"

"I have no idea," she said, suddenly confused. "I haven't seen myself in years."

"You haven't seen yourself? But . . . you don't have a mirror? When you didn't offer me one to use when I shaved, I thought maybe you had it in your room, mounted on a wall."

She shrugged. "We used to own one, but Jurgen dropped it when Papa was teaching him to shave."

David laughed, then spun her around. "You are without a doubt the most surprising woman I've ever met."

"What do you mean?"

"Let's just say that most women I know would trade a year's supply of butter and eggs rather than be without a mirror."

She shook her head, not understanding why anyone would prefer something so useless as a mirror when they needed food to survive. But then, she'd have plenty of time to learn.

"I'll carry your things to the plane and get ready for take-off. Do you want some time with Tommelise?" he asked gently.

"Yes." She looked at her mare, who watched them with interest and, Analisa suspected, a bit of confusion.

"Don't be too long," he said gently. "My gelding is hobbled near the pond. We'll need to put them together, I suppose."

She nodded, already walking toward Tommelise.

When David walked away, she lay her hand against her mare's neck and stroked, her eyes filling with tears.

"This is good-bye, my friend," she said hoarsely. "I'm going away with David, someplace I can't take you. I would if I could. Believe me, I don't want to say good-bye, but I have to go with David."

Tommelise turned her head toward her, bumping Analisa's shoulder with her soft muzzle as she so often did when she wanted attention.

"You be good for Charlie, you hear?" she whispered.

"You know I'll always love you." Her lip trembled as she sniffed back tears. "I'll always remember you."

She hugged her mare, burying her face in Tommelise's long, dark gray mane.

"What about Charlie?" David asked from behind her.

She pulled away, wiping her eyes. "We've already said our good-byes."

"I'll miss him too."

Analisa nodded. "Let's take her across the meadow with your gelding. Maybe she won't be as frightened by the plane there."

"Okay, but hurry."

They did, taking time only to tie the mare and the gelding along the tree line by the pond, where they should feel safe from the noise of the engine. "You never did name your horse," Analisa said, wiping away the last tear.

"No, I didn't. Charlie will name him. They'll be good together."

They walked quickly back toward the plane. Analisa didn't look back, because she knew that she'd see Tommelise once more, as they flew into the sky. She looked instead at the rainbow, arching bright and strong across the eastern horizon, grabbed David's hand, and began to run.

"What about Louie and Marie?" Analisa asked breathlessly as they reached the plane.

"Already on board," David answered, pointing behind the seats. "I put the crate on the floor so they wouldn't slip around."

"And my chest?"

"Strapped in and ready to go."

She took one last look, then lifted her foot onto the first step.

He helped her into the plane, then showed her how to

buckle the straps across her lap. The confining harness did nothing to calm her nerves. Suddenly, the idea of flying seemed odd and frightening. But David did this all the time. He knew what to do. She repeated those words to herself as he kept up a steady stream of words and phrases she didn't understand, flipped things he called switches, and peered at round, glass-covered things called gauges.

"Ready?" He turned to look at her for the first time, sending her a reassuring smile.

She took a deep breath, then nodded. "I'm ready."

He started the engine and the plane filled with noise. She nearly jumped from her seat when they began to move. So that's why the harnesses were important!

"I'm going to perform a short field take-off," David said as they bumped along the meadow toward the northwest. "That means that the noise is going to increase because I'm giving the plane full power, but applying the brakes. When we start down the meadow, we'll pick up speed very fast."

"How fast?"

"About eighty-five miles per hour."

"Miles per hour?"

"Yes. That means that in one hour, we can go eighty-five miles."

"Really? It would take a rider two days to go eighty-five miles!"

"I know, but that's how fast you have to go before the airplane will lift off. The wind coming under the wings makes it leave the ground."

"Will we go that fast very long?" she asked, clutching the edge of her seat. In the back of the plane, Louie and Marie were getting restless too, moving around and making distressed noises as the sound of the engine increased.

"We'll level off at an air speed of about a hundred miles an hour. This should be a short flight," he said, flashing her another smile.

"Yes, it should only take a hundred and eleven years," she replied, trying to relax even though her heart was pounding right out of her chest.

David laughed.

"Can we fly over the cabin?" she asked. "I'd like to make sure Charlie knows we're gone."

"Yes, I have enough fuel for that. After takeoff, we'll circle the cabin and the meadow, then climb to the altitude of the rainbow."

Analisa leaned down to look out the window and into the sky. "Look!"

David peered to his left, then smiled. "That's a sign if I ever saw one."

Analisa continued to stare as the second rainbow continued its arch inside the first. "A double rainbow," she whispered.

"Of course. We'll need two to get you home with me, don't you think? One for you, one for me."

She nodded, then slammed back against the seat when David increased the power and took off the brakes. Suddenly they were streaking down the meadow, faster and faster, the trees whipping by in a dark green blur. "David!" she squealed, feeling the plane move up and down.

"That's float," he said calmly. "I've used about ten degrees of flaps to help us lift off before we reach air speed. We'll bounce a couple of times, then be in the air."

"Bounce?"

They did. Analisa stuffed her fist into her mouth so she wouldn't scream as she felt the incredible sense of rising above the earth. Outside, the meadow seemed to slip away like a leaf sinking beneath the surface of the water. She saw the tops of trees, the pond, and the prancing shape of Tommelise between branches as they climbed higher into the sky. Then all she saw was blue, blue sky as David turned the plane until she was sure they were going to roll to their side. Her stomach churned until she felt the urge to swallow and clench her teeth. He eased it straight again before she lost what little lunch she'd eaten earlier in the day.

"You can relax now," he said with a trace of amusement. "The tough parts are the takeoffs and landings. The flying is a piece of cake."

"A piece of cake?" she repeated nervously. She didn't want to think about food!

"It's easy. You could even fly the plane now."

"No!"

"Charlie did," David said calmly.

"I don't care," she said, gripping the edge of the seat. "I'm just going to sit here and think about landing."

"There's an old saying," David started, turning the plane in the other direction this time, "that goes like this: The second biggest thrill in the world is flying. The first is landing."

"That's makes me feel so much better," she mumbled.

"The cabin's out your side of the plane," he told her.

She looked down, amazed at how small it seemed. Still, she could see everything clearly. Charlie stood in the yard, waving his arms, smiling so widely she could tell from way up here. Bernard and Beatrice leaped around their pen while Daisy ran for cover. Even Rose trotted toward the protection of her tree.

Then they were all gone, out of sight. David maneuvered the plane sharply right, then left.

"I'm waving good-bye to Charlie," he said soberly.

She thought she saw a trace of moisture in his eyes.

Then they were over the meadow, making a big circle so she could look down once more on the place where her best friend stood, no doubt trembling from the excitement of the plane. But David's gelding was beside her, a calming influence. Tommelise would have a new friend, and Charlie would take care of them both.

"I'm ready," she said softly.

"Okay, then. I'm going to put on these," he explained, holding up a half-circle with two small cups on each end, "so I can get our location and communicate with the airport in Jackson. I'll be talking to people on the ground, so don't be alarmed and think I'm talking to you."

She nodded, not understanding how people on the ground could hear someone speak from way up here, but knowing that David was experienced in these things. She sat back and tried to enjoy the view, which was spectacular. Except for one thing . . .

"David, there's no rainbow!"

"We can't see the rainbow from up here. We aren't at the right angle. If everything happens like it did before, though, we should feel a tingling sensation and see rainbow colors just briefly as we pass from your time into mine."

They climbed higher into the sky. The river ran far below, a brown snake through the green grass of the valley. She saw several lakes and canyons and mountains not high enough for snow.

"We should be just about there."

"Do we need to do anything?"

He thought for a moment. "We should make another wish. I'll go first, okay?"

She nodded.

"I wish to return to my time with Analisa, my own

fairy princess, whom I will love with all my heart, and accept with all my soul, for the rest of my days.''

She looked into his dark eyes. ''And I wish to travel to David's time, to be his wife and a mother to his child, and to love him for the rest of my days.''

He squeezed her hand, then looked at the gauges. The sounds of flying faded away. The sunlight dimmed ever so slightly.

''Eighty-two, eighty-three, eighty-four. Now!'' he whispered fiercely, and suddenly the inside of the plane sparkled with rainbow colors that seemed to pass right through them, tingling with the strangest sensation. And then the colors were gone and once again the plane flew on, the engine a steady hum, the wind streaking by.

Analisa gripped the seat tightly as David turned the plane. She closed her eyes, praying, praying that they'd made the wish at the right time. That they'd gotten back to where David belonged—and where she belonged now too.

When she opened her eyes, a different vista stretched below them. Brown and gray lines cut across the green meadows. Part of the earth seemed marked with squares and patterns, and she could see that some of the objects below were houses and barns.

''We're here,'' David said, grinning, grabbing her hand. He turned the dial of some device, then listened intently.

''Yes!'' he shouted.

In the back of the plane, Louie began to quack.

''Two-one-two-five-Robert to Jackson Unicom,'' David said. Analisa started to respond, then remembered that he was talking to someone on the ground. She looked out of the side of the plane but saw no one below.

''Request permission to land.''

He listened, then said, ''Roger.''

When he turned to her, grinning like a schoolboy, she asked, "Who are Robert and Roger? Are they the people on the ground?"

David laughed. "No, but I'll explain later. Right now I've got to land this plane."

"We're back in the right place?"

"Absolutely, although I should have asked the date. I've totally lost track of time."

"I did too, a long time ago."

"We'll be on the ground soon, and then we can find Holly and Jamie. As a matter of fact," he said, turning a dial again, "I'll switch over from 122.8 to my own frequency and see if Holly just happens to be manning the radio."

"Two-one-two-five-Robert calling base. Come in, Holly."

He listened, then a grin split his face. "Wait a minute. I'm switching to speaker."

"David? What's going on? We lost radio contact with you."

"I know, but I'm back know. Holly, I have the most incredible story to tell you and Jamie. Is she there?"

"She's outside."

"I'll be on the ground in a few. I can't wait to see both of you."

"Okay. Over and out."

The inside of the plane was silent once more. Even the ducks stilled.

"How did you do that?" Analisa asked.

"It's called a radio. We can talk to people anywhere, all around the world, in fact, through satellites. We've talked to astronauts in space, and on the moon."

"Men on the moon?" He couldn't be serious!

"Yes. And there's more, more than I can tell you before I land this plane. But don't worry. You'll have plenty of time to learn. A whole lifetime.''

She nodded and watched as the plane drew closer to the earth, as the gray and brown slashes became roads, and she saw the cars David had described move rapidly along them. In a fenced pasture, horses grazed. She read signs with brightly colored letters, and saw other airplanes, sitting on the ground. Her breath caught in her throat as the ground rushed to meet them. Then David landed the airplane with a bump and a jolt as the wheels touched the earth once more. They rolled for a long time, it seemed, then he turned and they rolled some more.

''When I stop at my hangar, Jamie will be there. I don't know what she thinks about why I've been gone, and I haven't even thought about explaining you or where you're from. But all that doesn't really matter, does it?''

''What do you mean?'' she asked when he stopped the plane.

He turned to her. ''All that matters is that we love each other and I want to make you happy. I want you to be free to be whatever you want to be, fairy princess or farmer, sculptor or mother.'' He lay his callused palm against her cheek. ''Most of all, I want this to be your home, and I want us to be a family.''

She leaned toward him and parted her lips, feeling the touch of his mouth not as possession but as sharing. She kissed him back with all the love in her heart, matching his strokes with a passion that built as quickly as the ride through time.

And suddenly, the prospect of this future world didn't seem frightening, just exciting. A new life waited just beyond this airplane. All she had to do was step outside.

She broke the kiss and smiled at David. ''We're home. Now it's time to meet the other member of our family.''

"Don't worry, love," he replied with a grin, glancing toward the flat, gray surface between the plane and the building. "She'll be here in just a few seconds. And the two of you are just made for each other."

Just like us, Analisa thought, waiting for the little girl whose faith in magical worlds had brought them all together.

David didn't know what to expect when they landed, but he was extremely relieved that Holly was still operating the air charter service, and that Jamie was here with her. Poor baby. How could he explain that he hadn't wanted to be separated from her, or that his wish had sent him back in time to find Analisa?

Jamie might just understand, though. Hadn't she insisted on his flying across the rainbow—an act that wasn't a "normal" request from a six-year-old? Since she believed in magic, she could possibly accept the fact that he'd traveled in time to find the fairy princess she wanted for her new mommy.

He smiled as she ran toward the plane, a huge grin on her face, her short legs pumping. Good thing he'd splurged on those new athletic shoes, since she looked as though she were trying out for the 2008 Olympic track-and-field team.

As a matter of fact, he thought as he looked closer, Jamie looked exactly as she had the last time he'd seen her. Red overalls, a striped T-shirt that she'd insisted on wearing, even though he'd had reservations about whether the yellow and blue stripes matched well with red. But Jamie had very strong opinions about her clothes, as she did with most things.

Poor baby. Had she worn that same outfit every day, hoping her daddy would come home? That sounded like something she'd do, since she believed so strongly in

347

magic—and, perhaps, good-luck charms and superstitions.

Like rainbows that brought her fairy princesses, he thought with a smile to Analisa. God, he couldn't wait to show her his world, and to start a new life for both of them, together.

Then Jamie flung open the door and shouted, "Daddy!"

Daddy jumped down from the plane, then picked her up and hugged her so tight that she yelped.

"Sorry, Muppet. I'm just so glad to see you."

Daddy looked so messy. His hair was awfully long and he didn't smell as good as he usually did. But he was still her daddy. "I'm glad to see you too, Daddy, but you almost squished me."

"Were you worried about me?"

"Just for a minute. Did you hear me, Daddy? I told you I couldn't see you no more."

"Any more," Aunt Holly said.

Jamie turned around. "Okay, okay. *Any* more."

"I'm so sorry," Daddy said. "I know both of you must have been worried sick." Then he hugged Aunt Holly really hard too.

"David, what's going on? You look like you've been through . . . well, a war or something. And how did you get so dirty?"

"Yeah, Daddy. Why do you look like that?"

"I've had a big adventure, Muppet," he said, leaning down and smiling at her.

"When did you have this big adventure?" Aunt Holly asked.

"When I was gone," Daddy said, looking very confused as he straightened up. "I don't even know for how long. What day is this, anyway?"

Aunt Holly put her hand on Daddy's forehead, just like she did when she thought she was sick. "Are you feeling okay?"

"I am now. And you didn't answer my question: What day is this?"

"It's the same day it was when you left, you big doofus."

"The same day?"

"David, you're scaring me! Did you black out or something up there?"

Daddy had a big grin on his face; then he started laughing. "I thought I did at first, but really I did have an adventure—a trip. And there's a surprise inside the plane."

Jamie got all excited. She loved it when Daddy brought home new surprises, and since he'd promised to make a wish, she knew this one was going to be really good.

He turned around and put his hand inside the plane. Then Jamie saw the most wonderful thing—a real fairy princess. She had long blond hair and wore a beautiful blue dress just like in all the books . . . except she wasn't wearing a crown.

"Daddy! You brought home the fairy princess!" Jamie jumped up and down, her new tennis shoes squeaking on the runway.

"She's not a real fairy princess, Muppet. This is Analisa Ludke, and she's going be my wife and your new mommy."

The princess smiled like she was real shy, but Daddy tugged on her hand and made her get out. He even lifted her down from the plane! Jamie started to run over and hug her, but Aunt Holly made her stop.

"Where are your manners?" she said. "And David, would you like to tell me how you managed to smuggle this beautiful young woman on board, and why you don't know what day it is, and why you look like that?''

Daddy laughed. ''I will, Holly, I will. But first, I want you to meet Analisa. She came here from . . .'' Daddy looked at the princess just like a prince was supposed to. ''She came here from very far away.''

''How could she—''

''It's a long story. And I didn't smuggle her aboard the plane before I left.''

Jamie ran over and threw her arms around the beautiful lady's legs. ''I'm so glad you came, Princess Analisa. I like your name. You look just like my Barbie doll. My name's Jamie Catherine Terrell and I just turned six. I promise I'll be really, really good.''

''I'm sure you're a wonderful child,'' the princess said, and Jamie looked up at her and smiled back.

Princess Analisa leaned down and smiled. ''Your daddy has told me all about you.''

''Really? That's neat.'' Then Jamie heard this really weird noise from inside the plane. ''What's that, Daddy?''

''Another surprise,'' he said, and he laughed as Princess Analisa's cheeks turned pink.

Jamie climbed into the plane and looked in the back. Then she turned around and clapped. ''Aunt Holly, come look! Daddy brought home a real princess *and* the goose that laid the golden egg.''

And everyone laughed. Jamie knew that now they'd live happily ever after.

Epilogue

Analisa waited until the summer's end to excavate the site where her cabin had once stood. Jamie was now in first grade, a momentous occasion in her young life. Analisa knew that her stepdaughter would be an excellent scholar, because she already knew so many words and numbers. And she was bright . . . so full of life and love that she made everyone around her smile.

Jamie had done more than smile last week when they'd told her the latest news, Analisa remembered, touching her stomach. Jamie's brother or sister would be born near the end of March in the year 1998, even though he or she had been conceived in a rainy meadow at the end of June 1886.

David was ecstatic.

"Are you ready?" he asked, breaking into her most recent memories.

"Yes," she said, smiling at her husband. "I'm ready for whatever we find."

351

"Are you sure? Because if you'd rather, I could—"

"David, quit talking and start digging," she said with a laugh. She'd learned in the last two and a half months that she could tease and command David in a good-natured manner whenever he got too "bossy," as Holly called him.

"Okay, but if you start feeling bad—"

"Dig!"

He smiled, shook his head, removed his shirt, and began to shovel away the years from the hillside where her cabin had once stood.

She settled on a boulder—one that must have tumbled down the hill because it hadn't been there before—and watched the play of muscles beneath David's golden skin as he worked. She hoped their child had his coloring, since Jamie was blond and paler in complexion. As a matter of fact, most people who met them for the first time assumed she was Analisa's daughter too.

Jamie had taken to that idea right away, and now called her Mommy. That was a welcome improvement from Princess Analisa, which she'd insisted upon for the first week, Analisa recalled with a smile. She'd changed to simply "Analisa" after the wedding, and now "Mommy."

Analisa had found her family, and with the grace of God, she'd bring their newest member into the world before the spring.

"I think I've found something," David announced.

Analisa walked to the site and leaned down, staring as he continued to push aside dirt and small rocks. Soon she could see the planks of a heavy door—and hinges she recognized from her cold room.

"That's it!" She clasped her hands together, her heart beating faster. "How long will it take before you can open it?"

"Maybe a half hour. Just relax, love. I'll call you as soon as I dig it out enough to open the door and get inside."

"Okay." She hugged her arms and walked away, willing herself to relax. She had another reason for being here, so she retrieved her tote bag and made her way across the site, now dotted with white-barked, yellow-leafed aspens and golden-brown grasses.

Beyond the stream, her mother's grave was marked by a granite headstone, commissioned by David to duplicate the wooden one her father had made many years ago. Analisa suspected that the mounded earth and piled stones beside her mother was Charlie's final resting place, but she didn't like to think of him that way. To her, he'd been a spry, middle-aged man just two months ago.

She and David had talked about the oddity of time that had brought them together, allowing weeks to pass in the past while less than a minute had gone by in 1997, according to Jamie and Holly. While they had no answers, they agreed that somehow their separate times had come together through a rainbow. David called it a "fold of time" that allowed him to live for weeks in the past and come back at the same moment he'd left the present. She didn't understand the science that he spoke of; she and Jamie would always think that rainbows were magic, for what better explanation could there be for such a miracle?

From the leather satchel, she pulled a bouquet of roses and placed them in the stone vase at the base of the headstone. "I brought your favorites," Analisa said. "Pink ones this time. The florist in town has a different color every time I go there."

She knelt on the ground, knowing her jeans and sweatshirt—two marvelous inventions she'd discovered in the stores in Jackson—would be covered in dirt before the day was through. She planned to climb into the cold room if necessary to pull out whatever Charlie had stored there.

Of course, there might not be anything there. An accident could have claimed him before he'd had time to secure a box of treasures. But she hoped . . .

"I have some news, Momma. I'm going to have a child next year. That will be 1998, you know. Isn't it marvelous? I'm hoping for a boy, but David says he doesn't care. He already has a houseful of women, he claims, and one more won't make a difference."

Analisa chuckled as she always did when she recalled the way he'd claimed to be "henpecked." What a funny term! She'd told him a boy would help even the odds, but he'd just shrugged and smiled.

"Now we're trying to find the things Charlie promised to save for me. I hope they're there, Momma, because I want to know what happened after I left. I've thought about it a long time, and I know that I'll never regret my decision to leave. I'd just like to know that Charlie and everyone had a good, long life. And even if they didn't, at least I'll know why there's no trace of our cabin to mark the spot. I've seen other cabins built a hundred years ago, Momma, and they're still around."

"Analisa!"

She looked up at David, waving beside the hill, then turned back to the grave. "I've got to go, Momma. I'm going to find out what's inside that room. I'll see you next week, and I'll tell you all about it."

She pushed herself up from the sandy ground and walked quickly toward her husband, hugging her arms and praying for answers that would reveal the past she'd left behind.

* * *

Late that night, Analisa again took the fragile, yellowed diary from the leather-bound trunk and placed it carefully on her desk in the room David had designated as her studio. Here she created magical creatures from the natural clay near her old homestead, feeling a link to the past with each one she sculpted.

Because she couldn't keep them all, she sold them through a gift shop in Jackson. She'd become very successful, according to David. She figured he was just being kind, but she enjoyed the income that allowed her to purchase a few items for Jamie and the coming baby.

She shook off the thoughts of her life now and concentrated on the past. Earlier that day, after they'd unearthed a sealed wooden box and brought it back home, she'd gotten her first glimpse of what had happened since she'd flown away to the future. Inside were her trolls, fairies, and goblins, carefully wrapped in an assortment of newspapers from 1903.

David had read the crumbling headlines telling of a controversial treaty concerning a canal in Panama, the first motion picture, *The Great Train Robbery,* and a cable across the Pacific Ocean that allowed President Theodore Roosevelt to send a message around the world in twelve minutes.

He'd enjoyed the published glimpses into the past, but she preferred to labor through Charlie's sometimes difficult handwriting. He'd told her in earlier entries that he'd asked the Shepherd's oldest son to write the first ten years, which explained why she'd had such an easy time reading those. But he'd "learned his letters better," he'd said in 1897, "so's I can rite to you myself."

She knew that he'd kept Beatrice with Daisy but sold Bernard to a neighbor who had a small herd of nanny goats but no billy. Beatrice had gone on to produce many offspring, and Charlie sold them to the incoming homesteaders as milk goats and billys.

A new settler came in with several sows and a boar, so Rose produced several litters of piglets. Charlie did not mention what happened to them, just that they'd been purchased by other families.

Sweet Sue passed away peacefully in 1890 of old age. Lucy contracted an infection and had to be put down that same year. Little Red breathed her last in 1891, a very old age for a weasel, and Charlie buried her in a pine box near the cabin; he included a map for Analisa, which made her cry.

David's gelding, whom Charlie named Big Red, had proven a strong and steady trail horse. When big-game hunters began flocking to the area at the end of the 1880s, Charlie became a guide and earned a "fair amount of cash" for his efforts. He assured her that he always hired the Shepherd's son to look after the homestead when he was away. That brought a smile to Analisa's face.

Now the hour was late, Jamie was in bed, and David was working in his home office on a charter for next week. There had been no mention of Tommelise in the diary, and Analisa knew that Charlie should have written about her by now. In the entries from 1903, the last year she and David had read, her beloved mare would have been thirty-one years old—very aged for a horse.

Charlie had written of his plans to travel to North Carolina by train that winter. He'd leave before the snows closed down the trails south so he could hook up with the railroad in Border. From there he'd go to Chicago, then south to North Carolina. She sensed his growing excitement over the trip.

This entry was dated June 1904. "I seen the flight last December. I looked toward that event ever since David told me about it, but when I saw them men with that spindly aircraft, I nearly laughed. It weren't nearly as pretty as David's plane. I still remember how it felt to go up in the sky with him. The flight that he told me about on December 17 was short and not too high off the ground. Not nearly as high as David took me. I treasure that memory every day, and I send him my thanks again for his kindness to me.

"I am an old man now, Annie, but I remember things from the past as clear as day. The world is fast changing and I can only hope I'll see a good many years before my time is up. My pappy was born in the year 1798, and I remember him teaching me to trap. And now I'm in the twentieth century, the same as you, Annie. Life is a wonderful gift. I sure hope you're happy in that time."

"I am, Charlie, I am," Analisa said with tears in her eyes. She wiped them away and continued to read.

"I have sad news this year. Your mare passed from this earth in May. She was healthy nigh to the end, except she lost the sight of her eyes during the winter. I have a sheep dog, and he guided her around the little pen on the sunny days when I let her outside. She was a good horse, Annie. I paid the young man who used to write for me to dig a grave, and we buried her at the base of the hill, forty feet southeast of the cabin. We placed a mound of stones there to show you where. I hope you can find the place."

Analisa placed the diary on the desk and closed her eyes. The tears escaped, rolling down her cheeks and dropping on her folded hands like warm summer rain. Just like that last day in the meadow, when she'd said good-bye to Tommelise. Now she'd say her final good-bye, knowing where her beloved mare rested for all eternity.

She wiped her eyes, overwhelmed by the kindness Charlie had shown to her all these years. He'd been the most loyal friend a person could have had.

She had to know what had happened to him. Turning the fragile pages as quickly as possible, she found the last date, June 1920, and read aloud from the weak, spidery script.

"I figure I am eighty years old now, and my health is not good. I feel the cold in my bones and find that even setting a fire is difficult for me. I think my time on this earth is growing short, but I have no regrets. You were like a daughter to me, Annie, and I think of you often. I still remember the way you looked at David when he came to the cabin that summer of 1886, and I knowed that the two of you were meant to be together.

"I'm sealing up the trunk this year, Annie, and going to live in the town of Jackson with a fine widow woman, Mrs. Collins, and her son. They will care for me in my last days. When I pass on, I've asked to be buried next to your mother. I sure hope you don't mind. I want my bones to rest in these mountains and I figure the homestead is the right place to be."

"It is, Charlie, it is," Analisa whispered, brushing away a tear.

"I told no one of your travel into the future, and I packed the two magazines so no one would find them and wonder what they were. This diary will be my only record to you, except for maybe a certificate of my death.

"I've decided to leave the land to the Shepherd boy, now a man of forty-some years. He's been my helper for thirty years, and has his own house and family. I sure hope that don't affect David's deed."

"It didn't, Charlie," she whispered.

"As I leave this property, I will have the cabin taken

apart and moved so that another settler can make use of the logs and boards. Hardware is still scarce here, so that will come to good use. The chimney will be broken apart and moved. The cold room will be covered with dirt and stones to save this record of the past for you, just like you wanted.''

Analisa felt the tears flow again as she thought of Charlie, an old man now, still preserving the things that had been important to her and had come to mean the world to him too. She'd heard his suggestion to write to her and save her things only two and a half months ago, but for Charlie, thirty-four years had passed.

"The last thing I will leave you, Annie, is a photograph of me taken this past summer in the automobile owned by Mrs. Collins's son. I attended Frontier Days when they drove me to the fairgrounds. I saw an airplane again that day, and it was much improved from that Wright Brothers' contraption. Tell David that the planes are still not as good as his, but I suspect he already knows that.''

Analisa laughed despite the tears flowing down her cheeks. She removed the sepia-toned photograph from behind the page and stared at the old man seated in the front passenger seat of an automobile very different from David's pickup truck or Holly's small car. He wore a hat, a shirt buttoned to his neck, and a vest over trousers that were tucked into boots. He had aged, but she recognized Charlie's chin and eyes, and she smiled at the memory. She placed the precious photo on the desk next to the open diary.

"So, this is good-bye. I had a good, long life and no regrets. When you get this diary, I hope you are happy in your new time and have many years ahead. You will see the next century, Annie, and I hope it is as grand as this one. Of all the people I have known, I miss just you and David. Someday I hope that I will see you again in life ever-after. If we do meet, I'll ask David to give me another ride in his plane, because I'm sure he'll be flying up there in the clouds. Good-bye, Annie-girl. Your friend, Charles Porter.''

She cried for some time before she felt David's hands on her shoulders. He leaned his cheek against her hair and comforted her with his strength and warmth. The tears slowed, then stopped.

"I never knew his last name," she whispered. "I never asked."

"It wasn't important," David said. "But now that we know, we can go to the public records and see when he died. I'd like to do something special in Charlie's name. He was the last of his kind."

"He was my best friend, David, and I don't think I ever really knew that until I read this diary."

"I think you knew. I know he did."

She swiveled around to look at her husband's dear, dark eyes. "Do you think so?"

He nodded. "He did many things for you, but you did something even more important for him. You gave him a home, a reason to live, and a way to provide for himself."

"And you gave him a glimpse of the future that he held on to all his life," she said.

"Yes, he did."

She wound her arms around David's waist and lay her head against his stomach, right below his steady heartbeat. "If we have a boy, I want to name him Charles Porter Terrell."

David stroked her hair. "I think that would be a fine, proud name. Charlie would like that." He paused, then tipped up her chin. "Are you sorry you didn't stay to see the things Charlie wrote about?"

"No," she said quickly, firmly. "You and I were meant to be together. We have a lifetime in front of us, raising Jamie and our own little Charles Porter. Just like Charlie, we'll see the dawning of a new century. I wouldn't give up these years with you for anything. I love you, David."

He folded his arms around her. "I love you to, my princess from the rainbow kingdom, more than you'll know in a thousand lifetimes."

She reached back and closed the diary. The past wasn't time as much as it was memories . . . and life was indeed a magical journey.

AUTHOR'S NOTE

For purposes of this book, I included Menor's Ferry, which wasn't in operation until the early 1890s, and I took some liberties with the number of settlers in 1886. For more information on Jackson Hole, I suggest *The Early Days in Jackson Hole,* by Virginia Huidekoper, available through the Grand Teton Natural History Association in Moose, Wyoming, and *Wyoming Handbook,* by Don Pitcher, Moon Publications.

Victoria Chancellor would love to hear from readers. Write to her at P.O. Box 852125, Richardson, TX 75085-2125. For bookmarks and information on her next releases, an SASE is appreciated.

FOREVER & A DAY

VICTORIA CHANCELLOR

When Linda O'Rourke returns to her grandmother's South Carolina beach house, it is for a quiet summer of tying up loose ends. And although the lovely dwelling charms her, she can't help but remember the evil presence that threatened her there so many years ago. Plagued by her fear, and tormented by visions of a virile Englishman tempting her with his every caress, she is unprepared for reality in the form of the mysterious and handsome Gifford Knight. His kisses evoke memories of the man in her dreams, but his sensual demands are all too real. Linda longs to surrender to Giff's masterful touch, but is it a safe haven she finds in his arms, or the beginning of her worst nightmare?

___52063-X $5.50 US/$7.50 CAN

BITTERROOT

TIMESWEPT

VICTORIA CHANCELLOR

Bestselling Author Of *Forever & A Day*

In the Wyoming Territory—a land both breathtaking and brutal—bitterroots grow every summer for a brief time. Therapist Rebecca Hartford has never seen such a plant— until she is swept back to the days of Indian medicine men, feuding ranchers, and her pioneer forebears. Nor has she ever known a man as dark, menacing, and devastatingly handsome as Sloan Travers. Sloan hides a tormented past, and Rebecca vows to use her professional skills to help the former Union soldier, even though she longs to succumb to personal desire. But when a mysterious shaman warns Rebecca that her sojourn in the Old West will last only as long as the bitterroot blooms, she can only pray that her love for Sloan is strong enough to span the ages....

_52087-7 $5.50 US/$7.50 CAN

DON'T MISS OTHER LOVE SPELL TIME-TRAVEL ROMANCES!

Tempest in Time by Eugenia Riley. When assertive, independent businesswoman Missy Monroe and timid Victorian virgin Melissa Montgomery accidentally trade places and partners on their wedding day, each finds herself in a bewildering new time, married to a husband she doesn't know. Now, each woman will have to decide whether she is part of an odd couple or a match made in heaven.
_52154-7 $5.50 US/$6.50 CAN

Miracle of Love by Victoria Chancellor. When Erina O'Shea's son is born too early, doctors tell the lovely immigrant there is little they can do to save young Colin's life. Not in 1896 Texas. But then she and Colin are hurtled one hundred years into the future and into the strong arms of Grant Kirby. He's handsome, powerful, wealthy, and doesn't believe a word of her story. However, united in their efforts to save the baby, Erina and Grant struggle to recognize that love is the greatest miracle of all.
_52144-X $5.50 US/$6.50 CAN

VICTORIA BRUCE

"Victoria Bruce Is a rare talent!"
—Rebecca Forster, Bestselling Author Of *Dreams*

A faint scent, a distant memory, and an age-old hurt aren't much to go on, but lovely Maggie Westshire has no other recollections of her missing father. Now she finds herself on a painful quest for answers—a journey that begins in Hot Springs, Arkansas, and leads her back through the years, into the strong arms of Shea Younger. He is from a different era, a time of danger and excitement, and he promises Maggie a passion like none she has ever known. And while she is determined, against all odds, to continue her search for her father, Maggie doesn't know how much longer she can resist Shea's considerable charms, or the sweet ecstasy she finds in his timeless embrace.

_52064-8 $4.99 US/$6.99 CAN